THE 13TH APOSTLE

Dr Richard Heller
and Dr Rachael Heller

WINDSOR
PARAGON

First published 2007
by
HarperCollins
This Large Print edition published 2008
by
BBC Audiobooks Ltd by arrangement with
HarperCollins Publishers Ltd

Hardcover ISBN: 978 1 405 68602 0
Softcover   ISBN: 978 1 405 68603 7

British Library Cataloguing in Publication Data available

LP

Printed and bound in Great Britain by
Antony Rowe Ltd., Chippenham, Wiltshire

Acknowledgments

We wish to express our deep appreciation to the following people:

Mel Berger of the William Morris Agency—by far the finest agent in the world. His brilliant flashes of insight, coupled with thoughtful and incisive advice, his creativity, quick wit, brevity of comment, years of experience, his caring, hard work, and willingness to put all he has into a project he believes in combine to make him the best agent and the best friend any writer could ever have.

Publisher Liate Stehlik and marketing director Adrienne Di Pietro, HarperCollins for their essential leadership and guidance.

Caroline Ridding, Managing Director of Avon UK, for her enterprise and love of literature.

Sarah Durand, our truly outstanding editor, for her understanding of this project, her earnestness, wise counsel, remarkable editorial expertise, and for her very hard work. We deeply appreciate Sarah's commitment to producing only top-notch work.

Maxine Hitchcock, our superb Avon UK editor, for her intelligence, vital experience, commitment to excellence, care, and remarkable energy. Her constancy, concern, involvement, and love of a good story has brought out the best in us and in this book.

Keshini Naidoo, for her incredible energy, keen eye, and fine mind and perfectly delightful personality.

Emily Krump, for her infectious enthusiasm and terrific attention to detail.

Head Design, our creative and skilled cover designers, whose excellence brought the soul of the story out of the pages on onto the cover.

Cathryn Summerhayes of William Morris Agency, for her involvement, care, commitment, and great expertise.

Charles D. Besford, Senior Executive Managing Director, Tokyo Disney Resort, for his early and enthusiastic encouragement and insight.

To Charles D. Besford,
For his fine mind, caring heart,
and generosity of spirit.

Among the most sacred of texts it is written:

In each generation there are born thirty-six righteous souls who, by their very existence, assure the continuation of the world.

According to Abraham's Covenant, once each millennium, God shall return to earth and count among the many, those who remain righteous.

Were it not for these tzaddikim, the righteous ones, who stand in God's judgment, mankind's fate would be in grave and certain peril.

These tzaddikim have no knowledge of each other; neither have they an understanding of their own singular importance. As innocents, they remain unaware of the critical consequences of their thoughts, their faith, and their deeds.
Save for one.

To this tzaddik alone, is the granted knowledge of his position, for to him is entrusted the most sacred of tasks.

PROLOGUE

Six months ago, London

Professor Arnold Ludlow opened the ancient diary. The musty smell filled him with excitement. This was the manuscript that had eluded him for four decades, its existence supported by a few obscure references and unsubstantiated rumor. Still, he had not lost faith. Now he held it in his hands and translated, from the Latin, the words of one long dead.

The Courtyard of Weymouth Monastery
The First day of May 1097

There was no stake onto which the monks might secure the prisoner, so Father Abbot John gave orders that the heretic be tied to the great elm. The tree was half-dead, having been struck by lightning last spring. One half of the trunk had turned to dry, brittle wood and would provide a quick hot flame at the start. The other half had exploded with new green growth and would now ensure a constant renewal of the flames of salvation. With the application of enough oil to the dry wood, the fire would burn steadily enough to allow the prisoner to renounce his heresies and so, at the last moment, snatch his soul from the waiting hand of the devil.

With the conclusion of evening vespers, novice-master and three novitiates fetched the

1

prisoner from his cell. The heretic walked among them, head held high, eyes forward. He did not protest as others had; neither did he beg for mercy.

Under the watchful eye of their instructor and the monastery's full register of monks—more than a score in all—the three novitiates bound the heretic to the tree, hand and foot. Each took a turn, loosening the coarse jute, then pulling it taut. With every tightening, small pieces of flesh were torn from the prisoner's wrists and ankles, leaving small rivulets of red in their wake.

The other monks drew closer and watched in silence. From time to time, each nodded his approval and, in solemn tones, expressed his hope for the heretic's repentance. Yet, even, as they watched the novices secure ropes around the prisoner's neck, waist, then across his groin, their breathing quickened. Although weighted down by heavy robes, Brother Jeremiah, the youngest of the monks, appeared to be greatly aroused.

At novice-master's nod, each of the monks, in turn, made his way to the shed and returned with a large bundle of faggots so that each, by his contribution, might share in the glory of the redemption.

The parcels of sticks were placed carefully around the feet of the heretic, then piled high to his waist. The packing of the wood was critical. If faggots were too lightly mixed with straw, the fire might go out, requiring a second or third attempt; wood too densely packed would produce a fire so hot that it might bring too rapid a surcease of pain. Much practice and skill was required in order to produce the perfect flame with which to burn a man alive.

And still the prisoner stood motionless.

In silence, the monks prayed for the heretic's soul. Only one among them did not.

I, alone, prayed for a miracle; some divine intervention that might spare the man whose soul needed no redemption; this brave knight who had fought so valiantly in the Holy Land and who now offered up his life, yet again, in service to God and his fellow man.

Head still bowed, I ventured one quick glance. Tears flowed from the prisoner's eyes, yet he offered no protest. Though I stood well within his gaze, he did not look in my direction.

Guided by novice-master's hand, the oldest of the novitiates ladled oil about the great pile of faggots, careful to spoon the greatest portion over the bottommost sticks, diminishing the application as he approached the top of the pile. The oil had been freshly rendered only that morning from the fat of the foulest of slaughtered livestock, a peasant's old pig, diseased and pocked, that had gone to its death squealing in pain and terror, in full earshot of the prisoner's cell.

Two rags soaked up the remainder of the oil. These novice-master used to anoint the heretic. As he smeared the foul-smelling viscous fluid over the prisoner's bare shoulders and shaven head, he continued his instructions to his charges. The oil must be

3

smeared evenly over the exposed flesh so as to encourage the start of a flame, then soaked into the jute to sustain the burning.

Amidst the instruction, the heretic continued in silence.

Novice-master signaled the novitiates to retreat, then stepped back to join the monks' circle.

All waited, eyes cast toward the sky. In accordance with the Inquisitor's Dictates for Redemption, the fire would be started at the moment when the light of the first star pierced the night. I beseeched God that, although the skies would grow dark, no star would appear. And for a time none did.

In the fading light, three birds flew across the horizon and disappeared into the heavens, one leading the two. They called loudly into the approaching night, one to the other, staying in perfect formation, flying as one. I knew this to be a sign that One far greater than we mortals waited to guide the prisoner into heaven.

A single star blinked and was gone. This was the signal for which all had been waiting. Father Abbot emerged from the shadows and approached the circle, an oil-soaked torch in one hand, a candle in the other, his eyes fixed upon me.

With sudden terror, it came to me that the Abbot John might command me to light the fire. Could even he require me to enact such a deed in order to prove my fidelity? If so, I could not comply. Though my sacred vows to the Church would be broken, though the repercussions of my rebellion might echo through eternity, this, Dear God, I could not do.

But Father Abbot John had other intentions. He lit the torch with the candle then passed it to one of the other monks, motioning me to remain by his side. It seemed to me that a smile crossed the Abbot's lips but nothing more was said. Then, in the light of that sputtering candle, he turned so that his prisoner could not fail to witness the only act that might yet bring a cry of repentance. From beneath his robes, the Abbot withdrew the moldering wooden box still wrapped in tattered cloth.

The heretic's gaze fixed on the bundle and then found me. Only then did I see fear spring to his eyes; fear not for himself but for something far greater, that which lay within the crumbling wooden box. As we had in our youth, I shared with the man they now called heretic a single terror, like none other before. Might the Abbot yet commit an atrocity far greater than the taking of a single innocent life? Might he yet commit a sacrilege against man and against God too terrible to imagine?

Professor Ludlow frowned. Hints, suggestions, intimations. Nothing more. He eyes fell on a small piece of parchment that had been wedged into the hand-sewn binding. It had been hastily written, it seemed, but the ink remained dark and clear.

With care, the Professor inched the hidden message from the binding. He read the words, smiled, sighed deeply, and closed the diary for

ONE

Present day
Day One, early evening
The New York City Grill

In the dim light of the restaurant, Gil Pearson strained to check his watch. He'd give the Professor and Sabbie ten more minutes to show. No more. He was tired and hungry and wanted to go home, grab something to eat, and crawl into bed. This was the last sales pitch dinner that George was going to get him to agree to.

What a way to start a weekend.

'Do this one as a favor to me,' George had cajoled. 'You know you're the reason they come to us. All any client wants is a chance to meet the man who helped rid the world of CyberStrep. You're a celebrity, for God's sake. You know they'll pay triple just to be able to brag to their friends they have you watching over their systems,' George added, trying to appear as endearing as his three chins would permit.

Although Gil hated to admit it, George was right. Since graduating top of his class from Massachusetts Institute of Technology two decades ago, Gil's anti-hacking discovery had changed the way virtually every major data protection company in the world approached the securing of high-risk and top secret information. For three years running, he had been named Man of the Year by the National Association of Artificial Intelligence, yet no client ever referred to these accomplishments. Only when the *New York Times* reported that Gil was the creator of the computer program that had eradicated the data-eating virus that held the Internet hostage for almost a month, did anyone take notice. The whole thing might have faded if *People* magazine hadn't jumped on the story. They spent three-quarters of the article describing his 'rugged good looks' and barely mentioned his work.

Lucy had teased him unmercifully. Within days of the article's publication, an ever-hungry storm of reporters and paparazzi began to beat a path to his—or rather to CyberNet Forensics, Inc.'s— door.

The company's worth had gone through the roof, Gil's salary had more than quadrupled, and he had been dragged, kicking and screaming, from the privacy of his little computer room to the bright lights of celebrity.

That had been four years ago. It couldn't have come at a worse time. Lucy had just been diagnosed with pancreatic cancer and, though every minute away from her felt like the greatest betrayal he could imagine, Gil had convinced himself that he had to cash in on his fame so that he could pump up his salary while he could. It was the only way he could be sure that Lucy would get the best possible care in the hard times that lay ahead.

A sour taste of bile rose in his throat.

Son-of-a-bitch doctor.

Right from the beginning the bastard had known that Lucy didn't have more than six weeks left. Had the quack told Gil the truth, he would have spent every precious minute with her. But,

8

instead, the doctor had led him to believe that because of her youth and strength, Lucy's decline would be unmercifully slow. Months—maybe a year—of painful deterioration were inevitable, the doctor had said; an unthinkable time in which Lucy's pain could be eased by the best medical care that money could buy.

Instead, she was gone in less than a month, only two weeks before her thirty-fourth birthday. Gil had spent much of that time away from her, in endless interviews, answering asinine questions posed by one stupid reporter after another. Less than a week after it was over, one tabloid cover sported his photo, snapped at the cemetery. The inside copy reported that he was recently widowed and implied that after a suitable time of mourning, he would be an excellent catch.

Gil swallowed against the lump in his throat and forced himself to think about something else.

I'm out of here.

He rose and kicked his chair back hard. As he reached to keep it from falling, something caught his eye.

Gray hair flying, short fat legs waddling, and looking a great deal like the White Rabbit in *Alice in Wonderland*, Dr. Arnold Ludlow, Professor of Antiquities and consultant on Early Christian Artifacts to the Israel Museum, arrived.

Breathless and dripping, he pealed off his wet raincoat and draped it on his seat back then settled into the chair.

'Sorry I'm late,' he began without introduction. 'Your taxis, you know. You can never get one in the rain.'

Gil managed a nod before the Professor

continued an account of the many difficulties he'd confronted in a city that seemed bent on preventing him from making this meeting.

'Sabbie didn't show at the airport but no worries,' Ludlow added, 'that's not unusual for her.'

Gil surrendered to the mounting wave of disappointment. It didn't really matter anyway. He would sit and wait while the old man prattled on and, when enough time had elapsed so that he could do so without seeming terribly impolite, Gil would reach for the menu.

But he never got the chance.

TWO

A few minutes later
Hotel Agincourt, New York City

Abdul Maluka stepped from the shower and stared at his reflection in the bathroom mirror. Black hair dripping, dark skin glistening in the bright light, he liked what he saw. He was short by Western standards, but every inch of his frame was pure muscle. He patted his flat stomach and surveyed his tan shoulders.

Not bad for an old man of forty.

The crescent-shaped scar across his right cheek was the perfect finishing touch. It made him look interesting. Even . . . sexy.

He had sustained the injury as a result of one of his father's infamous thrashings, in this case as a direct result of Maluka's refusal to stand silently by as his father announced to the family that his advanced age no longer permitted him to participate in the Fast of Ramadan.

'You are well enough to lie with your whore whenever she will tolerate you,' a twelve-year-old Maluka had sneered. 'How can you say you cannot keep the Fast?'

His father had attempted to stare the boy down. Maluka's mother had been in easy earshot. The older man's discomfort fueled Maluka's outrage.

'Surely, you can forgo some pleasure in the name of Allah. Or can you not even wait until the sun sets to bury your face in the flesh of that pig,' the youth had added with a laugh.

His father had ripped the worn brown leather belt from the waist of his Western suit of clothes and had beaten the young Maluka with all the strength he could muster. Only when the boy fell to the floor under the torrent of blows, did his father's fury subside.

'You are not my real father,' the young Maluka had declared. 'My father is the spirit of Islam. The poorest devotee to Allah is more my father than you.'

His father added one final blow for good measure; one the boy would never forget. The sharp edge of the buckle caught Maluka across the cheek and left a gash from which blood poured. It was only then that his father smiled with satisfaction.

'Let your faith heal that for you, boy!' he had said triumphantly, then turned, left, and never spoke of the matter again.

Nearly three decades later, the token left by his father's fury now declared to the world, proof of

Maluka's commitment to Islam. With age, the wound had transformed into a perfect crescent shape whenever he smiled. Not that he smiled all that often.

Maluka pulled on a pair of finely tailored slacks and selected a new silk shirt delivered fresh from his New York shirtmaker, then entered the living room.

Aijaz Bey looked up guiltily. His bulbous bald head, set on a thick neck and huge shoulders, would have made him look unintelligent even if he were bright—which he was not. At six foot six, weighing two hundred and eighty pounds, he was indeed as dangerous as he appeared—and as obedient; two essential attributes which made him the perfect assistant.

The remnants of torn plastic wrappings, wadded up linen napkins, and empty plates, littered the rolling dining cart. Maluka shook his head in resignation. Although Aijaz's huge hands were skilled at carrying out whatever delicate act with a knife was required, and his skill with a gun was quite remarkable, the man seemed incapable of removing his dinner from a room-service tray without making a mess.

'Couldn't wait,' Aijaz explained with a shrug and an obsequious smile.

'No problem.'

Aijaz breathed a sigh of relief.

At the sound of the knock at the hotel door, both men straightened.

Aijaz waited for instruction. Maluka raised his hand and silently signaled him to halt. At the second knock, Maluka nodded and Aijaz opened the door.

Clearly startled by Aijaz's bulk, the man hesitated, then entered. Though no more than forty years of age, his bent back and the downward thrust of his head betrayed the attitude of a man who had been broken on the rack of life. Tall and gaunt, his gray hair slicked back from an overabundance of grease or sweat, their guest offered his right hand to Maluka in greeting. Seeing that no such gesture was about to be returned, he hesitated, then withdrew his hand.

'Sorry, I guess you chaps don't shake hands,' he muttered with a nervous laugh. 'My error.'

When no smile was forthcoming, he checked his watch.

'Look, I'm sorry if I'm a tad early. I just thought that with the weather being what it is, well, you know, better to be early than late. Of course, if I interrupted something . . .'

His gaze darted from Maluka to Aijaz and back again, desperate for any indication of how to proceed. Maluka was pleased. Robert Peterson, assistant to Professor Arnold Ludlow, was not going to offer any resistance. It wouldn't take more than fifteen minutes for Maluka to get all of the information he needed. Twenty at most.

THREE

She slid into the chair next to Professor Ludlow's, finished her phone call, and snapped her cell phone shut. She summoned the waiter and ordered her wine and, still, never acknowledged Gil's presence.

The special smile she flashed the Professor was returned with unabashed adoration. She settled back into her chair and, only then, set her gaze on Gil.

'Have you ordered yet?' she asked, as if continuing an ongoing conversation.

'No, not yet,' Gil answered.

She was striking. Not beautiful, but remarkable looking; tall, with dark straight hair to her shoulders, and high, full breasts that strained against her ivory silk blouse. Gil forced himself to focus on her face.

She was not what he had expected. From day one, Gil's three-year Internet relationship with Sabbie Karaim had been strictly business. Sabbie was one of a dozen consultants around the world that Gil used as translators.

Whenever he was conducting an investigation for an Israeli client, which was getting more and more frequent, Gil sent the data to Sabbie for translation from Hebrew into English. Her transcription formed the basis for all his analyses, for all of the testing that he hoped would reveal

14

patterns of illegal activity that might help catch a cyber criminal dead in his tracks.

He used her on his most important cases, as well. Whenever an Israeli government agency hired CyberNet Forensics to set up a sting that involved cross-national Internet coverage, Gil would design the English version of the Internet bait intended to lure the cyber criminal into taking the next and, hopefully, fatal step. Then he'd send the cyber bait to Sabbie for translation into Hebrew and for posting on the net. She'd never let him down.

Her work was meticulous, and he had come to rely on her without question. She was not without her idiosyncrasies, however. Her rules were simple but firm: no communications outside Internet business. No matter how urgent the job, he was never to phone. And, surprisingly, she wanted no feedback after the cyber criminal had been caught.

Unlike Gil's other translators from South America, Germany and France, who took great satisfaction in knowing that their the work had put a criminal behind bars, Sabbie had made it clear that her involvement ended when her translation was complete. She was a professional from head to toe and, as Gil felt his excitement rise, that particular head to toe suddenly took on a whole different meaning.

Any erotic musings he might have been enjoying, however, were quickly expunged by Sabbie's first words of greeting.

'There's one thing we should get clear from the start,' she began. 'You're used to giving the orders. The Professor has put *me* in charge so, on this job, you'll be working for *me*.'

15

Gil stared in obvious surprise.

'If that's a problem,' Sabbie continued matter-of-factly, 'I need to know that now.'

That was it. Like she owned him. No smile, no 'Hello, it's nice to finally meet you.' Nothing. Just now hear this: I'm the boss. You're the slave. Get over it.

Ludlow rushed in to avoid a face-off.

'Oh, I'm sure that's not a problem, Sabbie. Mr. Pearson's such a lovely young man. I'm sure you two will make an outstanding team, just like you always have. Now, where was I?

'Oh, yes,' Ludlow continued, unabated. 'Early Christian artifacts. That's my area. Though officially I'm retired now, I still do a bit of consulting work at The Museum of the Shrine of the Book. In Jerusalem, you know,' he added proudly. 'My colleague, Dr. Anton DeVris, actually he's the Director of Acquisitions for the Israel Museum, well, he thought it would be best for me to speak to you in person . . .'

Gil emptied his water glass in one long gulp then crunched the single remaining ice cube between his teeth. Ludlow was a gem; an antique from some bygone era. The old guy had probably convinced himself that his pathetically obscure discovery contained some extraordinary secret hidden away for centuries; most likely, a map to hidden treasure or the like.

God, what people wouldn't do for one last chance at immortality. George must have been out of his mind to get them involved in this. What could he have possibly been thinking? If Sabbie had come to Gil first, he would have turned her down flat. She must have known that or else she wouldn't

16

have gone over his head.

Instead, she simply bypassed him and went straight to George. The shortest distance between two points, of course. She was smart. He had known that. And she had guts. He had known that too. What he hadn't suspected, however, was how exciting the combination could be.

FOUR

A few minutes later
The New York City Grill

Lucy used to say that, during the first year of their marriage, she discovered Gil had an amazing talent: he had perfected the art of sleeping with his eyes open. Whenever Gil found himself on the receiving end of one of her stories, some incident that had marred or made her day, she could expect Gil to appear to listen intently, nod at just the right times, ask the appropriate questions, and have absolutely no idea of what she was talking about.

Sleep-talking, as Lucy called it, was a skill that Gil had become rather fond of and one that had gotten him through almost every relationship since the first grade. But with Lucy it was different. He abandoned the practice long before their second anniversary. By then, he had discovered, much to his amazement, that he cared more about the little things that happened in Lucy's day than his own desire to veg out.

Now, in the restaurant with Ludlow droning on, he had been sleep-talking once again, letting the old man continue his monologue while retaining virtually none of the details.

'. . . And so we have come to believe that the document might contain a hidden message that would tell us where a certain artifact is located—a copper scroll that dates back to the time of Jesus. The thing is, we're not sure, it might just be a metaphor that the author of the diary used,' Dr. Ludlow concluded.

'Of course,' Gil confirmed, nodding.

'That's where you come in,' Ludlow added.

'Where . . . exactly?' Gil queried, trying desperately to appear as if he knew what the hell was going on.

'Why, telling us if the text of the journal contains any sort of pattern that could be concealing a hidden message,' Sabbie interjected.

'Do you mean a code?' Gil asked. 'You know, I don't do codes.'

'No. Not a code, that's the whole point,' Sabbie interrupted. 'If we needed a cryptanalyst, we wouldn't have called *you*.'

'Well, thank you very much,' Gil snapped back.

Ludlow interceded again. 'Look, if we're right, the person who wrote this journal would have been afraid to use an encrypting paradigm. He would have been concerned that, if he had embedded his message into a complex code, by the time the document was found—maybe centuries later—no one would have been able to decipher his message. We're pretty sure he would have chosen a simpler means of concealing any message. We just haven't been able to figure how he did it, and Sabbie said that with your talent in pattern recognition, well . . .'

Gil straightened and began to fire one question after another, in hopes of bringing himself up to speed. Sabbie remained silent, perhaps trying to understand why Gil seemed so lost in a conversation that had seemed so clear. Fortunately, the Professor's answers were long and detailed. They gave Gil just the information he needed to fill in the conversation he had missed.

A diary, written by an eleventh-century monk, had been discovered at an ancient monastery in Weymouth, England, sold to a local dealer of antiques, who had contacted Ludlow, whom he knew would be interested in the crumbling journal. For the moment, the diary remained safe, back in England, in a place known to Ludlow alone. At the appropriate time, it was to be smuggled or, as the Professor put it, 'relocated' by Dr. Anton DeVris to the Israel Museum.

'DeVris says that until we know exactly what information the diary contains, it makes no sense to bring it to the Museum. He says that even though he's the Director of Acquisitions, the Museum wouldn't accept the diary without some proof of its relevance to religious history. I suppose he's right, though I would feel a great deal better if it were safe with them, under lock and key.' The old man shrugged his disagreement with DeVris' decision to keep the diary to themselves but was apparently resigned to go along with the Director's decision.

'Do you think it's wise? Holding on to so precious a document?' Gil asked.

He had no clue as to what value this nameless old journal might hold, but he hoped that a little more wiggle room in the conversation might make him look like he was up to speed with the conversation. Ludlow's response was anything but what he expected.

'Well, it's only a matter of days now anyway,' the Professor replied jovially. 'As you know, George has assured us that, Monday morning, as soon as the last of the financial arrangements with CyberNet Forensics have been finalized, you'll be on your way to Israel to join us.' Ludlow threw Sabbie yet another adoring glance.

Gil stared blankly. He would have thought the old man crazy had he not known that George was more than capable of making such a promise. But Gil knew George. Too well.

Sabbie surveyed Gil questioningly. 'We were told you would be able to leave immediately.'

The Professor and Sabbie waited for Gil's affirmation, which he had no intention of giving. Damned if he was going be carted off to the Middle East at George's whim.

He wasn't going and that was that. George could be counted on to go through his typical routine. He would argue that the company needed the revenue and without it, they'd be facing pay cuts or worse, layoffs. When that failed, George would pull some other manipulation out of his hat. The big guy had been alluding to the fact that since Lucy's death Gil had become a recluse, so he'd probably argue that a little adventure would be good for Gil's soul.

Good for CyberNet's coffers, you mean.

Gil shook off the imaginary conversation. He had no intention of going anywhere. It was as simple as that.

'Why would I be going to Israel if the diary is in

England?' Gil asked, a bit argumentatively.

'No matter. No matter. That's where you'll be doing your work.'

Not on your life, old man.

He flashed the Professor his most sincere look. 'You know, considering what's involved, I think it would make far more sense to bring the diary to CyberNet's facilities,' Gil explained. 'So, with your okay, Dr. Ludlow, I'm going to recommend that CyberNet assign your project our best team here in New York. In that way, you'll get the best minds . . .'

'A team!' Ludlow gasped.

'Well, yes, but don't worry, it won't cost you any more. Actually, for the cost of transporting and housing me, it might even be cheaper in the long run . . .'

'Are you out of your mind?' Sabbie asked angrily. 'How could you make such a suggestion? Either you're a fool or you haven't heard a word Dr. Ludlow has said. In either case, you're wasting our time.'

She rose, nodded to the Professor, and made her way toward the restrooms. Ludlow mopped his forehead with his napkin, excused himself, and followed in the same general direction.

Gil shook his head in disbelief. What the hell had just happened? Had he really screwed things up that badly? Apparently so.

He slumped into his chair, prepared to offer the required apologies as soon as they both cooled down and made their way back to the table.

By the time the waiter came for their second drink order, Gil knew the bitter truth. Ludlow had walked out. And so had the girl.

Gil's eyes fixed on Ludlow's dripping raincoat,

still slung on the chair, and his umbrella lay half open on the floor under the table. Everything was exactly as it had been, save for the fact that Ludlow and Sabbie were gone. Gone from the table and, evidently, gone from the restaurant.

Had he thought to look up from the three square inches of tablecloth that occupied his field of vision since their departure, he might have seen them leave. But he had waited, like a schoolboy, for his punishment; ready to make amends, so that he might go home, get some rest, and let George have it—but good—on Monday morning.

Now, it appeared, there was no one left to apologize to. What started out as a bit of a pain-in-the-ass dinner had escalated into the meeting from hell. Gil's gaze fell on Ludlow's vacant chair. A single thought brought him to his feet and sent him striding in the direction he had last seen the Professor and Sabbie disappear.

Sabbie would never have allowed the old man to leave without his coat and umbrella. Not on a night like this.

FIVE

A few minutes later
Hotel Agincourt

'Do you think we should leave him alone in there?' Aijaz asked anxiously. 'I mean, he could just leave with the money. The stuff in the envelope could be worthless, right?'

Maluka glanced at the bedroom door that

separated them from Ludlow's assistant in the living room and motioned Aijaz to keep his voice down.

'No need to worry, my friend. Peterson isn't going anywhere until we're done with him. He may require our financial help again in the future and he knows it.'

Aijaz waited for clarification.

Maluka tossed the thick envelope onto the bed. 'This is of little importance. What I want isn't in the envelope. What I want lies within the man in the next room.'

Aijaz nodded, desperately trying to keep up.

'Getting what you desire is easy once your adversary thinks he's already given it to you,' Maluka explained.

The big man looked down, not knowing what to say.

'It's okay, Aijaz. I take care of my part. You take care of yours.'

Aijaz smiled with gratitude.

'Now we wait just long enough. Another three minutes should do it.'

Persuading noncooperative people to take seriously their moral obligations was Maluka's forte. As a boy in Halab, Syria, he had been obsessed with playing 'monks and demons,' a game that dated back to the fourth century. Having convinced one of his many cousins to dress in rags, Maluka would don his carefully assembled costume and assume the role of the holy man. With great ceremony, the young Maluka would summon the evil spirit that lurked within the heart of his playmate and challenge it to combat. Though small for his age, Maluka had been remarkably muscular, able to pin down a child several years his senior and to extract, at his demand, confessions of iniquity and promises of repentance. In so doing, Maluka invariably succeeded in exorcising the evil spirit and making the world safe for the Pure of Heart.

Once having played the game with him, a child would rarely do so again. Maluka couldn't have cared less. Having savored victory over any particular foe, he had no need for a rematch.

Now, decades later, Maluka had transformed the physical game of his childhood into the psychological game he used in the service of his Faith. Whenever he had to resort to physical persuasion, however, he preferred to delegate that responsibility to Aijaz.

Both men returned to the living room. The still-unopened envelope remained where it had been tossed on the bed.

Ludlow's assistant rose from his seat, waiting for Maluka's judgment on the envelope's contents.

'Excellent. Excellent. You have managed to obtain some very useful documents,' Maluka began.

A look of relief crossed Peterson's haggard face and betrayed what Maluka had suspected. Peterson was frightened Maluka would discover that he had been given information that was virtually useless. Although Peterson must have included some of Ludlow's personal notes on the diary, as Maluka had requested, and perhaps some background history on the Monastery at Weymouth where the diary was found, in all likelihood, Peterson had not included anything of any real importance. Maluka smiled with satisfaction. If there was one thing that he knew, it was people. He had no illusions about them, he could always expect the worst, and they rarely ever disappointed him.

'So, you've met your part of the bargain and we're all set,' Maluka concluded with a studied good humor.

Peterson's fingers reflexively patted the package of money in his jacket pocket. He smiled gratefully, stood, and walked toward the door, most likely convincing himself that he had been concerned over nothing.

Maluka offered the handshake that had not been forthcoming at Peterson's arrival. Peterson responded in kind and turned to go.

'Oh, I almost forgot,' Maluka said offhandedly. 'What is this business about a copper scroll?'

Peterson's smile faded.

Before Ludlow's assistant could respond, Maluka probed a little deeper. 'I'm sure it's not really significant or the Professor would have mentioned it in his notes more than that one time. I was just wondering if you included it because you thought it might be important.'

This was the part Maluka enjoyed the most. He'd set the trap, caught the rat, and now he got to watch him slowly wriggle. Best of all, with each squirm, Ludlow's assistant was providing Maluka with exactly the information he wanted.

'Copper scroll?' Peterson asked innocently. 'Oh, no. That's not why I included that page. I forgot it was even in there!'

Because you were so very careful to remove any possible reference to a scroll, weren't you? I knew it! I didn't even need to look at the pathetic pile of trash

25

you tried to pawn off on me. You must truly think me the fool!

Peterson continued, trying desperately to cover his tracks. 'Don't worry. The copper scroll thing's not important. On one of the pages of the diary, Ludlow and DeVris apparently found some mention of a copper scroll being hidden somewhere in Weymouth Monastery. They couldn't even agree if that's what it really said. Ludlow is certain that it's what the whole diary is really about. DeVris thinks it's nothing more than a reference to a copy.'

'A copy of The Cave 3 Copper Scroll they found in Qumran years ago?' probed Maluka.

'Right. And that you know is in the Book of the Shrine already. DeVris says the diary's just talking about a *copy* of The Cave 3 Scroll, not a new scroll. The monks probably sold copies of The Cave 3 Scroll by the dozens to bored knights in search of treasure. Anyway, the only reference to any scroll, new or old, was on some old scrap of paper Ludlow found stuck in the binding, so how could it be what the whole diary is about?'

'So DeVris says there is no scroll, or, if there is one, it's nothing more than a copy of The Cave 3 Copper Scroll?'

'Yes, nothing more than an old man's wishful thinking.' Peterson straightened and set back his shoulders.

'If you ask me, they're both crazy. I mean, here are two intelligent men debating and transcribing, then going back and debating it all over again. Just like the fight about who would keep the diary—that went on for a month! The Professor won, of course, ownership is nine-tenths of the law. But now with DeVris in Israel and the diary with Ludlow in London, Ludlow spends half his day uploading bits and pieces of it onto a secret website on the Internet. If you ask me, it would have been a lot easier if he had just let DeVris keep the damn thing.'

Maluka nodded and smiled. Fearful people explain too much. That always gives them away. If you can spot it, it always works in your favor. The greater the number of words they use to cover up their lies, the greater the opportunity to get more information.

'Ludlow's paranoid,' Peterson continued. 'He keeps every e-mail, every printout, even his own notes, locked up like they're the Crown Jewels.'

Peterson explained that even if he had needed to work with diary-related information, he had to ask the Professor to retrieve it.

'I must be confused. I thought you had access to Ludlow's safe,' Maluka asked.

'I do. I have access to his safe in the *den*. But there is another safe in the kitchen, in what looks like an oven.'

'In an oven! Really?'

'Yeah. The thing is bizarre. It's got a fake back—the oven I mean—which releases if you enter the right numbers in the right succession on the oven timer. It's one of those digital things—a smart board, Ludlow calls it—and you'd never know that it wasn't part of the kitchen equipment.'

Peterson explained that, on one particular occasion when he had attempted to heat his lunch in the oven, Ludlow's wife happened upon him just in the nick of time.

'She's just a little old lady but she pushed me

27

halfway across the kitchen. She said to never touch that oven again, that Ludlow built the safe inside to keep her valuables in,' Peterson explained. 'As a child, she was a prisoner in a Gulag. You know, a Soviet forced labor camp, and apparently she's still terrified that people will break in and take away everything she has. Not that she has anything worth stealing from what I can see.'

'And now . . .' Maluka prompted.

'And now, since Ludlow got hold of the diary, he's taken to putting almost all of his papers in the oven safe, which I don't have access to. Which is why I couldn't get you more,' Peterson concluded with a half-apologetic grin.

'No matter,' Maluka said congenially. 'You've given me all that I needed. Chances are this whole thing will come to nothing. Most importantly, let's hope the money you've earned gives your little girl the extra help she so desperately needs.'

Peterson's eyes shot to Maluka's as if seeking to confirm the sincerity in his words. Maluka put on his most sympathetic face. Peterson smiled his gratitude, then opened the door.

Maluka hesitated. He wanted to frame his next question carefully. He required only one final piece of information.

'A safe journey to you, Mr. Peterson. I assume that you and Professor Ludlow are heading back to London in the next day or two?'

'Yes. Tomorrow night. Though I'm not looking forward to the long flight.'

'Yes, yes,' Maluka said brusquely and closed the door.

Even as Peterson made his way to the street, Maluka had already snapped open his cell phone

28

to reserve airline seats for himself and Aijaz on the first morning flight to London.

SIX

Day Two, late evening
Regent's Park Tube Station
Camden Town, London

Professor Arnold Ludlow struggled up the steps, two heavy suitcases in tow. Sweat from the strain dripped into his eyes, and his back hurt like the dickens. A welcome bit of cool air wafted from the street above. He breathed it in, then with a sigh renewed his climb.

Sarah would be furious. She had begged him to arrange for a private car from the airport but he had refused. They had not put away enough money in the safe yet, he had protested. If Sabbie should need it . . . Neither Ludlow nor his wife had allowed themselves to linger on the thought.

'Until there is a comfortable cushion of funds, the tube will suit me fine,' he had concluded. 'Besides, the exercise will do me good.'

Sarah had kissed him on the bald spot on his head and had given his shoulders a squeeze. Now, she'd be rubbing his back with her infamous Chapman's Liniment for a week.

'Bloody stuff is made for horses,' he would protest.

'That's what you get for acting like an ass,' she'd be certain to counter.

Ludlow smiled.

He had reached the street and, revived by the cool air, he headed toward Upper Harley Street and the pleasures of home.

The walk was surprisingly invigorating and his apartment house greeted him like an old friend. Perhaps if his back hadn't been hurting him so badly, he might have realized something was wrong. Perhaps he might have become alarmed at seeing the apartment windows dark when he knew Sarah would be wide awake and anxious to hear the details of his trip. In any case, he still would have walked unknowingly into their apartment and into the stark terror that awaited him.

Two strong arms seized his and pulled him into the room, even as he struggled to free the key from the lock. They encircled him, and with one great wrench against his chest, left him breathless and in agony from ribs that splintered and gave way. Ludlow slumped to the floor. The room, suddenly flooded with light, seemed oddly filled with white. Two huge figures towered above him, each in clothes devoid of color and faces devoid of expression.

Only Sarah brought color to the moment, her face, hands, legs, and nightgown, all covered with the sickening brown-red of fresh blood. One eye was swollen shut, and a red trickle ran from her ear, but she was alive.

'Please, take what you want. Take it all,' Ludlow pleaded. 'Just leave us alone. We're old. Take whatever you want and go.'

'You know what we want,' the first intruder said softly.

Sarah's sob broke the silence that followed.

While one tormentor held Ludlow's head in

place so that he would bear witness to the scene that was to follow, the other walked toward his beloved Sarah. The intruder hesitated for a moment, smiled at Ludlow, then kicked the prone woman full force in the side of the head.

Ludlow heard the crack of her neck as it snapped the life out of her. For a moment, the room was silent, save for a tiny exhale of her last breath.

'No!' Ludlow shrieked. He was on his feet, and his hands found the face of the executioner. Ludlow held him by his hair as one eye yielded its soft viscosity to his death grip. Ludlow's screams of rage drowned out his victim's cries of pain.

The old man heard nothing, saw nothing, knew nothing. His body did what it had to do and continued grasping and flailing, even as the second intruder pulled him from the first and beat and kicked him until his body could no longer bring muscle and nerve together to move.

'Now give it to us,' the murderer demanded.

'I don't know what you want,' Ludlow mouthed. His chest spasmed with unreleased sobs. 'I don't know what you want,' he whispered again.

'The diary, you old piece of shit! Just give us the diary and we'll let you die in peace.'

'The diary?' Ludlow whispered, confused.

Another kick to his back. 'Like you didn't know,' his torturer snickered.

Ludlow struggled to clear his thoughts.

That's what this was all about? The diary! No, it couldn't be. It was all too fantastic to imagine.

He had warned DeVris that powerful people had powerful reasons to get control of the diary. DeVris had laughed at him. Sabbie had indulged

31

him his secrecy and had gone along with his emergency preparations, though she had thought him over the top about it. Sarah, too. But none of them had ever considered him anything but paranoid about the whole matter. Even he doubted his own concerns. And, now, son of a bloody bitch, he had been right all along.

Ludlow smiled; a tiny raising of the corners of his mouth, an insignificant movement that echoed a greater victory than any round of cannon fire.

He had what these murderers so desperately wanted, but they had left him with no reason to give it to them. They had taken everything; his Sarah, his desire to live, and his body's ability to continue to endure their abuse. He was dying and he knew it. Yet this, the only thing they really wanted, they would not get.

SEVEN

Day Four, early morning
CyberNet Forensics, Inc., New York City

CyberNet Forensics was one of the top-rated, though not one of the highest-grossing, Internet Investigative Services in the country. While the identities of clients were usually kept pretty hush-hush, all of the company's top cybersleuths, including Gil, knew that their clients were some of the most powerful individuals and agencies in the world.

CyberNet's website claimed their computer programs had helped spot, prosecute, and put an

32

end to more identity theft, online child pornography, money laundering, fraud, and potential terrorist schemes than all the other Internet forensics companies combined. Oddly, though, according to the company's annual financial reports, CyberNet continued to remain in the red.

At least once a month, George, as division supervisor, addressed the company's team of cybersleuths or, as he preferred to call them, his Internet Forensic Specialists. It was always the same old pep talk about how their programs were helping to keep cyberspace safe for the innocent. Most of them no longer listened to the plethora of words and lack of action. George could never explain why, as the accounts grew, budgets shrank. Morale dropped accordingly.

When Gil first came to the company, fresh out of graduate school, it had been a different place entirely; full of excitement and hope. These were the crème de la crème; young men and women, not necessarily tops in their classes but independent in their thinking and dogged in their persistence.

Every one of them was a loner, content to work in some tiny windowless office for days on end, hacking into 'unbreakable' data bases and Internet sites, in order to track down a target, find proof of the cyber crime, and present enough solid evidence to back up an arrest and conviction.

'You get paid to break into top secret files?' Lucy asked incredulously on their first date. 'Can't you be arrested or something?'

No, he couldn't be arrested. He was registered with the National Securities Administration, the only organization that hired more forensic investigators than CyberNet. And, no, he wasn't being paid the big bucks, such as they were, to break into systems; he was paid to figure out how identity thieves had made their way into the systems and to make sure that no one else could ever do the same.

The truth, however, was that like every other cybersleuth, it was 'nailing the target' that Gil loved. Once he had proof positive of a crime and the identity of the perpetrator, the task of making the system secure for the future didn't run anywhere near a close second. It was the very love of the hunt and his dislike for the cleanup that ended up being Gil's salvation.

While looking for a shortcut in order to patch up the FBI's payroll system, he'd written a set of computer instructions designed to sniff out the gaps in the original program. He called his subprograms Dobermans because, once set in motion, they hunted down their prey and pounced on it, holding it at bay until he gave them the okay to obliterate it. A single tap on the return key and the security breach in the system was literally gobbled up.

At the time, George had been beside himself with joy. He predicted that, with Gil's Dobermans in action, the world would be beating a path to CyberNet's door. Which it had, though the money never seemed to find its way beyond George's office on the top floor. Gil looked around at his own small, windowless office.

Well, so much for the Trickle-Down Theory of Economics.

Gil swiveled to face the largest of his three computer screens and settled back to savor his morning bagel and cream cheese as he perused his e-mail. It was early, George wouldn't be in for a couple of hours, and Gil would have plenty of time to figure out how he was going to play down last Friday's dinner fiasco with Ludlow.

The familiar 'You've Got Mail' alert interrupted Gil's final sip of coffee.

Jesus! What's he doing in this early?

Obviously, someone had already informed George of the problem. Nothing but a potentially lost source of income would get the big guy in at this hour.

A piercing alarm proclaimed that Gil's main computer had gone down and the rest were about to follow. He rushed to delete George's message. He was too late. The screens on his two alternate computers and the lights on his Internet server went dark. Gil held his breath as he waited for the whirr that would confirm that the backup system had kicked in. He sighed with relief. The backup system's welcome drone promised that, within a few minutes, everything would be up and running and more than seven terabytes of information would have been saved from oblivion.

Until recently, George's e-mail would have simply meant yet another pain-in-the-ass communication that required Gil's attention. For the past two weeks, however, any incoming e-mail bearing George's screen name sent Gil's computer network crashing.

Gil had warned George that if he continued to refuse to incorporate RSA security codes, they were inviting a major hacking catastrophe. George refused to discuss the matter. Gil offered to brave George's maze of computers to try and tease out the problem. George refused. Finally, they came to a truce. Gil agreed to drop the whole thing with the promise that George would phone, rather than send any e-mail until Gil figured out a workaround. The cease-fire lasted two days. By the third day, the big guy was sending e-mail messages as if there had never been a problem.

Each time an incoming e-mail shut Gil down, George would claim, as if for the first time, that he was doing his best to remember. 'After all,' he would add with a shrug and an innocent smile, 'I guess I'm just a creature of habit.'

Gil pulled his chair in close to the largest of the monitors and rapidly typed in a series of commands. Line by line, he examined the high-end security program he had designed for himself only days before the trouble had first begun.

What was triggering the goddamn thing to crash? And why only with George's e-mail?

Even his Dobermans couldn't find the source of the problem. Gil grabbed the phone and dialed George's extension.

'I'm coming. I'm coming,' Gil said as he continued to type. 'And for Christ's sake, don't send any more e-mails.'

Gil shook his head. What a waste. A brilliant mind like George's imprisoned in a four-hundred-pound body. With the maturity of a preadolescent, to boot. Nobody at work had ever seen the mountain of a man with a friend or had ever known him to go out socially. George simply shuffled from home to the offices, eating and sitting in front of one computer or another or playing with his latest tech toy. Though George had no one to blame but himself, still, it was a

36

pathetic waste of a life.

Given that he was probably terribly lonely, or maybe because of it, George wasn't half bad to work for. Though he was smart as hell, he wasn't competitive. He spoke his mind when he didn't like the way something was going but, in general, he appreciated Gil's work and told him so quite often. George was okay and just self-conscious enough about his appearance to make him easy to get along with. All you had to do was tell George there had been a noticeable decrease in his ample middle, and he'd beam at you like a happy five-year-old. Just a big old puppy dog—a greedy but lovable big old puppy dog.

The last computer kicked in and, before George could send yet another e-mail, Gil headed for what could be loosely referred to as George's office.

EIGHT

A few minutes later

The top floor of CyberNet Forensics shuddered with the combined boom of two televisions and a radio. On-screen reporters offered details on the latest disasters against a background of country music.

Since George had come on board, two finance people who had been working in rooms adjacent to his office had been moved to other locations. Another had taken a leave without pay until the company could relocate him to a lower floor, and one of the bookkeepers had just up and quit.

Management had changed the location of George's office twice before exiling him to the far end of the longest hall in the building. George couldn't have been happier. The huge man simply could not bear to work in silence. Even normal levels of noise were not enough. Surrounding himself in the clamor was not a mere idiosyncrasy, it was a necessity. And one that afforded him some extra perks.

'What can I say?' admitted George with a devilish grin, when the last person on the floor finally fled. 'It leaves all that extra space just for me.'

Gil approached the office and steeled himself for an even greater rush of sensory overload; a few minutes of audio abuse was all he could endure. He had given up on asking George to turn down the volume. His request always met with George's self-analysis: 'News, computers, and country music. Them's all I know, them's all I love.'

Gil knocked and, without waiting, walked in on the all-too-familiar scene of George stuffing his face with food.

This morning, the big guy was polishing off the last of his high-fiber breakfast cereal. It was a daily ritual that never seemed to make any difference in his health, weight, or, as George so often explained in far too much detail, his regularity.

Gil entered. George did his best to rise to his feet. He looked as if he had been caught doing something quite obscene. In the ensuing confusion of dislodging his bulk from his rolling chair, George overturned his plastic bowl and spoon. The remainder of the soggy cereal and a half-opened container of low-fat milk flowed over the jumbled spread of computer printouts that were strewn across his desk amid research reports, memos, graphs, and journals that lay one on top of the other. All became potential blotters for the fast-spreading white liquid. In a half-hearted attempt to contain George's most recent food-spill disaster, Gil reached below the soggiest section of paper and lifting it, turned toward the trashcan. George tripped over himself in an attempt to stop him.

Gil shook his head. 'Why do you *do* this?'

'Do what, eat cereal?' George asked. He flashed Gil what was supposed to pass for an endearing smile and attempted to sop up the milk with a single paper napkin.

'I'm serious. This is nuts. You probably have two weeks' worth of downloads here from every crackpot website in the world.'

'I know, but I haven't had time to go over them yet. I spend a lot of time researching this stuff, you know, and some of it could be really important.'

Gil shook his head.

'You might be interested to know I've been saving one of these downloads for you!' George added.

Foraging through the pile, George carefully extracted one set of papers that had not escaped the sludge of cereal and milk.

'It's about your Ludlow job . . .' George began.

'Look, about Ludlow. I think we ought to . . .'

George pulled one of the pages free. 'Hold on. Where did I see it? Oh, yeah, here it is. Look at this. It's a reprint of a Reuter's news release from a while ago. It says that Ludlow, well, not Ludlow

39

himself, but DeVris, the guy he works with in Israel, has one already.'

'One what?'

'One copper scroll, you putz. It says that they already have a copper scroll. So Ludlow, acting all academic and everything, isn't just looking for this diary to lead him to any old scroll, he's looking for the mate to one that the Museum already has,' George concluded. He rubbed his thumb and index finger together. 'And, from what the article says, I would imagine the complete set could turn them a very nice profit.'

Gil shrugged noncommittally. He had no clue as to what George was talking about. Gingerly, he took the soggy article by its corner and held it high. 'Does this mean you'll be raising Ludlow's fee?'

George responded with unusual seriousness. 'Maybe, but that's not what I'm saying. There could be a lot at stake here, and you're going to have to act like a professional for once in your life.'

Obviously, Ludlow had been in touch. Better to get it out in the open then. Gil summed up the low points of Friday night's dinner meeting, stumbled over an apology, and explained that he had no problem with another consultant being assigned to the job.

'No such luck, goombah. Got an e-mail from Ludlow just a few minutes ago. He and the translator, what's her name . . .'

'Sabbie,' Gil said glumly.

'Yeah, Sabbie. Seems like they still want you, though I can't imagine why. Good thing you get by on your wits and good looks and not on your

40

personality. You're the only one for the job, they say.'

'For Christ's sake, George! That makes no sense at all. Sabbie walked out on me and took Ludlow with her.'

George stared blankly.

Hadn't Ludlow told George what happened? Now, that was odd.

'Look, George, just let me wrap up the project I'm working on. It won't take more than a couple of days. That can't make that big a diff—'

'This afternoon,' George interrupted. 'Got you booked on a red eye that'll get you into Tel Aviv mid afternoon. You can head for Jerusalem and the Museum straight from the airport.'

Gil looked to see if the big guy was smiling. He wasn't.

'You gotta be kidding! Pulling me off the project for who knows how long it will take, will send me back to square one. Five months' work shot to hell.'

'Oh, give it up. It'll do you good to not know exactly what's going to happen tomorrow. Consider it an adventure.'

George picked up the Reuter's release Gil had laid aside and thrust it back into his face. 'This ought to change your mind. Read it.'

'Look, there's no way . . .' Gil began.

'Read it,' George insisted. 'Then tell me what you think.'

BURIED TREASURE:
FOUND AND LOST
Arnold Narin, AP, Jerusalem

'In Horebeh that is in the valley of Ahur, under the steps going eastward at 40 long cubits: a silver chest and its content of a value of 17 talents. In the funeral monument under the third course: 100 golden ingots. In the large cistern, which is in the yard of the small peristyle, in a hidden recess of its bottom blocked by the alluvial deposits, opposing the upper opening: 900 talents . . .'

So reads one of sixty-four entries of The 3Q15 Copper Scroll, commonly referred to as The Cave 3 Copper Scroll of Qumran. The Cave 3 Scroll has been described as one of the world's most tantalizing mysteries and for good reason. The Valley of Ahur described in The Cave 3 Scroll is real, although contemporary historians cannot agree on its location. Many researchers are convinced that the treasures the Scroll described within are genuine; incredible riches from the Second Temple, rescued before its destruction more than two thousand years ago. Other scientists have been certain that the concealed fortune was the renounced wealth of an ancient sect whose members held themselves to a strict vow of personal poverty.

No matter what the source, however, the waiting treasure is said to add up to as much as 200 tons of gold and silver. Today, more than five decades since the discovery of The Cave 3 Scroll and after a remarkable state-of-the-art restoration, this priceless manuscript remains a mystery.

On special loan to the Israel Museum here in Jerusalem for the past year, it has been on exhibit at Israel Museum's Shrine of the Book, magnificent home to the Dead Sea Scrolls. This enigmatic piece of history will remain available for viewing to the public until March 20 of next year, the anniversary of its discovery. On that day, the Scroll and its promises of hidden treasure will be returned to the Museum of Amman, Jordan, where it will be sequestered.

'The decision to place this priceless document in safekeeping is commendable,' noted Dr. Anton DeVris, Director of Acquisitions at Israel Museum's Shrine of the Book. 'The thought that the Scroll will soon be secured where scholars may no longer have access to it, that is difficult to accept. Still, we are grateful to have had it here for this time,' added Dr. DeVris diplomatically.

One word of caution to all you would-be fortune hunters, however: Before you start packing your shovels and heading off to search for hidden treasure, you should know that since The Cave 3 Scroll's discovery in 1952, scholars have been debating as to the authenticity of the Scroll, the treasures it describes, and even the intent of its author. Some have decreed the scroll to be 'the work of a madman' or 'a forgery.' Some have declared its creator to be 'a charlatan' who had only a 'passing knowledge of the Hebrew language.' Others believe the Scroll's critics to be part of a sweeping cover-up.

Even more intriguing: some experts agree that the secret to The Cave 3 Copper Scroll lies not in its writings alone but in a yet-to-be-discovered mate to the Scroll; a second copper scroll that holds the key to The Cave 3 Scroll's secrets and to the location of the vast array of priceless treasures that wait to be unearthed. Dr. DeVris described the possibility of the existence of a second scroll as 'intriguing, but unlikely.'

And some final advice: If you want a close-up look at the unsolved 3Q15 (Cave 3) Copper Scroll, make plans soon. In only twelve short months, the exhibit at Israel Museum's Shrine of the Book will be gone—back under lock and key—perhaps forever.

Gil finished reading. 'Yeah, so?'

'I can't believe you don't get it! Look, right now the Museum has the first scroll in their hands, and Ludlow has the diary that may show them where the second scroll is hidden. If they can get their hands on both of the scrolls at the same time, they should be able to figure out where the treasure is hidden. The problem is, that within a couple of months, the Museum's got to return the first scroll. If you don't help them find the second scroll before they have to return the first, they can pretty much kiss the treasure good-bye.'

George smiled with satisfaction and continued. 'They're caught between a rock and a hard place with all their contributors watching. If you can find some hidden message in the diary that leads them to a second scroll, you can just about write your own ticket.'

CyberNet's ticket, you mean. Still, Gil had to admit it didn't sound half bad.

'You said this Reuters' article is how old?'

'Six months, more or less.'

'Which is it? More or less?' Gil asked.

'Ahah! Got your interest didn't it? Knew it would. Actually, the article's about eight months old. From what I can see, it was written before Ludlow and DeVris got their hands on the diary. Now, with the possibility that the diary might connect The Cave 3 Scroll with a yet-to-be-uncovered second scroll, they must be desperate. I'm telling you, we could get a bundle for this one.'

Shaking his head, Gil smiled at the big lovable manipulator he called boss. He was hooked and George knew it.

'Here are your plane tickets. You've got a red-eye that leaves out of JFK at eleven tonight. Ludlow's still on his way back to London, but I'll nail down the contract by fax within a couple of hours, that is, unless you still want me to pass this whole thing on to one of the other guys, in which case . . .'

'Shut up and give me something to write on,' Gil muttered, reaching for a pad.

Gil caught George's fleeting look of supreme satisfaction.

Think you know me so well, don't you?

In his eagerness to sell Gil on the idea, George had left out one vital detail. The news article carried none of the banners or pop-up ads that brought those websites revenue. Clearly, George had cooked up the article to sell Gil on the deal.

Gil shook his head. He had no idea why George

45

was trying so hard to pull this one off, but whatever the reason, he was game for it.

NINE

Day Five, early morning
Entrance Gallery, Shrine of the Book
Israel Museum, Jerusalem

Tuesday was Kids' Day at The Shrine of the Book Museum. Hassan Ben Gaza hated the weekly intrusion. He hated the indulged children. Most of all, he hated their infidel parents and grandparents who had expropriated the land of his ancestors.

A group of schoolchildren blocked his way. He skirted around them with practiced skill. Had he been seen, Hassan would have been forced to endure their taunts. Twisted across the shoulders and back, his huge skull looked as if it might topple off his misshapen body. A matrix of wrinkles crisscrossed his face. It was no wonder that more than one child, confronted by Hassan in the hall, had whispered the word 'mummy' to a giggling companion. Their derision held more truth than they would ever know. Like the mummies who filled the screens of the old horror movies that Hassan so loved, he too waited patiently to make his dream of retribution come true.

Four years earlier, Maluka had rescued Hassan from a life of misery and crime. Out of work and desperate for money in a city in which forty men competed for even the most menial of jobs,

Hassan had been spending his nights breaking into cars. The few shekels for which he risked his life and freedom were barely enough to pay for his family's basic necessities but kept them together as a family.

On the night that changed his life, Hassan lay flat on his back across the front seat of a car, attempting to dismantle the radio by flashlight. It was three in the morning and the street was deserted.

Maluka did not see the intruder until he was within a few feet of the car. Hassan had jumped up and caught Maluka with a stranglehold that Maluka did not attempt to resist. Hassan hesitated, uncertain whether to cut his victim's throat or run. Quietly, Maluka suggested that Hassan join him for a cup of coffee at an all-night restaurant. Hassan anticipated some unscrupulous but profitable offer. Nothing could have been farther from the truth.

During the next two hours, Maluka elicited Hassan's most deeply felt regrets and frustrations; a litany of the painful disappointments that had forced him to undertake such acts of desperation.

Never had Hassan met such a man. Maluka showed him understanding where others would have condemned him, offered compassion where others would have demanded punishment, and, in doing so, revealed himself to be the spiritual leader in whom Hassan could find hope and meaning.

Maluka put him to work as a gopher in his video production studio only a few miles from where he first found him that fateful night. Hassan's days were filled with the fetching and delivering of the million things that were needed to make the famous Muslims for World Truth Videos. Shown each night of Ramadan, Maluka's television specials were renowned for their powerful portrayal of the inhumanity of the West. Hassan never missed a broadcast. These were the product of Hassan's loins as great as any child.

When Hassan had proven himself for two years, Maluka rewarded him with an opportunity greater than Hassan had ever imagined. He had been chosen to serve as the eyes and ears of MWT—down within the very belly of the enemy.

'Where no hope existed, Allah has provided the way,' Maluka said gently. At any time in the past, it would have been impossible to place Hassan within the all-Israeli workforce at the Israel Museum. With the signing of the exhibition agreement between the two Museums, however, all had been changed. Included in the agreement, at the Museum of Amman's insistence, a minimal number of non-Israelis were to be added as long-term employees. It was only a token stipulation, meant to provide public relations opportunities intended to calm those opposed to the arrangement. Still, the stipulation provided the small window of opportunity that would allow Hassan to be interviewed, then hired.

'To others, your work will appear menial, to our cause it will be immeasurable,' Maluka explained. There, among the most sacred of Jewish and Christian archives and artifacts, within the Museum itself, Hassan would sweep floors and empty garbage while carrying precious information back to the man who had given him life.

He had been sent with one purpose: to provide

proof of the secrets the Dead Sea Scrolls held and that the Museum concealed from the public eye for decades.

'Imagine,' Maluka said, 'with each note you copy and photo you take, you will help us lay bare a conspiracy perpetrated by some of the most respected men in the world. The guardians of these antiquities, past and present, will stand naked, exposed as those who have helped to perpetuate the supreme hoax.

'Once revealed, the secreted messages within these scrolls will prove beyond doubt that Jesus was nothing more than a mere mortal man and that the Church has been but a means to enslave its people as well as our own.'

'And then . . .' Hassan urged.

'And then our people and our faith shall be vindicated,' Maluka said.

'And truth shall prevail,' Hassan added.

It had taken the first eighteen months of Hassan's employ to work his way into invisibility. Moving from corridor to office, his sad lowly figure was barely noticed. With each office cleaning, with each access to more secure storage facilities, he was able to avail himself of greater proof of the secreted messages of the Dead Sea Scrolls.

His daily ritual was unerringly secure; all possible relevant information was stored below the plastic bags that lined the garbage cans within each room. He remained well into the night with the excuse that he was a bit slow and was willing to work longer hours in exchange for the Museum's tolerance of his physical limitations.

'You pay me to get the job done, not punch a time clock,' he once remarked to the Director.

49

DeVris had smiled, most likely with the thought that Hassan had little else to do to fill his nights.

Quite the contrary. Hassan worked late into the evening. Each hidden document had to be retrieved from its trash can, scanned into e-mail, then sent to Maluka on one of the computers for which Hassan had secured the password. When all had been transmitted, each document or photo had to be returned to its original location or destroyed. They were long days and longer nights, but Maluka's e-mail of confirmation each evening made it all worthwhile.

Then all was changed in a heartbeat. It was a typical evening, and Hassan had been involved in the process of sending Maluka the translation of a relatively unimportant section of one of the scrolls. He was seated at DeVris' computer and noticed a new e-mail had arrived from Ludlow. The Professor had no say in the decision to keep the most inflammatory sections of the Dead Sea Scrolls out of the reach of the public, so his communications were not among those that Maluka required Hassan to monitor.

On that night, however, the subject line of Ludlow's e-mail to DeVris pulled Hassan's attention from his task. On impulse, he opened it. The 'secured the find' subject line on the e-mail was not explained in its message, but Hassan forwarded the e-mail to Maluka anyway.

In the three months that followed, Maluka had learned that an eleventh-century diary had been secured by Ludlow; one that could lead them to an artifact more valuable and more damning to the mythology of Jesus than any message contained within the Dead Sea Scrolls.

The cost of this knowledge had been sizable; two deaths of key personnel at the Israel Museum that the police attributed to a random mugging and an unforeseen suicide along with the temporary collapse of the Israel Museum's entire data base. The latter Maluka had not anticipated. Once he had infiltrated the secure portions of the system, an irreversible fail-safe mechanism triggered a shut down of the entire database. Fortunately, Maluka had time to access and download the information that he needed and then, in the few minutes before the shutdown, was able to introduce a tourniquet program that concealed the breach while affording future access to all e-mail.

'But what about all of the months of work?' Hassan had asked with some disappointment. 'Are we to leave all of that behind?'

'I have come to realize that the public is more fickle than I imagined. A sixty-year-old conspiracy holds no interest for them,' Maluka explained. 'Others tried to expose the cover-up in the nineties as the Vatican Conspiracy but people quickly lost interest. With the power of MWT Videos behind me, I believed I could inspire the public to demand the truth, though recently I have begun to doubt it.

'This, on the other hand,' Maluka continued, 'is a collusion in the making. And if we are able to procure the scroll described in the diary, if indeed—as Ludlow believes—it dates back to the time of Jesus, every eye in the world will be upon us. This, my friend, is a gift from the hand of Allah. A discovery so great that none will dare deny it. And, most importantly, one that might yet be acquired before the Christian Infidels can once

51

again swallow it up.'

Hassan had been reluctant to give up so easily. 'But if Ludlow and DeVris locate the scroll, they won't hide it,' Hassan had protested. 'Why don't we let them find it and bring it to the world?'

'As others before them did with many of the Dead Sea Scrolls?' Maluka asked pointedly. 'No, DeVris is a poor academic in a world of very wealthy supporters. He watches contributors, without blinking an eye, write checks for ten times his annual salary. He has become bitter and greedy and sees the scroll only in terms of the potential wealth it may bring him.'

'But Ludlow . . .' Hassan interrupted.

'Yes, Ludlow sees the scroll's worth in terms of the truth it may hold. He is honest but weak. A bad combination. If they find this scroll, DeVris will sell it to the highest bidder, and Ludlow will have no say in the matter.'

Hassan hesitated. He knew better than to contradict his mentor. His fear of making so great an error in judgment would allow him to give in. 'But they worked together on The Cave 3 Scroll,' Hassan protested. 'They were both instrumental in getting it here so that all the world might see it. Wouldn't they do the same for the new scroll?'

Maluka shook his head. 'Ludlow, yes. DeVris, never. When the two of them first arranged to get The Cave 3 Scroll brought here from the Amman Museum, DeVris had only one thing in mind. If he got the actual scroll in his hands, he hoped he might discover some clue to the treasure described in The Cave 3's writings.'

'The treasure that no one has yet uncovered,' Hassan echoed thoughtfully.

52

'Exactly. If DeVris had believed that he could extract favors or fortune by keeping it hidden, he would have done so.'

Hassan had thought long and hard about Maluka's answer.

If what Maluka says is true, what then might DeVris be willing to do in order to get his hands on the new scroll?

TEN

Later that morning
Office of the Director of Acquisitions
Shrine of the Book, Israel Museum

Dr. Anton DeVris glanced down at the caller ID on his cell phone. Just what he needed, a call from Nathan McCullum, CEO of White Americans to Save Christianity. DeVris braced himself for the quick thinking he required to keep track of all of the lies, past and present.

McCullum's voice was warm and sympathetic, almost believable. 'I just heard about Ludlow,' McCullum began. 'How tragic. So sorry for your loss.'

After having read an account of Ludlow's brutal murder on the Internet, McCullum could have been expected to act in a number of predictable ways: he might have voiced his displeasure at not having been informed immediately by DeVris of the turn of events; he might have demanded an earlier estimated time of arrival for the translation of the final section of the diary; or he might have

53

reminded DeVris how much he was paying him to keep things on schedule. A sympathetic acknowledgment of DeVris' loss, with not a single mention of the diary, was not only out of character, it was downright suspicious.

Ludlow had been working full-time at the Museum when McCullum had first contacted DeVris more than six years earlier. McCullum's initial phone call to DeVris was of a completely innocent nature, related only to a donation.

'My accountants say I can use a tax break,' McCullum had explained. 'And given all the negative press that Evangelicals are getting in the States these days, an ecumenical donation couldn't be bad for WATSC's image.'

WATSC, an acronym for White Americans to Save Christianity, was not your typical Evangelical congregation. Having risen from the back swamps of KKK country, WATSC—pronounced 'watt-see'—found fertile ground in twenty-first century finance. In his climb to the top, McCullum, grandson of the founder, traded in Bible pounding for handshaking of the most influential kind. The big money that backed him and his enterprises agreed with his far, far right view of the world and had a vested interest in helping steer the U.S. in just the right direction.

Ludlow had tried to convince DeVris that WATSC was far more than a powerful political-financial institution. The old man couldn't have been more vehement if DeVris were being courted by the devil himself.

'Please say you're joking,' Ludlow had gasped when he first learned of McCullum's initial donation. According to Ludlow, WATSC's Nazis, as he called them, were so right-wing they made Adolf Hitler look like a bleeding-heart liberal. 'I'm telling you, Anton, they're not like you and me. When they want something they'll do anything to get it. No holds barred.' When DeVris had refused to turn down the donation, Ludlow added his final admonitions. 'You're way out of your league with this one. I hope to God you don't live to regret it.'

DeVris had told McCullum about Ludlow's predictions of doom. They had a good laugh together about it. From that moment on, encouraged by McCullum's reaction, DeVris had begun to see Ludlow as little more than a past-his-prime academic.

Only DeVris' assurance that McCullum's contribution was a one-time occurrence had calmed the old boy down. God only knows what Ludlow would have done had he known the DeVris-McCullum connection would be ongoing.

In exchange for McCullum's continued contributions to DeVris' ever-growing personal retirement account, the Director had used his authority and veto power within the Museum to help McCullum's cause. The sum total of DeVris' memos, speeches, and power votes helped squelch any actions—within and without the Museum— that might have allowed nearly all of the Dead Sea Scrolls to be put on public exhibition. The translations that would have followed would have most certainly challenged some of Christianity's most sacred writings.

'The last thing we need right now is fuel for another attack on the Church,' McCullum had explained. 'Lord knows, we had enough with those trumped-up child molestation accusations.

Challenges to the historical validity of the Bible do no one any good, much less God-fearing Christians who do not need yet another test of faith.'

DeVris had accepted McCullum's point of view with grace, resisting temptation to add his personal thought that any such test of faith might have a considerable impact on WATSC's billion-dollar Evangelical empire as well.

To tell the truth, there were moments when Ludlow's disquieting predictions stirred a bit of fear in DeVris. A short phone call from McCullum, however, never failed to put the whole thing right.

Last year, Ludlow's decision to retire had come as a more than welcome announcement. The Professor's return to England had allowed DeVris the luxury of easy communication with McCullum. Not that DeVris was doing anything wrong. After all, he had never actually voted against his conscience. He simply allowed himself to keep an open mind to McCullum's insights. The fact that his votes helped to keep particularly provocative sections of the Dead Sea Scrolls under wraps was not as much testimony to his loyalty to McCullum as it was to the cogent points of McCullum's arguments.

Had others known of McCullum's support, they might have accused him of selling out. He would have argued that he simply was buying into a responsible approach to information sharing. Give the people what they can handle. No more. No less. It was better for them, and it was better for the world at large. And if, at the same time, McCullum's contributions helped make up for the

Museum's unfair and inadequate pension policy, so much the better.

Ludlow's rare visits to the Museum to do research were always preceded by a courtesy call to DeVris, as per the Director's request. Advance warning of the Professor's visits gave DeVris plenty of time to remove any trace of the McCullum influence. All in all, things had been moving along quite smoothly.

Then, two months earlier, the Professor procured a piece of antiquity that McCullum was hell-bent on acquiring. From the day that DeVris told McCullum about the diary, DeVris had been walking a tightrope, trying to maintain a balance between McCullum's determination to obtain the diary and Ludlow's terror of allowing the secrets that the diary held to fall into 'the wrong hands.'

Now, with Ludlow permanently out of the picture, and the diary apparently still secure within Ludlow's safe, housed behind the oven, DeVris was finally in control.

DeVris turned his attention back to the phone conversation. It was time for a contribution from him.

'From what the police told me when they notified me of the incident, Ludlow must have walked in on his attackers,' DeVris explained. 'The intruders must have been in the apartment for some time trying to force Ludlow's wife to tell them where the diary was, apparently keeping her alive until Ludlow came home.'

'Lucky you followed my suggestion and had Ludlow get the diary to you,' McCullum concluded.

Fear shot through DeVris' body. McCullum was testing him, waiting for DeVris to assure him, once again, that the diary was safe in DeVris' possession.

The Director broke into a cold sweat. Perhaps McCullum was giving him one last chance to confess that he had been lying. If McCullum suspected that Ludlow had never given up the diary, DeVris might do better to just admit it and take his punishment like a man.

But how could he admit he only had the bits and pieces of the diary that Ludlow had doled out to him? How could he say he had been stringing McCullum along for weeks?

It had seemed like a foolproof scheme at the time. Ludlow, unwilling to turn over the diary, had agreed to upload a small section of the manuscript each day for DeVris to translate directly off the Internet. In exchange, DeVris had paid the small fortune demanded by the antique dealer for the diary and had agreed to provide Sabbie's services, without whom Ludlow would not have been able to decipher the more esoteric passages of the moldy manuscript.

Though the exchange had been more than fair, at the last minute, Ludlow had insisted on maintaining strict control. By using a special copyright protection program, the Professor had ensured that DeVris could view each day's section of the diary on the Internet but had barred him from copying the material into a document or from printing it out.

At least, that's what the old guy believed. DeVris had worked his way past a similar program used by online booksellers for customers who searched the contents of books. By instructing his computer to take screen shots, DeVris had been able to photograph each page of the diary and save them as PDF files for printing, reevaluation, and compilation at his leisure. He had allowed Ludlow to believe he was in control. It made the old man happy and, most of all, kept him quiet.

Without actually having the diary, DeVris had been able to provide McCullum with the ever-growing manuscript translation and copies of the original text for which McCullum paid extraordinarily well.

It would have been the perfect plan if DeVris had not lived in fear that McCullum might someday demand to see the actual diary. When that day came . . . well, DeVris never actually allowed himself to consider what might happen.

With notification of Ludlow's death, DeVris had feared his pretense might be revealed but the gods had been with him. The police had indicated that Ludlow's wall safe had been broken into but made no mention of the oven safe. Both Ludlow's assassins and the police appeared ignorant of its existence and DeVris had every reason to believe that it was still intact, the diary safe within.

All of his warnings to Ludlow to tell no one but his assistant, Peterson, of the existence of the oven safe had paid off . . . in spades.

It had been DeVris' additional good fortune that Ludlow had uploaded the last of the diary's pages only two days before heading for his meeting in the States with CyberNet.

As soon as things calmed down a bit, DeVris would fly to England, gain access to the apartment, get Peterson to open the oven safe, and bring the diary home with no one any the wiser. Piece of cake. Until then, the Internet photos that DeVris had taken would continue to convince McCullum that the diary was secure within DeVris' hands. And, for all intents and purposes, it was. As Ludlow would have put it, what the top WATSC Nazi didn't know wouldn't hurt him.

'So Ludlow's murderers never got what they were looking for?' McCullum reiterated.

'How could they?' DeVris replied with as upbeat a tone as he could muster.

'Good,' McCullum concluded, seemingly satisfied. 'By the way,' he added nonchalantly. 'Interesting turn of events, this Peterson thing, don't you think?'

DeVris froze. 'What Peterson thing?'

'Oh, didn't you know? Ludlow's assistant has been missing for two days now.'

ELEVEN

Later that afternoon
Main Entry Gate, Israel Museum

The cab pulled into the grand circle driveway. Beyond the great gates lay an unending boulevard walk. Buildings on both sides of the boulevard seemed miles away.

'Can't you get any closer?' Gil asked. Although he had landed at the airport with more than three hours to spare, customs inspections and mid-day traffic had eaten up almost all of the time. He had less than a half an hour to get to DeVris' office in the Shrine of the Book before the Director left for the day. Gil could have called and said he was running late if he had had the time to charge his cell phone, which he hadn't, so he couldn't.

'This is as far as I can go,' the driver said. 'You could take the old-people's shuttle to the Entrance Pavilion Information Desk if you like,' he added with a grin.

'Some sage advice,' Gil retorted. 'Don't make fun of the customer 'til after you get your tip.'

'Some sager advice,' the driver replied. 'Don't assume the tip isn't already built into the fare.'

The buildings, crosswalks, and soft grassy areas that made up the Israel Museum complex covered more than twenty acres. The maze that led to the Shrine of the Book was indecipherable. He was lost. The simple map provided by the security guard at the gate was useless. Asking three people for directions yielded four different sets of instructions in what Gil had quickly termed 'Heblish,' for the indistinguishable blending of Hebrew-English lexicon.

A final request to a passerby brought help in the form of a Canadian who, taking Gil by the elbow, steered him past the Youth Wing of the Museum to where they presumably could get a better view.

The white, mushroom-shaped roof in the distance rose to a peak in the center, jutting into the cloudless blue sky. Black walls rose in stark contrast. 'That's the Shrine of the Book,' the Canadian said softly. 'She's a beauty, ehh?'

The grandeur of the architecture was unexpected, as was Gil's reaction. With each step, he felt less sure of himself and more in awe.

A simple map in the lobby of the white-capped

building, its legend in English and Hebrew, pointed the way to the Museum offices. Pulling open the heavy door to that wing, Gil stepped into the cool, dark corridor. Though light streamed in, the labyrinth of layered walls more resembled a cave than a hall. Gil walked slowly, finding the appropriate turnoff at the end. Reluctantly, he left the peaceful passageway and entered the glaring efficiency of the faculty offices.

The secretary greeted him with a smile that was only as friendly as it had to be. Gil explained that he was already late and would appreciate it if she would tell Dr. DeVris that he had arrived.

She shrugged and turned back to her phone conversation.

'Yes, I know,' she whispered loudly. 'Isn't it a tragedy? And he was such a dear man. Always so polite.'

God, this could go on all day.

'And they were such a lovely couple. So sweet. Their golden wedding anniversary was only next week,' the secretary continued.

Gil resisted the desire to grab her by her skinny little shoulders and force her to dial the Director's extension. Lucy used to say that he didn't do powerless well. A definite understatement.

Gil jumped at the sound of his name. 'He expecting you,' the secretary announced. She pointed to the appropriate door with the phone she still clutched in her hand. 'Knock before you go in.'

Gil did as instructed. A voice from within told him to enter.

'You can tell a lot about a man from his back,' Grandpa Max used to say. 'That's the part he's less

likely to be able to control.'

The back of the figure that greeted Gil sported a perfectly tailored suit and a head of hair that looked more sculpted than cut. It remained standing and stared out the window, then it spoke.

'I didn't want you on this project.'

Gil hesitated.

'It's nothing personal,' the man continued. 'It's just that I think this whole thing is . . . well, to be blunt . . . beyond you.'

'Dr. DeVris?' Gil asked, hoping to find that an error had been made.

DeVris turned and seated himself behind his desk and surveyed his guest. Without waiting for an invitation, Gil took a seat and waited.

The office itself appeared to match its occupant, understated to the point of pretension. Gil surmised that it was no accident that the tones of DeVris' suit and tie as well as the color scheme of the office were in shades of gray. The color scheme perfectly complimented the silver highlights of DeVris' salt-and-peppered hair. The message from his behavior and office décor was clear and simple. 'I am a man of taste. I am confident and cultured. Know with whom you are dealing.'

He's trying too hard! Gil smiled broadly.

'I don't have time for games,' DeVris continued. 'The point is that your boss and Dr. Ludlow considered you the best choice, so neither you nor I had any say in this matter.'

'Just two kids whose mothers have dumped 'em in a playpen,' Gil said with an easy grin. 'Question is, are we gonna play nice?'

DeVris considered Gil's comment. Apparently,

63

this was not the response DeVris had anticipated.

From Gil's experience with George, the big guy probably told DeVris he could expect Gil to be hotheaded and egotistical, certain to respond in anger to an antagonistic challenge, but smart as hell; a description not entirely without precedent but perhaps a little over the top. DeVris probably figured that an outburst of temper from Gil would have been just the thing to have him removed from the project. A change in plans that, obviously, would have suited DeVris to a 'T.'

I'm not going to make it that easy for you. If you want me out of here, you're going to have to do better than that.

DeVris seemed to be considering his next move. 'Why did you accept this assignment?'

'Because I was told to,' Gil answered simply.

'So, if I understand you correctly, you're going to help us find any pattern that may reveal a hidden message in the diary which, in turn, may help us locate the scroll, all because you've been told to?'

'Well, for the most part, yes.'

'And you expect nothing for yourself? Other than your regular pay and perhaps a bonus?'

'Not really. I mean, I think all of us want to leave something behind. That's man's nature,' Gil added.

'Bullshit,' DeVris said simply. 'I know who you are. The truth is you're interested in wealth, fame, and maybe a little adventure. There's nothing wrong with that. Truly successful men not only admit to their ambition, they embrace it.'

DeVris' voice softened. 'It's funny, you remind me a great deal of myself.' He resumed the stance

64

in which Gil had first found him. 'I wasted a good part of my life pretending that all I wanted was to make the world a better place. In truth, I wanted a whole lot more. But,' DeVris added, with a sigh, 'I don't think it's going take you half as long as it took me.'

DeVris turned back from the window and detailed what he expected of Gil. A small room next to DeVris' office would be made available. Gil would be given a photocopy of the diary to examine for patterns that might contain a hidden message. He was to decipher any pattern or message he discovered with the expectation that it might relate the location of the Weymouth Scroll. If Gil proved himself useful, he would have earned the right to continue with the project and to share in the notoriety. If not, CyberNet would be paid for his time and the consultation would be considered terminated.

DeVris turned, once again, to look out the window.

Taking his cue, Gil made his way to the door.

Without turning to face his new employee, DeVris added one sentence of encouragement. 'You're going to do well,' he said with unexpected warmth. 'Now get yourself a good meal and some sleep. We're going to work you hard. I'll expect you bright and early in the morning.'

Before he closed the door behind him, Gil glanced back at DeVris. The red rays of the setting sun seemed to reflect as a halo. Each silver strand of hair, each highlight of his clothing, glowed with a fluorescent-like red. The grays and silvers of the room radiated crimson and scarlet. The luminescence was so great that, for a moment,

DeVris appeared to be encircled and caressed by flames. It was an odd illusion, gone in a moment, replaced by shadows, with the shifting of the final rays of the sun.

TWELVE

A few minutes later
Office of Dr. Anton DeVris

'Hold on.' DeVris spoke into the empty room. After a few moments, he walked to his door, looked down the hall, then returned to his desk.

'Okay,' he announced. 'He's gone.'

The Director smiled to himself, then spoke into the air again.

'Sabbie, on your way in, bring me a cup of coffee.' Reaching down, he switched off the intercom that had been left on during Gil's interview and waited.

A kick at the door announced her arrival. He rose, slowly walked to the door, and opened it.

'Inconsiderate bastard.' She shoved past him, one cup in each hand. 'You could at least leave the door open so I don't have to claw at it like a dog.'

He took his seat behind his great desk. 'Scratch,' he corrected.

'Scratch?'

'Cats claw, dogs scratch,' DeVris said coolly. 'Technically, you can't claw like a dog.'

Sabbie slid DeVris' cup to him across his desk, fast. She knew it would get a rise out of him, but he was certain she had no idea in what way.

She looked particularly beautiful; shiny hair, flushed cheeks.

'We need a new intercom,' she announced. 'Everything sounded scratchy. It was like listening to an old phonograph record.'

'Need a recap?' DeVris asked.

'No, I heard enough. The guy's a schmuck,' Sabbie concluded. 'Dump him. Just tell CyberNet you've changed your mind. Worst comes to worst, you'll lose your deposit. No big deal.'

'So you think he's not capable of the job. Is that why you walked out on him at the restaurant?'

'That and because I thought we were being followed,' she replied. Her gaze never left his eyes. 'Are you saying Ludlow and I should have stayed?' she challenged.

'Well, it's not the best way to start off a working relationship.'

'So you're going to keep him?' she asked incredulously.

DeVris hesitated. She was hiding something. Why was she pushing so hard?

'And who would you recommend in his place?' DeVris asked. 'There's nobody else and you know it.'

Sabbie stood abruptly and headed toward the door.

'You know what? Do what you want. I'd just like to know why in the hell you even bother to ask my opinion.'

Because methinks the lady doth protest too much. And because I'm trying to figure out if you're more interested in screwing me figuratively or Mr. Pearson literally.

She was arrogant and opinionated. Had he not

felt that he had to have her around, under whatever pretense was necessary, he would never have hired her. She was the best translator in the field. She had a working knowledge of Aramaic, Greek, Ancient Hebrew, and Classical Latin. She was tech savvy and a workaholic. A perfect assistant were it not for one undeniable fact.

Beneath her brilliance and her easy antagonistic joking was a hardness that DeVris never wanted to put to the test; a coldness that came from seeing the world without illusion and, perhaps, without hope. He had not known her before the assault and often wondered if, indeed, it was that violence that helped sculpt her unpretentious directness. The very quality he found so damn seductive.

THIRTEEN

Day Six, morning
Office of the Translator, Shrine of the Book
Israel Museum

'You're late,' Sabbie said. She looked up casually, then returned to sorting papers on the great desk. From the look of the place, she'd been there for hours.

Gil stared at her in surprise. The last time he had seen her, she was headed for the Ladies' Room at the restaurant in New York, never to return again.

Sabbie smiled at his confusion.

'Just kidding about you being late. You're right on time. Good morning,' she added with uncharacteristic bonhomie.

Gil smiled back with relief. Apparently, his concern that she had changed her mind about working with him had been way off target. Good thing. No matter how bitchy she had been in the restaurant, he hadn't been able to stop imagining what it would be like to savor every inch of her.

Best of all, since he was already at the Museum, and since they were not about to send him home for just looking, Gil allowed himself a good long and unashamed look at the object of several of the most erotic dreams of his life.

She wore loose men's khaki slacks with macramé suspenders and a man's big white shirt that made her look small and surprisingly feminine. The pattern of lace from her bra was visible through the cotton fabric of the shirt, and beneath the lace, the hint of café-au-lait-colored nipples beckoned him to come and explore. Gil caught his breath and struggled to keep control.

As if reading his mind, Sabbie suddenly became all business again.

'Come to my office,' she said.

Gil followed, surrendering his thoughts to the movement of her perfectly rounded bottom.

She closed the door. Still standing, she faced him and began.

'First, a few ground rules. All work is to be done in this office only. All translation and decoding will take place here. No discussion, not even a casual comment, will be exchanged in any other room.'

'The lighting sucks,' Gil said sharply. If she had her demands, he had his.

'I'll see if we can have another lamp brought in but it may have to do.'

'Why can't we work on that big table in the main office?'

'Because I said so, that's why.'

Gil folded his arms and shook his head. If she wanted to treat him like a child, he might as well act like one.

'Look,' Sabbie began, 'when I state something unequivocally I have a very good reason for doing so. Anyone who knows anything about current technology knows that no place is safe. Open up your pc and anyone within a couple of hundred feet can access all your records via your wireless connection. Make a call on your cell phone and that info is up for sale within minutes. Even your personal phonecard is fair game at any airport.'

'Well, I would assume you don't exactly have identity thieves running around one of the most prestigious museums in the world,' Gil said with an intentional smirk.

'Identity theft would be the least of our worries. When you're in this building, you're always on, Jack.'

'Gil,' he corrected, broadening the sneer.

'Whatever. Appropriate steps have been taken to protect this office. Let's get to work.'

Well, this is lovely. By the end of the day, we should be eating each other's carcasses.

She settled down in the seat facing Gil and handed him several pages of translation. 'The translation of the diary was relatively simple. I tried as much as possible to keep to the original word count and order in case that was important.'

Gil nodded his approval. Not bad. That bit of detail could spell the difference between finding a

70

pattern and missing it completely.

She sat forward. 'Now, here's the deal,' Sabbie continued. 'These pages appear to be an accounting of the sales and deliveries of tapestries made by the monks at Weymouth Monastery. On the surface, it's pretty straight-forward.'

'But . . .' Gil prompted.

'But I don't think that's what it is at all,' she said, half to herself. 'The sentences are logical and correct in their grammar but the words convey little more than medieval gossip. To make matters worse, the ramblings about the people of the town are interspersed with dates and numbers and the whole thing is put into an accounting format. I don't understand why whoever wrote this would do that.'

'Do what?' Gil asked.

'Why he would put long nonsensical sentences onto accounting pages,' she said with obvious frustration. 'It just doesn't make sense.'

'So what's the problem?' Gil asked calmly. He was hoping to push her until something snapped, until she could give him the connection she didn't even know that she knew. He was hoping, as well, to avoid the likelihood of her breaking a chair over his head.

'The problem is,' Sabbie continued, 'if we don't find anything in this section that mentions another scroll, something—anything—about a mate to The Cave 3 Scroll, we might as well just give up.'

'And . . .' Gil prompted again.

'I really wish you wouldn't do that, it's incredibly irritating. Anyway, although I know there's something in here, I just can't figure it out.'

'What makes you think there's something in

here?' Gil asked.

'I don't know, I just do.'

'*How* do you know?'

'I told you. I don't *know* how I know it's there! I just do!' Sabbie bellowed.

She was clearly at the end of her patience, exactly where Gil wanted her. George always said that if you wanted to get someone's attention, first you had to shoot them in the leg. Well, finding any hidden message in the diary might well depend on Sabbie's intuition, and this little control freak wasn't going to trust her instincts unless she was pushed—hard.

'So, somehow you just *know* it,' Gil said sarcastically.

She looked like she was going to haul off and slam him.

'Works for me,' he said with a sudden smile. 'That's exactly what forensics depends on. That and some terrific technology. When you get that feeling, when you just know there's something hidden just beyond where you can see it, you're almost always right.'

'And when you're wrong?' she asked.

'Then you've screwed up. But, more often than not, you're right.'

Sabbie didn't look convinced. Gil knew what she was thinking. A fifty-fifty chance of finding a hidden message in the diary was better than nothing, but not as good as a hundred percent.

Careful, my sweet. That's what makes gamblers into addicts.

'Okay, show me what you got,' Gil said.

She handed him the printouts. They were fuzzy and too light, barely readable. They looked like second-generation copies of scanned pages that had been posted on the Internet or put through the dishwasher.

'I need something better to work from.'

She reminded him that he already had her translations. Besides, she said, since he didn't understand Latin anyway, it didn't seem essential that he work from pristine pages.

'I look for patterns,' he explained. 'Even in other languages. So I need the original to look at, too.'

She was immovable. This was all they had. He would have to depend on her.

'Why can't we work directly from the diary?'

'Not possible,' she answered and indicated that the matter for discussion was closed.

'Okay, we'll do it your way,' he said with a shrug, 'but it's going to take a lot longer. Let's try doing it by ear instead. Read it to me.'

At first, the translated sentences made no sense at all. Then, after a few minutes, something seemed to call to him from beyond the words, like a melody he couldn't quite make out. If he could just . . .

Gil placed his hands on either side of his head. The ride was about to start. 'Read it again,' he said excitedly. 'The same first few sentences. Read them over and over. Keep going.'

26th day of January 1097 in the year of our Lord

1-18 1 4 19 I am here with Elias. A poor simple monk living outside Caston within the great city walls of Halcourt near Weymouth Monastery.

27th day of January 1097 in the year of our Lord

5-8 3 1 79 He knows I put lies in this tale and wrongs to ink.

25th day of February 1097 in the year of our Lord

4-12 3 6 9 He angers for I have no fear that one day all shall come to be lost.

3rd day of March 1097 in the year of our Lord

14-2 13 26 7 He rages should I never again fail to try and do so.

For over an hour she reread the same word salad, until they both knew it by heart, backward and forward. She was starting to lose faith, and it showed.

'This is getting us nowhere,' she began. 'Why don't you try decoding it?'

'What are you talking about?'

'You know, substitute letters or whatever you do. Come on, *I* shouldn't have to tell *you*!'

'I told you I don't do codes,' he said simply. 'I look for patterns. Or changes in patterns. Look, if you're married, a change in patterns tells you that your spouse has been cheating on you. If you're a bank president, it clues you to the fact that your employee has been embezzling money. If you're a cybersleuth, it alerts you to a predator trying to lure a child into an abusive relationship. Even terrorists are easy to spot if you know what patterns to look for.'

This diary held a hidden pattern. He could hear it. Loud and clear. It was something he couldn't explain. He wanted to tell her that you don't find it by telling your brain where to go, you let it take you. That was the thrill of it. You just went along for the ride and you never knew where you were going to end up. And the pattern was here, calling him like sirens used to call to the sailors of old. The same sailors, Gil reminded himself, who ended up crashing to their death against the rocks.

Bad analogy. Get back to work.

Something was clicking. The words echoed in his mind.

'Read it once more. Quick!'

Without protest, she began again.

'Okay, now slowly,' he said, scrambling for a pen and paper.

Sabbie recited the first few entries.

'Again,' he shouted. 'Faster. Faster.'

She read it twice more.

'Son of a bitch. I think we got it!' he announced triumphantly. 'Son of a bitch! And it was so damn simple.'

FOURTEEN

A few minutes later
Muslims for World Truth (MWT)
Video Production Studios
London

News of Ludlow's death was shocking but not surprising. It made all the sense in the world. Maluka, himself, with the able assistance of Aijaz, had had similar plans for the Professor. Only the presence of two large and very muscular young men, apparently making their way to Ludlow's apartment a few steps ahead of him and Aijaz, had deterred Maluka from his immediate objective.

As they left, he and Aijaz had spotted two others, dressed in the same white jeans and sweaters as the first two. The second pair waited at the elevator door.

At the time, Maluka considered that the men might have been hired to protect Ludlow and the diary. As far as he knew, no one had intentions of taking the diary by force. And Maluka had known nothing of McCullum's Angels of Death. Now he knew better.

They had come, they had killed, but, apparently, they had not obtained what they had sought. From all reports he had accessed, official and otherwise, Maluka found no mention of the oven safe or, as per Peterson's description, the diary within.

The thought that a team of professional killers had failed to persuade the old Professor and his wife to reveal the diary's location perplexed Maluka. Another thought, however, concerned him more.

While Ludlow had lived, DeVris had been kept within a modicum of restraint. The DeVris-McCullum connection had blossomed with the Professor's retirement and move to England. Nevertheless, the threat of Ludlow's ever-watchful eye and his willingness to report any obvious infraction to the Museum administration, had kept DeVris from doing any real and permanent harm.

Now, with Ludlow completely out of the picture, the fate of the diary and the scroll would lie entirely in DeVris' hands. If, indeed, the scroll proved to bear witness to the existence of Jesus as nothing more than a mortal man, it would matter little to DeVris. Though the manuscript might contain proof of Islam's most sacred teachings, DeVris was quite likely to simply sell it off to the highest bidder whether their intention was to disclose the manuscript's sacred message or keep it hidden forever.

'We cannot wait,' Maluka informed Hassan. 'Ludlow's death is a sign from Allah that the time has come for action. Focus on the girl and the American. There will come a time when they will follow the trail dictated by the contents of the diary. We shall let them lead us to the scroll. Then we shall claim that for which our people have waited far too long.'

'What if the scroll bears false witness?' Hassan asked. 'Suppose it claims that Jesus was, indeed, the son of God?'

'Then it shall be melted down and returned back to the earth, where it belongs.'

FIFTEEN

A few minutes later
Office of the Translator, Shrine of the Book

'It couldn't be that simple,' Sabbie said softly.

'That's the beauty of it,' Gil said. 'Look, first disregard all the dates, punctuation, and numbers. They're meant to misdirect you. Now, read the first two words, skip two words, read two words, and skip the next two. Go ahead.'

26th day of January 1097 in the year of our Lord

1-18 1 4 19 **I am** here with **Elias. A** poor simple **monk living** outside Caston **within the** great city **walls of** Halcourt near **Weymouth Monastery.**

27th day of January 1097 in the year of our Lord

5-8 3 1 79 He knows **I put** lies in **this tale** and wrongs **to ink.**

25th day of February 1097 in the year of our Lord

4-12 3 6 9 He angers **for I** have no **fear that** one day **all shall** come to **be lost.**

3rd day of March 1097 in the year of our Lord

14-2 13 26 7 He rages **should I** never again **fail to** try and **do so.**

'But it's so obvious,' she protested. 'It could be seen by anybody.'

'That's what makes it work. The best place to hide a tree is in the forest. Look how long it took us to get it. And we knew it was there,' he added.

'What are you talking about?'

'Elias knew that people see what they expect to see,' Gil explained. 'It's one of the oldest tricks in the book. The ancient Greeks used to tattoo secret communiqués on the shaved heads of slaves. They'd let the hair grow in and send the slave off to the intended recipient. The recipient would shave the slave's head and read the message. No enemy along the way expected a message to be tattooed on the scalp, so no one ever looked for it.

Elias knew the best way to keep his message safe was to be sure that no one knew it was there.'

'Seems much too risky to me. I don't think he'd take the chance,' she argued.

'Look,' Gil continued, trying another approach. 'You said it yourself. Most people couldn't read back then and even if they *could* read and they *were* looking for a hidden message, chances are they'd be looking for a simple code, a substitution system—letter for letter.'

'Like I was,' Sabbie said thoughtfully.

'Exactly.'

She was up out of her chair, gathering papers, using the two-word pattern to translate and dictate phrases as fast as Gil could write them down. With alternate two-word phrases discarded, sentence after sentence revealed itself, simple and powerful in its honesty and its pain.

The words were those of Brother Elias, monk of Weymouth Monastery in England.

To Elias, there had been given a scroll, made of copper and brought from the Holy Land by William, Lord of Weymouthshire and knight of the Crusades. Lord William was Elias' brother though not by birth. The monk and the knight were brothers, the monk explained, by 'spirit and upbringing if not by blood.'

Lord William's story was both heroic and tragic. While serving God and King in the Holy Land, he had been wounded and left among the legions of dead and dying on their battleground near Qumran. A Muslim in soldier's garb brought the knight to a cave nearby, where he tended William's injuries and brought him food and drink.

Each morning the Muslim soldier left the cave

and joined the fighting legions that William could hear in the distance. Each night, the soldier returned, bringing fresh food and drink. They shared no common language but were able to make themselves understood, one to the other, of their intent and their feelings. As the days passed, William grew strong yet he wondered if his benefactor would ever permit him to leave.

On the morning that William was first able to stand on his own, the soldier brought him to the backmost section of the cave and revealed to him an ancient copper scroll secreted in a wooden casket. William appreciated well the importance of this find and knew, as well, that for some reason the soldier did not wish it to fall into the hands of his Muslim comrades. In words that he hoped the soldier might understand, William pledged his liege to protect that which was so important to one who had been so merciful.

That evening the soldier left and never returned.

William waited for several days, consuming what food and drink remained, then in the dark of night, he left in hopes of making his way home. As he had promised, he took the scroll with him.

After many long months, William returned to his beloved England. Home, however, did not afford him the sanctuary he anticipated. While he had been away, sustaining wounds in the name of the Church, the local Abbot had usurped William's castle and lands and was now unwilling to return so profitable an acquisition.

Upon hearing of William's prize from the Holy Land, which the knight had brought to his brother, Elias, for translation, Father Abbot declared the scroll to be the work of the devil and called for ritual redemption by fire. As was the law, upon the death of the knight, the Church would become the beneficiary of all property, land and otherwise, previously held by the heretic.

William was executed, burned at the stake, though not before Elias revealed to him the true contents of the scroll. Elias realized William had discovered the writings of one who walked and talked with the messiah, Yeshua, which is what he might very well have been called at that time.

'Jesus!' Gil exclaimed.

'Exactly,' Sabbie replied. 'If what this diary says is true, the scroll William took from the cave contained the only firsthand account in existence of the life and the death of Jesus, then called Yeshua.

'Can you imagine what such a find would mean?' she continued with excitement. 'To know, with certainty, exactly what happened in Jesus' life, to see it as if we were there?'

Gil shook his head at the enormity of it.

'There's more,' she said. 'Remember, the last section of The Cave 3 Scroll says that he who finds its mate will discover the key to the locations of the many treasures described in The Cave 3 Scroll. If Elias' scroll turns out to be the mate to The Cave 3, it could be expected to hold even more than priceless proof of the life of Jesus. At the same time it may very well provide a map to a storehouse of riches beyond measure.'

Before Gil could respond, Sabbie continued, her face far more serious than it had been a moment ago. 'It also means that any person or organization that seeks power or wealth, religious vindication or domination, will do anything they can to get hold of this scroll. Anything, including killing anyone who stands in its way. They may have begun already,' she added thoughtfully.

'But we still have no idea where the scroll is.'

'Yes, but they don't know that,' she said.

'Well, I don't know who "they" is,' he said, trying to minimize her latest detour into paranoia. 'All I know is that this is all that Elias left behind, so there must be a clue to where the scroll is hidden in these.' Gil held up a stack of deciphered pages.

'Or somewhere else,' Sabbie said.

Gil looked up in surprise.

She walked to the safe, opened it, and handed Gil a new stack of papers. These copies were crisp and clear. Each was formatted in the same accounting layout as the muddy copies they had just deciphered but these pages were easily read. Most importantly, these pages contained information he had never seen before.

'The pages we just deciphered comprise only half of the diary, the second half,' she explained. 'These new pages make up the first half of the diary.'

'So Elias' story was actually part two?' Gil asked.

'Exactly.'

'Then why didn't you give me the first section in the beginning?'

'Nobody has a copy of this,' she said.

'Not even DeVris?'

'Especially not DeVris. Ludlow has never trusted him. Said the man has no conscience and . . . no soul.'

'And what's your take on DeVris?' Gil asked.

'I think Ludlow was being kind.'

Gil picked up a pencil and began to circle every other two-word combination.

'That's not going to work,' Sabbie said. 'The words in these pages can't be arranged into sentences. They are simply names and places. They document who bought which tapestry and for how much, just like any other accounting journal.'

'Because that's exactly what it is,' Gil said simply.

This diary, both parts of it, was almost certainly one of the Church's Books of Record, Gil explained. Elias was probably the most literate of the monks. It would have been natural to choose him as the official Keeper of Records for his monastery.

From what Gil could surmise, Elias had used the first section of the diary for the record-keeping for which the book was intended and had used the second half of the book as his personal diary. By putting his hidden message into the same format as the accounting pages that filled the front of the diary, then placing it in the back part of the book, all of the pages looked alike from start to finish; especially to those who couldn't read.

'But what if someone *could* read?' Sabbie asked.

'Elias must have thought that wasn't likely or he wouldn't have done it this way,' Gil said.

He shook his head slowly. There was something else he wasn't seeing. It kept popping into his thoughts, then disappearing before he could get hold of it.

'But you think it's in here?'

'The location of the scroll? Yeah, it's got to be,'

Gil concluded. 'I'd bet my life on it.'

Gil waited for Sabbie's usual comeback. She looked up with no trace of a smile. Her silence scared the hell out of him.

SIXTEEN

Day Seven, mid-morning
Office of the Translator

Gil had been hard at work since seven in the morning and, with the exception of a raging headache, he had nothing to show for it. Sabbie, on the other hand, strolled in at her own leisure.

'Well, how nice of you to join us,' he said sarcastically.

'I had some things to take care of. I should have told you I'd be late.'

'Among other things,' Gil continued.

Sabbie looked up in surprise.

'You know you might have warned me that the guard last night was going to give me a better feel than I've had from anyone in years,' he said.

She smiled at his description.

'Or that almost every piece of paper on my person, including my used Kleenex, would be open to inspection,' he went on. 'I expected it on the way in, but why did they do it last night, on the way out? Never did that before,' he mused.

'As of yesterday, you were moved up to a Level Three Security Risk. Once you saw the diary, you gave up the right to physical privacy. That's the trade-off.'

Gil threw her a dirty look.

'You don't want to know what an Aleph or Bet have to go through,' she laughed.

'Then how come you get to pass by the friendly hands of our Gestapo Museum guard with only the lightest of pat-downs?'

Her smiled faded and a soft sadness crept across her face. 'You don't want to know,' she said quietly.

'Yes, I do. Come on. How come you get special treatment?

She moved closer, her face only inches from his, and smiled impudently. 'Because most people, especially men—but women too—feel funny about touching someone who's been raped. Even if it's nothing more than a standard security frisk, it makes them uncomfortable. In my case, they would rather risk my smuggling sensitive information out of the Museum than chance offending me and creating a scene.'

Gil struggled to sort through her comeback. If Sabbie had wanted him to know she had been raped, she had chosen a particularly lousy way to tell him. No accident, he concluded. She wasn't about to waste the shock value of it. He wasn't certain what she expected but he wasn't buying into the game.

'I didn't know,' he said simply. He stared back unblinkingly.

'About which, the rape or people's reactions?' she asked haughtily.

'Either.'

'Well, it's true. Once people know you've been raped, they never treat you the same again. Every time they see you, the first thing they think about is the rape. You can see it in their eyes. It affects how they treat you, how they speak to you, certainly, how they touch you.'

Her tone, though it had started out as defiant, had become honest and passionate.

'It's probably a lot like being fat or being a nun,' she continued. 'Few people are able to get past that first big fact. In my case, it works to my advantage. I get to bypass the groping sweaty hands that wait for you every time you leave the building, while you get a free thrill every time,' she added with a mischievous grin.

'Thanks a lot!' he said sarcastically.

'So, how's it going?' she asked.

'What, the pattern-hunting? It's not,' Gil admitted.

'What would help?'

'A good smack in the head with some particularly heavy object might do the trick. Look, as far as I can see, Elias' message says nothing about the scroll. Nada, zilch, zippo,' he concluded with a pop of his lips.

'Come on,' she said warmly. 'You need a break.' She took him by the hand and walked toward the door. 'I'm going to show you what you've been working for.'

The next two hours passed as if they had been minutes. The Museum's plethora of riches, beauty, ingenuity, and sheer antiquity were overwhelming. He had expected to see Judaica, historical finds of disintegrating paper and rusted metal. He was met with fourteenth-century sculptures of Venus, astounding riches of Turkish Sultans, the works of Pollock, Ernst, Rembrandt, Rodin, and hundreds of other treasures that, each in itself, would have warranted its own place of exhibit.

'It's not like anything I've ever seen before,' Gil said.

'When I first came here I felt like I had found a time capsule that contained the best of mankind. Now, I don't get to see almost any of it,' she said. 'Some of the exhibitions remain but there are always new ones. I promise myself I'll come more often, but unless I'm taking someone around, I never make the time.'

'What a shame.'

'Yes.'

They stood in the Art Garden surrounded by fig trees and olive bushes. Massive sculptures rose like the rock islands of Japan. She guided him to one of the largest monuments.

'This one's by Ezra Orion,' she said.

The five-story concrete staircase seemed to lead to heaven.

'Isn't it amazing?' she asked. 'It almost beckons you to ascend, to be something greater than you are. Like a promise that is waiting to be fulfilled.'

'The morning after the rape, I came here,' Sabbie continued. 'It was dawn. I wasn't working at the Museum then, I sneaked in through a small break in the front fence near the rosemary bushes. I never told anyone where the opening was, so I could always come back. They say they found me unconscious on the sculpture's first step. They couldn't understand why I didn't go to the hospital first but I needed to come here, to this staircase. I knew I would find what I needed here.'

Gil nodded to tell her that he understood, though clearly he did not.

They stood, side by side, without speaking then

continued through the garden. Water flows sprang from a fountain-sculpture, and the small stones of a Zen Garden crunched under their feet.

'It's paradise,' he said simply.

She nodded and squeezed his hand.

'There's more,' she said. 'Come on.'

SEVENTEEN

A few minutes later
Side Entrance Hall, Shrine of the Book

Sabbie led Gil through the cave-like hall that he had navigated on his first day. With one hand softly touching the back of his arm, she guided him into the great exhibition room of the Shrine of the Book. They stood in silence, dwarfed by the great room.

'This building was designed to reflect a sanctuary that seeks to convey sacred messages,' she explained. 'The mushroom-shaped white dome with the center peak symbolizes the lids of the jars in which some of the Dead Sea Scrolls were found. They say the black wall opposite the building mirrors the tension between the spiritual world of the "Sons of Light" and the "Sons of Darkness' described in the scrolls. Two-thirds of the building remains within the ground, and the building is surrounded by a pool of still water.'

'Who pays for all of this?' he asked.

'That's the most amazing part. Contributors from around the world keep it alive. Founders, benefactors, sponsors, patrons, members. They give what they can and, in almost all cases, their gifts and monies are used wisely.'

'*Almost* always?' Gil asked.

'There are always a few bad apples, though a lot fewer here than in most places. More about that later.'

They had moved to a showcase that held nine small white marble rectangular boxes. Within each box lay a green strip of metal, its etchings barely visible through the glass. A large framed copper sheet with clear deep etchings provided background to the nine little caskets.

'There it is. It's on loan from the Archaeological Museum in Amman, Jordan,' Sabbie began. 'We're going to hate to see it go back.'

'I know,' Gil said, remembering George's pathetic attempt at replicating an Internet press release.

'Its official title is The 3Q15 Copper Scroll of Qumran. The numbers in its name reflect the archeological section in which it was found. Everybody here just calls it The Cave 3 Scroll or The Copper Scroll.'

She moved to the side to allow Gil full view and continued.

'Supposedly it contains the locations of sixty-four places in Palestine where portions of the treasure of the Jerusalem temple were hidden, but no one has ever been able to find any of the treasure. See that, the last section? That's where it promises a mate will be found that holds the key to locating the treasures.'

So George did get his facts right.

'When the scroll was discovered,' she continued, 'it had been rolled up for so long that it was feared that unrolling it would damage it beyond repair. It was carefully cut into strips so it could be read. That large copper sheet in the background there is a facsimile of what it would have looked like if it had been unrolled intact.'

'Facsimile?' Gil quipped. 'I thought you guys went for nothing but the real thing.'

'It's not always possible,' she retorted. 'When we can, we show the original find. When we can't, we exhibit either a facsimile or faux facsimile.'

'How can you have a fake reproduction? That's what a reproduction is.'

'Our facsimiles are just what they sound like, copies of the original. A *faux* facsimile is an approximation of the original. It looks like the real thing but doesn't contain all of the details. To use your phrasing, people see what they expect to see, so sometimes it's enough to just make an approximation of the original.'

Gil pointed toward the other exhibition cases. 'So some of these may be fake?'

'Not in this museum! If it's not the original, we say so. There's been some pressure lately, mostly from DeVris, to put the good stuff away and display facsimiles but so far the Museum's Artificer has managed to keep DeVris in line.'

'I thought an artificer was a worker of magic,' Gil said thoughtfully. He would have kept any conversation going rather than break the mood and lose the gentle resting of her hand on his shoulder.

Sabbie laughed lightly. 'Well, Sarkami is that, too. A worker of magic. But around here we use the term as it was used in the Bible; to refer to someone who is an extraordinary artisan of metals.'

She explained that this Sarkami fellow lived in England and donated his talents and time, crafting metal facsimiles and faux facsimiles whenever the Museum needed them.

'He does much more than facsimiles, of course,' she continued. 'He's a brilliant artist.' Her face glowed with admiration. 'And an amazing man.'

Gil had listened to enough. He didn't need to hear her sing the praises of some old guy who spent his life making fake scrolls. Besides, her hand no longer rested on his shoulder—or any other part of him for that matter.

'Let me ask you a question,' he said with a grin. 'All of those exhibitions my father dragged me to all through my childhood; are you saying they may have been nothing but faux?'

He didn't wait for her answer before offering his punchline. 'In that case, one might say I was a victim of a "faux pa"!'

Gil chuckled at his pun. Sabbie was not amused.

She refused to walk him back to the office after that. He needed some time out, she said. He was running on fumes, and it was affecting his mind.

Gil gave her a few minutes lead time, then caught up with her as she entered her office.

Sabbie closed her door after him. 'Yesterday, you said that you wished you could figure out what you were missing.'

Gil nodded.

'I think this is it.'

She slipped on white cotton gloves and, from a small wall safe, removed a plastic zip-lock bag. Gingerly, she withdrew a browned piece of paper and slid it onto another plastic bag that she laid on the desk. 'This ought to help but, whatever you do, don't touch it!' she cautioned.

He had no intention of doing so.

'If you have to turn it, touch only the plastic it sits on. Don't even breathe on it, okay? I'm serious.'

She reached back into the safe and placed a typed sheet of translation into his hands.

She waited as he read.

Forty-four years ago, in the year of our Lord 1053, they found me, abandoned and near death's door, still encircled within my dead mother's arms. It is said that upon returning home, The Lord of Weymouth Castle laid me in William's arms. Barely out of swaddling clothes himself, William was said to have laughed with joy and would not allow them to remove me from his loving embrace until, late into the night, when he was overcome by sleep. From that first moment, we were brothers, bound tightly as any two might be, by fate and by spirit, if not by parentage.

Yesterday, I took into my arms what remained of William's tortured body, his face blackened and cracked, his flesh still smoldering. With unrelenting hope for his salvation, I gave him back to the earth. I fear that the very treasure for which William willingly gave his life may likewise meet a fate not unlike his. As may I.

Only this diary, then, may remain.

It is my humble hope that this shall not come to be and that these words may stand as a signpost and a testament to that which has been sacrificed but not lost. Then the heavens shall beckon and the sound of angels shall open the heart of the righteous one, for they sing to him as in the words of those who have come before. May they live forever in the song of renewal and the promise of continuance.

'What is this?' Gil asked. He waited for the answer he hoped she'd provide.

'It's a piece of the diary that was hidden in the binding, probably put there by Elias himself nearly a thousand years ago.'

Gil's heart pounded with excitement. This was the last piece of the puzzle. The part he knew was there without ever being told. This was what he had been waiting for.

'No one else knows about it,' she said.

'No one?'

'No one.'

'Not even DeVris?' Gil asked.

She shook her head.

'Does Ludlow know about it?'

'He did,' she said softly. Her face tightened.

'What do you mean?' Gil asked.

He waited for her answer, knowing she was about to put into words what he already suspected.

'Ludlow's dead,' she said simply and turned to slip the browned piece of paper back into its zip-lock bag.

Gil grabbed her by the shoulder and pulled her to face him. The fragile piece of antiquity fluttered to the floor. Sabbie gasped.

'What do you mean, he's dead?' Gil demanded.

'He's dead, okay? He's dead. That's all there is to it.'

'No, it's not okay and that's not all there is to it. I have a right to know what happened to him, you know. I mean, after all, I knew the old guy. You can't just say he's dead and leave it at that,' Gil retorted.

Sabbie's heart pounded in her neck but her voice remained steady. Her face betrayed no emotion whatsoever.

'First of all,' she began, 'you only *met* Ludlow once, that's all. You didn't *know* him. If you could even think of him as "the old guy," you didn't know him.'

She stooped and carefully retrieved the brown piece of paper from the floor. Still, with gloved hands, she lovingly sealed it in its thin plastic bag.

She continued in the same irritating cool manner. 'Second, in your self-indulgent temper tantrum just now, you could have destroyed the very thing "the old guy," as you put it, gave his life for.'

Gil stared at the ancient paper. He wanted to know all that she wasn't telling him. Asking her was useless. Worse than useless. Whatever Sabbie knew about Ludlow's death, she wasn't about to reveal to him. Whatever she was feeling, she was not about to reveal either. Always in control. Oh, how he'd love to see her break. Just once.

Apparently finished with the conversation, Sabbie turned and walked to the other side of the room to return the ancient paper to the wall safe.

Images of Ludlow lying dead from a dozen causes flashed across Gil's mind. A deep sadness washed over him. *Poor old guy.*

Remembering Sabbie's belittlement of the phrase, Gil raised a third finger in the air toward the back Sabbie had turned toward him. It was a stupid, impotent gesture but, save for smacking her in the head, it was all he had available to him at the moment.

God, what a bitch she was.

EIGHTEEN

Later that morning
Office of the Translator

It only took four steps to cross the tiny office. Gil had been pacing for an hour and, as far as he could figure, he must have covered the same ground several hundred times.

Where the hell is she? She can't keep disappearing like this.

He had found Elias' message! It was right there in the message he had hidden in the binding. Not a number substitution, not a word frequency count. Nothing a code breaker would have looked for. This was a cybersleuth's kind of pattern. It made you work for the pleasure of the discovery and, once you nailed it, it put you to work all over again.

The sound of the door opening stopped Gil mid-pace.

'Where the hell have you . . .'

'Uh uh uh,' DeVris said as he entered. He shook his index finger in mock rebuke. 'Thou shalt not curse within these hallowed halls.'

'Sorry, I didn't expect you.'

'Obviously.'

95

DeVris sorted through a stack of books on the floor. He opened each volume and riffled through the pages.

'Everything okay?' Gil asked. He had not seen the Director since his first day at the Museum. At the time, he had seemed quite intimidating. Now, outside the confines of his richly decorated office, DeVris looked a great deal less impressive.

'Do me a favor,' the Director said, pointing to Sabbie's old oak desk. 'Reach into the top right-hand drawer and see if there's a three-by-five yellow index card in there. It should have all the phone extensions of . . .'

Gil stared at the open drawer. It held a yellow index card, a pair of white cotton gloves, and one more thing; a very small, very shiny revolver.

'Oh, the gun. Don't mind that,' said DeVris with a smile. 'She won't use it on you unless you give her a hard time.'

Gil stared at him.

'Hey, I was only joking,' DeVris said.

Gil nodded, closed the drawer, and stepped away from the desk.

'Look, this is Israel,' DeVris began.

'And do most of your translators carry guns?' Gil asked.

DeVris admitted that it was not common practice but added that Sabbie's personal history made her actions quite understandable.

'It was not a simple homicide,' DeVris began. 'The man she killed was one of those who had sexually assaulted her. The others remain free. Who knows, she may still be in danger after all these years, so carrying a gun makes all the sense in the world.'

96

She killed one of them!

DeVris continued. 'If the Military Board of Aleph had not turned their back on her, she . . .'

'They threw her out of the army?' Gil asked.

'No, Aleph is a Special Police Unit, the crème de la crème of counterterrorism. It started out as a branch of the Yamam but later became an independent SWAT force unto itself. Sabbie was one of Aleph's best.'

She had gotten her training in the Lochamot MaGav, the Women's Border Police, DeVris explained. An excellent sharpshooter and brilliant strategist. Her skills and her drive had 'anti-terrorist unit' written all over them. When her first tour of duty with the Border Police was completed, Yamam snatched her up for Aleph, a special elite and highly experimental SWAT team.

'It was the first of its kind, a SWAT team for women, hence the name,' DeVris explained. 'When Aleph broke ranks with Yamam, Sabbie chose to go with them. If she's one thing, she's loyal.'

DeVris continued to rummage through the books as he spoke. 'It never made sense that, after she was arrested, Aleph turned on her like they did. Not a single one of her fellow officers ever testified for her at her trial. They claimed that when they found out she had gone after the other men as well . . .'

'*Other* men? She killed more than one?'

'You should really be discussing this with her, you know,' DeVris concluded, and took a step toward the door.

'Wait a minute,' Gil interrupted. 'I can't just say to her, "Oh, by the way, I hear you're a convicted murderer."'

'You're overreacting,' DeVris said. He made it a point to look Gil in the eye for emphasis.

'Look,' DeVris continued, 'she was tried and found guilty, that's true, but she was given a suspended sentence based on an elaborate rehabilitation plan. She went to England, enrolled in graduate school and, essentially, turned her life around. Now, her love of antiquities and her dedication to their translation has become her life. Still, if she's sometimes overzealous, I think we can afford to be a little compassionate.'

'How come she's back in Israel?'

'Ludlow met her at the University of London, where he was doing research and teaching. Actually, Ludlow was introduced to her by one of our off-campus artisans, a man by the name of Sarkami . . .'

Gil looked up sharply at the sound of the name.

DeVris registered the reaction and continued.

'Anyway, Ludlow and his wife, Sarah, apparently took Sabbie under their wing. So, when he brought her to me a couple of years ago and begged me to give her a real job, how could I refuse?'

Gil shook his head.

So Ludlow's death must have hit her like a ton of bricks. But she didn't mention it for days . . .

'I have to ask you not to relate any of this to her,' DeVris added. 'I'd hate to see any animosity come out of all of this. She wasn't so sure you were right for the job, you know.'

'And why was that?' Gil asked.

'I think we better drop the whole thing. Could you do that, please? I think we can afford to cut her a little slack, don't you?'

'Why? Because of all she's been through?' Gil asked, a little more scornfully than he intended.

DeVris' voice softened. 'No, because there's something very special about her, don't you think? Something you can't quite put into words. She draws you to her and, when she pushes you away, she pulls you right back in. I'm not just talking about sex appeal, though that's certainly there, too.'

DeVris waited a moment, then abruptly changed the subject.

'If you like, you can use the computer in the next room. For security reasons, you can't send out any e-mail, but it might help you pass the time until she comes back.'

Gil readily agreed and settled into the pleasantly familiar experience of the keyboard and screen. A few minutes earlier, he couldn't wait for Sabbie to return. Now, he was hoping she would take her time. He needed to know more about her than DeVris could provide; sure as hell, a lot more than she would ever tell him.

DeVris quietly left and closed the door behind him.

The yellow index card remained untouched in the drawer of the desk next door.

NINETEEN

Later that afternoon
Office of the Translator

He had completed his Internet searches and had been waiting for more than three hours. Now she walked in like she didn't have a care in the world.

'Where the hell were you?' Gil asked.

'I beg your pardon,' she said sarcastically. 'You're not talking to me like that, are you?'

'You're damn straight I am. I've been sitting here for God knows how long with my thumb up my rear end, waiting for you to get back. You could at least have given me your cell phone number,' Gil added.

'And what would you call me with?'

He had never noticed. There were no phones in the room. He didn't remember seeing any in the outer office either. And the guard confiscated his cell phone for 'safe keeping' every morning, not that it would have worked here anyway.

Gil continued to glare but considered it wise not to respond.

'If you're ready to take your foot out of your mouth and your thumb out of your rear end, I'll tell you what I found out at the library. It took a while because I had to cross-reference several collections of medieval history, but I think it was worth it.'

Sabbie kicked off her high heels and walked over to the desk. The thought of her opening the drawer, removing the gun, and shooting him in the middle of the forehead fast-forwarded across Gil's mind. She opened the left-hand bottom drawer, removed a pair of sneakers, then joined him on the other side of the room. She sat down on the floor, and laced them up.

'I realized we needed to know more about Elias,' she began. 'Do you remember a CNN interview you did about tracking down the inventor of the CyberStrep computer virus so you could figure out how to stop him?'

Gil looked up in surprise

'First rule of Internet forensics, you said, is to know your man. You said, "Once you can think as he does, finding him comes easily." '

'You remember that?' Gil asked in surprise.

'Of course. I thought it was brilliant as well as amazingly chauvinistic. You made it sound as if only men could be cyber criminals. Your approach to tracking one down, however, was unusual to say the least.'

The creator of the CyberStrep virus had been in police custody when Gil had been called in. A backdoor to the virus program had been found, but no one had been able to figure out the password.

Whenever an attempt was made to disarm the virus, it would offer the prompt, 'Say, "Good Night," ' and wait for the correct response in order to allow access. A legion of cryptanalysts had typed in the obvious responses in every language and code they could come up with. Nothing worked.

Gil had taken a different approach. He spent several weeks learning everything he could about the creator of the program and never even looked at the virus in action. In the end, the simple knowledge that the inventor of the virus was a devotee of old radio shows, especially Burns and Allen, gave Gil all the info he needed.

After listening to a dozen Burns and Allen's radio recordings, Gil knew the correct response.

'Say "Good night,"' the CyberStrep program prompted, refusing entry until the proper response was supplied. '"Gracie,"' Gil responded. There were the famous parting words of the Burns and Allen radio show, held in affection by all of the show's fans. By taking the time to know the man behind the code, Gil had conquered the worst computer virus the Internet had ever known. And he had done it in less than five minutes at the computer.

'So I went in search of Elias, and here's what I found,' said Sabbie.

The life of a monk, she explained, was spent less in devotion and more in making money for the Church. Prayer services took place every three hours, day and night. At the time when Elias would have entered the brotherhood, the few monks who could read and write divided their hours between meditation and study. Those who were illiterate were privileged to be allowed to work long hours in order to support those devoted to higher spiritual pursuits. As the years passed however, things changed. A monastery's devotion came to be judged far more by the magnitude of its contribution to mother Church than by the pious meditation and scholarly achievements of its monks.

The luxury of devotion and study quickly gave way to a lifetime spent in copying manuscripts or weaving tapestries for the wealthy. The Church sanctified the work as holy. Monks, holed up in scriptoriums or weaving rooms for the duration of their lives, were told they were engaged in the highest form of devotion; a prayer through action.

'Sort of like a monk's sweatshop,' Gil bantered with a wry smile.

'Actually, you're more on target than you know.'

For centuries, she explained, abbeys held the monopoly on the copying of texts and the making of tapestries in what now would be called a kind of price-fixing scheme. Some monasteries grew enormously wealthy and powerful. A somewhat cut-throat competition sprang up between abbeys as to who could contribute the most to the Church. The greater the contributions, the greater the preferential treatment for the Abbots, if not for the lowly monks.

Sabbie checked her notes. 'From odd bits and pieces of his entries in the diary, it seems that after Elias' brother, William, was put to death, the Abbot took possession of his lands. He had Elias moved out of the scriptorium and banished to the weaving shop where the old monks, or as Elias put it, "those who were stupid, old, or infirm," were set to work making mediocre tapestries for the rich. All of the tapestries were designed by the Abbot, leaving a weaver nothing to do but work like an automaton on someone else's brainchild.'

'Sounds miserable. I wonder why he stayed.'

'Good question. Look, I want to show you this.' She handed him a page from the second half of the diary. Like the others, it was in Latin, and bore her red markings of two-word by two-word deciphering.

103

'It says that Elias beseeched the Abbot to allow him to design a tapestry of his own. He describes how important the design of his own tapestry was to him and how he wished his brother could have seen it. Now that I've said it out loud,' she continued, with a sigh, 'it sort of sounds like a medieval soap opera. Don't you think?'

'Just the opposite,' Gil announced triumphantly. 'It all makes sense.'

At first, Gil had assumed the missing page Sabbie had given him could not possibly hold the key. How could a couple of paragraphs that contained no apparent pattern possibly tell them where the mate to The Cave 3 Scroll was hidden? The answer was that it couldn't! The brevity of the note was not the problem, it was the *answer.*

By making the shortest entry the most important one, Elias ensured that anyone trying to uncover a covert communication would quickly realize that it contained no secret pattern and, therefore, no hidden message.

'Look,' Gil said. 'It's right here in the last paragraph.'

It is my humble hope that this shall not come to be and these words may stand as a signpost and a testament to that which has been sacrificed but not lost. Then the heavens . . .

'I don't get it,' Sabbie said.

'Haven't you ever noticed that the real reason that someone calls you is the last thing that person brings up right before they say "good-bye"? That's what Elias is doing here. He's saying that, beyond everything else, this diary is a testament and a signpost. A signpost!'

She still didn't make the connection.

'There are basically two ways to hide something while keeping it in full view. The first is misdirection, where your attention is pulled *away* from the object that someone wants to hide. Like the magician that has you look at one hand while he'd doing things you never notice with the other. The second way of hiding things in full view is to reveal only a piece of it at a time, while at the same time, telling you where you need to look for the next piece of the puzzle. Essentially, it sends you on a hunt. Actually, it leads you, like a signpost that tells you which way to go to get to your goal. It's simple and it's obvious but, at the same time, easy to miss,' Gil concluded.

'But a thousand years ago nobody would have thought to use the term "signpost,"?' she protested. 'So how could Elias have used it intentionally in a hidden message?'

'The idea was there, even way back then, and Elias understood it. I think he's trying to tell us to keep going, that there's more to the diary than we know.'

'Like the location of the scroll?'

'I don't know. But there's more to come.'

She looked like she was going to argue, then decided against it. Gil knew she was unconvinced but the truth was, she had no other option but to go along with his hunch.

'All right, let's look at what we know right now,' she said.

'First, according to the two-word alternating entries, we know there is, indeed, a second scroll, and that the scroll contains a firsthand account of the messiah, Yeshua,' Gil said.

'Not *the* messiah, necessarily. A man who is viewed as *a* messiah and who is also named Yeshua,' she corrected him.

'Okay,' Gil agreed. 'We can't be absolutely certain the scroll tells the story of Jesus, The Messiah, until we find it. Satisfied?'

She nodded and Gil continued. 'Next, we know that the scroll was taken from Qumran to Weymouth Monastery in England, where Elias lived and William was killed. And where the diary was found.'

'And,' Sabbie continued, 'because Elias says the scroll was found by William in an area that sounds very much like Qumran, if it turns out to be made of copper, Elias' scroll could be the mate to The Cave 3 Scroll and could point the way to riches that have been buried since the time of Christ.'

Last, and most importantly, Gil added, they could be pretty sure the diary was left as a signpost to tell them to search within Weymouth Monastery.

'Unless I miss my guess, we need to find Elias' tapestry,' Gil said.

'Why his tapestry?' Sabbie asked.

'This diary is a signpost pointing to the tapestries, to one in particular. How did you put it . . . ? Yes, you said that Elias described how important the design of his own tapestry was to him and how he wished his brother could have seen it. Don't you get it? Find Elias' tapestry and you find the scroll,' Gil concluded.

She spoke softly, as if allowing the depth of Elias' sacrifice to sink in. 'So, that's why he stayed, to write the diary, weave the tapestry, and protect the scroll.'

'And to make certain it was found by those who would someday come to rescue it. This can't only be about the gold and silver mentioned in The Cave 3 Scroll,' Gil added.

'To some it will be,' she said thoughtfully, then seemed to change direction. 'We're wasting our time here. We should be on our way to Weymouth.'

'One more thing,' she added. 'What about the rest of the page?'

. . . Then the heavens shall beckon and the sound of angels shall open the heart of the righteous one, for they sing to him as in the words of those who have come before. May they live forever in the song of renewal and the promise of continuance.

'What's that about?' she asked.

'I don't know,' Gil said simply. 'Elias hasn't told me yet.'

TWENTY

Later that afternoon
White Americans To Save Christianity (WATSC)
Headquarters
Near Stone Mountain, Georgia

'This information is very important to us,' McCullum said. 'But of course, you know that.'

They had been speaking for less than an hour

but, within that time, McCullum had learned more about DeVris' day-to-day activities and moment-to-moment deceptions than he had ever suspected. His guest's willingness to initiate contact with WATSC, make the trip, and offer facts unknown to McCullum—without expectation of compensation —was a clear sign of loyalty.

'My granddaddy always said that friendships were forged by the exchange of vital information,' McCullum continued.

'And services,' his guest added.

'And services.'

'If I may speak freely, Anton DeVris not only did you an injustice by lying to you, and putting your future acquisition of the mate to The Cave 3 Scroll in jeopardy, he insulted you, your family, and this incredible institution. We are, none of us, responsible for our parentage. I would be the first to acknowledge that fact, but I think one must draw the conclusion that DeVris is little more than Jewish scum.'

McCullum couldn't have been more pleased. His first impression had been accurate. Appearances notwithstanding, here was someone who could be counted on to support, in both word and deed, the cause of white supremacy.

Best of all, WATSC's newest supporter came replete with personal connections and singular experiences that, in the near future, might prove extraordinarily useful. God had provided the perfect person to fill a most unusual niche, and McCullum was most grateful.

He offered his guest a brandy-dipped cigar. 'If you don't mind my saying it, appearances being what they are, one would never suppose your allegiance.'

His guest accepted the amenity and nodded with agreement. 'I learned a long time ago that prejudice can work for or against you. You can allow the assumptions of others to prevent you from getting what you want or you can use their blindness as a layer of invisibility that prevents them from seeing your true actions.'

'People see only what they believe,' McCullum agreed.

'Some. Others believe only what they see.'

'And which are you?' McCullum asked pointedly.

'Now that's a whole other conversation.'

McCullum apologized for his lack of consideration. He was aware that his guest had traveled a long distance and, understandably, might be a bit tired. A chauffeur and town car, WATSC's VIP penthouse suite, and personal chef awaited. If desired, companionship could be provided.

'Let's talk in the morning before you leave. I'll be traveling so call me on my cell and I'll call you back on a secure land line. I have some ideas I want to run past you. I think you'll agree that this may be the start of a beautiful friendship,' McCullum added. The quote from his favorite Bogart movie, so perfect in this context, was completely lost on his guest.

TWENTY-ONE

Day Eight, mid-afternoon
Office of the Translator, Shrine of the Book
Israel Museum

Sabbie closed the door behind her but held onto the knob to prevent the lock from making any noise. Gil looked up in surprise. The mix of emotions on her face was unreadable. She was pale and her breathing rapid. From under her arms, dark circles of sweat spread onto her pale blue blouse.

'What's wrong?' he asked anxiously.

'How long have you been here?' she whispered.

'Just got here, why?'

'Did you walk through the lobby?'

'No, I flew in the window,' he retorted. 'What's going on?'

She was trembling. He suddenly remembered the rape.

'Hey, I was only joking. What happened?'

'Shhh. Keep your voice down.' She opened the safe with one hand and, stretching as far as she could, picked up some papers from the desk with the other. 'Here, take these and shred them. Only a few sheets at a time. The last thing we need is for that thing to jam.'

'Hey, these are my notes,' Gil protested.

'I can't believe I didn't see it. Neither of us did,' she continued.

'Neither of us saw what?'

'Not you. Ludlow. He said McCullum was bad

news, but it never occurred to him that . . . Never mind,' she said roughly. 'Here do these, too.'

Gil shredded as directed. He didn't need the notes anyway.

'Come here,' she said, still sorting through the safe's contents.

With one movement, she had unbuttoned his slacks and pulled his shirt free.

'Suck in your gut,' she commanded.

'What?'

'Suck it in.' He stood motionless as she thrust a thick wad of paper between his bare skin and his underwear, then spun him around and performed a similar action on his backside. She ordered him to button up.

Only the fear on her face kept him from joking.

'Got any coffee?' she asked.

It was cold, Gil told her. She didn't care. She ordered him to open the shredder and dump the coffee onto the topmost bits of paper. He rolled his eyes and shook his head, then complied.

By the time he turned back, she had pulled off her slacks and was struggling into a pair of pantyhose. Within seconds, she had stowed the remainder of the notes, divided equally next to each thigh. Gently, she withdrew the diary from the safe, carefully removed the hidden page from its plastic bag, placed the sheet between the diary's cover and first page, slid the diary back into the zip-lock, and unceremoniously stuffed the entire book in the crotch of her pantyhose.

The comment slipped out before he knew it was coming. 'Attractive,' he said. 'But it's going to make you walk a little funny, don't you think?'

She looked up in surprise.

'We don't have much time. Right now McCullum is probably confirming that DeVris was lying to him about having the diary. That's the only thing that would have brought him here. If he figures out that DeVris doesn't have the extra page of the diary, he's going to realize that someone has been playing DeVris while DeVris was playing him. And he's going to be mad as hell.'

The giant from Jack and the Beanstalk crossed Gil's mind. 'Fee, fi, fo, fum.' As a kid, the image always terrified Gil. It was not a comforting thought now.

'Who's McCullum?' he asked.

'He's CEO of White Americans to Save Christianity, a far right-wing Evangelical organization that "stands alone and controls the many," as the newspapers describe it. It's an offshoot of the old KKK and, when called to action, can make the old organization look like a bunch of choir girls. It's sanctioned by no one but bigger in finance than you want to know. They are intent on making the U.S. a one-religion one-race country or, better yet, world. McCullum's more like the Grand Wizard than the CEO and to see him, you'd think he was just another mover and shaker from Wall Street, which he is,' she added.

There were at least three balls in play, she explained: DeVris, McCullum, and somebody else. While each would do anything to get hold of the scroll, separately they were limited. McCullum had the power, influence, and money. DeVris had up-to-date info on their progress, or so he thought. It was the third one that troubled her.

'We don't know what he brings to the pot. There could even be others involved for all I know.'

Sabbie continued rearranging the office. She said that, in the beginning, she thought the unknown player was someone on the inside, working within the Museum complex. Her computer terminal had been accessed and her drawers carefully jimmied, but nothing was ever missing. The intruder had never gotten to her safe; at least, not to her knowledge. She realized that the whole thing could be chalked up to one of the workers accessing pornographic websites at night and looking around for some money. When she saw that George's system had been breached, however . . .

'Wait a minute! George who?' Gil interrupted.

'George. Your George, whatever his last name is.'

'*My* George! How do you know his system has been breached? Which? His work files or his e-mail?'

'Both. That's what made me realize he was involved,' she explained.

'Involved in what, getting hold of the scroll? Because he broke into his own systems?'

'No, because he didn't tell you,' she explained.

Gil protested that there could be a thousand reasons why George didn't alert him to a hack-in.

'Name one,' she said.

'Well, for starters, he's the laziest son-of a-bitch in the world. Even if he knew there was a breech, unless it was bad for business, he'd just as soon turn the other way.'

'Look, do you have any idea what's at stake here? Can you even conceive of how much the scroll would be worth to someone who wanted to exploit it or, worse, to destroy it?'

113

'Enough to kill for it,' he said, hoping she would disagree.

'We've had three murders in three months, including the so-called suicide and a mugging, so you tell me. As far as I can see, McCullum's the big player here. If DeVris gets the scroll he'll turn it over to McCullum. The same with George—I know, you think there's no way George is involved—anyway, WATSC has a tremendous stake in this. If the scroll turns out to testify to the fact that Jesus was the son of God, McCullum will hold the proof in the palm of his hand.'

'And if it doesn't?' Gil asked.

'Then the scroll will disappear from the face of the earth.'

'Suppose the scroll is nothing more than the mate to The Cave 3 Scroll?'

'Then it unlocks the locations of great treasures. So much the better,' she said. 'For McCullum and his organization, it's win-win-win. God, he's fucking brilliant.

'One thing for sure,' she added, as she turned to leave. 'If McCullum's involved, nothing's sacred.'

'Did you say "sacred" or "safe"?' Gil asked.

'Both,' she answered.

'In that case, don't forget the gun in the upper right-hand drawer,' Gil advised.

TWENTY-TWO

A few minutes later

Gil followed the directions Sabbie had written on the back of the yellow index card. She had walked ahead of him and, while she chatted with the guard, he had used the payphone to call the phone number as instructed.

After hitting zero twice to get an operator he carefully, very carefully, pronounced the phonetic representation of a single word. As Sabbie had instructed, Gil hung up the phone, held his coat in front of him, and plastered a smile on his face.

On cue, he walked up to her amid the blaring alarms and scurrying guards, and was given a quick one-handed pat-down, then waved on through.

'They're looking for a stranger with a bomb who just called in the threat. If you weren't with me, you'd be flat on the table with the guard's . . .'

'Please, I can do without the details,' he said, thoroughly relieved to be out of the building. 'Can't they put you in prison for calling in a false bomb threat?' He thought better than to make some reference to her previous involvement with the law.

'I didn't call it in, you did,' she said over her shoulder. She had led him well out of sight of the guard's door and into the bustling campus of the Museum Complex.

They walked quickly toward the gate where taxis waited hungrily for new passengers.

'I just wish I could have taken the diary with us,'

she said thoughtfully. 'It was a judgment call and I was afraid to risk . . .'

'You left it behind?' Gil asked in surprise. He had seen her stuff it in her crotch not ten minutes earlier.

'Of course not. I dropped it in the Museum's overnight mail box.'

'Won't they check all the mail?'

'Only the incoming mail. I just wish we had the translation with us, especially the hidden page,' she added thoughtfully. 'I have a feeling we're going to need it.'

'Me, too,' Gil said. 'So I thought it would be a good idea to bring it along.'

Gil pulled his wallet from his pocket, from the wallet a wad of U.S. currency. The first and last bills in the pile appeared unremarkable, but on every other bill were carefully printed notes; duplicates of the hidden message that Elias had stuck in the binding of the diary and copies of the translations that now lay shredded and soggy with cold coffee.

'They never look at your money,' he announced. 'Even without your bomb scare.'

'*Your* bomb scare,' she reminded him flippantly, but her smile was warm and she nodded in silent confirmation of a job well done.

Her mood changed suddenly. 'Jesus! If they had searched your wallet, they would have gotten the whole translation, all deciphered, everything, even the hidden page.'

'Yes, but they didn't,' Gil said.

'That was the most stupid-ass thing you could have done.'

'I didn't know you cared,' he said teasingly. He

waited for her response.

'You could have blown everything,' she answered with a shake of her head.

'Well, I didn't, did I?' he countered sharply. 'Your guards, like all security people, follow protocols. That's what gives terrorists the edge. So the notes were never in danger. And, by the way, you're very welcome.'

They had arrived at the entrance gate to the complex and a taxi, anticipating their need, had pulled up.

'Airport,' Sabbie instructed the driver.

Gil slid into the back seat next to her.

'By the way, here's your yellow card. Never got to shred it,' he said, handing her the index card from the top drawer of her desk.

'Never saw it before,' she said. 'It's not mine.'

TWENTY-THREE

One hour earlier
Office of Dr. Anton DeVris

Each of the twin hulks was six-foot-six at least, with blond hair, broadshouldered, and dressed in a white jumpsuit. With faces that bore no trace of an expression. McCullum's identical Power Angels guarded DeVris' door. Inside, the man they would gladly give their life for, questioned the Director of Acquisitions.

McCullum puffed his cigar as he spoke, taking obvious pleasure in the discomfort on DeVris' face.

'I have learned . . . not from you . . . but from an altogether other source . . . that, contrary to your assurances, you are *not* in possession of the Weymouth diary.'

'Yes, that is true, technically speaking,' DeVris began nervously.

WATSC's leader rose to his feet, and reached a beefy hand across the Director's desk. His grip half encircled DeVris' neck.

'No bullshit,' McCullum said. He released his hold, returned to his seat, then picked up a large book from the table next to his chair and browsed through it as DeVris spoke.

The Director chose his words with care. 'It is true that, at this moment, I am not in possession of the Weymouth diary. I should not have represented myself as such but . . .'

McCullum sat forward to indicate his displeasure.

'I should not have misrepresented that fact,' DeVris continued.

'Lied,' McCullum corrected. He continued to casually thumb through the book.

'I should not have lied. May I explain why I did it?'

'If you can do so in two sentences or less.'

DeVris searched frantically for the best defense; an excuse that would take the onus off of him without placing it on McCullum.

Even as the words left his mouth, DeVris knew he had taken a wrong turn.

'I just wanted to spare you . . .' he began.

The power behind the book coming flat against his head threw the Director against the wall. Blood trickled from his right ear, and the cold terror that

118

swept up from his stomach made him fear he would urinate in his pants. He retained hearing on one side only.

DeVris pulled himself up to his chair. He pushed past the shock and pain and considered his next statement carefully. He might explain that the facsimile he had printed covertly from Ludlow's program would serve McCullum's purposes just as well as the diary itself. He could assure McCullum that within a fortnight he would be able to gain entrance to Ludlow's apartment and open the oven safe in which the diary was hidden. He rejected both statements. Either justification, if spoken, was tantamount to suicide.

DeVris took the only safe path possible. 'I was wrong to deceive you,' he said.

McCullum nodded.

'There is no excuse. I will never do it again.'

Another nod.

'Now tell me what I need to know,' McCullum said. And DeVris did; every thought, every belief, every fact he knew to be true about Sabbie and Gil, Ludlow and the diary, and his own plans for securing the mate to The Cave 3 Scroll. Each sentence was presented simply, with no pretense.

'Is there anything else you want to tell me?' McCullum asked.

DeVris considered a repeated apology, then thought better of it. He shook his head.

'One question,' McCullum added as he rose to leave. 'Should I be concerned about Sabbie's reliability? Given her history and Ludlow's recent demise, is she likely to convince her new American friend to join her in some foolhardy adventure?'

'She may be up for it,' DeVris confirmed, 'but

not him. He's a monkey with a coconut.'

As McCullum's guest on a hunting trip to Kenya the previous year, DeVris had witnessed natives trap monkeys by the use of a coconut and an earthen jar. The opening at the top of the jar was slightly larger than the coconut, so there was just enough room for the coconut to slide in. The jars with the coconuts were left tethered to trees at various points around the compound. When a curious monkey reached in and tightened his little fingers around the coconut, he discovered the opening was not large enough to allow him to pull his treasure out.

Throughout their journey, DeVris and McCullum witnessed monkeys, their arms stuck in jars, trapped by their unwillingness to let go. There they remained until they were shipped off on a boat or until they starved to death.

'This American is just another greedy monkey determined to get the prize no matter what the cost,' DeVris affirmed.

'You think so?' McCullum asked. 'I was just wondering if this one might just crash the earthen jar to the ground and run off with his prize.'

'No need to worry,' DeVris declared with certainty. 'This little monkey's not going anywhere.'

TWENTY-FOUR

Later that afternoon
Ben Gurion Airport, Tel Aviv

'First, some ground rules. Give me your cell phone,' Sabbie demanded.

'Why? It doesn't even work outside the U.S.'

'So you won't miss it.'

'It's got all my phone numbers on it,' he argued.

'You'll live.'

'I hope so,' he retorted.

He could barely keep up with her giant strides. 'Look, it really would help if you would just take a second and explain some of your more bizarre actions,' Gil suggested.

She sighed, rolled her eyes, and slowed to a moderate pace. '*You* may not be able to use your cell phone here, but it's got a Global Positioning System in it, right?'

'So what?'

'Didn't it ever occur to you they work in two directions?' she asked. 'You might as well have one of those little chips implanted into your brain. Anybody with big bucks can find out where you are anytime they want.'

'Who'd care?'

She held her free hand out. 'Give me your credit card.'

'Why?'

'You really have trouble with this trust thing, don't you?' she asked.

'Yes, when I'm running to keep up with a

121

woman with a gun who's got my cell phone and has me call in a bomb scare to a world renowned museum and is now demanding my credit card without explanation, yes, I do have a problem with that, I guess.'

She stopped and turned to look at him. 'Listen, I'm going to say this one time and it's going to have to last. This isn't a game. We're playing with the big kids now. There's more at stake than you can ever imagine. We're not just talking about a mate to The Cave 3 Scroll. We're probably looking at something far greater than a first-hand-account of Jesus' life and death.'

Her words would have been enough to communicate the seriousness of the situation, but the look on her face brought it home.

'These people have probably already killed three times, four if you count Ludlow's wife, Sarah, and that's without knowing what the diary says about the scroll. Imagine what they'll do when they find out what we know.'

If he hadn't been certain she was overreacting, Gil might have been truly frightened. She was beautiful and convincing but she was, at the same time, more than a little paranoid. She suspected a connection between the mugging and the suicide that claimed the lives of two faculty members several months before Ludlow's tragic death. No matter that the police saw no association. She claimed the police were blind and too busy with more political concerns.

While she and Ludlow might have considered Nathan McCullum to be a big, bad scary man, Gil had seen the man's name inscribed in large bold letters right there in the lobby, on the Museum's

Wall of Benefactors. Obviously, not a man the Museum considered a major threat to security.

Her conspiracy theory pointed to a ring of villains whose identities changed from moment to moment and, at last count, she'd even begun to suspect George.

Why not add the strange little guy who picks up the Museum trash to your list of subjects? After all, if we're going to make it a paranoia free-for-all, we might as well go all the way.

From the little he remembered from Psych 101, she was an example of classic post-traumatic stress syndrome. Almost certainly from the rape. On the other hand, she was the only game in town and, if he didn't want to go with DeVris, which for some reason he didn't, he'd better stick with her. Eventually, her conspiracy theory would fall apart and she'd come to see how crazy the whole idea was. At least, he hoped it would.

They were approaching the El Al counter for flights to the U.S. He handed her his credit card, and she booked two first-class seats to New York.

'Aren't we going to Weymouth?' he asked as he signed away half his checking account balance.

She stomped on his foot. Hard but deftly so that the attendant did not notice.

'Yes, dear. But I thought we'd spend a few days in Manhattan before heading for Weymouth, Massachusetts.' She smiled at the agent and helped Gil limp toward the boarding gate.

'Lucky for you there's a city in the States with the same name. From now on, let me do all the talking,' she said.

Sabbie handed him the ticket receipts. 'Hold onto these. You'll need them to get your refund,' she said, then tossed his cell phone in the open trash can.

He knew she was up to something but this was not the time to ask for an accounting.

'Can't they trace the phone back here?' he asked.

'I'm betting on it,' she said.

With only forty minutes before boarding time they had to hurry. They made it to the British Airways counter, this one selling seats for Europe-bound flights. She talked her way to the front of the line, using a sob story about her dying mother-in-law. Gil figured that his look of distress probably did much to add to the believability of her performance.

'Give me your credit card again,' she said.

Without even bothering to protest, Gil handed over his American Express card and watched in disbelief as she pulled a ballpoint pen out of her jacket pocket, then dragged the tip of the ballpoint pen across the magnetic strip on the back.

'Now watch and learn,' she said, as they stepped up to the counter.

The airline ticket agent, unable to process the card, apologized profusely.

'I am so sorry. Once a card is rejected, we are prohibited from entering the numbers into our systems. It's for your own protection,' the agent added. 'Do you have another card?'

Sabbie frowned and shook her head. 'But it was working five minutes ago!' she said loudly. 'I don't know what you did to it. What are we supposed to do now?'

Timidly, the agent asked if Sabbie and Gil might have the cash necessary for their first-class seats.

Sabbie explained that they had traveler's checks that could be cashed in for coach fares. She added that she kept the traveler's checks for emergencies and was quite unhappy with not being able to use their credit card. She made a point to call the agent by name and to repeat her feelings of dissatisfaction. Five minutes later they were walking away with first-class seats on a flight to London, having been graciously upgraded from coach.

'The first-class seats were just an afterthought,' Sabbie explained. 'I figure we're going to need to get some sleep while we can. The real goal was to pay cash but not have them realize we *wanted* to pay cash. When it comes to airline tickets, cash payments on the day of departure are red flags and more than enough reason for investigation. Since we requested a credit card charge that *they* couldn't comply with, we're not considered suspicious.'

'But we're holding seats on two different flights bound for two different countries,' Gil pressed. 'I know how these systems work. When they pick up our double booking, the computer could cancel all of our reservations and leave us with no seats at all.'

'You give them too much credit. Our bookings are with two different airlines. They never exchange info unless the flight is a code share or something like that.'

They had only twenty minutes to get through security and make it to the U.S.-bound flight, she said.

'But what about our flight to England?' Gil asked.

'Trust me, there's a method to my madness,' she said with a mischievous grin. 'No time to get into the details, just give me your N.S.A. card.'

She took his hand and pulled him to a near run. 'C'mon,' she urged.

Gil struggled to talk in a near whisper, pull out his N.S.A. card, and run beside her at the same time. 'Its authorized cyber-entry only. Unless you plan on accessing someone's database before we get onboard . . .' He reached for his wallet to prove the limits of the pass.

'For crying out loud, Gil!' She grabbed the wallet, located the card, and returned his wallet in less time than it took him to slide it back into his pocket.

The security line was at least a half-hour long. Sabbie cut past the obedient passengers and pulled an airport security inspector aside.

'Who's your immediate superior?' Sabbie asked authoritatively.

The young agent looked around frantically and signaled to a short, round woman. Sabbie propelled Gil by the elbow and met the supervisor halfway. She flashed Gil's N.S.A. card and handed the supervisor their passports and their boarding passes.

'I'm Agent Sabra Karaim from the U.S. National Security Administration,' she said, 'and I need your help.'

The supervisor snapped to attention, which added a good two inches to her less than five-foot-tall frame.

'We need to get this man on board with as little fuss as possible,' Sabbie explained. 'He shouldn't give us any trouble, it's a white-collar crime and he knows that I'm trained in Lotar. I would like to get him to his seat without alarming any of the passengers.'

The supervisor glanced down at Gil's free hands and at the strong hold Sabbie had on his elbow. Sabbie's explanation seemed to resolve any remaining concerns.

Sabbie continued her reassurances. 'If you can accompany us to the gate and arrange pre-boarding, I won't have to place him in handcuffs. I'll hand off my weapon to you at the gate and if you place it in your Safe Box, I can retrieve it once we land,' Sabbie added. 'Needless to say, we have no luggage.'

'Aren't there supposed to be two of you when you transport?' the supervisor asked, hesitantly.

'There are,' Sabbie answered, nodding toward a tall, well-dressed middle-aged man at the front of the line. In response to Sabbie's smile, he nodded back, and confirmed the illusion.

'Well, you folks are supposed to clear this with my boss,' the security agent said over her shoulder, as she moved toward the outside aisle.

'He's just been apprehended,' Sabbie explained, 'and we have sixteen hours to get him back to the States before our extradition warrant expires.'

'I guess it'll be okay, as long as you turn over the gun.' Seemingly satisfied, the little round supervisor marched ahead, leading the way for this, her most important task of the day. Gil and Sabbie were seated immediately.

'See? No problem,' Sabbie said with obvious satisfaction. 'If we were trying to get the gun into Israel it would be a different story, but taking it out of Israel presents no difficulty. Besides, they're always impressed as hell when a foreigner knows Lotar.'

'I don't know Lotar,' Gil complained. 'What the hell is it anyway?'

'Israeli Martial Arts. It works on the idea that the simplest instinctive method of self-defense is the most effective,' she explained. 'And I didn't say *you* knew it, I said a foreigner did. That's me, the American N.S.A. agent with the pass, remember?'

'But it has my name on it,' Gil whispered loudly. 'You could have gotten us both arrested as terrorists!'

'They never read the passes. An N.S.A. card with the official seal can get you past almost any roadblock.'

'I'll remember that next time I plan to hijack a plane or need to cut a security line,' he said. 'Wait a minute, doesn't your passport say you're Israeli?'

'Shhh. Here come the passengers.'

There was no time to force her to answer even if he had had the will to do so, which he hadn't.

'Clean cup, clean cup,' he muttered to himself. He was at the Mad Hatter's tea party and he was never going to get a straight answer. With a shrug to himself, he put all logic behind him and put his life in her hands.

The flight for New York took off on time and without a hitch. Gil started to doze, even as the engines were revving. The soft sound of Sabbie's voice on the airline phone was comforting in the background. He was asleep by the time they taxied out to the runway and didn't wake until they had returned to the gate and the flight attendant had initiated instructions on exiting the aircraft in this time of emergency.

'Don't tell me. Bomb scare,' he said.

She shrugged.

'You really need a more extensive repertoire,' he whispered.

'What can I say, you work with what you got,' she retorted.

'It's a good thing both planes are leaving from the same terminal,' she added more seriously. 'We couldn't have made it if we had to go through security again. We have less than twenty minutes to get to our next flight.'

'Of course we do,' he said flatly. 'I should have known.'

As Gil breathlessly raced to keep up with her strides, Sabbie explained that the reason for the airline marathon was simple and surprisingly logical. Anyone following their trail would be sure to spot the American Express charge for their flight to New York. The airline's records would show that they had boarded the plane for the U.S., so there would be no need to check any other flights. Their tickets to London, on the other hand, had been paid in cash and were untraceable.

'But won't the airline be suspicious that we didn't reboard the U.S. flight?' Gil asked.

'Are you kidding? One little bomb scare and half your passengers cut bait and run. Especially . . .'

'I know, especially in Israel.'

Once settled into their seats aboard their England-bound flight, Sabbie filled him in on a set-up she'd put in play earlier in the day.

'Early this morning, I stopped at DeVris' office supposedly to give him an update. I said you weren't making any headway in decoding the diary.'

'And he believed you?'

'No problem. He said from the start you'd never get past square one. He only agreed to take you on in order to satisfy Ludlow.'

'Oh, really?'

She hesitated, then continued. 'Anyway, I told him I thought you needed a break, that I'd take you to the library in the afternoon to do some research on Weymouth.'

'Wouldn't he figure we could do that in the office on the Internet?'

'That was a euphemism, you moron. I implied that I'd be giving you some incentive to work harder.'

'And he doesn't object to that sort of thing?'

'Who? DeVris? Are you kidding? He'd sleep with you himself if it would get the job done.'

'And when we don't come back for the rest of the day?' Gil asked.

'He'll figure you were just getting that much more motivated.'

When Gil asked her *why* she had set up DeVris not to expect them back at the Museum that afternoon, she said it was important that she and Gil get enough lead time to get to Weymouth Monastery before DeVris realized they were missing.

She arranged all this before she ever saw McCullum. She is good. Really good. Whatever she was up to he was glad she was on his side.

'So, what's next?' he asked.

They'd be landing in London in less than five hours, Sabbie said. She held out her hand, palm up. 'Give me your passport for safekeeping.' He thought to protest, but let it go. After all, what's

130

she going to do with it, sell it on the black market?

'Get some sleep while you can,' she said. 'You'll be needing it.'

Of course he would. Of that, he had no doubt.

TWENTY-FIVE

Later that evening
London

The car on the South West train from London to Weymouth was empty except for a sprinkling of passengers in the first few rows of their car. Gil took a seat next to Sabbie at the back of the coach. He relaxed into the seat and pulled a blanket up to his chin. Tel Aviv or London time, either way you sliced it, it was the middle of the night.

'Shouldn't you be reading over the diary notes?' she asked.

'I've already memorized them. They say, go to Weymouth and use the good brains God gave you.'

'Then let's go over the itinerary, okay?' Her voice had softened. It was warm and held an intimacy he had never heard from her before.

She was so transparent. Obviously she couldn't sleep, but she didn't know how to say she wanted company.

Instinctively, he reached to touch her hair, then stopped short. The look of uncertainty on her face told him that he was moving in new territories. He thought of Lucy. The memory of her face was not as clear as it had been only a week earlier. His chest tightened with guilt.

Sabbie leaned over to turn on his reading lamp. Her breast brushed his arm. She seemed not to notice; he pretended as well.

'So here's how we're going to handle Weymouth,' she began.

'I'm all ears.'

'We'll be lovers,' she explained with a mischievous smile.

Gil laughed out loud.

'What, it seems so impossible to think we are lovers?' she asked in a mock tone of challenge.

'No, not at all. After all, technically . . .'

She cut him off. 'Good, then we shall be very intimate. Enthralled with each other. That way, should we go for a long moonlit walk, no one will think it odd. We will have a perfectly acceptable reason to not want to talk with anyone. You shall have eyes only for me.'

'And what about you?'

'I shall have eyes on everything that is going on around us,' she answered.

'That doesn't seem fair,' Gil continued. He was unwilling to let go of the banter.

'This is important. We must be convincing as lovers. It's not as easy as you think,' continued Sabbie.

'I can bite the bullet if you can.'

She deftly changed the subject. 'Let me fill you in on what I know about Weymouth and the Monastery.'

Gil nodded unenthusiastically.

'The Monastery at Weymouth was one of the first in Europe. Over the years, it has gone through some extraordinary changes. It survived ten centuries and some pretty rough times—though

132

maybe saying it survived is giving it too much credit. Except for one section, the whole thing had to be torn down, repaired, or rebuilt. They were able to stay true to the architecture and to salvage a few of the statues and most of the tapestries but, other than that, very little of the original Monastery remains; just a lot of reconstructed walls laid out according to what architects believe was the original floor plan.

'Still,' she continued, 'the town considers the building to be the same Monastery that it has always been *and*—I'll tell you more about this, later—some of the townsfolk have reported some unusual happenings.'

Gil began to drift off to sleep.

She shook his arm to rouse him.

'Anyway,' she continued, 'the town of Weymouth is situated at least four hours southwest of London by bus, when the bus is running, which it doesn't after four o'clock in the afternoon. That's why we had to take the train. Besides, it ended up saving us almost an hour and a half.'

She explained that the Monastery was a good forty-minute walk from the center of the town—an apparently important point because it guaranteed a bit of solitude. According to her Internet printout, there was only one road to the Monastery and the best way to identify it was to use the oldest pub in town as a starting point.

Gil started to fade once more and let his head fall back onto the headrest.

She shook him again, harder than before.

'You're a cold woman.'

Sabbie continued, leaning over him to speak into his exposed ear.

'The Monastery is generally deserted. There haven't been any monks there since the eighteen-hundreds. Volunteers give tours of the place, but their schedules are erratic, depending on how many people sign up. If we need info on the history of the place, we'll have to go to the Weymouth Library, which may seem odd given that we're supposed to be lovers on a romantic get-away but we'll think of something if we have to.'

Gil sat up, suddenly awake. 'Wait a minute. Go back to what you were saying. Tell me about the strange happenings.'

According to local legend, she explained, there was a buried casket somewhere on the Monastery grounds. Some claimed that the casket was made of silver, while others claimed it to be of gold or copper. The townsfolk were divided on the spiritual nature of the casket. Some claimed it was evil, a trap set by the Devil. Others said it was a gift from God. A few believed it to be blessed by Christ and that it held the power to heal.

'They swear it bears the formula for eternal life which Jesus himself imbibed, even as he was being crucified,' Sabbie continued. 'Visitors from the surrounding countryside pay regular visits to the Monastery Chapel, which is still intact. Some come out claiming that they have been healed or have found a renewed sense of peace by the simple act of praying. They believe themselves to have been in the casket's presence even though they have no idea where it actually resides.'

According to what Sabbie had read, there was one old couple who supposedly moved to the town because the woman was dying of some rare cancer. They believed that if they went to the Monastery

134

every day, she'd be cured.

'What happened?' Gil asked.

'That was eight years ago. They still walk the grounds every day.'

'Anything else?'

'Nope, that's it,' she said. 'What do you think?'

'It's incredible. The best thing you could have said.'

There is a pattern to the way people think, Gil explained. Whether they were trying to hide something for someone to discover a thousand years later or simply deciding what to eat for dinner, people followed patterns. When it came to making up stories, people continued to follow predictable patterns. Scratch the surface of a myth and you discover a real event. It may have been twisted and used by vested interests for ulterior purposes but, at its start, it was real.

'Let's start with fact number one,' Gil said. 'In the diary, Elias wrote that the scroll his brother brought from the Holy Land was encased in a wooden box.'

'A casket!'

'Exactly. And the townsfolk think it's evil . . .'

'Because they burned William at the stake!'

'And the rest, the part about Christ?' he prompted.

'Don't tell me that you think . . .'

'Don't you? Doesn't it fit perfectly with what Elias wrote?' he asked.

'Things are never that simple,' she said.

She was a tough cookie, he'd give her that, but she didn't fool him. She was hoping just like he was, that the Weymouth myth was all about Elias' scroll. And neither of them could wait to find out.

135

Side by side they sat in silence, listening to the rumble of the train, rushing toward Weymouth.

Gil watched her eyelids fall and her breathing grow deep and relaxed.

And your patterns, Sabbie, hot and cold, caring then distant, sexual without intimacy, control at any cost. What do they say about you? A hard life even before the rape. Pain and betrayal. No one could be trusted. Only special, safe people like Ludlow and his wife. Now, they were gone, too.

He understood her. Like Lucy in her last days, when there was no one left to blame, she blamed herself. It was a hard choice and a very lonely one. To all the world it looked as if she had no need for anyone. Nothing could have been further from the truth.

An old familiar ache rose in Gil's chest. He wished he could be certain that he'd be able to lead her to the secret that had waited two millennia to be set free. He knew how desperately she wanted to find it and protect it. He wanted to tell her to sleep well, that everything would work out. He wanted to promise it all. But he knew things were never that simple.

TWENTY-SIX

Later that evening
Muslims for World Truth (MWT) Video Production
Studios London

Many hours had passed before Hassan informed Maluka of McCullum's unexpected appearance. Precious hours in which Maluka might have taken action, now lost because Hassan had failed in his duty. Perhaps Hassan was becoming as self-indulgent as those he had been sent to observe. Perhaps their greed and indolence had seeped into his soul. Or perhaps, as he claimed, Hassan had been so ill as to require a nap in the storeroom of the Museum.

The final thought would have given Maluka the greatest peace of mind. Unfortunately, he had a difficult time believing it. Hassan had never missed time at work due to illness, either at Maluka's video studio or at the Museum. Neither high fever nor racking cough would have kept him from completing his duty. It was one of those things by which some men define themselves and in which they take great pride.

If it were not for the particularly bad timing of Hassan's so-called infirmity, Maluka might have been merely surprised. As it was, a sudden illness that prevented Hassan from knowledge of McCullum's arrival at the Museum seemed more than coincidental.

Maluka had answered Hassan's phone call with caution. This was not the time of their prearranged communication. An unexpected call could not be expected to bring good news.

'I don't know what to say,' Hassan began. His voice cracked with apparent emotion. 'If only I had been here, I would have called you immediately.'

Maluka remained silent as Hassan offered the few details he was able to glean from the other maintenance staff.

'McCullum arrived with two bodyguards,' Hassan began.

McCullum's choice of Power Angels would reveal the purpose of his visit. Each of McCullum's three pairs of Power Angels bore a name taken from angelic folklore or scripture, usually from Talmudic and Islamic teachings, a particularly ironic twist given McCullum's contempt for both traditions. Each bodyguard was chosen with care, paired with another of similar yet complementary talents, then groomed to perform a singular function.

If McCullum arrived accompanied by Nakir and Munkir, named for the questioning angels who, according to tradition, decided whether a soul goes to Heaven or Hell, one could assume that the intent of McCullum's visit was information gathering. On the other hand, if Ahadiel, who bore the name of the angelic enforcer of the law, and Azareel, the heavenly curer of stupidity, were seen at McCullum's side, one could expect that there would be a meting out of his particular type of punishment. Two other Power Angels were said to remain at WATSC headquarters, their help enlisted only as required. Their names and special attributes remained a mystery to almost all outside the elite members of the White Americans To

Save Christianity organization.

'Whom did he bring?' Maluka asked.

'Nakir and Munkir, the fair-haired twins,' Hassan answered.

'So, McCullum came only to question DeVris. Most likely about the diary. What else?' Maluka asked.

'I discovered a book on DeVris' floor, one that is particularly precious to him, one which he would never leave lying about. A few of its pages were bent and there appeared to be a spray of blood on the back,' Hassan reported.

DeVris must have not been forthcoming with his answers and McCullum had deemed it necessary to offer some incentive.

'And when I asked DeVris if I might empty his wastebasket, he did not hear me. He claimed to have an ear infection.'

McCullum's blow must have been to DeVris' head.

'And the outcome of the meeting?' Maluka asked.

'Strangely friendly. McCullum was said to be smiling, his arm around DeVris' shoulder, as he left.'

So, DeVris revealed everything, for the time being, McCullum is satisfied that there is some plan in the works that offers promise of attaining the diary and, perhaps, the scroll.

Next, Maluka inquired as to the progress of Sabbie and Gil. Hassan explained that they had taken the day off.

'They told DeVris they were not making significant progress and needed time away from the confines of the Museum for, quote, unquote, research purposes,' Hassan concluded with a disdainful grunt.

Maluka straightened in surprise. The news was the worst Hassan could have given him. Of all he had heard, this was the most alarming. Sabbie would never abandon translation of the diary for a mere sexual encounter. If she were not at the Museum, it was probable that she had learned what she needed from the diary and, in all likelihood, was in pursuit of the scroll.

DeVris was blind to Sabbie's power and determination. In light of the American's reported lack of progress, DeVris would have probably seen her request for a day off as unremarkable. As far as the Director was concerned, he and McCullum were the only game in town. He would have assumed there was no reason to rush the translation.

Sabbie probably suggested to DeVris that she would maintain more control over Gil as long she continued to provide the promise, or reality, of her favors. All the more reason to allow them some time off together.

DeVris would have granted them leave, allowed himself to linger on what carnal deeds they might engage in, and have thought no more of the matter. Maluka, on the other hand, recognized in Sabbie a resolve that, under certain circumstances, could easily make her a most prodigious opponent.

'She has left and has either taken the American with her or has disposed of him. She has almost a full day's head start. That is of great concern!'

Maluka's instructions to Hassan were precise. If they acted quickly, they might yet be able to recoup the time they had lost and might yet

140

overtake her. After all, Sabbie had no awareness of Maluka's existence, much less his involvement.

If all went as planned, she and the American would make the discovery of the millennium, experience an exhilaration that few would ever know, then deliver the prize into Maluka's waiting hands.

But now there was so much to arrange. He had lost precious time. The question of Hassan's loyalty would have to wait for another day.

TWENTY-SEVEN

Day Nine, early morning
Weymouth Train Station
Weymouth, England

The Weymouth Limousine Service was the model of dependability, when the owner was in town. Which today, he wasn't. According to the stationmaster, the specific instructions that Sabbie left the day before on the company's voice mail would probably be retrieved just in time for spring thaw and the onslaught of vacationers.

'It wouldn't have killed them to include that vital piece of information on the answering machine message,' she complained to the stationmaster.

'The sky is blue,' Gil muttered.

'What?' she asked, apparently more than ready for a fight.

'It's something George always says. "The sky is blue, the grass is green, and people are stupid."'

'Meaning?'

'Meaning you can't change any of them, so why try?'

She shot him a cold stare.

The stationmaster told them they could catch a private cab. Only a few taxis bothered to come down to the station when it wasn't tourist season but, with a bit of luck, they'd find one parked at the far side of the parking lot.

Gil spotted a gray cab amid a sea of silver-colored cars. 'There it is, over there.' He waved the driver over. 'You know what I always say. Best place to hide a tree is in the forest.'

'Great idea. Why bother to make a cab easily visible?' Sabbie muttered.

It was a quick trip to the hotel and the check-in was effortless—until the desk clerk asked to hold their passports, as was the custom. Sabbie left Gil to finish up the details of the registration while she had a private word with the manager. Gil had anticipated a repeat of the intimidation tactic Sabbie had used in the airport but, even from a distance, he could tell she and the manager seemed to be getting on famously.

The desk clerk handed Gil the key to their room and made one final request. 'Would you please fill in an address and phone number on this traveler's check?' he asked. 'Your friend has signed the check but has neglected to finish filling it out.'

Gil struggled to remember the address of the Museum then settled on as near an approximation as he could conjure.

'Just there, under your name, Prof. Ludlow,' the desk clerk said.

Gil's gaze dropped from the clerk to the

traveler's check; one of many traveler's checks that had been paying their way. Only one name appeared on the traveler's check: Professor Robert Ludlow. Next to it, awaiting the manager's decision, lay a passport which contained Gil's picture and, under his photo, the name of a dead man.

TWENTY-EIGHT

Later that afternoon
Weymouth Monastery

A break-in, whether at the Monastery or any other building, required two essentials: planning and the right tools. Such was the world according to Sabbie. Gil didn't bother to ask what previous experience provided her with these words of wisdom. He didn't want to know.

Her plan was simple: get a look at the Monastery by day, preferably from the inside, then to return in the evening to search for the scroll. Time, however, was not on their side.

'DeVris may have already realized we've gone. If not, we have one day, maybe two before he figures it out.'

'After that?'

'Not sure. If DeVris decides to use official channels, Scotland Yard could be called in. Or, he could get McCullum to send his Power Angels.' She explained the purpose and tactics of McCullum's WATSC Nazis in far more detail than Gil would have preferred.

143

'So, I'm not sure that it matters who is after us,' she concluded wryly.

'Well, Scotland Yard sounds a lot more appealing than McCullum's goons.'

'Don't be so sure.'

'But you think we have a day or two, right?' Gil asked.

'Yes, but I could be wrong.'

'Great,' he said sarcastically. He did not do powerless well.

She ignored him as usual. 'Food, information, and a hardware store. That's what we need, in that order.'

They got their food and information at the same place, and both were equally bad. The waitress who served them runny eggs, also informed them that tours at Weymouth Monastery were on hold during off-season.

'Not enough demand, you know,' she added, then left them to their inedible meal.

'Never take one person's word on anything,' Sabbie advised, as she pushed the untouched plate aside. They grabbed some coffee and stale muffins and headed for the Weymouth Tourist office.

'Monastery tour? No problem,' the pleasant young woman informed them. Best of all, they were able to book a tour for that afternoon.

They spent the morning buying supplies and walking the streets of Weymouth in order to get a lay of the land. They divided their purchases between several establishments so as to not cause suspicion and had to cash in four more traveler's checks.

Several hours of feigned nonchalant shopping yielded everything from crowbars and wire cutters

144

to the biggest backpack Gil had ever seen. Fully loaded it must have weighed fifty pounds. Although Sabbie said they would trade off carrying it, Gil refused to hand it over.

'Don't you think we're overdoing it? How much money do we have left?' Gil asked.

If they were going to find the scroll, Sabbie said, they needed all the help they could get. They had nothing to depend on but the diary and their wits.

'Yeah, and enough tools to furnish a Home Depot,' Gil added. The reference was lost on her.

'I suppose you prefer prying open doors with your fingernails?'

Until that moment, Gil had never really contemplated what would be involved. Breaking into the Monastery suddenly took on a whole new wood-splintering-window-smashing-spending-your-life-in-jail kind of feeling about it.

What's this, my third crime in two days, counting the bomb scare at the Museum and my string of forgeries? Terrific.

He had lost count.

The afternoon tour was a welcome distraction. The Monastery was imposing—huge stone walls, towering spires, an expansive circular cobblestone courtyard led to wide stone steps. Two great wooden doors towered above them. Their tour companions, three women and a young man, paused to take pictures, and approached.

'Our little crowbar is not going to make a dent on those,' Gil whispered.

'Shhh.'

Last to arrive was the tour guide. She could have easily doubled as a Women's Army Corps sergeant left over from the Second World War.

145

Square-shouldered and broad of hip, she addressed her little group of visitors in front of the Monastery's great double doors. In keeping with her appearance, she wasted no time on pleasantries. Rules of behavior were listed with precision, as if speaking to new recruits in a tiny and somewhat odd-looking army.

Gil, Sabbie, and the other four hapless sightseers that made up the group were instructed to stay together, abstain from eating, drinking, smoking, and especially from touching anything that might be found within one's natural reach.

'And you think *I'm* tough,' Sabbie whispered.

The guide paused, possibly aware of the disappointment she was about to engender. 'In addition, the taking of photos or video is strictly prohibited.'

Each of the tourists, heavily laden with now-useless cameras, snacks, and bottled water, sighed deeply and grumbled their complaints. Her directives complete, the guide turned and walked past the great doors, and disappeared into a small, side entrance. The rest of their little band filed behind like ducklings with Gil and Sabbie bringing up the rear.

The tour began in the buttery, which the guide noted had nothing to do with butter but, rather, had served as a storehouse for casks of wine and beer.

'The sell-air-ium,' the guide explained with more enthusiasm than Gil thought justified, 'has nothing to do with sun and air . . . it is not soooolarium . . . it's *sell-arium*, spelled c-e-l-l-a-r-i-u-m. It means underground, which is where the food was kept to minimize spoilage.'

'Jesus, lady, get a life,' Gil muttered under his breath. Sabbie threw him a disapproving look.

They spent fifteen minutes learning more than any civilized human being needed to know about preventing the decay of food. 'And now, on to the cow-le-factor-y,' the guide announced with precision.

Gil couldn't help it. It was one of those thoughts that begs to be spoken, so witty that it must be shared by another. Gil whispered the comment that demanded to be heard. 'Cow-le-factory? Isn't that where they used to build French bovines?'

It didn't sound as nearly as funny coming out of his mouth as it had sounded in his head. Sabbie distanced herself from him and concentrated on the guide's explanation that a calefactory was a warming room where monks found a few moments of welcome conversation as well as respite from the ceaseless cold of their unheated cells and workrooms in winter.

Sabbie scribbled something on her notepad then coughed a bit to mask the noise as she furtively tore off the page and handed it to Gil.

Her note was brief but to the point. 'Get a grip.'

Gil forced himself into a semblance of sobriety.

The tour guide's current banter on the changing architectural features inspired Sabbie to take copious notes. Gil, on the other hand, needed some quiet and solitude, a chance to think.

Suppose he didn't have enough time to decipher the diary's vague message! A list of accountings that made mention of a tapestry, that was his only signpost. The discovery of a priceless scroll bearing witness to Jesus' life depended on that alone . . . and on him. His stomach tightened.

'We'll be finishing up in the Chapel,' the guide announced. 'But, first, we'll tour the gardens and make our way around to . . .'

He had to get some God damned peace and quiet! He needed to get away from the drone of the guide's unending commentary and eagle eye.

'Follow my lead,' Gil whispered to Sabbie. 'I've got to get some time alone to look around.'

Approaching the guide, Gil spoke softly, as if no one else could overhear. 'Excuse me, I need a word in private with you.'

Reluctantly, the guide obliged. Out of earshot of the others, Gil explained.

'I have diabetes and I'm not feeling well. May I just sit down for a while?' he asked.

The guide hesitated, eyeing him suspiciously.

He had placed her on the horns of a dilemma and each of the points was equally uncomfortable. If she didn't grant him this small act of kindness, she'd have to take him for medical attention, which would necessitate canceling the tour halfway through. As this was the only tour of the day, the group was bound to be mighty unhappy. On the other hand, his request was clearly not within her narrow guidelines.

'I've taken my pills and I need to rest a while. I won't bother anything,' Gil added. Feigning exhaustion, he slid to a sitting position next to the wall, head bent, and eyes closed.

Sabbie sprang to his support. 'Please,' she said, earnestly. 'If you just give him a few minutes to rest, he'll be fine. He'll wait right here until we return. You did say we'd swing back through here, didn't you?'

Sabbie's indication that she would be continuing

the tour seemed to lessen any remaining doubt the guide still entertained, and Sabbie's question, which required a response, provided a final distraction.

In the end, the tour guide seemed satisfied to keep Sabbie as a tour hostage should Gil take it into his mind to commit some unspeakable profanity. Within a few minutes, the group had vacated, Sabbie in the lead, leaving Gil a half hour to himself.

He was on his feet even as the door closed behind the departing group. At best, there wasn't a second to spare. At worst . . . well, he didn't want to think about that.

At the end of the one corridor that the group had not yet explored, Gil found himself faced with two choices. On his right, a long dark hall snaked between two massive stone walls. The narrow passage turned and trailed off, with no doors or openings in sight. On the left, a hall that, according to a small wooden sign, led to the Chapel.

He walked quickly to the right. The chill air of the hall cooled his sweaty neck.

How long does this damn hall go on? Shit! I must have lost five minutes already. I'm going to have to turn around if it doesn't lead some . . .

He never saw the end of the dark hall coming. He turned as the passage twisted and raced as fast as his pounding heart could manage. He rounded the final curve and barely escaped a collision with a large unpainted wooden door.

Surprisingly, it was unlocked and it opened with ease, revealing a wealth of tapestries. The room was filled with the smell of antiquity. The scene

149

before him reminded Gil of a large carpet store gone unattended for a couple hundred years. Dozens of tapestries hung on the walls, lay piled on the floor, or draped over racks. Knights on horseback, ladies and their attendants, dogs, even dragons were intricately woven into the designs. In their day, their colors must have been bright and rich, but the tapestries he could see had greatly faded.

Surely these works could not be the 'mediocre tapestries woven by the old, stupid or infirm' that Elias had described in one deciphered bit of diary text. Each was an intricate work of precision and beauty. There was something oddly consistent about them, as if they had been made by the same hand.

What was it that Brother Elias had written? The Abbot had designed all of the tapestries—with the exception of only one that Elias had been permitted to conceive and create on his own? Well, Elias' tapestry may have been special to him but among all of these, it was just another face in the crowd.

Gil glanced at his watch. He was running out of time. The jog back through the passageway seemed to take longer than the forward run. He was late and, if the guide returned and found an empty entry way where he was supposed to be resting, there'd be no way to explain it. Putting on a burst of speed, he found with relief that the group was not yet in sight. He had barely seated himself when the group trooped in from the garden. Gil struggled to control his labored breathing, then turned to allow the guide full view of his pale and sweaty face.

Sabbie stooped to wipe his wet forehead with

the sleeve of her sweater. 'You're clammy and white. Are you okay?' she asked.

The yellow cardigan smelled vaguely of vanilla, and he longed to lie flat on the cool stone floor and have her continue to keep mopping his forehead.

'What did you find?' Sabbie whispered.

The guide called to them to join the group in the Chapel.

'Good stuff,' he whispered back. They hurried to catch up with their little band.

The massive stone columns of the Chapel rose high into the air and, although the vast chamber contained the same dirty glass windows as the tapestry room, the Chapel seemed far brighter and warmer. A great pipe organ loomed at the far end and, next to it, a simple altar sat upon a huge stone slab. A small wooden bench peeked out from under the organ keyboard as if inviting the next pious soul to bring the old pipes to life.

Gil's body ached. He had never felt quite so tired. His head slipped backward and rested on the back of the wooden pew.

The guide's voice seemed to come from afar. Next to him, Sabbie took notes.

'This, of course, is our Chapel, the part most of you have been waiting for,' the guide continued. 'You may have heard about the healing power of the Chapel, but we strongly discourage that sort of talk. This is not Lourdes and we caution visitors not to expect any kind of miracle here. Some people report a feeling of peace or well-being.'

Others have described it as a renewed sense of faith, she added. Some claim that the rejuvenation springs from the power of some ancient object that

151

has been hidden within the confines of this building. Most of the Friends of the Monastery agree that the source of the experiences doesn't matter so long as it continues to bring replenishment and spiritual healing to those in need.

Having completed her obviously well-rehearsed speech, the guide stood straight and proud, a confident witness who now spoke in her own words; no longer fearful of saying the wrong thing. Her words were simple and carried a new warmth.

'Scientists may not be able to explain it to their liking, but sitting here in this Chapel, something comes over you. People say it's like being in the company of something holy. I will tell you that it's a presence; a good, loving, and protective presence.'

Got to get some sleep. Need to close my eyes. Just for a minute.

Sabbie poked Gil with her elbow. The guide had begun moving the group to the exit. Their few minutes of Chapel healing time was up. Dutifully, he stood and filed out with the others.

Their little group quickly disbanded. 'Well, so much for healing,' Gil said. 'I didn't feel a damn thing.'

'Maybe we're just not believers,' Sabbie replied with a shrug. 'Still, it must be nice to believe,' she added thoughtfully.

'I prefer reality,' he said.

'Well, speaking of reality, we need to . . .'

'I found the tapestry,' he interrupted.

'Where?' she asked excitedly.

'In there, in the tapestry room.'

'What does it look like?' she asked.

'I don't know. It was somewhere among fifty others,' Gil answered.

She pinched him. Hard, on the soft underpart of his arm. It really hurt. 'That's not funny,' she said.

'Oww! Don't do that!' he protested.

'Then stop joking,' she snapped. 'Now, how will you know which tapestry is Elias"?'

'I thought you said you trusted me,' he replied, and continued to rub his bruise.

In the fading light of day, they returned to town over the unpaved rocky shortcut that cut across the field. Neither spoke. Both made mental notes of the rugged terrain that they would need to negotiate on their return to the Monastery that evening. There'd be no light save for that from a crescent moon.

TWENTY-NINE

Later that evening
Weymouth Harbour Hotel

As arguments go, this one was a beaut. And the timing couldn't have been worse.

It started when Sabbie asked Gil how he would be able to spot Elias' tapestry among the fifty or so odd pieces he had seen during the tour.

'We can't just break into the Monastery and *hope* you get lucky,' she argued. 'You've got to have some kind of a plan!'

'I just need to relax and let it happen,' he said.

The *it* that needed to happen had always been the same. Whether he was hot on a drug dealer's cyber trail of money laundering or setting up a program that would pinpoint a child molester's next most likely move, if Gil had to think about it, it just didn't work. He had to stop thinking and just put himself on automatic.

'You must have something better in mind than that,' Sabbie demanded. 'As far as I can see, this is going to be our only shot at finding it.'

'Once we're inside the Monastery, I'll know what to do,' Gil repeated coldly. He wished he felt half as confident as he was acting.

Her panic was starting to get to him. She was afraid that Elias' tapestry might no longer be at the Monastery or that it might not exist at all but she wouldn't admit it. Not to him, not to herself. She was afraid there wasn't enough time. And she was right. But pinning him to the wall sure as hell wasn't helping things.

Finally, he put an end to the whole thing. 'Look, I'm going to the Monastery tonight,' Gil said simply. 'I'm going to trust myself—and you—to figure out which tapestry is Elias' and what it has to tell us about the scroll. You can go or not. Do whatever you want.'

He hoped the bluff would work. He had no intention of going it alone.

Sabbie didn't acknowledge his ultimatum but continued to check over their tools for the night. Backpack, flashlights, extra batteries, a blanket, two Swiss Army knives, hammer, wooden wedge, duct tape, and tape measure. Some of the items made no sense to Gil, but she said they might need them, so he went along with it. That seemed to change her mood for the better.

After all, what's ten more pounds in your

backpack when you're already carrying fifty?

Over sandwiches brought in for a picnic on the bed, they made plans for that evening's break-in. Any thought Gil might have entertained of spending the afternoon in bed together was quickly squelched. Sabbie was all business.

Their first challenge was the massive entry doors, she explained. Hopefully, they would be able to jimmy the lock on the side door Sabbie had seen on the tour. Once in, they had to be aware of the light from their flashlights. The Chapel's exterior walls were not visible from the village but, from what Gil could tell, the windows of the tapestry room faced the town. The blanket would have to be used to block the beams from their flashlights so as to not invite investigation.

Timing was crucial. They had to walk right past the busiest pub in town and, if they wanted to avoid being noticed as they headed down the path that led only to the Monastery, they'd have to wait until the pub closed at around 2:00 A.M. By dawn, the bakery would be offering up breakfast to its usual bunch of bleary-eyed townspeople. Given the load in the backpack and the darkness, it would take a good half-hour to walk to the Monastery by way of their newly discovered shortcut and hopefully a little longer back, assuming they were successful and the load was heavier. That left them a little more than three hours to find Elias' tapestry, make sense of its message, locate the scroll, and put things back in order.

Gil had his doubts. Serious doubts. He guessed that she did, too.

155

THIRTY

The walk through town had been easy; fair enough moonlight, downhill slope on paved sidewalk, and crisp air. But once they passed the pub, everything changed. The backpack seemed to double in weight.

While Sabbie made her way easily along the jagged path in darkness, Gil strained to keep up. His chest ached straight through to his back, and he couldn't shake the image of dropping dead from a heart attack just as they entered the Chapel; of the townspeople finding him lying face down, arms out and Christ-like in front of the altar.

That would certainly put an end to all the talk about the healing power of the Chapel.

Sabbie moved easily ahead of him. 'First we'll go to the tapestry room,' she said. 'You don't think you'll have any trouble finding it in the dark, do you? I mean, with just the flashlights?'

Gil didn't answer. He barely had breath to keep up with her, much less offer an explanation.

'Look, working by the seat of my pants is not just something I do when all else fails. It *is* my talent. I do best under pressure,' he said with his last gasp of air. The wheeze did little to instill confidence.

In the distance to the right, fine white sand stretched to the edge of the sea.

156

That beach is where we ought to be. A nice young couple, enjoying the pleasure of each other's company.

Instead, he was stumbling in the dark, fighting the rocky path and the terror that this time, he might finally come up empty.

The dreary ramparts of the Monastery rose against the blackness of the now cloud-shrouded sky, its silhouette reminiscent of a city's skyline. Gil's foot slipped into a maze of roots and he went down hard. His extended hands, meant to break his fall, skimmed into jagged plant debris. Something pierced his right hand.

'Shit! I just got skewered.'

Sabbie whipped the blanket from his backpack, threw it over them like a tent, then switched on the flashlight.

A three-inch twig, bent at an odd angle, protruded from his palm. Blood dripped freely from the twig's hollow center. Gil reached to pull out the piercing weed.

'Don't touch it,' she commanded. 'Don't move.'

She bent closer and took hold of his hand to steady it. Gil assumed she was coming in for a better view. In two swift movements, however, she had bent his hand back to better expose the stick, then with her teeth, quickly and deftly wrested the remaining splinter from his flesh. She spit repeatedly into the dirt.

'Jesus Christ! What the hell are you doing? You took out a whole chunk of my hand!'

Slapping the flashlight into his good hand, Sabbie pointed it toward the wound. A wide trickle of blood dripped from his fingers. 'Keep the light on it,' she ordered.

157

He was too surprised and in too much pain to think of doing anything else.

Sabbie retrieved something from her pocket. She unwrapped the object and before Gil could get a fix on it, laid it onto his wound. She quickly secured it with duct tape, torn in sections with the powerful incisors Gil was getting to know far too intimately. Only a thin white cord protruded from the lumpy-looking dressing.

'Is that a tampon?' he asked incredulously.

She moved behind him, pinching the back of his neck—hard.

'Are you out of your mind?' he yelled. 'That hurts more than my hand.'

'That's the idea.' She calmly gathered up the tampon wrapping, turned off the flashlight, and stuffed the blanket back in the backpack. 'It's hard to hurt in more than one place at a time. We'll need that hand more than your neck, so tell me when it starts to throb and . . .'

'Like hell I will. You'll probably bite it off at the wrist,' he protested.

The twig looked like it had come from an oleander bush, she explained. Every part of the oleander was poisonous. People had died from using its branches as skewers for roasting hot dogs. The poison worked like digitalis.

'First, your heart starts pounding, then your pulse gets weak. Eventually your whole cardiovascular system shuts down. You could be dead in a matter of hours. Maybe less. I wasn't sure if it would still be poisonous once it was dried out, but I thought we should play it safe.'

'So why didn't you just suck the poison out of me instead of taking a chunk of me with it?'

'You're welcome,' she said, then turned and continued up the path.

They approached the great doors of the edifice, and she stopped short, staring straight ahead. Gil set his heavy load down and glanced at her profile in the moonlight.

Her face was set. She was tight and determined. No wonder. For Sabbie, it was a lose-lose situation. If they were unable to find the scroll, she had no place to go. She couldn't go back to the Museum, not after taking off on a rogue treasure hunt. If DeVris figured out that she had the diary, he'd have the police on her tail. She couldn't show her face back in Israel, especially with the theft of the diary added to her previous felony. On the other hand, if they were successful and found the scroll, DeVris would be after her for the prize. With McCullum behind him, there was no telling what DeVris might do to her.

Or to me.

Gil pushed away the rising panic his thought triggered. He turned to her in the darkness. 'We're going to find it,' he said calmly. The tenderness in his voice rang with unfamiliarity. He repeated his reassurance, adding nothing more.

'I know,' she said simply. 'That's what I'm afraid of.'

THIRTY-ONE

A few minutes later
Weymouth Monastery Courtyard

The side door of the Monastery offered no resistance. The blade of her Swiss Army knife slipped easily between the door and the jamb and released the bolt.

'Army training,' Sabbie said with a smile.

Their footsteps echoed in the entryway. The sound hadn't been noticeable during the afternoon tour. Now, the noise echoed and felt large in the darkness.

'Don't turn on your flashlight yet,' she said. 'Wait until we get to the tapestry room and put up the blanket.' Sabbie hooked her arm around his, and he led her in the direction he had taken earlier that day.

As Gil worked his way through the dark, she detailed her version of their game plan. 'Now, we'll give each tapestry a quick once-over to see if it looks like it could be Elias,' she explained. 'If we limit ourselves to two and a half minutes for each, at fifty tapestries that's just over two hours. Hopefully, Elias' tapestry won't be the last one we come to. Assuming it gives us pretty clear directions as to where the scroll is hidden, we'll still have a full hour to . . .'

Gil stopped in his tracks. 'No,' he said firmly.

'No, what?'

'No, we start in the Chapel.'

He expected her to argue or at least to demand

160

an explanation. But she remained silent.

'This is where Elias prayed for inspiration,' Gil said. He told her that he needed her to be quiet; to just let him sit and let it happen.

She murmured an okay, then said nothing as they moved to the Chapel.

A dozen strategies flashed across his mind. Some of them so intricate Gil could hardly have put them into words. He rejected them all. This was a different kind of puzzle. It required a different kind of thinking.

For ten minutes they sat in silence in front of the altar. Something in his mind was changing. He had to give it time to work itself through. He could almost grab the thought as it flew by. Almost. But not quite.

'What are you thinking?' Sabbie interrupted. He could feel her shivering in the cold. 'You're not waiting for one of those mystical experiences the guide talked about, are you? You know, we don't have all night.'

'I'm trying to think like Elias. This is where he came to pray. I need to understand what would have been on his mind.'

'I don't know about him, but I have one thing on mine. I say let's go to the tapestry room. While you think, I can start going through each of those tapestries . . .'

'That's it!' Gil cried. He threw the backpack over his shoulder and grabbed Sabbie's elbow with his good hand. He guided her in long strides down the corridor in the beam of her flashlight.

'Brother Elias had one goal—to help us find the scroll,' he explained. 'We don't have to look for bits and pieces to help us retrace his actions, we just have to stay sharp and keep an eye out for the clues Elias left behind for us.'

'I don't understand the difference,' she said.

'Look, imagine we're trying to follow Hansel and Gretel—you know who Hansel and Gretel are, don't you?' Gil asked.

'Yes . . .'

'Well, imagine that we're tracking Hansel and Gretel to see where they've gone. If they weren't expecting us to follow, we'd check the bushes to see if any branches were broken by their passing or we'd inspect the ground for evidence of child-sized footprints. That's what you do when you look for clues. On the other hand, if we knew they *expected* us to come looking for them, we'd keep an eye out for something they intentionally left behind, something they knew would help us follow their trail. Like breadcrumbs they would have scattered on the ground as they walked. Understand?'

'Not really. In either case, you're looking at the ground,' she replied.

'Yes, but you're looking for two completely different things. We shouldn't be trying to figure out which tapestry belonged to Elias, we should be looking for the clues he left for *us.*'

Sabbie shrugged then pushed ahead of him into the tapestry room. She tried to fix the blanket to the old window frames but found that no tape or clips would support the weight of the blanket.

He waited, arms crossed.

Though she turned her flashlight on him, she seemed to take no notice of his resistance. 'We'll just have to hope that no one sees the light,' she continued matter-of-factly.

Gil waited.

You're not going to ignore everything I just said!

Sabbie walked around him, aimed her flashlight at the first hanging piece, and began to slowly examine it.

Gil reached for her elbow. This time he pulled her around, hard.

'Look, we do this my way or we don't do it at all. At least, I don't. Right now, I'm the expert here and, like it or not, you're supposed to be helping *me.*'

'I don't have time for this,' Sabbie said. She turned back to the first tapestry.

'No, *we* don't have time for this. You go through each tapestry, one by one, and by the time 6:00 A.M. comes, you aren't going to be any closer to finding that scroll than you are now. Except you'll be out of time and out of luck.'

Panic crept into her voice. 'So what do we do?' she asked.

'First, let go of your logic. Stop thinking. We're looking for something special, something different. But something that, at first glance, looks like everything else,' Gil explained. He unrolled a particularly large tapestry. 'Something Elias *wanted* us to find.'

Gil moved to the other side of the room. His flashlight beam moved from tapestry to tapestry.

'Just be a kid and follow where your eye takes you,' he said as he continued his inspection. 'Stand in front of the first few and list all the things they have in common.'

'Uhhh, they're all about the same size, they're all pretty faded, and . . .'

'No!' Gil shouted, moving back to shine his flashlight on Sabbie's tapestries. 'No kid would say that. Tell me about the scenes. Remember the game you played as a kid, "What's different in this picture?" Talk about what's different.'

'Well, these two tapestries have two horses and this one has three,' she recited in an impatient voice. 'This is stupid, we're just wasting time.'

'Look, you're doing it already. Now just walk around the room and let your eyes wander. Move the tapestries around so you can get a good look at all of them.'

If she found a tapestry that made her stop and take notice, Gil said, she needed to describe it out loud, even if she didn't know why it caught her attention. *Especially* if she didn't know why.

Gil went back to his own side of the room.

'It doesn't matter whether you're a forensics specialist, a poker player, or a kid trying to learn to ride a bike,' he continued. 'Sometimes you just have to let go of the control and trust that little voice inside you.'

Sabbie continued her review of the weavings and, in her own inimitable fashion, commented on what she saw.

'Ladies in long gowns, they never bathed, probably stunk to high heaven,' she said.

The time passed quickly. Too quickly.

With each new tapestry, Sabbie's comments grew more cutting. 'And angels, and more angels and cherubs. If you thought Elias' reference to angels was going to be helpful, think again.'

Gil talked as he wandered. With his good hand, he pulled hidden weavings from the piles. 'Here's one with palms and cedar trees,' he muttered. 'The desk clerk said the cedars in Dorset are over two hundred and fifty years . . .'

Sabbie was beside him instantly, her flashlight over his shoulder. 'What did you just say?' she asked anxiously.

'I said that the desk clerk recommended a trip to see the cedars . . .'

'No,' she demanded. 'About the palms and cedars.'

Gil continued to move his light from tapestry to tapestry. 'Oh, one of these had cedar trees but they are all full of plant life of some kind or another. That's a common theme . . .'

'And palms? Did you say "palms"?' Sabbie interrupted.

'Yes, here it is. Some palms and cedars and a couple of angels. Why?'

'When have you seen palms and cedars growing side by side?' Sabbie asked excitedly.

She didn't wait for an answer. 'You don't,' she continued. 'Cedars can only live where there are cold winters and palms need a tropical climate. Besides, palms didn't exist here in Elias' time. They weren't brought to Britain until the seventeen hundreds by some Duke of Argyll or something.'

Sabbie explained that, in Elias' time, tapestries depicted gardens as they actually existed. Monks wove the pieces from sketches, commissioned by the owners of estates, who would later exhibit the pieces as testimonies to their wealth. While Elias' Abbot would have had his say on the overall design and the decoration of the tapestry, when it came to the still life, they always portrayed an optimized vision of reality.

'There would be no reason for a monk to weave a tapestry with palms and cedars together. It would

165

have been a product of his imagination. Unsaleable, essentially worthless,' Sabbie concluded.

'Maybe that's exactly what Elias had in mind,' Gil said thoughtfully. 'That way it would stay here . . .'

'Because no one would want it!' Sabbie finished with a nod of confirmation.

Within the limitations of his ascetic life, Elias had managed to figure out that, by making the tapestry unmarketable, he could ensure that it would remain at the Monastery. It was brilliant, inspired. Elias had the kind of mind that every cybersleuth would love to spar with. And he lived almost a millennium earlier.

'We're going to find it,' Gil said quietly.

'What? The scroll? What do you see?'

'Elias thinks like I do, actually like *we* do. Maybe a little better, but in the same direction. He'll show us where the scroll is because we all see with the same eyes. And he's been waiting a long, long time,' Gil added.

Sabbie turned back to the palm and cedar tapestry.

'There are only two angels in this tapestry,' she said. 'All the others have five or six. I don't know what that means but it's different from the rest.

'Quick, get your wallet,' she continued. 'Find the bill with Elias' hidden message and read me the last few lines. Exactly.'

Then the heavens shall beckon and the sound of angels shall open the heart of the righteous one, for they sing to him as in the words of those who have come before.

166

May they live forever in the song of renewal and the promise of continuance.

'These are the only angels that are singing,' she said. 'Okay. Let's see. "Then the heavens shall beckon . . . Then the heavens shall beckon."'

Sabbie's next words came slowly. 'It's there, right there, in the clouds. Oh, my God, it's right there in the clouds.'

Gil strained to see. There were no clouds. Nothing but a few faded patches of sky.

'No, look carefully,' she insisted. 'Right there between the angels. See, the thin horizontal threads that run between them. And, in between those lines, are clouds.'

Gil shook his head.

'Okay,' she continued. 'Just imagine the whole thing vibrant with color, like it would have been before it faded. When you look at it that way, the lines form a musical staff, you know, the parallel lines that you write musical notes on.'

Gil stared at the tapestry, straining to make sense of what she was saying.

She took his index finger and pushed it into several spots of the tapestry. 'Here and here and here. Don't you see it? The clouds are notes, musical tones that the angels are singing.'

She might as well have been pointing at a blank wall.

Sabbie pulled him back a few steps and focused the beam from her flashlight. 'Try from back here. Don't you see?'

Nothing. She was growing impatient. He was doing his best but it just wouldn't come.

'Look,' she insisted, 'the clouds are way too

small and well defined for the rest of the picture. They should fill up the sky like they do in the other tapestries.'

He strained, tried to imagine what she was seeing, then, suddenly, they were there; little puffs, resting on soft shadowed lines. 'I get it. I think. They're tiny, almost the size of the flowers on the palms, just not as long, right?' he added.

Her gasp made him think that someone had found them. He turned his flashlight on the door, hoping to blind any intruder in the beam.

Sabbie grabbed his flashlight and focused it back onto the tapestry. 'No, here, here!' she said.

'They're flowering palms,' Sabbie said. She was silent for a moment. 'So it's true,' she added with a sigh.

There was no time to tell him all she knew, she said, but this much he needed to know.

'Listen to me.' She put her fingertips gently over his mouth. 'This is important.'

She explained that among the most sacred of texts, it is written that in each generation there are born thirty-six righteous souls who, by their very existence, assure the continuation of the world. Were it not for these tzaddikim, who stand in God's judgment, mankind's fate would be in grave and certain peril.

These souls have no knowledge of each other; neither have they any knowledge of their own singular importance. As innocents, they remain unaware of the critical consequences of their deeds.

When these righteous souls have completed their task on earth, they are rewarded with the knowledge that upon their death, among those

168

who have loved them, whose lives they have touched, there will emerge new souls who shall rise to take their place.

'Interesting myth,' Gil said, not certain what the story had to do with finding the scroll and getting the hell out of there.

'You don't get it. The tzaddik is described and praised throughout the Bible, from the Proverbs to the Psalms. The Bible says that the tzaddik is "the foundation of the world" and Psalm 92 specifically says that the tzaddik, the righteous one, will flower like a date palm and grow tall like the cedars of Lebanon. That's why Elias put all of that in the tapestry.'

'What does that have to do with the scroll?' Gil asked.

That's the whole point, she explained. Ludlow spent his lifetime looking for one thing, an ancient message that would point the way to the mate of The Cave 3 Scroll. He believed The Cave 3 Scroll was a trap for the greedy, a detour for those who would see only the promise of riches and disregard its true message. The last entry in The Cave 3 Scroll says simply that there is another copper scroll that holds the key to treasure. The mention of the existence of another scroll comes after the description of dozens of storehouses of riches and their locations.

'Like the last sentence in the telephone call you talked about, the *real* message of The Cave 3 Scroll is its last entry that says there is another, more important manuscript, yet to be discovered. Don't you get it?' she asked excitedly. 'Elias is calling out for the tzaddik, the righteous one, to seek out the second scroll and to uncover the true

169

treasure it alone holds.'

Gil shook his head. 'So, what's the *true* treasure?'

'We won't know that until we figure out what these musical notes mean and find the second scroll.'

THIRTY-TWO

They were so close to finding it; incredibly close. They knew Elias' message was concealed in the puffs of clouds that dotted the heavens of the tapestry. Only one problem remained. Neither of them could read music.

'I had two months of piano lessons when I was seven or eight,' Gil offered lamely.

He remembered something about moving up and down the scale one note at a time and that each note landed on a line or in between the lines but that was just about the extent of his expertise. He never did understand sharps and flats. He had once learned a trick to help keep track of the names of the notes. It involved using the first letters of each words in the phrase, 'every good boy does . . . something or other,' but he had no idea how to use the mnemonic.

'I know where middle C is on a keyboard and that's it,' Sabbie offered, then muttered something about the blind leading the blind.

Gil copied the tapestry's placement of lines and clouds onto his hand. It was beginning to look less and less like a staff with notes. Something was wrong. It took him a minute to figure it out. When he did, the answer made the whole question of a musical message a moot point.

'Look at the musical staff,' Gil said tensely. 'Only four horizontal lines.'

'So, what does that mean?'

From what he could remember, modern notation used five lines and the spaces above, between, and below each line to represent the notes of an octave. If the tapestry showed only four lines it meant that the musical notation was written in the four-line tradition of Elias' time or that, even worse, the clouds didn't represent musical notation at all.

'Either way we're screwed,' Sabbie said.

'Wait a minute, it may not be that bad after all. When you read music, what are you doing? You're following a pattern,' he answered, not waiting for a reply. 'Let's assume these clouds and lines do represent a musical notation. Even though we may not know the absolute notes, we know the relationship of the notes.'

Sabbie looked unconvinced. 'And if it's not a musical notation at all?' she asked demandingly.

'*Then* we're screwed.'

'So, what do we do now?' she asked.

'We just repeat the pattern starting with every key on the keyboard,' Gil answered.

'Try it on what?'

'On the organ in the Chapel,' he said excitedly. He scooped up their gear, and headed for the door.

'That's it?' Sabbie asked in disbelief. 'Hit or miss? That's your plan? We've got less than two hours left!'

'That's the only way I can see to do it, unless

171

you've got something better in mind.'

Gil grabbed her hand and ran back down the passageway to the Chapel. With each step that brought him closer to the great chamber, his stride became more sure and easy. Elias was with them, calling to them to hurry. Gil knew where he was going as if he had walked these halls a thousand times before.

THIRTY-THREE

Twenty minutes later
Weymouth Monastery Chapel

Gil shook his head in disbelief. How could he have been so stupid? He had been thinking only of the tapestry's musical notes and never took it to the next step. Now, with one of the three hours already gone, it might have been a fatal oversight.

If, beneath the cloth that covered the organ keyboard, organ keys were found to be missing, or if the great pipes failed to produce any sound, there wouldn't be enough time to go back to the tapestry room and start over. Either DeVris or some of McCullum's WATSC Power Angels could be expected to arrive any time. There'd be no second chance.

Sabbie held both flashlights while Gil slid the cloth from the organ keyboard. He steeled himself for the almost certain disappointment of a crooked line of yellow, crumbling, half-missing ivories; a contingency that even Elias might not have thought to provide for.

The sight that greeted him, however, bore witness to countless years of dedicated care. The bench and organ looked as if someone had just vacated them and might be returning momentarily. Their surfaces were spotless, oiled and buffed so that they shone even in the near darkness; the keyboard, though yellow with age, was smooth and clean.

A new fear tightened in his chest. If someone had put in the time and energy needed to keep the huge organ in such fine repair, couldn't they have accidentally hit upon the combination of notes he and Sabbie had discovered in the tapestry? He knew the answer even as the question was forming in his mind. A sense of certainty made him smile.

No, Elias would have thought of that. He would have figured a way around it.

'That's middle C,' Sabbie said pointing to a central key. 'That's all I know.'

Gil circled the organ's great pipes and considered its workings. As far as he could see, it utilized a bellows system. He was going to have to pump the bellows while she pressed down on the keys.

Sabbie ignored his plan. She knelt in front of the bellows and waited for him to seat himself at the organ. 'By now your hand should be hurting like hell,' she said.

In fact, the pain had deepened and spread up his arm. Funny, until that moment he had barely noticed it.

'You should start feeling a numbness creeping up your arm,' she added, matter-of-factly. He did and there was no reason to lie about it.

'That's the poison from the oleander. If we

173

could, we'd immobilize that arm. The last thing you need to do is exercise it.' She began to pump the bellows.

'Why? What'll happen?'

'I'll take care of the pumping. You start picking out notes. Hold the flashlight in between your teeth,' she added, 'so you use only your good hand on the keyboard.'

'What happens if I don't?'

'Don't worry, it won't kill you,' she laughed. 'Wait, I have a better idea.' Sabbie dug into their supplies, pulled out what she needed, then deftly secured the flashlight to his forehead with a circle of duct tape and did the same for herself. She returned to the bellows and pumped them in a slow rhythmic pulse. A soft grunt escaped with each push and pull against the bellows' powerful resistance. Gil turned back to the task at hand.

With middle C as a starting point, he hammered out the note sequence they'd seen in the tapestry. He waited, not knowing what would happen but hoping that somehow, something would. Nothing did.

Systematically, Gil moved up and down the keyboard using each new key as a starting point. At first, he paused at the end of each combination, waiting as if in front of a slot machine, hoping for some unidentified payoff. As the minutes passed, however, the starting points and sequences began to run together.

Sabbie caught each run-on sequence and cautioned him, repeatedly, to keep each combination distinct.

'The way you're playing, even if you hit the right starting note, we'll never know it. It's becoming

174

one big jumble of notes.'

Gil forced himself to stay focused. Time was slipping away. They had a little more than an hour left and, except for dimming flashlights and frazzled nerves, they had nothing to show for their effort. Though she denied it, Sabbie had become visibly exhausted. She could barely pump enough air into the organ to get it to play more than three or four notes in succession. He didn't have the heart to keep pushing her but his arm, no longer numb, was on fire.

Gil willed himself to concentrate. Twice more he lost track of his starting key in the sequence. Like a man lost in the desert, he seemed to be walking around in circles. Perhaps all of it was for nothing. He had been going on instinct; a hunch at best. He could have been completely off base.

Gil heard it first, a sort of crunching sound. Frantically, he tried to repeat the sequence of notes he had just played.

'Wait!' Sabbie called. 'Shhh.'

Gil ignored her. He needed to make sure he wouldn't lose the sequence.

'Stop!' she commanded in a hushed tone.

The crunching sound grew louder. It was accompanied by the rev of a motor as a car continued up the drive to the Monastery.

'Cut your light and don't move,' Sabbie whispered. She disappeared into the darkness, and he saw the door open, then quickly close.

Gil slid to the floor and sat, in the dark, motionless, his back against the bench. Outside a car door opened. With each approaching step, the steady crunch on the gravel grew louder. A rustle was followed by the sound of a low moan. Then silence.

He groped along the wall in the darkness and made his way to the side door at the Monastery entrance. Slowly and silently he inched it open. Sabbie's silhouette was clear against the pre-dawn sky. She crouched at the foot of the steps, a supine figure at her feet, the car door still opened. Gil slowly approached.

'Get me the duct tape in the basket,' she ordered. 'And the Swiss Army knife. And turn off his car lights, first!

'Now, before he wakes up. Hurry!' she barked again.

Gil hesitated. He wanted to know who was lying unconscious at their feet. He wanted to know what they were going to do with him. More than anything, however, he wanted to make sure that the man lying on the ground was bound good and tight before he regained consciousness. Gil returned quickly with the tape and knife.

'Now, give me something to stick in his mouth,' she ordered.

Gil considered his shoe, then his fist. Nothing seemed workable. He reached into his pocket and pulled out his wallet then, thinking better of it, clumsily stuffed it back.

'Never mind. Get the blanket,' she ordered.

Gil was back in a moment. 'Who the hell is he?'

'This isn't exactly the time for a discussion.' She cut a strip from the blanket, pushed it into the intruder's mouth and secured it with duct tape.

Sabbie slid her arms under the man's back and arms. 'Pick up his feet.'

Gil crossed his arms and shook his head. Hot pain from the oleander puncture shot up his arm.

176

He winced, then stood tall to communicate his steadfastness. 'I'm not going to be part of this.'

'You're already part of this. What do you call breaking and entering?'

'Yeah, well, it's not murder,' he said.

The moon moved from behind the clouds and brought an eerie light to the macabre scene.

'Don't be a baby. Does he look dead to you?' she asked, pointing to the wet spot that was spreading across the crotch of the prone man's pants.

A wave of nausea swept up Gil's throat. The helpless form lying at his feet was too terrible to comprehend, either as victim or predator. Even worse was Sabbie's apparent lack of concern.

She's had lots of practice. The nausea doubled.

'Who is he?' Gil demanded.

'Just the maintenance guy. He tidies up and gets things ready for the tours,' Sabbie explained. 'He wasn't supposed to show for another half hour.'

'You *knew* he was coming?' Gil asked incredulously.

'The tour guide talked about him when we were all out in the garden. He's her brother-in-law.'

'Terrific.'

Sabbie spoke quickly and with a tone one might use when describing why dinner would be ten minutes late. 'The way I see it, between the guy at the hardware store who was curious about our purchases, your diabetic drama during the tour, and, now, him,' she nodded at the unmoving figure at her feet, 'the police ought to have no trouble figuring out who's responsible for the break-in. The blanket will be pretty easy to trace and our fingerprints are all over the duct tape.'

177

'So wipe it off!' Gil said.

'The sticky side, too?' Sabbie asked. 'We have a little more than an hour. Do you want to continue talking or do you want to find the scroll?' She turned and headed back to the Chapel.

Gil caught up to her in three strides. 'What are we going to do with him? With the car?'

'I wanted to make him more comfortable by putting him in the backseat, but you didn't want any part of it, so I guess now, he'll lay out there on the gravel "til they arrive for the first tour around noon. By then, we'll be long gone, with or without the scroll.'

'Noon? Won't somebody miss him before that?'

'No, he's a drinker,' Sabbie replied. In the semi-darkness of the courtyard, she changed flashlight batteries as deftly as if in full light.

'You know what the problem is?' she asked.

Damn straight.

'No, it's not me,' she said, as if reading his thoughts. 'It's you.'

'Me?' Gil said in disbelief.

'Yes. You said you work by the seat of your pants, that's what you do best, but you've just spent the last hour sitting at the organ, doing everything in the most methodical way you could. You've played it perfectly logical and safe. And all wrong.'

She was right. Once he had discovered Elias' message in the tapestry's clouds, Gil had used it in the same way that anyone else in the world would have. That wasn't Elias' way and it shouldn't have been his.

Gil knew exactly what had to be done. It was getting light and he wasn't sure they still had time.

178

'Here, take this dollar bill and read me the last part of the hidden message again,' Gil said. 'Start with the heavens beckoning part.'

'"then the heavens shall beckon and the sound of angels shall open the heart of the righteous one . . ."'

'Yes. Okay. We did that already, now the rest.' Gil insisted.

'". . . for they sing to him as in the words of those who have come before. May they live forever in . . ."'

'That's it!' Gil shouted. '"in the words of those who have come before."'

'Who came before?'

'The diary may be written in Latin but, if the scroll was created at the time of Jesus, it should be in ancient Hebrew!'

'Or Aramaic. Backwards . . .' Sabbie added softly.

'That's right. We've been playing the sequence in the wrong direction.'

Gil sat down at the bench and waited for Sabbie to take her position at the bellows.

'Pump!' he called.

His mind was clear and focused. He kept track of every combination and permutation of notes to be tried, then he repeated the sequences but now in reverse order—from right to left—as in Hebrew, the ancient tongue of those who had come before.

It didn't happen until the end of the sixth reverse note combination. The great creaking sound echoed in the silence; then changed to a deafening grinding sound that filled the Chapel. The whir of wheels, gears, and counterweights, silent for a millennium, groaned into motion.

The altar table shook and threatened to fall. The Bible slid to its edge, and the large cross at its center wobbled dangerously. Gil jumped from the organ bench and, by the light of the flashlight still taped to his head, caught the beautifully carved cross in one hand and the Bible in the other. The pain from his injured hand coursed up his arm to his shoulder. The table's altar cloths slipped to his feet, and he scooped them up with two fingers of his good hand just in time to step back from the sliding stone slab that was inching toward him.

Sabbie made her way to his side and focused her flashlight at his feet. A large dark rectangular hole appeared where only a moment ago there had been a stone slab. She bent down to get a better look. Her flashlight revealed the top of a stone staircase at the edge of the opening. They stood together and stared into the darkness beyond the circle of light. The moving slab halted abruptly.

Gil gently placed the Bible and cross back on the now-still table and ripped the flashlight from his forehead. With the light held carefully in his injured hand, Sabbie's hand in his other, Gil descended into the dark recess that had been waiting for nearly a thousand years.

THIRTY-FOUR

A few minutes later
The Chapel Altar

Gil led the way down into the underground chamber. The smell of mold was overpowering. The beam of his flashlight flickered and began to grow dim. The beam illuminated only a few feet ahead and proved almost useless. The base of the stairway remained in darkness.

At the eighth step, he hit bottom, straightened, and smashed his head against the ceiling. The force of the impact was immediate and unforgivable. Rough damp stone scraped the soft skin of his scalp, and the pain of the impact shot through his neck and shoulders. Instinctively Gil reached out and pulled Sabbie down before she could meet a similar fate. Then, as he remembered that she was a foot shorter, he let go of her hand and allowed himself the luxury of sinking in pain to the floor.

'Come on,' she said. 'We don't have any time to waste. Just keep crouching but make sure your head stays higher than your heart. It'll keep the swelling down.'

'Army training, right?' he snapped. His hand explored the growing egg that was rising at the top of his head and came back wet and sticky. The familiar smell of blood needed no further confirmation of the source.

No smart repartee was returned by Sabbie and, for once, no instructions. In the silence, Gil imagined that the grave-like room had swallowed her up.

We aren't wanted here. I can feel it. Like the guys who discovered King Tut's tomb, we're going to be knocked off one by one until . . .

'Don't start getting weird on me,' she said, as if reading his mind. 'Elias wants you here. All you're doing is following the breadcrumbs he left behind.'

A sudden, inexplicable calm washed over Gil. He was okay. More than okay. They weren't intruders, they were invited guests; compliments of a monk who had been waiting for them to finish the task he had begun.

Gil rose carefully to his feet and, as he swung his flashlight in wide circles, strained to see the room in its entirety. He sensed, rather than saw, that it was empty. His heart sank.

'I don't understand. If there's nothing here, why would Elias have dug this chamber?' Gil asked. Desperation rose in his voice.

'Don't be an idiot,' Sabbie answered. 'Elias wouldn't have built such a huge chamber for one little scroll. Even if he wanted to for some reason, he couldn't have dug it out without any of the other monks seeing him. No, chances are, this is one of dozens of chambers that were built long before Elias' time. These old monasteries endured countless attacks and lootings by French soldiers, Spanish sailors, even pirates. After each raid, those monks who had been spared, would typically rebuild the edifice, adding hidden passages where, in the event of another attack, they might hide any future artifacts they might acquire. The result was a long-forgotten rambling maze of underground tunnels that crisscrossed beneath a monastery

182

much like those of an ant colony. The monks often added crudely-dug chambers for refuge, placed at random, so that in the event their tunnels were discovered, they might still survive to begin the process all over again. Over the centuries, the chambers that were dug at random were often forgotten. My bet is that Elias discovered this one and had realized that by securing entrance to it with the musical passage, he had found the perfect hiding place for the scroll.'

'So, if the scroll were going to be found anywhere, it would be here?' Gil asked, hopefully.

'Yes,' Sabbie replied, 'unless someone else has beaten us to it.' Sabbie had moved forward. She followed the now flickering beam of her flashlight and systematically examined the walls, covered with beads of moisture and dark patches of unidentifiable growth.

'Smells like death,' she said simply.

Death of a dream. Sorry, Elias. Looks like somebody got to it before us.

Gil continued to swing his flashlight in an arc to get as much coverage as possible and half-heartedly made his way along the wall to a spot opposite from where Sabbie stood. It was a useless endeavor, but she would insist on a thorough once-over. They might still discover some clue as to who had discovered the scroll before them.

His right foot hit it first. In a corner, on the floor. It was angled in so deeply that he might have missed it if he had depended on the dim beam of his flashlight. Gil straightened in surprise and again smacked his head on the ceiling. He couldn't have cared less.

Sabbie said something. It didn't matter. He

183

knelt on the cold hard dirt for a better look and saw a small heap of dark cloth covered with the same moldy substance that clung to the walls. The beam of his flashlight brightened, then faded to darkness. He shook it vigorously and made it come to life one last time, then the light was gone.

'Come here!' Gil called.

Sabbie was already at his side.

'Down here, at my feet.'

The tar-covered wooden chest sat on a flat-topped stone no larger than a serving platter. The patches of dark fabric that clung to the box gave it an appearance more like that of a huge moldy loaf of bread than a potentially priceless discovery. The wood had rotted away at the corners of the box, leaving small openings through which a dull green reflected back in the beam of Sabbie's flashlight. Tar still sealed the box and made it impossible to open without damaging it.

They squatted, almost butting heads, squinting to make out the detail in the fading light. Sabbie's light flickered and died.

'Son of a bitch,' Sabbie exclaimed. 'They probably pawn the old batteries off on tourists,' she muttered, half to herself.

They stood together in the darkness, the promise of treasure at their feet. Gil's mind raced to come up with a logical course of action.

Sabbie hit it first. 'The camera,' she cried.

'Great! The flash will give us enough light to get it packed up.'

'No,' Sabbie explained. 'I meant that we need to take some pictures. We're certain to be challenged as to its authenticity. Besides . . .'

'Pictures can be doctored,' Gil retorted without

184

thinking, then dropped the subject. If she wanted pictures, pictures she'd have. And he'd get the light he needed anyway.

Sabbie inched her way toward the steps. In a moment, she called from the top of the stairs.

'Ready? I'm going to shoot from up here.'

'Yeah.'

The first flash was blinding. Gil closed his eyes too late and, as he waited for the red ball to dissipate and for her to get all the photos she needed, he considered how to best protect their find. By feel, he wrapped the box in the blanket, and hoisted the package under his arm.

A surprising warmth radiated from the spot where the bundle rested against his side, and the pleasant heat spread to his back. Sabbie continued to snap pictures to give him light.

'Don't just stand there. Start making your way to the stairs,' she called.

But he couldn't move and he couldn't tell her why. He was weak with joy and filled with power at the same time. The hand that had been throbbing from Sabbie's less-than-delicate removal of the oleander stick tingled with lightly pricking pins and needles. Instinctively, Gil put the wound to his mouth. The warmth spread from his hand to his lips, flushed down his throat, around to the back of his neck, over the crown of his head, and across his chest. His heart leapt, pounded hard for a moment, then fell into a slow powerful rhythm. Never had he felt such a sense of well-being.

With the bundle tucked beneath his arm, Gil made his way toward the pre-dawn illumination that beckoned from the Chapel above. As he emerged from the darkness, he took what seemed like his first breath. It was sweet and cool, and it filled him with a sense of joy he never imagined possible.

Oblivious to any change in Gil, Sabbie rambled on about ways in which they might return the slab to its original position, how many photos they still had left, and what remained to be documented.

The Chapel looked as if it were lit from within. Filled with an overwhelming tenderness, he waited patiently for her to finish her litany of 'must do's.

She's scared. The plans make her feel more secure.

'The slab will close and the underground chamber will return to oblivion once more,' he said softly. 'Don't worry.'

'How can you be so sure?'

He didn't respond.

At his direction, Sabbie took up her former position at the bellows, and Gil played the keyboard sequence as if he had practiced it for years. It was the same phrase of notes that had caused the slab to move and had opened the entrance to the chamber.

With one hand securing the box next to him on the organ bench, Gil played the musical passage that had opened the chamber. This time he played it in reverse. The gears and pulleys set the stone slab into motion and removed all evidence of the chamber below save for some fresh scratch marks on the stone floor beside the platform.

Sabbie murmured her relief. Gil had no such reaction. He knew it would work as well as if Elias had whispered the directions in his ear.

'I'll be right back,' Sabbie said. She disappeared out the door. She returned moments later and informed him that the maintenance man was still out cold.

'Are you sure he's okay?' Gil asked.

Sabbie ignored his question and picked up the backpack. 'Are you ready?' she asked. 'Bring it over there. There's more light.'

Gil joined her at the window.

Carefully, they cut through the tar and gently pried open the ancient box. There, before them, lay the treasure that Elias and his brother had given their lives for. Within its words, a message, two thousand years in the waiting, that would soon be revealed.

Though Gil cradled the open box in his arm, he did not touch the scroll. Sabbie hesitated as well. To touch it would seem a desecration. A single shaft of light lit the spot where they stood. Now, in the new morning, the scroll that had not seen the light of day for a millennium, reflected back the sun's welcome radiance and seemed to beckon them.

Gil took Sabbie's hand, gently placed it on the scroll, and let the voice of antiquity enter her and speak for itself.

THIRTY-FIVE

Day Ten, dawn
Monastery Road, Weymouth

Sabbie spotted them at a distance.

Moments before, the hotel entrance had looked inviting, a sanctuary that welcomed them home from their long night at the Monastery and offered them the chance to explore their incredible discovery. Now, according to Sabbie, the same facade concealed their would-be assassins.

She squatted behind a pile of bagged garbage and pulled Gil down beside her. The stench of the rotting refuse was overpowering.

'Don't make a sound,' Sabbie whispered. 'Breathe through your mouth and the smell won't get you.

'There are two of them,' she continued. 'They're right there in that little space where the tall hedge stops and the trees begin.' She pointed to the far right of the hotel's entrance. 'One is small. The other's large and heavy. The big one doesn't look like he can move quickly, but the small one can and that's all that counts.'

Gil squinted into the early morning sun and tried to discern their alleged pursuers.

Two men in front of a hotel entrance. That's all they were. They could have been waiting for anyone. Gil tried to talk reason with her. She was adamant. They couldn't go back to the hotel.

'I'm not staying here in the garbage just because you're getting paranoid.'

'Shhh,' she cautioned. 'Look, you're the one who keeps saying I should trust my instincts. And I'm telling you something isn't right here.'

He had to admit her logic, as well, wasn't half bad. No car, no bus, no taxi could pull up within fifty feet of where the men were standing. If they were waiting for a hotel guest, there were a dozen more comfortable spots to choose. They were barely talking, but they continued to face each other and look over each other's shoulders. There

188

could be no other logical reason for such odd behavior. Most of all, she added, she just knew it.

'They're here for us . . . and this.' She put her hand on the backpack as if to protect their precious cargo. Her heart pounded in the hollow of her neck. 'God, I can't believe they found us so fast. I thought we'd have at least until this afternoon.'

'At least until this afternoon for what?' he whispered back.

Sabbie ignored his question. 'Stay low and follow me.'

He started to protest.

'I'm betting they won't be able to tell it's us at this distance. Be quiet and do what I say,' she ordered. 'Walk slowly but don't make it obvious. Look nonchalant. Keep your eyes on me but don't act like we're together. If I stop, you stop. Stay about thirty feet behind. If anything happens, grab the backpack and run like hell. Whatever you do, don't run in the same direction as me . . . if I'm able to run.'

'What?'

'On the count of three. One . . .' Sabbie was up, moving fluidly along the building. She headed away from the hotel, back in the direction from which they'd come. As instructed, Gil followed. He turned his head to get a fix on both men but the space where they were standing was now vacant.

Gil looked back to tell her the good news but she was gone. In that moment, she had disappeared, probably into one of the buildings. He shook off a wave of panic. Maybe he should go back and try to find where she had turned off. No, better go ahead and find a break in the buildings

189

to the next street. Maybe shed was waiting there for him.

A strong hand grabbed him by the shoulder of his sweatshirt, another covered his mouth. He was dragged backward into a small alley. Gil struggled to stay upright, regained his balance, and kicked the feet out from under his assailant.

'Great work, Sherlock,' Sabbie whispered. She got to her feet. 'Follow me, this alley goes straight through to the next street.'

Luck was with them. The alley continued for three blocks. They emerged at a more-than-comfortable distance from the hotel and the shadowy figures.

Sabbie steered Gil toward a passing cab that she had signaled.

'Where can we get a good breakfast?' she asked the driver.

La Maison was five minutes away. It catered to the business elite who minimized the sting of early morning meetings by sweetening up their clients with caramelized French toast smothered in Devonshire clotted cream.

By the time the driver finished praising the restaurant's cuisine and denouncing their prices, they had arrived.

'We need someplace public but quiet,' she told Gil. 'This will do.'

Public or not, he appreciated her choice of refuge. He hadn't eaten dinner the day before, and he was starving. Inviting odors filled the entryway, and his stomach grumbled in anticipation. Sabbie's imaginary foes were gone for the moment and he'd be eating soon. If, before he was finished eating, he found himself involved in a shoot-out scene straight out of *The Godfather*, at least he'd die a happy man.

The maitre d' allowed a slow downward gaze to communicate the inappropriateness of their jeans and sweatshirts. A quick glance at his reservations' list indicated the inappropriateness of the unanticipated arrival. A silent frown suggested that both transgressions could be overlooked for the right compensation.

Sabbie discreetly placed a bill in the hand of the maitre d' and, in a warm voice that Gil had never heard before, asked for help. She explained that their unanticipated arrival and overly informal attire was due to the airlines loss of their baggage, and added that she was hypoglycemic and felt a bit faint for lack of food.

They were seated immediately and reassured that the serving staff would be informed of her medical condition. The few occupied tables were well out of earshot, most likely to accommodate the most private of business discussions.

A pimply-faced youth brought them steaming coffee and inquired if they preferred tea. He was replaced by a gruff, ill-tempered waiter.

Gil ordered quickly, not caring what he selected as long as it was hot and there was a lot of it. With his meal on its way, he formulated the best way to approach a discussion of Sabbie's latest bout of paranoia.

Suddenly, her body stiffened, and she stared oddly over Gil's left shoulder. 'Don't look now,' she said. 'I mean *really* don't look now. Just keep smiling and chatting.'

'Okay,' Gil said through a wide, fake grin, barely moving his lips. 'What am I not looking at?'

'That man who just walked past us. He came in after we did and he's being seated already. Something's wrong.'

'Yeah? Well, he just took a seat two tables behind you,' Gil said. 'Maybe he topped your hypoglycemia story or offered the maitre d' more money. Or, now here's one, maybe he had a reservation!' he added sarcastically.

Sabbie ignored his tone. 'I don't think so. I saw their reservations list. Their next seating isn't for an hour. Besides, I'm almost sure I saw him on the train and then again at the hotel yesterday afternoon.'

'What's strange about that? He's probably here for a business meeting like the rest of them.' Gil motioned to the clusters of involved discussions around the dining room.

'He's following us,' Sabbie concluded. 'He's not one of the two from outside the hotel. That's not good.'

'Correct me if I'm wrong, but when somebody's tailing somebody, aren't they supposed to stay hidden, you know, out of view?' Gil laughed.

'Not if they're smart or if they want to be seen. Besides,' she added with a shrug that seemed to conclude the matter for the moment, 'they have to eat, too.'

At Gil's request, the eggs and sausages arrived first. Twice, although they were not yet finished, the waiter attempted to remove their plates to indicate that they had lingered too long. Their French toast, plunked down in front of them, clattered as he impatiently removed the protective china covers. Gil declined the waiter's overly polite offer to refresh his coffee, fearful he might be inviting third-degree burns. Sabbie remained silent and watchful.

'Tell me what he's doing now,' she said.

Gil peered over Sabbie's shoulder and reported with sarcastic exaggeration. 'Well . . . now here's something suspicious . . . he's . . . yes, he is, he's eating breakfast. Very odd if you ask me. I mean, look at this, we order eggs and sausages. Bingo, so does he and . . .'

'I'm going to the Ladies' Room,' she said, rising. 'Just watch and see if he follows me.'

'You said not to look,' Gil retorted.

'Stay here,' she said, steadily looking into his eyes. 'Please.'

She rose, made some comments about their upcoming imaginary anniversary, kissed him lightly on the top of the head to project the image of a loving couple, then headed to the rear of the restaurant.

Gil gazed at the man two tables away. Middle-aged, nondescript, and looking decidedly British, the poor fellow sat alone as he read a newspaper and continued his meal. Gil closed his eyes and surrendered to his tiredness. It had been a long, incredible night. His body ached for sleep.

Gil closed his eyes for what seemed like just a moment then woke with a start. The man, only halfway through his meal, had vacated his seat and was headed in the same direction Sabbie had gone.

Gil could think of endless explanations for the man's hasty exit, starting with pure coincidence and ending with the guy having irritable bowel syndrome. Still, the scene was far too reminiscent of his first restaurant encounter with Sabbie and Ludlow.

Gil watched the man walk toward the restrooms. Perhaps Sabbie would emerge before the man disappeared from view and she'd see how foolish she had been.

The telltale bulge beneath the man's left arm sent Gil's heart racing. He had noticed the same curve to the jackets of each of the guards at the Museum security gates.

He's got a gun under that arm.

No more pretense, no more jokes. Gil knew the truth. While he had been busy trying to dismiss everything Sabbie had been saying, she had been busy trying to keep them alive and to save the scroll—though he wasn't sure in which order. He had made fun of her because it was a hell of a lot easier than admitting the truth; the importance of the scroll might well have rendered their lives insignificant.

He was scared, not just for himself. Whoever was following them was far more interested in her than in him. Here he sat, the scroll in his backpack, while the guy went after her.

Went after her!

He had to do something. He could call the maitre d' and say . . . what? That a man with a gun went to the restroom? He could race to the back and try to warn her—or help her, if she needed it. And what would he do with the scroll?

The hell with the scroll. I can't just sit here.

In the end that's exactly what he did. He waited, silent and miserable, simply because that's exactly what Sabbie asked him to do. Before she had left the table, she had planted a lover's kiss on his head and had asked him to please stay where he was. No matter what. So, this time, for once in his life, he

194

did.

Several minutes passed. Sabbie appeared, her face pale, her manner calm.

'You okay?' Gil asked with relief. 'You know I have this tendency to lose people who go to restaurant bathrooms.' His voice trailed off, remembering the last time he had seen Ludlow and Sabbie together and the fate the Professor had met less than twenty-four hours later.

More soberly, Gil tried again. 'So, was he following you?'

'Not a problem.'

'Not a problem as in, he wasn't following you or not a problem as in . . .'

The waiter appeared and handed them the check to indicate he had no intention of bringing them anything else, then disappeared.

She explained that they still had an hour to kill until the car rental agency opened. The word 'kill' echoed like never before. 'What about taking a train back?' Gil asked hopefully.

'No trains for hours—engineering works. We'll drive.'

The waiter reappeared. Sabbie produced another traveler's check and passed it to Gil to sign. He hesitated, shrugged, then signed Ludlow's name without argument. What was one more felony added to the list?

The waiter nearly pushed them out the door and slammed it closed behind them, happy to rid his restaurant of their unsightly presence. They waited on the busy street, hoping to hail a passing cab. Sabbie's gun was secreted somewhere on her person, of that he was certain. But gun or no gun, with the backpack slung on his shoulder, Gil had never felt more exposed and vulnerable.

The next seating of breakfast customers had begun to arrive and, with them, several taxis. Grateful for the security of the cab, they slid into the back seat. Only then did Gil realize that Sabbie had never given him a straight answer about the man who had followed her to the restroom. Nor, now that he thought of it, had Gil ever seen the man return to his table.

THIRTY-SIX

A few hours later
Weymouth Car Rental Agency

They needed a luxury sedan, Sabbie told Gil. A car big enough for her to spread out the scroll. 'You can't unroll a piece of history in the backseat of a subcompact,' she added.

To pay for the rental of the car, Sabbie had produced a credit card with yet another name, Sarkami. The name rang a bell. As far as Gil could remember, Sarkami was the metalsmith guy she had talked about. The Great Artificer or something like that. The one who introduced her to Ludlow. Whatever.

Gil knew better than to ask her how she came by Sarkami's credit card. She wouldn't have told him the truth anyway. If she did, he probably wouldn't have believed her, so what was the use? Besides, if Sarkami's credit card would get them the car they needed to leave Weymouth, who cared?

'I'll get in the backseat with the scroll and take a stab at the translation,' she said. 'You drive. Remember to rest your hand,' she said gently. 'Also, keep it as high as you can.'

Gil looked at her in surprise then down at his injury. Somewhere along the way he must have removed her makeshift dressing without thinking. He extended his hand for her to see and as a way of making a statement he could not explain.

The puncture wound that had been red and swollen from the piercing oleander stick was barely visible. The red trail of poison up his arm had disappeared and with it the pain and numbness that gave testimony to the spread of the plant's toxin.

Sabbie had never seen so fast a recovery, she said. 'You must have one hell of an immune system.'

'Immunity doesn't work on toxins unless you've built up a resistance, which I haven't,' Gil said. When they were in the Monastery, the ache and numbness had steadily increased as the night progressed. At the altar, when he caught the cross that teetered off the wobbly table, the pain had been excruciating. But from the moment he had first held the scroll, all discomfort had disappeared.

Gil reached to touch the bump on his head, the reminder of his abrupt encounter with the chamber's stone ceiling. He knew what he'd find before his fingers made contact with the injury. No knot, no discomfort. Where there had been swelling and a throbbing ache, not even a twinge of pain remained.

Gil shook his head in wonder. She nodded hers

197

in confirmation. There was no need to put into words what they had just witnessed.

They had two hours of driving ahead of them, she said, three if they allowed time for cross-town London traffic. Once they got to the outskirts of the city, she'd direct him to a place that was safe. Until then, he'd have to drive and navigate on his own. She needed to focus on removing the scroll from the box with as little damage to either as possible.

'The box will be needed for authentication, if it ever comes to that,' she said. If the scroll turned out to be made of the same delicate copper sheets as The Cave 3 Scroll, unrolling and translating them while in a moving vehicle would prove as impossible as any undertaking she could imagine. But, she added, they had no choice.

There was another hitch that concerned Sabbie. Elias' diary bore testimony to a scroll that, during his time, was considered blasphemous. Apparently, it challenged the very foundations of Christianity. The problem was, there was no way of knowing whether this message would reveal anything new or exciting today.

'Interpretations of what others have purported to be Jesus' teachings and actions have changed over the centuries. What was considered sacrilege at one time, might now be considered the proper practice of faith,' Sabbie concluded.

Still, no matter whose view in today's world the scroll upheld, the immensity of the discovery of Jesus' teachings, teachings dictated in His own words and recorded by one who lived at His side, was simply too great to imagine.

Gil glanced back at her in the rear view mirror.

'This could challenge the whole enchilada,' he said.

'Which is more likely the case, *if* you put stock in what Elias' wrote in the diary,' she added.

Gil looked at her reflection in surprise.

'And *if* you believe what is inscribed in the scroll,' she said without expression.

'What reason would Elias or the author of the scroll have to lie?' Gil asked. 'What would either of them have to gain?'

'What reason do any of us have?' she countered.

Sabbie shrugged. Gil turned back to his driving, she to the scroll that she continued to gently unroll. Word by word, the message revealed itself to her. It filled her with joy, then sadness. Its story of betrayal echoed her own, its promise of renewal, a pledge of redemption. When she had unrolled the scroll as far as she dared without risking damage to it, she began to read it aloud, so that Gil, too, might share in the greatest story never told.

THIRTY-SEVEN

Thirty-three years before the Crucifixion
Southwest of Jerusalem, main route to Hebron
and Egypt

The cloths the young girl held in readiness for the newborn were finer than anything she had ever seen. It was rumored among the other domestics that the master of the house had been presented with these rich fabrics by a Roman general who was so high in rank that it was said he reported directly to Pontius Pilot himself.

The maidservant considered herself fortunate to be part of a household where the fame of the master was great and whose friendship was courted with the spoils of Roman campaigns. For a moment, she allowed herself the pleasure of caressing the edge of the exceptional material, imagining what it might be like to be mistress of this great home complete with all of the luxuries and pleasures that money could buy.

A sudden shriek from her mistress shook the young girl from her daydream. She turned in time to see the midwife pull the bloody infant into the world. 'That's the last battle he'll ever have to fight,' she heard the old cook remark to the wet nurse as they stood watching from the door. 'Little bastard will want for nothing.'

The young maidservant flushed at so bitter a comment and hoped her mistress had not overheard. She was summoned to help bathe and swaddle the child in his first silken wrappings, and all concern vanished.

Haggai ben Asher waited by the inner court fountain, alone by choice. The cry of his firstborn brought with it the relief Haggai sought. The child lived. Today was born a son to the house of Asher and his name would be Micah, may God be praised.

For more than a score of years his wife had diligently applied the plethora of tinctures and balms prescribed by the ministers of such therapies but there had been no pregnancies. Fully aware that it was forbidden for Jews to do so, he had begun to consider taking a second wife in order to ensure that his legacy would pass to future generations. But now, with God's blessing, all was right with the world.

He had worked hard and had succeeded in trading and securing great and varied consignments of fine metals. Yet, until now, he had been unable to claim what the most ignorant peasant was granted without thought or concern— a son—a fine and beautiful son.

When out, among his friends, Haggai blamed his wife for their lack of offspring. Alone in his private quarters, however, he had sometimes wondered if in a way unknown to him, he had offended the Lord. Perhaps his pursuit and accumulation of riches had been so great as to win him disfavor. Yet, like his father and grandfather before him, he sought the security that wealth could buy, gold and lands that could be traded for freedom in times of unrest in Jerusalem, or, if need be, purchase a Jew's very life. Now the high-pitched wail of the infant filled his heart with joy, and he knew that God had, indeed, smiled upon him.

Some people thought him a traitor, an appeaser of the enemy, a Roman-lover. Some assumed that he favored only those of similar aristocratic birthright. Others claimed that because he traded with the lower and middle-class Pharisees, he had turned his back on his Sadducee heritage. In truth, he cared not a whit for either sect's endless pontifical discussions over the rightness of oral versus written Jewish law. And, if it should ever come to pass, as it had during previous centuries, before the Roman occupation, when no fewer than eight different world powers had dominated the

Jews, those same critics would be the first to beg for his help, for the money he had worked so hard to accumulate, pleading that his hard-earned fortunes might well be used to save their unworthy lives.

No, he neither had time for their religious debates nor defense against their criticisms. He was a practical man, a family man now, and he knew too well how far their philosophic discussions would get them when they stood at the end of a Roman sword. Still, the wagging of too many jealous tongues was making life in Jerusalem unpleasant. His wife complained of a change in the servants' attitudes and, though he had not confirmed her suspicions, he knew their gossiping had gotten out of hand.

Now all of that would change. He would move his newborn son and his wife into the great house being erected on the edge of the sea, near Qumran. Building so great a home a fair distance from Jerusalem was an unusual move. Friends and family warned that his choice of location would mean hardship for his wife and son but Haggai was certain that his wealth would bring all that they needed to their door. Above all else, he prided himself on his independence and the cherished thought of removing his family from the judgmental eyes of others made his choice a most logical one.

The huge estate that awaited him, his wife, and his baby son, Micah, however, remained empty for the moment, watched over only by a single houseman until the day that Caesar Augustus' new census and taxation determination would be completed. Perhaps if King Herod had not been granted a one-year postponement of the census, this birth might have taken place in their new home. Oh, what a blessing that would have been! Still, Haggai had to admit to himself, the delay in moving had meant another year before he would have to pay the higher taxes that came with the great house and that was a blessing in itself. Yes, all was good. Just as it should be. After all, he had worked hard for this good life. It was only right that he should enjoy it.

*   *   *

Six miles away in a manger, the high-pitched wail of another newborn son was heard. There was no maidservant in attendance, no fine swaddling clothing in which to wrap the child, and no promise of a great estate in the country where a child might be protected and pampered. There was at this birth, however, as there was in the house of Haggai ben Asher, great joy at the arrival of a firstborn son, healthy and strong, with his whole life yet before him.

THIRTY-EIGHT

Day Ten, mid-morning
North Circular to London

'Why did you stop reading?' Gil asked.
    'Because that's where Micah stopped, when the second baby was born. Besides, I need a bathroom break. Stop at the next petrol station.'

Gil nodded his agreement. They needed gas anyway, and something else was bothering him. A pit-stop would give him a chance to test out his suspicion. No need to alarm her unless he was sure. Until then, he'd keep it light.

'So, what do you think so far?' he asked.

'I'm not sure,' she answered. 'My Aramaic is rusty, and this PDA translation program is practically useless. Still, if the second baby turns out to be who I think it is . . . Why, what are you thinking?'

Gil straightened out the rearview mirror and, for the tenth time in as many minutes, checked out the road behind them. 'I thought the scroll was autobiographical. At least, that's what Elias said in the diary, isn't it? So far it reads like the story of someone else's life. The author of the scroll doesn't mention a word about himself.'

'And he's not about to,' she said.

In a voice too filled with amusement for Gil's liking, Sabbie explained the reason for the third-person view of the births. In all likelihood, she said, the story that was being told in the scroll *was* autobiographical. Two thousand years ago, however, no one would have thought to describe his own life in 'I' terms. Everything was written as if it were a story about someone else. First-person wasn't even a known concept.

'Think about the Gospels from the New Testament. Imagine how odd it would sound if Luke said, "So, on this day, me and Jesus were discussing such-and-such, and this woman came up to us . . ."

'Back then, everything was described as if it were being witnessed by another, although the

204

author, himself, may have been involved. Even a thousand years later, when Elias described his brother being burned at the stake, he wrote it in the storytelling method of the day. The last part of Elias' description of the burning, in which he talked about his own feelings, was not only unusual, it was unheard of.

'And probably constituted heresy,' she added.

'So the author of the scroll would have naturally told the story of his own life as if he were describing the life of another,' Gil said.

'Yes, but no one would have ever considered just telling the story of his life two thousand years ago. The whole idea that we're important enough to have a story to leave behind is a modern concept. If you consider how little the individual mattered two thousand years ago, if you think about the fact that the "I" in storytelling didn't even exist, then to record the history of your own life, and to engrave it into a copper scroll, would never occur to anyone unless . . .'

'. . . unless the story was so important . . .' Gil continued.

'. . . or someone else in the story was so important . . .' Sabbie added.

'. . . that the story had to be told,' he concluded.

'Exactly.'

There was nothing more to say. They'd have to wait for the scroll to tell them the rest.

They were fast approaching a gas station. Gil kept his foot on the gas until they were almost past the turnoff. Then, without signaling, he swerved onto the off ramp.

'Hey,' she called. 'I'd like to keep this in one piece for the moment.'

'You or the scroll?' Gil asked teasingly, then added, more seriously, 'That's exactly my intention.'

His eyes remained fixed on the rearview mirror, in search of the black town car that had been following them for the past twenty minutes. No car followed them into the gas station. Gil looked back to the highway in time to see the black town car pass on its way to London, apparently a threat only in the drama of Gil's making.

He filled the tank while she hit the ladies' room and, as she headed back to the car, signaled that he was on his way for a similar break.

The green sedan wouldn't have caught his attention except for the odd coincidence of the license plate. It was red, like the plate on their car, and like the plate on the black town car that he had been concerned about. His bladder could wait. He wasn't leaving her alone.

'I thought you had to go to the bathroom,' she said, surprised at his quick return.

'Tell me one thing,' he asked as he stepped on the gas. 'Do all rental cars in England have red license plates?'

'Never used to,' she answered. 'Why?'

No need to alarm her over nothing. 'Just curious,' he said. 'I used to play license plate games when I was a kid and I was just wondering. It's not important.'

Sabbie shrugged and returned to her translating.

He drove with his eyes fixed more on the rearview than the front. Although no car, in particular, remained behind them, Gil knew that they were, indeed, being followed. The answer to

206

the question of who was following them and in which car was one he couldn't answer. Not yet.

Thirty minutes had passed before Gil realized he had not paid for the gas that now propelled them to London. He smiled and shrugged.

Just add it to my rap sheet.

THIRTY-NINE

Seventeen years before the Crucifixion
Midway between Medeba and Bethlehem

Micah held back the tears until he reached the cave. Safe inside, in a place that no other knew existed, he could allow himself the luxury of his true feelings. Tears cut rivulets down his dust-layered cheeks. At least he had not given them the satisfaction of knowing they had made him cry. After all, it had been three years since his Bar Mitzvah and, even if his father's business associates still treated him as a child, it was considered that he had come of age among his fellow Jews. After all, four of the apprentices in his father's workshops were married by the time they were his age and one had already fathered a boy of his own. Yet each acted more like a child than the younger boys who followed after them and begged for their attention.

This morning, in a great show of their prowess, the three eldest sons of his father's oldest business associate had forced Micah to flee. Each had chosen a pilum from the best of the newly forged swords and together they formed a circle around a young goat. Each took turns throwing the spears at the terrified kid. In the end, it crawled to its mother's side, bleeding and bleating, and died—the boys' weapons still dangling from its flesh.

When Micah had cried out in protest and threatened them should they continue their cruel mischief, they had ripped their weapons from the dead goat and set out after him. At any other time, they might have been concerned about the consequences of laying a hand on the son of Haggai, but on this day they were so taken with their power that they cared not for the consequences.

Jonah, his father's chief metalsmith, had misdirected them so that Micah had enough time to get away. Micah's father would have been livid had he but known of Jonah's actions. Haggai put great stock in a man's ability to counter violence with violence. Even greater would have been his anger had Haggai known of Jonah's ongoing instruction to his son. Micah was, after all, the eldest son in the wealthiest house in the district and destined for greater things than could be imparted by a mere metalsmith.

To Micah, however, the hours spent under the metalsmith's tutelage had been the best in his life. At Jonah's side, he had learned to see the world in a scrap of metal and in the skill and touch he brought to the moment.

'No, no,' Jonah would exclaim. 'Don't gouge the silver. The metal is like a woman. It should be warmed gently, only when it is soft and flowing, will it move as you wish. Remember, with metal, as with women, or as with life, you must wait for just the right moment. That is a most important and most difficult skill.

'Patience, always patience,' Jonah added. He ruffled Micah's hair. 'It is the difference between a good metalsmith and a master craftsman. And true as well if you wish to be a good husband.'

At the time, Jonah's wisdom was lost on Micah. Meaningless, also, were the older craftsman's caustic criticisms of the barbaric treatment of the poor and the enslaved. In the years to come, however, Jonah's wisdom would reach out like a lifeline, guiding Micah when no other was there for comfort or advice.

Had Micah's father ever learned of Jonah's instructions, craft wise or worldly, it might have meant Jonah's life. The old craftsman's radical ideas, including equal treatment for all men, were nothing less than heresy.

Micah sensed that his mother knew of the hours he spent with Jonah but that she chose to ignore it. Micah never broached the subject with her or any other living soul. Not even when he was told that Jonah had died, not even when no cause of death was given and no body was ever seen for ritual burial. Not even then. Micah kept their secret, grieved in silence, and tried desperately to remember the wise and loving counsel he had taken for granted for so many years. In so many ways, Jonah had been more of a father to Micah than Haggai would ever be.

The voices of Micah's tormentors could not be heard deep in the cave where he sat among his collection of tools and scraps of precious metals. He breathed deeply. They would never find him here.

Micah pulled a lumpy piece of copper sheeting

209

toward him. He reached for the wooden mallet and felt cloth that were as familiar to him as his own two hands. Gently, he pounded the metal on the flat rock that served as his workbench and gave himself willingly to the hypnotic rhythm. As the copper sheet thinned and smoothed to a fine luster, the pain that lingered from the cruelty of his persecutors slipped away.

It seemed as if it had always been thus. Though he longed for acceptance and camaraderie with all his heart, both were as elusive as the stars—easily seen but beyond his grasp. He was too much of this or not enough of that. In spite of all the time he spent at the Essene settlement nearby, the keepers of the faith still considered him an outsider. Jonah said they didn't trust Micah because of his father's wealth, but he knew it was more than that.

Though he was drawn to them because of his respect for their compassion and ideals and, perhaps, because Jonah so admired them, Micah could not bring himself to commit to their ascetic ways. Their lives, devoid of worldly possessions and personal relationships had, at first, offered an attractive alternative to his father's world of riches and power. After a while, Micah had come to realize that among the most religious, man's avarice did not disappear, it simply changed form, replacing a hunger for wealth with that of a spiritual materialism.

Even among the youngsters, orphans and outcasts that the Essenes adopted and who lived in far less comfortable circumstances than his father's poorest servant, a young man's worth was measured by his devout service to God. No matter if he were cruel to the man who had taken him in when none other would spare him food or shelter; no matter if he did nothing for the other children or for the community of fellow devotees who accepted him as one of their own. So long as he appeared most pious and, in word and action deferred to God's will, among the Essenes he would be afforded the greatest of respect. Micah thought it wrong to place so great a value on one's devotion to God and so little on his action to his fellow man. He could never be an Essene.

At the same time, Micah could not imagine himself a Sadducee, conspiring for power, always in the name of the Almighty; nor a Pharisee, caught up in endless debates over the minutiae that supposedly proved one's devotion to God, a God who, to Micah, had seemed to distance Himself from the needs and struggles of the very men who worshipped Him.

Micah's chest filled with an indescribable longing. He yearned for a friend, a confidant, either man or deity—it didn't matter which—someone that might understand, love, and care for the young man who struggled from the depths of his soul to find meaning and goodness in life; a caring soul who dreamed of equality for all men and dared to see the justice in equality for women, servants, and even slaves.

His dreams were as great a burden as was his father's wealth, for the first beckoned him to explore the world while the second prevented him from doing so. In reality, he was not free and, he feared, would never be so. He owed too much to a father who had showered him with such luxury that even the son of a Roman Centurion might envy. Too, there was an obligation by birthright to his mother, young sisters, and the family servants, all of whom counted on him to carry on the family's financial legacy, and to support them in their later years.

His life of adventure and discovery had been traded on the auction block for a life of obligation long before he knew what such words might mean. There was no way out. His lot was little different from that of the poorest of Jews the Romans used as slaves. They were both held captive by another. The only distinction was simply that of how well appointed was one's prison. Upon sharing this insight with Jonah, the elder craftsman had grown pale with fear.

'Never speak of such things to your father,' Jonah had cautioned sternly. 'It will be the end of all. Never even think of it again.'

Jonah was right. To speak of such matters would be to cross the unspoken line that each person knows exists within another; to confront that which is so unthinkable as to make further relations impossible. If he had tried to express his yearnings to his father, if he had even hinted that he was less than content with the life Haggai had crafted so carefully for him, he would have denigrated all that his father held meaningful. And it would have profited him nothing.

When the responsibilities of a life so completely preordained seemed too overwhelming, Micah sought the solitude of his cave and his metalwork. While his father's men crafted swords for the taking of lives, Micah crafted only things of beauty, that which would harm no other in its transmutation.

In the half-light of the cave, Micah continued to

pound the copper sheeting. The rhythm lulled him, and he imagined himself walking freely into the sunlight, tall and unafraid, bringing truth and peace to his fellow man, then ascending to the heavens where a benevolent God awaited him.

The thought of a heavenly father was suddenly replaced by an earthly one, probably filled with fury by now, as he awaited a son who had forgotten the birthday celebration so carefully planned on his behalf. Micah's mother, Ruth, would be worried, begging his father to be patient, calming his sisters, and praying that no ill had befallen her firstborn.

With this birthday, his father had promised to fulfill Micah's wish to accompany him on his upcoming expedition along the great Silk Trade Route. He knew that Haggai regretted the promise, and Micah's lateness would now provide his father with a perfect excuse to put him off for yet another year. Quickly setting aside his metalwork, Micah ran from the cave, barely observing his usual precautions to emerge unnoticed.

FORTY

Day Ten, noon
North Circular Road to London

Sabbie looked up from the scroll and caught Gil's eye in the rearview mirror. 'We've got a problem,' she said.

How the hell did she know?

213

Gil had been watching the green sedan follow them for over a half hour. Since they left the gas station, it had remained exactly one car length behind them. Although the road changed direction and the sun was no longer reflected off the windshield of the sedan, Gil could not get a good view of the driver.

In an attempt to force the car out of its position, Gil switched on his flashing hazard lights and slowed to a crawl. The sedan slowed to a matched speed. There was no doubt about it. They were being followed, and the driver had no intention of hiding the fact from them.

'Any suggestions?' Gil asked.

'Yes, I think we're going to have to cut it into strips,' she said without looking up from the scroll.

'What?'

Sabbie repeated her recommendation. 'I hate to do it but there's really no other way,' she added.

'How do we do that in a moving car?'

'Oh, not me. That's not my expertise. But, remember I told you about the man that makes the faux facsimiles for the Museum? He ought to be able to handle it.'

'What? Cut up the scroll?' Gil asked incredulously.

'Of course, the scroll. What did you think I was talking about? I can translate a bit more of it, actually quite a bit, but I can tell by the tightness of the roll that there will come a point where we'll risk damaging it if we try to go too much further. It's going to have to be cut in strips like The Cave 3 Scroll.'

'I thought you were talking about the car that was following us,' Gil said. While he had been trying to shield her from concern about their safety, she had been free to debate the pros and cons of how best to expose the final section of the scroll. It was time for her to come down to the level of reality he'd been dealing with for the last half hour.

'What? You mean the green sedan?' she asked without looking around.

Gil nodded.

'No worries. He wouldn't think of approaching us on the highway.'

'You know who it is?' Gil asked hopefully.

'No,' Sabbie answered, and returned to her translating.

'Then how can you be sure?' Gil asked. He looked for her answer in the rearview mirror.

'Army training,' she mouthed, and went back to her reading.

'Look, I'm really sorry to interrupt you,' Gil protested sarcastically, 'but I have this fondness of knowing who might be after me with intention of doing me bodily harm. So, what's going to happen when we get off the highway?'

Sabbie sighed, annoyed at being interrupted once again. 'Number one, he's not after you. He couldn't give a shit whether you live or die.'

'Well, that's comforting.'

'Actually, it should be,' she replied.

'So, he's only after the scroll,' Gil said.

'And me,' she added.

'Why you?'

'Because I'm one of the world's best translators, if you put any stock in what DeVris says, though you wouldn't know it from my paycheck. Now, if I can get back to what I do best . . .'

215

'What happens when we get off the highway?' Gil insisted.

'You turn right.'

'Don't be an ass. What happens to the scroll and what happens to you?'

'It's all taken care of,' Sabbie answered.

'Oh, just like that?'

'Just like that.'

FORTY-ONE

Seventeen years before the Crucifixion
Medeba, East of the Sea of Salt

Micah's birthday outing was indistinguishable from any of his father's usual business trips.

'First, I need to stop at the shops of two clients. Then, if we have time, we'll take some refreshment at Saul ben Simon's house. There is much business I must discuss with him, so I want you to make yourself busy when we get there. You can find yourself something to do around the city, as long as you don't go too far. If Saul's youngest son, what's his name—Tobiah—is home, then you may wish to play with him.'

It was useless to inform his father that he no longer 'played' with other boys. Even if he still engaged in such juvenile pursuits, Tobiah was not a companion he would choose. The boy was three years his junior and a girlish gossip to boot. Micah could not bear the thought of spending yet another useless evening dodging Tobiah's attempts to pump him for some morsel of scandal that might be used on the morrow. Micah's desires, however, mattered little. His father sought neither his opinion nor preferences with regards to the itinerary, on this or any other day. He bent down and patted the ambling horse for which he felt far more affection than his father and took silent pleasure in his dislike for the man who always rode just a few paces ahead.

By the time they arrived at Saul ben Simon's house, it was well past dark. The city was crowded in celebration of the repeal of the Roman tax levy that had been so drastic as to bring the people close to rebellion. The Jews of the city counted its revocation as a victory, but Micah believed their triumph would be short-lived. Within a few months, the Romans would impose a new tax, once again. The new tax would be smaller in amount but wider in scope. In time, bit-by-bit, the taxes would continue to rise, though never at so great a rate as to warrant revolt. It was a clever trick that the Romans had learned to use to their full advantage.

On arrival at ben Simon's house, the effeminate young man met them at the gate. All hopes that Micah held of avoiding Tobiah's presence were quickly dispelled. Not only did the boy appear eager to engage Micah in discussion, he announced that he had been waiting all evening to spend time in town with him.

'They're celebrating the tax repeal, you know, and everything will be open late in town tonight,' Tobiah announced joyfully.

Micah spent the next hour in misery, walking the streets with the boy, enduring endless prattle about meaningless actions by meaningless people.

217

To cool himself off and as well as to escape his irritating companion's ceaseless chatter, Micah suggested a drink and dessert bread from a nearby shop. He positioned himself and his annoying charge on a low stone wall where they might see the revelers as they partied past. The boy ceaselessly waved to passers by—many of whom appeared to move along far more quickly after being hailed. Refreshed by his repast, Micah found himself a little more tolerant of his companion.

'Hey, look over there,' Micah said, jabbing his elbow into Tobiah's side. Four young women walked without a chaperone. The prettiest of the young women shot Micah a flirtatious look. She glanced backward as she walked and smiled with triumph at the confirmation that his eyes had followed her down the street.

Micah's mood rose. This was fun. 'Let's look for more girls!' he said, then remembered Tobiah's limited preferences.

The boy seemed to be growing more tired with each passing minute, and Micah had no desire to take him home. To keep him awake, Micah engaged Tobiah in conversation about the passing crowd.

'Look at those,' Micah laughed, pointing to two drunken men who attempted to navigate three asses through the street. 'And those!' he added, noting two sparsely dressed women of ill repute, openly advertising their more-than-abundant wares. The boy nodded, more asleep than awake.

Suddenly, for Micah, the crowd seemed to fade away. A young man, about Micah's own age, came into view as he walked down the center of the street. The stranger moved among the tumultuous

218

crowd, yet he walked as if alone. On all sides, people laughed with drunken revelry and made lewd comments to passersby. Some pushed and jabbed those who came too close or for no reason whatsoever. Others hurled insults at those around them in their frustration and impatience. Still the young man walked effortlessly amidst the crowd. He moved with a serenity, the likes of which Micah had never seen.

The stranger's dress was not as those bedecked for revelry. This young man wore a simple caftan of white coarse cloth and a head covering of a woven pattern unknown to Micah.

'Who's that, Tobiah?' Micah asked, as he elbowed his companion into wakefulness. 'See, there, the one in the middle.'

'I know a little about him. Why do you ask?' questioned Tobiah, waking in an instant for the possibility of fresh gossip.

'It's just that he's so different looking. You know, interesting.'

'Interesting?' Tobiah smirked with a knowing smile.

Not like you think, you depraved little wretch, Micah thought. Knowing that Tobiah would offer far more information if he thought he might gain some inside gossip, Micah kept his thoughts to himself and nodded.

Tobiah, fueled by what he now assumed to be their common predilection, related to Micah all of the rumors to which he was privy.

'His name is Yeshua, Yeshua ben Yosef,' Tobiah began eagerly. 'They say that around the time of his birth, there were those who proclaimed that the King of the Jews had been born, in Bethlehem of all places.'

Tobiah snickered at the absurdity of the thought and continued. 'It is said that when King Herod heard that the temple priests proclaimed that a baby had been sent to fulfill the prophecy of the Messiah, he became furious. He ordered a house-by-house search of Bethlehem for the baby. Now, I don't know if it's true, but they say that's where Herod's order for the slaying of all firstborn sons came from. I mean not necessarily because of Yeshua ben Yosef, but who knows, it was just about the time he was born.

'Anyway,' Tobiah continued, 'the day before the "slaughter-order," as my parents called it, was to be carried out, Yeshua's parents apparently fled with him to Alexandria, where they lived in the security of the home of Yeshua's father's rich relatives.'

'He does not dress as one of wealth,' Micah said absently, still unable to take his eyes off the slow-moving figure that seemed to glide through the crowd.

'They say he scorns the love of riches. He could be a man of means if he so desired. Supposedly, he's not a bad carpenter and a pretty good harness-maker and fisherman, as well—that is, when he works at it.'

'He doesn't look like he would shirk his responsibilities,' Micah mused to himself.

'Well, from what I hear, he's more strange than lazy. His family moved back to Nazareth when Yeshua was only a couple of years old, but he still wears clothes from every place he's lived.'

Micah nodded absentmindedly.

'But it goes far beyond his peculiar dress. He's

headed for big trouble, that one!' Tobiah announced with delight.

Micah turned with interest. 'What do you mean by trouble?'

'He's fashioned himself a teacher, questioning the wisdom of the high priests. He's making enemies in all the wrong places, if you know what I mean,' Tobiah added with a snicker.

Apparently Yeshua's radical talk against Roman taxes, fellow Jews he knew to be corrupt, and any issue he thought a crime against the poor, were earning him quite a reputation as a troublemaker. He had begun to beseech people to prepare for the coming of The Kingdom of God and to reject all false prophets. The most dangerous of his detractors was Ananus, the High Priest, who Yeshua claimed was culling his son and sons-in-law to follow in his footsteps in the hierarchy of the Temple.

Barely stopping to draw a breath, Tobiah drew in a little too close for Micah's liking and continued. 'Now I know this is none of my business but they say that when he prays he talks directly to his "Father in Heaven." He claims it's just as good to pray in the fields or on the mountainside or among the trees of the forest, as it is to pray in the Temple. Oh, how the Priests must just love that!'

Micah's heart pounded with excitement. How could one his own age and with no riches that would ensure his safety be unafraid to challenge the Temple priests?

According to Tobiah, the Romans and Temple priests were not Yeshua's only targets. He rejected the Pharisees, saying that they were hypocrites and dishonest. He had no kind words for the

221

Sadducees either, whom he believed to have grown rich on the suffering of others. He even managed to make enemies among the Essenes, though many were not certain what to make of him.

Suddenly the name 'Yeshua' rang a bell in the recesses of Micah's mind. 'He's Yeshua. I know who he is! I heard old Abidan ben Ehud talking about him just yesterday. He, too, said that this Yeshua was causing quite a stir!' Micah added.

'And all of it bad,' Tobiah added with a snort of self-satisfaction.

In his excitement, Micah lost sight of the subject of their discussion. Searching the faces of the crowd, Micah discovered that the form of Yeshua had disappeared from view. Only the image of the extraordinary young man remained, burned into Micah's memory.

'There might be lots of trouble now, but not half as much as there will be if he continues his foolishness,' Tobiah concluded self-importantly. 'Mark my words, Micah, you haven't heard the last of that one!'

FORTY-TWO

Day Ten, early afternoon
Central London

'If anything happens to me, there are a few things you need to know,' Sabbie began.

Gil had just completed the quickest cross-traffic change of lanes ever maneuvered in the history of driving and, as per Sabbie's instructions, was in the process of making an illegal U-turn, when she broached the subject of her imminent demise.

The green sedan was nowhere in sight, apparently left behind in the wake of Gil's stunt-level driving.

She was right. Not a problem after all.

'Look, could we discuss this when we get where we're going? If you ever decide to tell me where that might be,' he added.

'Get out and let me drive,' she said.

He ignored her order. The road ended one hundred feet ahead. 'Which way?' Gil asked. 'Left or right? Which way?'

'Right, and take it slowly. I'm trying to get the scroll back in the box. It doesn't fit anymore.'

'Now what?' he asked.

'Follow the signs to the train station,' Sabbie said. 'And tell me when you're a couple of blocks away.'

It was useless to ask her how he would know when they were a few blocks away when he'd never been there before. She was trying to coax the scroll into the rotted and disintegrating box. It was no easy job given that the scroll was twice as bulky as it had been before she unrolled it.

'The hell with this,' he heard her mutter, then he watched in wonder as she produced two huge reinforced paper shopping bags. Sabbie slid the blanket-wrapped scroll into one and, into the other, the ancient box.

Satisfied with her solution, she sat up and peered over Gil's shoulder.

'Good, we're almost there,' she said, as they approached the station.

So, we're taking the train.

It made sense, given that the green sedan would

be looking for their car.

'Now, do exactly as I tell you,' she said slowly. 'For once in your life, don't ask questions.'

Instinctively, Gil's gaze flashed to the rearview mirror.

There it is, as if we never lost it.

The green sedan was on their tail and, this time, it was not content to stay a car's length away. With each second, it gained on them. In less than a block it would overtake them, and it was obvious that was the driver's intention.

'Hard right,' she shouted. 'Now!'

Gil turned to see if the lane was clear.

'Now!' Sabbie repeated.

He gritted his teeth and cut the wheel without knowing what car might be coming in the opposite direction.

'Now drive straight, no matter what. Don't stop, don't turn, just go straight.'

Two curbs and three speed bumps slowed them down a bit, but Gil did as directed.

'Now, pull to the curb and get out,' Sabbie commanded as they approached the passenger drop-off area of the train station. 'Leave the keys. Follow me.'

Gil threw the car in park and left it running. He was by her side in a few strides. She was going full speed with the two shopping bags in tow. They ran into the railway station, across the slippery floor, and past the ticket windows.

He had no breath to ask her where they were going. It didn't matter anyway. He wasn't about to debate the matter.

The driver from the green car had abandoned his sedan and was in pursuit. Sabbie and Gil had the clear advantage for the moment but, at some point, they would have to come to a stop, and Gil could not imagine what good this race could possibly do.

Sabbie dashed toward a revolving door exit. As she approached, she apparently realized the slow-moving door occupied by even slower-moving people would put them in jeopardy. She hesitated, then changed directions. Gil almost ran into her. She turned, shoved aside a large trash can that blocked a glass and metal door, and pushed hard on the door. To his amazement, it swung open under the weight of her thrust and, in an instant, he and Sabbie were out of the building and onto the side parking lot.

The big black town car took Gil by surprise. It cut them off, nearly ran them over, then screeched to a halt in front of them. When the passenger door opened, Gil expected the worst. But Sabbie piled into the front seat and ordered him to follow her in.

'Slam it, slam the door,' she ordered, as the car began to move. They were off, away from their pursuer, away from the train station, just plain away.

FORTY-THREE

Three years before the Crucifixion
Bethany, East of the River Jordan

No matter how he positioned himself, Micah's back ached incessantly. The summer robes clung

225

and twisted about his body. The stifling air, filled with dust and the odor of animal droppings, filled his chest. He tried to remind himself of how fortunate he was to be riding on his old and faithful ass, while others walked such great distances, but the self-directed rebuke simply served to irritate rather than to humble him.

I am getting too old for this.

In his youth he would have eagerly anticipated the excitement of adventure. It had been a decade since he left his father's weapons enterprise and had established himself as a jewelry and metal crafter. He had endured more than his share of the filthy accommodations, barely edible food, and perilous encounters necessitated by his business excursions. It had become clear that no matter where one might journey, there seemed to be a commonality as to the best and the worst in man.

More than a decade had passed since he had walked these streets. They seemed not to have changed at all. The poverty, the filth, the debauchery, remained unaffected by the years. In his youth, Micah found his father's easy condemnations of the poor to be abhorrent. Now, he saw the miserable masses in much the same way.

As he liked to say, he had become a practical man. The dreams of his youth had died with the loss of his wife and yet-to-be-born first child. Their fate had been determined by a legionnaire who had urged his horse forward, trampling the young woman, heavy with child, who had been unable to get out of his way.

Lena was the love of his life, a free-spirited woman who would not tolerate an arranged marriage and had come to him as his equal. Strong and forthright yet soft and loving, she was all things. With her and for her, he had been happy to do anything.

After her death, nothing mattered. He had neither the desire to broker the sales of fine metals and crafts, nor the wish to take up his tools. Friends cared for him. They fed him when he cared not for food and housed him when he could not face returning home.

For one year Micah remained a dead man, rousing himself only to go to the temple to recite Kaddish, the traditional prayer by which her soul might be elevated to Olum Haba, The World to Come.

Then, on the anniversary of her death, as he recited the Kaddish prayer, Micah's pain was miraculously lifted. No longer twisted in agony, the reason for his Lena's death and that of their innocent babe had become clear. There was no reason, there was no deliverance, and clearly, there was no God. Tall, calm, and free, he left the temple never to return again.

With a new purpose fashioned from bitterness, he struggled to reclaim his craft and rebuild his life. He might have succeeded, for he needed little to survive, had not Herod Antipas levied yet another tax, this one on all goods bought or sold in Galilee. It had been the deathblow to far better established metalsmiths than he and, though Micah was willing to take on any type of labor, those few opportunities that still existed were given to men with families or high connections, both of which he no longer had.

His father had been right all along. Financial

security was more important than a righteous life and trust in self, rather than in God, was the intelligent man's only path. Now Micah was returning home, ready to face the man whom he had denigrated in his youth, and to ask forgiveness as well as help.

The night before he was to leave, as Micah packed for his journey, an old friend delivered an unexpected blow.

'You can't go home,' Jeremiah cautioned.

'Why not?' Micah asked. 'There is nothing here for me but poverty and debt. Those few who still have money know better than to flaunt their self-indulgence by wearing the jewelry I craft. It is useless. I have failed. I will go back to my family and beg for their forgiveness and help.'

'That door is no longer open to you.'

'You are wrong,' Micah said. 'A father's love does not so easily vanish no matter how many years have passed. And my mother, she will welcome me with open arms and tears. And, perhaps, a fine and lavish meal.' Micah laughed as his stomach growled loudly in anticipation.

'No, Micah, they won't,' Jeremiah said solemnly.

Micah stopped packing. 'What are you not saying?'

'After you left, your father did more than disown you,' Jeremiah admitted. 'Every night he went to the temple and said Kaddish for you.'

'He included me in prayers for the dead? No, he couldn't have!' Micah cried in disbelief. 'You must be mistaken.'

It had been true, however, for Jeremiah had borne witness to a father who would rather count his son as among the dead than to allow him to

228

make a life of his own. At the time, Jeremiah had not the heart to tell Micah what he had seen with his own eyes. As the years passed and Micah had traveled far from the home of his childhood, it seemed less and less important. But now there seemed little choice.

Much to Jeremiah's surprise, however, Micah, without so much as a word, resumed his preparations for his trip and, next morning at sunrise, bid his friend good-bye.

'But why would you go back?' Jeremiah asked.

'I don't know,' Micah answered. 'It is what I must do.'

'There is nothing there for you, my friend.'

'Nor is there anything here,' Micah concluded.

Now, after long days of travel, Micah approached Nazareth. It may have been the long ride, or the pounding heat, or the fact that today, on his thirtieth birthday, he had nothing to show for his life other than a few pieces of silver and copper he had crafted himself. Whatever the case, he was empty and directionless and, though a good meal and some respite from the blazing afternoon sun might have helped to heal his body, it would not have lessened the void that engulfed his soul.

The steady roll of his old mount, slower with each hour in the blazing sun, lulled him into a troubled sleep. Through his dreams came the sound of a woman's cries. Micah pushed away images of Lena that once again threatened to haunt him and forced himself awake.

His old mount had stopped to graze by the river's edge at a spot renowned to be the place where David escaped during Absalom's rebellion a thousand years earlier. This point along the

Jordan put them an hour or two south of Galilee.

Micah's journey had been swifter than he had anticipated, and he welcomed an unexpected rest at the place he had once loved as a boy. It was here, in the late afternoon, that the farmers' wives would come to rest and the soft background of their voices had often lulled him to sleep in the tall grasses.

Today, more than a hundred people had congregated on the banks; some huddled in small gatherings, some stood alone in silence. All watched one man, taller than most and broad across his tanned shoulders, clad only in a white sindon wrapped round as a loincloth. His dark hair and beard, dripping with water, shone almost golden red in the sun. Waist-deep in the river, he cradled a young woman, guiding her to shore, as she cried with exalted shouts of joy.

On their approach, an old woman seated among others her age, rose and joined the small group that waited at the water's edge. Though the crowd that waited seemed to close in front of her, the man in the sindon beckoned the old woman to join him. She took his hand and allowed him to guide her to the middle of the flowing water steadied by his gentle hold.

Two men joined them and gave support to the old woman as the taller man poured water about her head. When it all was completed, she silently made her way to shore. She appeared transformed and walked straight and steady, as if the years had been washed from her body as well as her soul.

Micah dismounted and approached her from behind. She turned as if knowing he was there, smiled, and embraced him. Then, without a word, she moved on, enfolded by the welcoming arms of some of the onlookers.

A sweet sadness overwhelmed Micah. He wanted to reach out and draw her back. Filled with a yearning, an almost imperceptible song that lingered just out of earshot, he longed to feel what she felt, to know what she knew, what he, too, had once known; that which life's pain and struggle had since worn away.

A prayer formed on Micah's lips. He entreated God to deliver him from his bitterness and his anger. Nothing more did he ask save for the chance to serve God once again, in word and action, and to bring joy and hope to others as did this man before him.

Then, as if he himself had received the ablution, Micah moved through the crowd. He had been transmuted to the man that a less painful life might have produced.

At Micah's urging, those who waited for baptism allowed the sickest and weakest to come to the fore. He insured that each was to be taken to the river according to his need. Micah's voice, calm and reassuring, engendered trust. Those who had been restless or quarrelsome now waited patiently. When the baptisms had been completed, Micah turned from the river and walked toward his horse.

'James,' called the baptizer to his friend on the shore. 'Go ask that man to remain, I wish to speak with him.'

'But tonight we were going to . . .' James argued.

'Quickly, James!' the man ordered. 'Quickly! Don't let him go.'

James did not move to the task.

Another, who called from the shore,

231

approached the baptizer and in a voice that Micah could overhear, explained James' reluctance. 'We don't know if it's a good idea for you to see him, Yeshua. James and I don't like it. He could be a Roman spy. Maybe someone from the Temple. After all, in the little time he's been here, he's practically taken over. The people seem more willing to listen to him than to either James or me.'

The baptizer ignored the explanation and called once again to the shore. 'James, stop him. Ask him to join me for the evening meal. Do as I say!'

Grumbling, James complied, moving as slowly as he might so as to be unable to catch up.

Micah moved slowly to ensure the invitation would be delivered and that he would accept.

*   *   *

They did not speak on the road to the nearby public house. James and Peter quietly disappeared. Once their mounts had been cared for, Micah and the baptizer settled down to a simple but much welcomed meal. Micah's host introduced himself.

'I am Yeshua ben Yosef,' he began. 'How came you to be who you are?'

Micah had no explanation for either his life or the transformation he had experienced that very day. 'I know not yet,' Micah replied.

'As do any of us. Perhaps that is why we meet today,' Yeshua said smiling.

Micah nodded. He could barely bring himself to gaze into the eyes of one who had inspired such respect as to make him feel almost unworthy.

Yeshua urged his guest to recount his past, and Micah spoke with an honesty he had not known since he talked with his beloved Lena.

'I could recite the journeys that make up a man's life, the trade routes I have traveled from Tyre and Sidon on the West or the caravan roads from Damascus to the Northeast. I could regale you with stories of my adventures along the great imperial highways that traverse the whole of Palestine or the knowledge I have gained in Antioch and along the Egyptian frontier. But I think that is not what you truly desire, is it?' queried Micah.

'No, it is not,' answered Yeshua. A smile of amusement spread across his face.

'Then I will respond to the question your heart wishes answered,' continued Micah. 'I have traveled far and wide. I have journeyed in search of knowledge and wealth, not always in that order. I have had the wisest of teachers and have been the most willing of students.'

In his youth, Micah explained, a loving and wise metalsmith showed him a world and the man within himself that he might otherwise have never known. After he left his father's home, Micah spent time exploring the world before pursing his own metal craft.

For a short time, he dwelt with Apollonius from Tyana, who believed that the practice of illusion was justified when it was used for the good. The great teacher, renowned for his knowledge of healing and pain-alleviating potions, also instructed Micah in the use of 'loving deceptions,' sleights of hand that caused an otherwise intelligent man to overlook that which appeared right before his eyes. From manuscripts and from those schooled in their teachings, Micah studied the simplicity of Lao Tzu, the wisdom of Confucius, and the discipline of Buddha. Only then was Micah ready to start raising the family that others had begun a full decade earlier.

Yeshua nodded. 'You were wise to travel and to learn. Now you are well versed in the ways of the world.'

'It is true,' Micah agreed. 'Yet nowhere in my daily life have I been able to apply these teachings nor the miraculous works they may allow one to manifest. Fortune has made me wise, but it has left me without purpose . . . until now.'

'And now?' asked Yeshua.

All was changed that day, Micah said. He had been compelled to bear witness to the futility of his life and the pointlessness of his existence. 'Now, I am changed. I have been returned to myself,' Micah said.

'You have not yet been baptized.'

'No,' answered Micah, 'nevertheless I have been transformed. I have touched those you have touched. The spirit was in them as it was in you and . . .' Micah looked steadily into Yeshua's eyes as he continued, 'and it has filled me with the purpose that lives in you.'

Yeshua seemed transfixed. He had ministered to countless converts, he said, and he had healed the minions, but none had spoken to him as did Micah. To others he was the leader, the healer, the father. To Micah, he was a brother. And this, he had yearned for, for too many years.

Long into the night they spoke, as old friends, as equals. Each related his story; each listened in turn. Teachings, understandings, losses, dreams and, most of all, purpose; they shared them all.

Together they were stronger than either had been alone. Though it was never put into words, it was understood that Micah would stay and join in Yeshua's ministry.

'One thing must be said,' Micah added. 'I want nothing of you. To be with you, help you in your work, share your journey, and to learn from you as I may. That is all I ask.'

'Did it ever occur to you,' Yeshua countered, 'that it is I who may learn from you? Those who call themselves my Apostles worry like old women. Though, I must add in all fairness, that they are not altogether wrong. They say I underestimate the anger I instill in those who are at cross-purposes with my teachings.'

'What do they advise?' asked Micah.

'Ah, there is the problem,' responded Yeshua. 'Though they observe a danger, they are at a loss as to how to thwart it. Perhaps, as I may teach you about the Kingdom of Heaven, you may teach to me all that you have learned about men and human nature and share with me the wonders of the many skills you have learned in those lands to the east.'

'It would be my joy,' Micah answered softly.

Concern clouded Yeshua's face. 'Not necessarily so.'

Yeshua explained that he feared that the twelve who traveled with him would not take kindly to Micah. 'As men will do, they have taken into their minds that no other may join our inner circle.'

They believed there must be only twelve apostles, Yeshua explained, as there were twelve tribes of Israel. To his Apostles, a greater number would be sacrilege. He did not agree, but he allowed them this indulgence.

'They are good men in their own right,' Yeshua, said, 'though they are neither as learned nor perhaps of such lofty thought as you.'

In the early hours of the morning an idea came to Yeshua, and a plan was set. He would bring Micah into the circle, not as another apostle, but as a scribe; one who would record their daily comings and goings for posterity or, should need be, for legal defense before a tribunal.

'We'll say you're going to record my life for all the future generations who might thirst for such details,' Yeshua announced with a grand sweep of his hand. Then, falling back in laughter at the absurdity of such an event, he continued. 'Or at least your writings may bear witness to my innocence should I meet a less noble end,' he added, raising a goblet of wine in toast.

'But I must warn you,' Yeshua added more soberly. 'While they will have no choice but to accept you as my scribe, they will make your life less than easy. I fear you shall, once again, be as an outcast.'

'I will trust in you and in myself,' Micah assured Yeshua. 'I came in hopes of finding welcome in my father's home. I have found it, instead, in the house of the Lord. I seek nothing so great as to be counted as one of your Apostles. If fortune has decreed that my task is that of a scribe, I will nonetheless consider myself blessed.'

FORTY-FOUR

Day Ten, mid-afternoon
Hillingdon Town Centre, London

He was tall for a Syrian and broad in the shoulders. Gray hair bristled in all directions, and his prominent nose, deep-set brown eyes, and dark skin combined to give him the look of a great ageing eagle.

Sarkami escorted Gil and Sabbie to his home through a back alley that weaved its way past tiny backyards, each groomed with meticulous care. White picket fences marked boundaries between properties, and neatly arranged, unblemished rubbish cans stoutly awaited their consignments.

For Gil, the short walk from the car to Sarkami's home was less than pleasant. Neither Sabbie nor Sarkami spoke a word. They didn't seem to need to.

Gil maintained his silence as well, though it was not a comfortable one. He was the outsider, forced to bear witness to the most intimate of wordless exchanges between them, and he longed to be somewhere else; anywhere else.

Sarkami carried one shopping bag, Sabbie the other. Gil walked behind, intrigued by the look of contentment on her face. This was a different Sabbie, the woman Gil would have loved to know, the product of a different life. Her face was soft and beautiful and she gazed often into Sarkami's eyes. They held hands and, as they walked, their bodies moved in step.

237

Anger rose in Gil's chest, and his face grew hot. What was he getting so angry about? He had no claims on her. All the same, he didn't have to watch her make love to the guy.

Four bolt locks barred entry to the sea-green backdoor of Sarkami's tiny home; a great deal of protection for so humble a dwelling. The scene that greeted Gil beyond the door, however, surprised and amused him.

The small, simple layout was not unlike his own apartment. Square, simple utilitarian furniture filled a minimum of space. The room was one of singular purpose, the comfortable and efficient completion of one's work.

In the area where Gil would have placed computers and display screens, the tops of two long tables and a desk held vices, cutting tools, engraving instruments, inks, scissors, paper and pens. Extension cords crisscrossed the floor.

One long folding table against the back wall appeared to be designated a clean zone. It was covered with a fine white cloth on which were carefully laid several small sections of parchment, a couple of faux facsimile scrolls, and more than a dozen strips of copper, not unlike The Cave 3 Scroll sections Sabbie had shown him at the Museum. Books, dust, scraps of paper, bits of metal, and sketches littered every surface of the room save for the clean table. This was the workshop that Sarkami called home. Gil understood the man completely.

Sarkami ignored Gil and turned to Sabbie. 'Was it very bad?' he asked.

She nodded.

'Did he know you were there, at the end?'

238

She nodded again. 'They left him there to die slowly and turned him so he had to face Sarah's body.'

'Did he speak?'

'He said he was sorry,' she began, then broke into sobs.

Sarkami looked puzzled. 'Sorry for what? He never gave them the diary.'

'I know. He was just saying he was sorry things turned out like they did.'

Sarkami shook his head sadly.

'Victims often blame themselves, you know,' Sabbie said softly with a slight shrug. 'Even though they could have done nothing to stop their assailants. A very wise man once tried to teach me that,' she added, and looked knowingly at Sarkami's gentle face.

Sabbie closed her eyes, opened them after a moment, and continued. 'He told me that he had wished he could have been there when it all came to be. I promised him we would not fail. He smiled and said we had better not. Then he told me to take everything from the oven safe and get the hell out.'

'No problem with the diary?' Sarkami asked.

'No problem. It was right there in the oven safe with the passport you gave him for Gil. Whoever killed him never knew it was a few feet from where they left him.' She choked back a sob.

'Something else?' Sarkami prompted.

Sabbie nodded. 'Next to the diary, he left a pile of several thousand pounds in traveler's checks. On top of the pile was a Post-it that read: "Take it. You'll need it."' Her voice cracked with emotion. 'Considering his salary, it must have taken years of sacrifice to accumulate that much money.'

She surrendered herself into Sarkami's open arms.

Gil watched in amazement. He hadn't thought Sabbie capable of such love, not for Ludlow, not for anyone.

Sabbie blew her nose into a handkerchief Sarkami offered, then continued. 'I should have known it was the work of McCullum's boys. It had WATSC written all over it, down to keeping Ludlow's wife alive until he arrived home and causing Sarah enough damage to . . .'

Once more sobs overtook her, and Sarkami held her as he had before.

She straightened and continued. Until she had spotted McCullum at the Museum, she hadn't considered him to be a player. McCullum must have gotten smart and stopped using e-mail to communicate with DeVris. Otherwise, she would have been able to pick up on their ongoing connection.

There was more, she added, and it wasn't good. 'McCullum wasn't the only one after Ludlow. As I was leaving Ludlow's, I spotted two men— definitely not WATSC—checking out the apartment. One of the men was very large, the other was small and dark. I think the smaller one had a scar on his cheek but I couldn't be sure.'

Sarkami's face became grim.

She added that she had spotted both men again in Weymouth, waiting outside their hotel. She didn't think they saw her on either occasion but, again, she couldn't be certain.

Sarkami asked if she had encountered anyone in Weymouth. By the way he emphasized the word 'encountered,' Gil was certain he was using the euphemism for Gil's benefit. Sabbie seemed to have no such reservations.

'I took down one in the restaurant bathroom and put another on hold at the Monastery. They weren't McCullum's WATSC boys. That's what really has me worried.'

'The guy in the Monastery?' Gil interrupted. 'You said he was a maintenance man!'

'We had more important things to deal with at the time,' she answered simply, then exited the room with Sarkami. Gil heard a door close behind them.

They returned a few minutes later.

'Give me your wallet,' she said. She held her hand out for Gil's expected offering.

Gil didn't move.

'I need the bills with the translation to give to Sarkami,' she said.

'Screw you!' Gil shouted.

He had put up with more than enough, he said. He added that he was tired of being treated like a child, a potentially dead one at that.

'You got what you wanted from me, so why don't I just go and leave you two to whatever you two want to do?'

Sabbie and Sarkami looked at him with shocked expressions, then both smiled, and shook their heads.

His anger soared. They were doing it again, only more so. He told them what they could do with their patronizing smiles as well as the scroll.

'You don't understand,' Sabbie said. 'We're not done with you . . .'

'So what, you're saying you're not going to let

241

me go?' Gil asked.

'No, we're not done with you because the scroll's not done with you. There is much more for you to do. When you're ready to know, it will all become clear . . .'

They were treating him like a schmuck once again. 'What is it?' Gil asked. 'Aren't I smart enough or violent enough or whatever it is you want to be part of your little game?'

Sarkami addressed Gil for the first time. 'Not violent enough?' he asked incredulously. 'Yes, that's true. Not violent enough to defend the scroll against those who would destroy its message? I think so. God, I pray so. You have a far greater task ahead of you, one which requires far more than the mere ability to spot pursuers and remove their threat.'

Gil waited for an explanation, but none came.

'What kind of task?' Gil asked skeptically.

'One that only you can complete,' Sabbie said. Her touch on his shoulder was electric. The warmth he felt when he first found the scroll surged through him once again. She held the scroll and was passing it to him.

'Take this,' she urged. 'Then protest if you like and we'll do as you say.'

Gil stared at her. He knew what he would feel even before she laid the scroll in his arms.

There was no anger. There was no distrust. A lifetime of betrayals had been wiped clean and with it the petty concerns and jealousies that had filled his thinking and his heart. Ludlow—God rest his soul—Sarkami, Sabbie, and he, together they now shared one purpose: to complete the promise of those who had gone before, to protect this

242

scroll, and to deliver the two-thousand-year-old message it bore.

Though, for whom the message was intended, Gil could not imagine.

FORTY-FIVE

Day One following the Crucifixion, morning
Home of Joseph of Arimathea, Judea

It was a dream filled with terror. It disappeared even as Micah reached to grasp hold of it. Perhaps it was for the best. Waking brought with it a dread almost too horrible to bear. Judas' betrayal, Yeshua's arrest, and the flight of the Twelve. Last night, in only a few moments, all was changed, all was lost.

Had he not been so foolish, so willing to be swayed by Yeshua's assurances, Micah might have seen it coming and, perhaps, might have taken some action, any action, to prevent it.

The last ten days had seemed interminable. From the moment that the Apostles heard of Pontius Pilate's intention to have Yeshua arrested, the debates raged without resolution. Simon wanted to approach the Temple Priests and try to appease their anger by promising to keep Yeshua out of Jerusalem and to have Yeshua tame his attacks on the Pharisees and the Priests. Bartholomew and James argued that all of their lives were in danger, and it was best that they not go to Jerusalem for the Passover celebration.

Yeshua, himself, claimed the best path was one

of non-resistance, saying, 'The Roman guards will seek me out wherever I go. I need not take others with me. Each of you has a far greater duty than to join me in prison or, even worse if it should come to be, to languish on a cross alongside of my own. Rather, if it is to be, I will die as I have lived, in the service of my Father's will.'

Now, as he looked back, Micah bitterly blamed himself for siding with Yeshua in his plan to celebrate the rest of the Passover in Jerusalem. All knew the danger that waited there, but Yeshua would not be dissuaded.

Late into the night, while the others slept, Yeshua had conferred with Micah. It was the evening before they made the journey, and Yeshua argued each point as only he could. In the end, when no logic remained to support Yeshua's intention, he stated simply to Micah, 'I must do as I must do.'

Micah knew that once he made up his mind, Yeshua would be as immovable as the Temple itself and, so, turned his attention to convincing Yeshua to make a quiet entrance into the city. Even here Yeshua held his ground.

'I come to Jerusalem to celebrate with my brethren. If they choose to recognize me and follow me, so be it.'

On arrival at the city, Micah's worst fear was realized. The reception at the city gates had been greater than any had imagined. With hoardes following him and praising his name, Yeshua made his way to the Temple. When he discovered money changers plying their trade on this holiest of Holy Days, Yeshua was enraged beyond words. Unable to contain his fury and fully aware of the possible repercussions of his actions, Yeshua drove the offenders out of the Temple.

That night, Yeshua spoke little during the Seder meal, although the few references he did make regarding the wine and bread seemed undecipherable to the Apostles. Only Micah, who lay close by Yeshua's side, understood too well the symbolism of the blood and body of which Yeshua spoke.

When Yeshua spoke of one who would yet betray him, several of the Apostles made light of the matter. To betray Yeshua would be as to betray themselves, they said, and they would speak of it no more. Micah, alone, recognized too well the import of Yeshua's portent of treachery. His heart, alone, ached with the knowledge of what was to come to pass.

At Yeshua's request, Micah joined the others and reclined in accordance with tradition at the Seder table, though he knew full well this might be their last supper together.

Micah was The Disciple, as the Twelve called him in derision. To them he would never be an apostle, always the follower, never the messenger. Within his bosom, however, Micah held the knowledge that Yeshua did not regard him as they did.

'Know this,' Yeshua had assured him. 'We are all disciples, followers of God's way. There is honor, not disgrace in being called thus. Be assured as well, my dear friend, that you are an apostle as much as any of the others. You shall carry my message to lands and times they cannot imagine. You stand forever as Protector of the Word. You, alone, are my beloved Thirteenth

Apostle.'

Micah had kept his silence as he partook of the Sabbath meal. He had been forbidden by Yeshua to speak of the play that was about to unfold. As they traveled together to Gethsemane he was overcome with certainty of the travesty that was about to take place. Weary after their journey, the Twelve slept. Finally, Micah was free to attend his friend who stood alone.

It was there, among the olive trees, that Yeshua spoke to Micah of the tzaddikim; thirty-six righteous souls born to each generation who, by their very existence, assured the continuation of the world.

According to Abraham's Covenant, Yeshua explained, once each millennium, God shall return to earth to count among the many, those who remain righteous. Only the tzaddikim, the righteous ones, standing in God's judgment, may ensure God's promise to Abraham, His Covenant of Continuance. Without these righteous souls, mankind's fate would be in grave and certain peril.

Yet these tzaddikim have no knowledge of one another, neither have they any awareness of their own singular importance. As innocents, they remain unaware of the critical consequences of their thoughts, their faith, and their deeds.

'All of this is known to me,' Micah said softly.

Yeshua looked up in surprise.

'Some say that you are tzaddik,' Micah added.

'I would not claim it for, in doing so, I would prove I was not,' Yeshua answered.

'Yet neither can you deny it,' Micah said softly.

Yeshua smiled.

'You are as wise as I counted you to be, dear

friend, for you know that of which I cannot speak.'

Micah nodded.

'Good,' Yeshua said, with obvious pleasure. 'Then let me add only this. If by God's good grace, I bear so divine a blessing and so great a burden as you know me to carry, and if I am unable to complete my sacred tasks, then when my soul has shed its mortal sheath, I pray that you, dear brother, shall rise and take my place.'

'Your prayer is mine,' Micah whispered.

'These are difficult times,' Yeshua continued. 'Things are not always as they seem. Nor are people,' he added, glancing thoughtfully at his sleeping Apostles. 'It will come to pass that those who cannot tolerate the truth shall take action to silence it. And to silence me, as well.'

Micah remained steadfast, his eyes fixed on his beloved Yeshua. Tears streamed down his cheeks. He understood.

'I ask only that which I know you will do . . .'

'Gladly,' Micah interjected.

'Yes.' Yeshua smiled. 'And that which you are uniquely qualified to do. I would ask that no matter what may befall me, you shall not let the truth die with me.'

'I could not bear it if . . .' Micah interrupted.

'Have I your word?' Yeshua insisted.

'Before God.'

Yeshua smiled and seemed content, yet he shivered in the cold. He wore no cloak for, on the road to Gethsemane, he had given his outer garment to an old man who suffered in the cool night air. Micah removed his caftan and persuaded Yeshua to place it on top of his own for warmth.

'Then you will wear nothing but a sindon,'

Yeshua protested. 'I cannot accept it. I will be fine.'

Micah argued that the sacrifice was of little importance. 'All that I am, all that I have, I gladly give in the name of God, Elyon.'

Yeshua smiled and accepted Micah's offering. 'Now, dear friend, leave me with Him.' Yeshua's face was beatific with peace.

Micah watched his friend, powerless to put a halt to Yeshua's prophecy of betrayal by one of the Twelve. Micah struggled in torment at the thought of that which would soon come to be.

Then, when he could bear the thought of the impending betrayal no longer, Micah's anguish gave birth to a plan that might yet save Yeshua's life. His heart soared. Yes, there was yet a way to save his friend! Were Yeshua to be arrested and sent to the cross, Micah could yet set him free. Fear was transformed to hope, anger to joy. It mattered not what any of the Twelve might do, Micah, the Thirteenth, scorned by the others, might yet save his beloved friend.

Micah rushed to Yeshua to reveal his plan but, even as he watched, Judas entered the garden and, with a single kiss, a signal to the guards who waited to arrest the recipient, betrayed both man and God.

Even as the Roman guards took Yeshua away, the Apostles scattered, fearful for their own lives. None remained in the garden; neither had any followed to attend Yeshua, to plead for him, or to stand by his side. The Apostles knew well that their fate would be the same as Yeshua's had they interceded and all had cared far more for themselves than for him.

Micah, too, had fled from the garden though not in pursuit of his safety. Rather, he had rushed to enlist the help that he would require to make preparations for the deception he had devised; a deception he had hoped would never be brought into play. Last night, Micah's plan had seemed little more than the result of fear-laden musings. Now, it appeared to be Yeshua's only hope.

FORTY-SIX

Day Ten, evening
Hillingdon Town Centre, London

They left Sarkami to do what he did best: to prepare the remaining section of the scroll for Sabbie's translation. It meant cutting the innermost section into strips. It was a tedious job that would take the rest of the night.

'We can't risk unrolling it after a millennium or two,' Sabbie said. Gil knew she was right but to both of them, cutting the scroll felt like a terrible sacrilege. One that could never be undone.

Remaining at Sarkami's was out of the question. Though he did all the restorations and faux facsimiles in England, he was still considered a member of the Museum's staff, the logical person Sabbie would seek out, and easily traceable. With a new set of players on the field, it was simply too dangerous. They made their way to a busy hotel and took up the all-night vigil. Sarkami would call as soon as he was finished.

Sabbie had requested two hotel rooms. It

seemed unnecessary, but Gil didn't object. A bit of time alone sounded wonderful.

'One room is for us, the other is for them,' she explained. 'We stay in one, keep the lights on, do whatever we want.'

The other room was for observing what was happening on the street. It would be a bit obvious, she said, if they turned off the lights every time they wanted to look out of the window, then turned them back on when they were finished.

'Now we just keep our eyes open and wait,' Sabbie added.

Gil fought the impulse to go to the window immediately and get a good look at the street, lights or no lights. He sat down on the bed, across from her. It was going to be a long night.

She had perched herself on the side of the big double bed, kicked off her shoes, and had begun to massage her feet. 'Ever play chess?' Sabbie asked.

She isn't suggesting we play chess to pass the time!
Gil nodded.

'Have you ever been castled?' she continued.

Castling was a powerful but greatly underused chess strategy. It involved removing the king from its normal position in the center of the board and placing it in a protected corner. With a single move, all of the plans that one's opponent had in the works were turned upside down. Gil knew it well. It was one of his favorite strategies.

'Well, now it's being pulled on us,' Sabbie explained. McCullum was no longer the only king on the board. Earlier in the evening Sarkami had pulled her aside and for good reason. She filled Gil in on the details.

Sarkami had wanted her to know that the two

250

men she had seen circling Ludlow's apartment were Abdul Maluka, head of Muslims for World Truth Video, and his bodyguard slash assassin, Aijaz.

'They are Syrian,' Sarkami had informed her.

'Countrymen!' Sabbie exclaimed. She understood how powerful the tie might be for Sarkami.

'No, Maluka was born in Syria like myself, but he is no countryman of mine,' Sarkami had answered. 'Maluka seeks to expose the message the scroll bears only if it suits his purposes. Otherwise, he will destroy it. He is no countryman,' Sarkami repeated.

'They are not so different, Maluka and McCullum,' Sabbie said.

She turned to Gil. 'The one who surprised us at the Monastery, didn't he look familiar?' she asked.

Gil tried to remember. The wrinkled face, twisted body. Yes, they belonged to a cleaning man at the Museum but, like so many, Gil had paid him little attention. Sabbie had known at once, even in the dark of the Monastery courtyard, but she had no idea he was Maluka's spy turned assassin.

'There's something else, as well,' Sabbie explained. 'Something we're missing.'

Sarkami had agreed, she said. The pieces were not fitting together as they should. McCullum's thugs and Maluka and his assassin had appeared at Ludlow's apartment at about the same time and, apparently, with the same intent. McCullum's man in the restaurant and Maluka and his men had arrived at the same time in Weymouth. The odds against such coincidences were overwhelming. And DeVris was conspicuously absent. It didn't add up, and the missing piece could mean a castle move was in the works, Sabbie explained.

Best to keep the scroll and the person best able to translate the document in two different locations. At least for the moment. Besides, Sabbie said, there was more that the scroll had revealed than could be understood in a mere translation.

'What did you notice about the Gethsemane scene?' she asked. 'You know, where Yeshua is talking to Micah, right before the Roman guards came to take Yeshua away? What do you remember from that scene?'

The only thing that stuck in his mind was the image of Micah giving Yeshua his caftan so that Micah was left with only a sindon, or whatever Sabbie called the loincloth. It seemed a strange detail to leave behind for others to read in the millennia to come.

'Perfect,' she exclaimed. 'That's the whole point. Why would Micah include that detail in particular?'

'You mean, besides the fact that he had probably shivered his ass off after giving up his caftan?' Gil asked with a laugh.

She wasn't smiling. Every word that Micah engraved in the copper took time and precious space. That detail must have held an important meaning, otherwise he wouldn't have included it. Gil seemed unimpressed.

'You don't get it,' she said in frustration. 'Look, that scene is the confirmation we've been looking for. It's what Ludlow would have given . . . Wait!' she exclaimed, in excitement. 'I know how to say it so you'll understand. That scene is Micah's *signpost* to us. Like the signpost that Elias left in

252

the hidden page of the diary. This scene says, "There is something important I must tell you. Look here for the clues." '

And extraordinary clues they were.

'In the section where they take Yeshua away, Micah tells us who he, himself, is,' Sabbie began. 'And the Gospels of Mark and John confirm it. The Gospels describe a disciple who was there in Gethsemane, in the garden, on that night after the Last Supper. The disciple wore only a loincloth. This man was, and I quote, "the disciple that Jesus loved." In the Gospels, John even talks about this same disciple lying close to Jesus at the Last Supper, just as Micah describes his position at the Seder meal. According to John, this beloved disciple asks Jesus, "Who is he that betrayeth thee?"

'Don't you get it?' she insisted. 'The very scenes that Micah describes in the scroll are the same that Mark and John recount in the Gospels. The beloved disciple they describe right there in the scriptures, that's Micah.'

'*Our* Micah?'

'Our Micah,' Sabbie said. 'To the Apostles, Micah was a disciple that Jesus loved above all others but still, only a disciple. To Jesus, he was an apostle, His Thirteenth Apostle.'

The words Micah recorded in the scroll were those of Jesus himself, etched into copper for all eternity, by the hand of one who was most loved by Him. They had uncovered the most important document in the history of mankind. It was too incredible to imagine. And far too important to allow it to fall into the wrong hands.

'So far the scroll confirms what the Gospels say

about His adult life,' Sabbie began. 'It's exactly what McCullum and his WATSC organization would love to hold up for the world to see. At the same time, the scroll's message is just what Maluka and his Muslims for World Truth want to bury forever. Both have a stake, and it is huge.'

But no one knew what the rest of the scroll would reveal, and there was the hitch. It could confirm the rest of the Gospels or dispute them. It could lay bare a whole new truth that no one had ever considered, one that could shake the very foundations of Christianity itself.

'Then the positions would be reversed,' Gil said with a certainty that he wished he didn't own. 'Maluka would want the scroll to be able to show it to the world as proof that Christianity is false to its core.'

'And McCullum would need to destroy any trace of its existence,' Sabbie added.

'Ever hear the term "tiger by the tail?"' Gil asked Sabbie. 'It means we're holding on to something too big to imagine, and we just hope it doesn't suddenly turn around and come after us.'

'More than that, I think we got a tiger in each hand,' Gil concluded.

'Maybe more,' Sabbie added thoughtfully.

FORTY-SEVEN

Day One following the Crucifixion, afternoon
North of Jerusalem

The Apostles gathered in the old, abandoned farmhouse. Over a day had passed since Yeshua's arrest but his friends and followers were filled with fear for his life. The Twelve had returned from their flight and, as they debated, those most loyal to Yeshua brought reports of him being shuffled from place to place and subjected to mock hearings and self-serving determinations.

Still, the Apostles continued their hypothetical arguments. When Micah could stand no more, he took the Twelve aside and presented his plan. Yet, even as they listened, word came that Yeshua was being crucified. No more debate. This was the time for action.

Micah's proposal involved quite a bit of risk, though not to the Apostles themselves. Each agreed and set to work immediately, procuring the herbs that Micah would need to prepare Apollonius' Elixir of Death, a potion he had learned to make on his last journey to the east. The sweet, aromatic solution would be given to Yeshua even as he hung upon his cross.

If all went as planned, a few minutes after its administration, the potion would make it appear that Yeshua had died. The antidote, to be used no more than two full days after administration of the elixir, would reverse its effects.

It was a simple enough plan with one great

drawback; the unpredictable nature of the elixir. Give too little and Yeshua would awaken too quickly, making it obvious that he was very much alive. Give too much and he might never wake again. The timing was critical. Likewise, the antidote did not always bring about the desired effect of restoring the near dead to life once again.

Give the antidote within two days and one man would rise; administer it at one day and another would not. Though the thought of Yeshua dying by administration of Micah's own elixir tore at his chest like the short sword of a Roman soldier, still, it seemed to be the only plan that offered any hope.

It was agreed that Micah would enlist the help of Joseph of Arimathea. The two would claim the body of Yeshua, and remove it ostensibly for burial. Once in the safety of a burial tomb, it would then be the job of the Apostles to administer the counteragent that would wake Yeshua from his death-like sleep. While the Apostles administered the antidote that Micah had prepared, Micah would rush ahead to the hills near Qumran and prepare his secret cave for their arrival. There in the seclusion and safety of the cave, they could all escape detection while Yeshua healed and grew strong once again.

For once there seemed no dissention among the Apostles. With careful and deliberate strokes, Micah drew a detailed map that would direct the Apostles to his cave. Micah then took his leave to join Joseph and to bring to Yeshua his Elixir of Death even as he hung on the cross.

Joseph of Arimathea, deeply grieving the imminent death of Yeshua, willingly agreed to offer his help. He pleaded with Pontius Pilate for the body of Yeshua. He pleaded hard and long and, with his promise of more than a few well-considered favors, in the end Pilate agreed. Pontius Pilate's consent was all that Joseph needed. He had already enlisted the help of Nicodemus, who allowed Micah to wrap himself in Nicodemus' clothes and ride his mule and, so, to pass as Joseph's assistant if any Roman guard should stop them.

Joseph led Micah to the place where Yeshua hung on the cross and, upon their arrival at Golgotha, Joseph presented Pilate's order for release of Yeshua's body.

'Not dead yet,' the fat Roman guard informed Joseph disinterestedly. He glanced at Micah, well concealed in rags, who appeared to be staring vacantly off into the distance. The guard turned back to his half-eaten lunch.

'Oh, no!' Joseph exclaimed, in frustration. 'They said he was in poor condition, that he wouldn't last more than a few hours. I cannot come back later. I don't have all day, you know.'

'What would you like me to do about it? I could put a sword through him if you would like,' the guard said, as he withdrew his sword from its sheath, 'but it'll cost you. Not supposed to give them a quick end, you know.'

The guard glanced over his shoulder to be certain that none of the other guards had yet returned. 'I mean your time must be worth a lot to you. It would be a shame if you had to wait here for hours, maybe days.'

It was common knowledge that the Roman guards who had been relegated to crucifixion watching had been demoted to such a duty because they were too old, too stupid, or too incompetent for any other duty. For those same reasons, they could be counted on to be the most corrupt as well. For a few gold coins, they would slit anyone's throat, including—if one wasn't careful—the throat of the one who had just offered payment.

With a knowing smile Joseph reached into his robe and withdrew a small pouch, which he offered to the guard. 'Well, I do have something here that might help to bring my waiting to a swift conclusion, if you know what I mean.'

The guard returned his sword to its sheath. Micah caught Joseph's eye, and they shared a moment of great relief. Interested only in the contents of Joseph's pouch, the guard snatched it from Joseph's hand, opened it, and poured the contents into the palm of his free hand.

'What's this?' he asked as his fingers bypassed the coins and picked up the vial that held the precious Elixir of Death.

'The contents of the vial will bring you the remainder of the coins in this hand,' Joseph said, holding up a larger and considerably fuller pouch. 'Pour the contents of that vial into a cup of wine and give it to the prisoner, the one who calls himself Yeshua of Nazareth. It will make the wine sour, but he will not be surprised at being given bitter drink.'

'That one? He will refuse it,' the guard countered.

'Tell him that Joseph of Arimathea brought it to ease his pain. He will trust you and he will drink it. But, fear not. Its only virtue is that it will make my

258

wait the shorter and you the richer. Then you and I will both be free to be on our way.'

'Why can't I just skewer him like the pig he is?'

'Because you were given clear instruction to let him hang and suffer 'til he died. Come now, don't get us both in trouble.'

The guard shrugged, then took the pouch and positioned himself so that no other guard might see his bribery in action. He quickly counted out the coins. He laughed and placed the money deep within his robes, then turned and walked off without a word.

Joseph retreated to where Micah had allowed the horse to amble. 'What's happening?' Micah asked. 'Is he just taking the money or is he going to do it?'

'I don't know,' Joseph answered. 'I'm not sure . . .'

They waited. As far as Joseph could tell, the guard was just as likely to give Yeshua the drink as he was to keep the money but do nothing. At any moment, he might signal the other guards to come and take Joseph and Micah away. They awaited their fate as much as Yeshua awaited his.

The guard, originally headed in Yeshua's direction, stopped and conversed with two other men who were not in guards' uniforms. They laughed and, as the minutes passed, it became clear that Yeshua's last chance was to be lost at the whim of a stupid arrogant lout.

The guard pounded his thighs in exaggerated laughter at some comment, then moved off into the distance where their Yeshua might yet be clinging to his last measure of life. Joseph and Micah strained to see. It appeared to them that the guard had climbed up and administered the elixir to one who hung upon a cross but at such a distance, they could not be sure. Slowly, after the guard stopped to relieve himself on the bottom of one of the crosses, he returned.

'It is done,' he announced. 'Now get him out of here quickly. If you ever speak of this to anyone, I will deny it, then I will make certain you never speak again.'

Joseph and Micah nodded their agreement, then hurried in the direction from which the guard had come.

'Wait,' the guard commanded. They held their breath. The guard raised his hand in the air and shook a non-existent pouch of money, to communicate what was expected.

Joseph hesitated. If he paid the guard now, the pig might easily take the money and refuse them entry. On the other hand, if he didn't show good faith, all could be lost. As he silently begged for God's help, Joseph reached into his sleeve and tossed the heavy pouch into the greedy hand that awaited it. Miraculously, it seemed, the guard stepped aside and allowed them to pass.

The enormity of the number of crosses was beyond their imagination. The faces, frozen in pain, covered in blood, were but one face. There was no way to recognize their beloved Yeshua. Still, they walked in the direction the guard had first taken until they stopped, both at the same cross, for they felt in whose shadow they stood.

Oh, that they might take his wounds as their own. They removed him as gently as they could and carried Yeshua past the small group of guards who believed him dead and demanded a few extra coins to allow them to pass.

The plan worked!

Once they had him secure at the sepulcher that Joseph had prepared for him, the Apostles would administer the antidote and Yeshua would wake. Oh, how he would laugh at the recounting of their deception and the victory they had extracted from the Romans. And Micah would welcome them to his cave where they would celebrate as one.

But all was not to go as smoothly as planned. Perhaps the Roman guard had not been as compliant as they had hoped or the other guards had grown suspicious. Perhaps Pilate had been bothered by rumors or, and this thought greatly worried Micah, perhaps one or more of the Apostles had betrayed their plan. But, in any case, Micah and Joseph were greeted at the burial room by Roman guards who had been stationed at the vault to guard the tomb in which Yeshua was to lie.

'What shall we do?' Micah cried to Joseph in desperation. 'He will not wake without the counteragent, and it cannot be administered until the effects of the elixir have had time to subside. If the antidote is given too soon or not soon enough, he will never awaken again.'

'Worry not,' Joseph assured him. 'The guards will allow me to come and go so that Yeshua may be prepared for burial. At sunset tomorrow, I shall go to the sepulcher and remove his body and bring him to the Apostles. There they will administer the antidote and all will be as you planned.'

'But how will we get him out of the sepulcher when the guards watch all that you do?' Micah asked.

'The guard changes watch at midday. The two who watch him now will not return until midnight,'

261

explained Joseph. 'When they return, in thanks for their consideration for allowing me to prepare Yeshua for ritual burial, I will arrange for a gift of wine to be delivered to them. They will be expecting some bribery, so all will seem as it should be. I know well those two who guard him. They will surely drink themselves into a stupor. I will have something added to the wine to help them on their way. After all, you are not the only one with knowledge of elixirs,' Joseph added in good humor, then he continued. 'As they sleep, I will bring Yeshua to the Apostles so he may take the antidote, and they will deliver him to you. I will join you all there, later, in the cave near Qumran where you wait.'

His voice grew ever more confident and Joseph continued. 'After I deliver Yeshua to the Apostles, I will quickly return to the sepulcher and, as the guards continue in their stupor, I will cover the opening to the sepulcher with a large stone so that they may not see that Yeshua is gone. I will explain that the stone will assure that none may enter or leave to do mischief or desecrate the body. These guards will not dare to tell anyone that they fell asleep from too much drink and did not see me move the stone into place. Since I shall have no complaint, who is there to question their obvious devotion to duty if they themselves make no trouble?'

Micah did not share Joseph's confidence. There were too many uncertainties for his liking.

I should have anticipated the possibility of the guards. What else might I have overlooked?

Joseph, placing a fatherly arm around Micah's shoulder, nodded in wordless understanding.

Good men blame themselves before they fault any other.

'Now, Micah, you must go!' Joseph announced. 'You must finish the preparation of the counteragent. By now, Bartholomew should be back at the stable with the special pungent myrrh you requested.'

Micah hesitated.

'Go,' Joseph commanded. 'The Apostles await you. In two days' time, you and Yeshua shall be together again.'

FORTY-EIGHT

Day Ten, late evening
Carlton Bay Hotel, London

Gil turned on the hot stream of water and washed off the dirt of the day. He could hear the sound of Sabbie showering in the room they had rented next door. By the time he was finished, she had returned; apparently with one objective in mind. Warm, welcoming, and completely naked, she waited for him stretched across the cool sheets. It was a dream come true and his body responded without hesitation.

'We both need a little tension release,' Sabbie said simply.

'What?'

'This will make us both sleep a lot better,' she continued soothingly.

A lump fought its way into his throat. Gil slipped under the covers and turned his back to

Sabbie. 'No, thanks,' he said over his shoulder.

'What? You're turning me down?' she said in surprise.

He could hardly believe it himself but he was still filled with the jealousy he had been plunged into at Sarkami's apartment. He was not about to let it go. He had been able to keep a lid on it by telling himself that as long as they were working as professionals, he had no right to feel jealous. But if they were about to get just about as personal as it goes, he had a right to his anger. The rush of pain he had felt when she looked at Sarkami would no longer be contained. Yesterday, Gil would have done anything to have her look at him in the way she had looked at that old eagle. Instead, she was offering to have sex with him as nothing more than a tension release.

Gil turned over and sat up. 'Do you realize that I know absolutely nothing about you?' he said accusingly. 'Not a goddamned thing.

'You're all business with me,' he continued. 'Then you're all warm and wonderful with everyone else.'

'Everyone else? Like who?' Sabbie retorted.

'Like Sarkami, like Ludlow.'

'Ludlow! My God, he was like a grandfather to me. He and Sarah took me in when I had no place to go. And Sarkami! You met him. Didn't you get it? He is simply the wisest and most principled man I have ever met. He would spare nothing, even his own life, to do what he thought was right. I don't know too many people like that. I doubt that you do either.

'What did you think?' she continued. 'That we were lovers? That I had a thing for older men?'

264

Gil flushed at the absurdity of his jealousy. What could he say? That he ached to hold her so much that he couldn't think straight, that he was crazy with his need to know her, to touch her mind and her body at the same time.

He shook his head, frustrated at his lack of words and his own asinine actions.

His search for the right words was fruitless. Even as the thoughts left his lips, he knew the tone was all wrong and that she was sure to misunderstand his intention.

'You never really say anything of yourself,' he said, far more accusingly than he felt. 'And you run hot and cold. First, you're all business, cool and professional, then suddenly you want to make love. I'm left hanging out to dry.'

'What do you want, one of those whining women who think that a litany of all the wrongs done to them in their lives is a prelude to sex?'

She was right. The fact that she didn't spill out her entire personal history was actually a pleasant and a welcome change. Still, there had to be some middle ground between spilling one's guts and playing the role of the ice maiden.

'Look,' he began, 'when you talk about the rape, you act as if it was . . .'

'The rape?' she said incredulously. Her face flushed with anger. 'Is that what you want? For me to tell you what it was like to be raped? What? You think that's sexy? Well, imagine this. A knife to your throat and four men tearing you apart and laughing at your agony. Watching your best friend's throat cut because she defended herself, then watching her body being mounted even as the last of her blood pours out. Imagine the hot burn

265

of piss on your face as your violators wring one last bit of degradation out of the experience.'

Gil stared, unable to move or to speak. Her images were burned into his mind forever and he was filled with shame at his own former arrogance.

Sabbie looked unblinkingly into his face, apparently struggling to hold onto the aloofness that had served her so well for so long. She nodded, almost imperceptibly, as if agreeing with the voice within that urged her to trust him with her secrets and her shame.

There was more to tell, she explained. A second rape, much more vile than the first. This one perpetrated by those with whom she lived and fought. The politics of the moment, it seemed, made it 'prudent' to forgo reporting the rape. Her superior officers at Aleph determined that the subsequent investigation of so sensational a crime might put the entire SWAT unit in jeopardy.

'I was told that, regrettably, the timing of my "incident" was less than ideal. Less than ideal,' she repeated. 'Aleph's budget was up for review and, given the changing public opinion about putting women in harm's way, the board of military advisors concluded that the less publicity about the incident the better.'

'But what happened to you had nothing to do with combat,' Gil said incredulously.

It made no difference, she said. 'They wanted no problems. I was a problem. Alana was less of a problem. She was dead. I demanded justice for both of us and they did what they had to do to shut me up.'

Sabbie had demanded a hearing. Aleph agreed. Her fellow soldiers and superior officers were in attendance. Those she counted on as character witnesses testified to her sexual promiscuity and lack of good judgment. Women who had fought side by side with her, women for whom she would have laid down her life, painted a picture of her as unstable and licentious. Friends, who had once urged her to date more, testified that she was a troubled young woman who regularly engaged in high-risk sexual behavior with multiple partners.

Her military service record, as well, was called into question. Small infractions, some of which she had never even been informed of, were magnified beyond recognition so that they might lend credence to Sabbie's lack of judgment and responsibility.

'You can make anyone look like anything if you really want to,' she said with a shrug.

'Alana's death was deemed inadmissible,' she continued. 'A separate hearing was slated for the following week. It was later canceled, of course, by request of Alana's parents. In the end, I did what I had to do.'

Sabbie had refused the honorable discharge Aleph had offered. Without explanation, she left in pursuit of the men responsible for the taking of her life as well as Alana's. Using skills Gil dared not imagine, Sabbie had extracted from the first of her attackers the names of the others.

'And, had it not been for Sarkami,' Sabbie concluded, 'I would have continued to take lives in hopes of a retribution that could never be realized.'

Gil straightened in surprise. Sarkami. What the hell did he have to do with all of this?

'Everything,' she said. Even as she put the last

bullet into her assailant's brain, Sarkami had happened unexpectedly upon the scene.

'I turned the gun on him,' Sabbie explained, 'though I didn't want to kill him. After all, he had done nothing to me,' she continued.

'To kill someone for what he has done to you or to another innocent soul, that was one thing. To kill someone simply because he has unwittingly witnessed your retaliation, that was another matter entirely.

'So we stood, face to face, I with my gun, the corpse at my feet. I don't know what I expected from him, horror, I suppose. Fear, at the very least.'

But neither was forthcoming. Instead, Sarkami calmly inquired as to how she intended to dispose of the body and whether it would be given an appropriate burial. With these words, Sabbie explained, Sarkami made her act of violence real to her and transformed her prey into a human being.

She told Sarkami her story, from beginning to end, in much the same way she was telling it to Gil, she added.

'Then he did the most incredible thing,' Sabbie said. 'He asked me how he might help.'

In that offering Sarkami had given Sabbie back her life. She was no longer an animal, fending for itself, in a world intent on consuming her alive. She was a human being capable of engendering sympathy in another. And compassion.

She had said all she had to say and she waited for Gil to say something in return. He struggled desperately for anything other than the usual words of comfort and sympathy.

In the end, he whispered only one phrase, a simple thought that came from his heart. 'I wish you hadn't had to go through all of that,' he said simply.

Sabbie looked at him with a wry smile, hesitated, then, without warning, it all fell apart. The wall. The anger. The distance. The horrendous hurt. Even what Gil assumed to be her rationalization of all that had happened.

It was all gone and she was crying, sobbing like he hadn't thought possible. Young and sad, terribly sad. Gil knew it was the first time that she had cried since that day when all had been lost.

When she had finished, he had held her, never speaking. He smoothed her hair, kissed her forehead, and had gone for toilet paper for a dozen nose blows. In the end, when she seemed all cried out, he covered her gently and brought a glass of water.

She reached for him, both arms around his neck and pulled him to her. Only then did they make love. Softly, strongly, honestly. They never stopped looking at each other, drinking up the sight, the smell, the joy of giving each other pleasure and of being alive.

FORTY-NINE

Day Eleven, early morning
Carlton Bay Hotel, London

It was a very sexy dream. Her body melded with his in perfect form and perfect rhythm. She rose to meet him with each thrust. Her excitement filled him with an anticipation he had never experienced and she climaxed with him, and he with her.

Gil awakened and cursed the shaft of sun that stabbed into his brain and pulled him from his sleep. Oh, how he ached to go back. Just a few more minutes. Just to smell her and touch her and pretend she was real. Then, in one warm wave of pleasure, it all came back to him. It hadn't been a dream.

He turned, reluctantly checking the time. 8:45. They hadn't fallen asleep until dawn. Even as he was drifting off she began to give him instructions on how to get the scroll back to the U.S. should he need to do it alone. He had tried to tease her out of her pessimistic predictions, but it had been of no use.

'You can put the scroll in the backpack and take it as carry-on luggage,' she had explained. 'It seems strange, I know, but there shouldn't be a problem. Even when it goes through security's X-ray machine, they won't question you. Their job is to look for anything that poses a potential threat. You're not about to blow up the plane with a scroll.'

Gil wasn't buying it. 'You just don't walk around

270

carrying an ancient copper scroll without someone asking you where you got it,' he argued.

'Actually, you do. When you get to customs in the U.S., they'll ask you if you have anything to declare. You say "no" because, in fact, you are bringing in nothing on their list of items for declaration. Chances are, they won't even check.'

'And if they do?'

'If they do, they'll check the scroll against a list of stolen items and your name against a list of felons. If neither you nor the scroll are listed, you pass right on through.'

The whole thing was moot, he concluded, given that she'd be coming with him.

'Oh, if I'm with you,' she said. 'That changes everything. I'm a convicted felon.'

She told him to get some rest while she went to the other room to check the street. No one had shown up all night. *A good sign*, Gil thought. Sabbie wasn't as optimistic.

'Please don't tell me you're one of those no-news-is-good-news people,' she said. 'I have no time for ostriches that bury their heads in the sand.'

Wisely, he had fought down the impulse to correct her misconception about animal behavior. It wasn't the time or place, he told himself. Besides, his track record had been far from sterling. Sabbie had been more on top of things than he had. Far more. More than he wanted to think about right then. And apparently, she required far less sleep.

Gil dragged himself to his feet and listened. No shower running. She was probably on the toilet.

He knocked on the door and got no response.

She was probably in the next room, checking out the street for the thousandth time. With anticipation he pushed the shower curtain aside and surrendered to the hottest, most satisfying shower he had experienced in a long, long time.

FIFTY

Day One following the Crucifixion, evening
North of Jerusalem

Micah paused to catch his breath. He had been walking as quickly as he could without attracting attention, and though Joseph said all was well, his chest was wrapped with bands of fear. He approached the stable carefully.

A faint light emanated from cracks in the stable wall. Was this a Roman trap? Set, perhaps, for the Apostles? Or for him? No, nothing could have happened with such haste. With the exception of the Apostles and Joseph, all thought Yeshua lay dead in the sepulcher.

Stealthily, Micah drew closer. Several of the voices were known to him. Clutching the precious bag of ingredients for the brew that would save Yeshua's life, Micah waited and listened.

Peter's deep voice was the easiest to recognize. 'We have to look out for ourselves as well. It was by the grace of God that we too were not arrested and hung on crosses beside him. His actions have angered too many. He has put us all in danger.'

'I agree,' Bartholomew concurred. 'And who would be there to save us? He has gone too far this

272

time, challenging the Priests and the Pharisees. I told you that we should have gone to Galilee for Passover. He would not have offended the authorities there.'

Micah flushed with anger. He peered through a crack as James began to speak. 'As long as he lives, he presents a danger to us all. You all know it is true. I will say what none of you has the courage to say. It is better for all of us if he never wakes.'

Thomas rose and, as was his custom, spread his arms wide to emphasize his words. 'We first followed him in the promise that he would become King of the Jews and that we would prosper as one of his inner circle. That promise is now like smoke from a fire; it rises and disappears. I for one believe it to be nothing more than good judgment to rid ourselves of the malevolence he will bring down upon us if he remains alive. He no longer serves our purposes or his own.'

'Or that of his God,' another added.

The cold breath of anger caught in Micah's throat.

Traitors! How much Yeshua had done for them and this is how he was to be repaid. Were these just words of dissatisfied rabble, chewing their cud of discontent, or were they really contemplating bodily harm to he who took them in and made them holy?

Only moments ago, such a display would have been unthinkable. Now he was bearing witness to words so dark and sinister that only Satan himself could have uttered them.

With all that had transpired the last few days, could it be that he and Joseph were all that stood between Yeshua and death? A darker thought yet, entered his heart. Could Joseph still be trusted or was he, too, part of this heinous conspiracy?

No, not Joseph, of that Micah was certain. Together they had carried Yeshua's bloodied and broken body from the hill and, with each step, the good man from Arimathea had wept deep silent tears of grief. Of all, he was to be trusted. Micah's face flushed with shame at so disloyal, if brief, a contemplation.

So this is was what it has come to.

The night was still and growing cool. Micah forced himself to continue to listen through the stable cracks.

Thaddaeus was next to speak. 'Could we not just spirit him far enough away so that we could be left in peace to continue our work?'

At last one who speaks for Yeshua!

The silence that followed gave voice to the condemnation of Thaddaeus' words.

Matthew, who had remained quiet, now spoke. 'We know three things about the Priests and the Pharisees: they hate Yeshua, they hold the reins of power, and they have the ear of Pontius Pilate. If Yeshua lives, the Romans would hunt him to the ends of the earth and, as we too would bear the stain of his name, we shall be hunted. I must agree with James say with candor what we all already know, that Yeshua serves us better dead than alive.'

Filled with his own certainty, Matthew continued. 'Yeshua's death will provide the people with a martyr, someone to worship and rally against the Priests, Romans, and Pharisees. We, his Apostles, will be exalted only if history does not view Yeshua as a rabble-rouser and troublemaker.

And that view depends on the decisions—hard decisions—we make here today. With courage, one of us still may be regarded King of the Jews.'

'God willing,' said another voice, and they all laughed.

Micah could no longer force himself to listen. He fought to get control of his fury and entered the stable. With ostensibly warm camaraderie, he related the tale of trickery that he and Joseph had perpetrated upon the Roman guard, their successful retrieval of Yeshua from the cross, and the placement of Yeshua in Joseph's sepulcher.

The others listened as Micah informed them of Pilate's assignment of Roman guards at the entrance of the sepulcher. Had he not heard their evil plans, Micah might have assumed the Apostles' concern was for Yeshua's safety, but now, with knowledge of their intent, Micah understood that each of the Apostles feared that Yeshua might yet recover and, in so doing, put each of them in danger.

With obvious relief and jubilance, they welcomed the news that Joseph of Arimathea planned to deliver Yeshua to them at the close of the Sabbath. Fighting back the tears, Micah understood why the news was so well received. He and Joseph would soon be delivering Yeshua's life into their hands.

Micah continued the charade that the others had begun. He explained that he must remove himself so that he might prepare the counteragent intended to revive Yeshua. He bid them good rest and told them that he would wake Peter when all was in readiness.

As he removed himself to a small shack adjacent

275

to the stable, Micah wondered if he, too, was slated for the same fate as Yeshua? Probably so, he thought, yet he had no fear.

As he prepared the antidote, Micah began to devise a way in which he might yet take back Yeshua's life from the hands of those who would rob him of it.

With each passing hour, Micah fought his body's demand for rest much as he would fight any enemy reaching to snatch Yeshua's life. His eyes grew heavy and his body ached for sleep, yet Micah worked through the night. As the preparation of the counteragent was completed, so was the secret plan that Micah prayed would succeed.

Micah mixed a few drops of the strong-smelling counteragent with some of the unfinished wine from dinner and poured the concoction into a small flask. He was sure that this 'false brew' would never reach Yeshua's lips. If Yeshua were to be saved, it would be up to Micah to retain the real counteragent.

Micah placed the flask that contained the false brew on the makeshift table where the still-sleeping Apostles were certain to find it and then prepared for his own journey. After he carefully siphoned the remaining counteragent into a small earthen vial, he returned the stopper and placed it within his travel pouch, taking care that it would not spill.

With the vial safely out of view, Micah roused Peter and informed him that the antidote was finished and had been placed on the table. Barely awake, Peter listened while Micah gave him instructions on how and when to administer the bogus brew.

After he concluded his instructions to Peter, Micah added that he was leaving for his cave immediately and would meet them all there, then he allowed Peter to drift back to sleep.

In the moonlight, Micah looked once more at the men who slept, the men who called themselves Yeshua's Apostles. Then he left the stable, mounted his mule and as the moon still hung heavy in the sky, headed for the home of Joseph of Arimathea.

FIFTY-ONE

Day Eleven, mid-morning
Carlton Bay Hotel, London

Ten o'clock came and went and still no Sabbie.

She wouldn't have gone out alone, not without giving me one of her in-case-you-never-see-me-again lectures.

Gil stopped short. Suddenly Sabbie's predictions of doom didn't sound quite so silly. No, he was being ridiculous. She had gone out for breakfast or a paper. She probably planned to get back before he had awakened but something had come up. Maybe she'd gone over to Sarkami's to get the scroll by herself.

Gil pushed the thought of a morning liaison out of his mind.

He longed to see her come through the door. He would yell at her for not leaving a note and they would have a good fight, then a good laugh about how silly he had been to be worried. The minutes passed. She didn't come through the door and she didn't call.

When Gil ran out of I'll-just-wait-five-more-minutes promises to himself, he formulated a plan. Three things had to be done. He needed to see if Sabbie had gone to Sarkami's and, if she hadn't, he needed to inform Sarkami that she was missing; he needed to get Sarkami's help in finding her; and he needed to get the scroll back. All of which involved making his way back to Sarkami's.

Gil had managed to get a look at the second intersection they passed when they left Sarkami's house the night before. The cab had stopped under a conveniently well-lit corner, and Gil had made note of the street names though, at the time, he had no idea why. Now, they were the most important two words in his vocabulary. The third was 'money.'

Gil dug into his pants pocket in search of the one credit card he had not surrendered to Sabbie. If he could find an ATM, he could get all the money he'd need and in the right currency as well. Then, all he'd require would be directions to the intersection near Sarkami's house.

A sudden recollection brought a smile of satisfaction. Gil reached into the back pocket of his pants and pulled out his PDA. He had not opened it since he left CyberNet. An ache of longing washed over him. He missed his work, his home, and his life. He even missed George. Well, almost.

Gil typed in a request for a local ATM, and the PDA's Global Positioning System sprang into action. Money awaited him out the door and two blocks to the left. He added a request for the

278

intersection. From there, Gil could reconstruct the trail back to Sarkami's by following the odd snaking back alley until he came to a green door equipped with four locks. His PDA offered a choice of maps or step-by-step directions.

Gil's mood soared. He would find Sabbie at Sarkami's, he was certain. Chances were, she had convinced herself it was safer for her to go out alone and intended to surprise him, still sleeping in their hotel room, with the scroll, all neatly cut into strips upon her return. Or else, she'd give him a spiel on why she couldn't be expected to wait around all day for him to wake up and add that she had every intention of calling him when she got a chance. In either case, he'd be glad as hell to see her.

Gil grabbed his clothes and made his way for the door. He was starting to feel like his old confident self again. So confident that he never even bothered to check out the street before he left his room.

FIFTY-TWO

Day Two following the Crucifixion, morning
Home of Joseph of Arimathea, Judea

Joseph, face set, sat unmoving. 'I need not ask you if you are certain of what you heard,' he said.

'I wish that it were untrue but I swear to you, Joseph, it is as I have described. I bring this antidote to you and beg you to administer it. I know not who else to trust.'

'But the false potion you left them, what if they administer it to Yeshua?'

'It will do him no harm, but I know it shall never reach his lips,' Micah added with sadness. 'You must go to Yeshua and remove him to safety before they can reach him. I can do nothing else for him now.'

'Then it is up to me,' Joseph agreed. 'I thought to bring Yeshua to them long before morning. The guards known to me shall come to the watch at midnight. But now I am afraid to wait . . .'

'Peter and the others sleep soundly and will not be awake until morning,' said Micah.

'As if they might enjoy sleep of the just,' Joseph said bitterly, then waited for Micah to instruct him further.

It was all laid out in a matter of minutes. Joseph insisted that Micah take his horse rather than Micah's ass, arguing that the steed would get Micah to the cave more quickly in order to make things ready.

'I have no use for my horse,' explained Joseph. 'If I am successful and I am able to bring Yeshua to you, it would be best for both of us to ride separate asses. The sight of both of us on a single horse would draw too much attention. We must each ride separate asses so as to not draw anyone's attention. If, God forbid, I am unsuccessful and am unable to remove Yeshua from the sepulcher, I will have no need for the speed that a horse could provide.

'You, on the other hand,' Joseph continued, 'will do well to have a steed for your use should you need to make a rapid escape from the cave.'

They embraced, for a moment longer than they

had on their partings in the past, and with more unsaid than spoken, bade each other well.

*   *   *

Micah's ride to his cave at Qumran had been swift and uneventful, yet his mind had been filled with far too many fears and too great a sadness to find any pleasure in the journey.

He entered the cave of his youth. The smell of damp earth welcomed him with a fragrance that was pungent and wonderfully familiar. All was exactly as Micah had left it. In the many years since he had been to the secret cave of his childhood, not a rock had been moved and, as far as he could tell, no one had entered his hiding place. Within the loving cool walls of the chamber, his tools and his precious hoard of silver and copper awaited his return.

He was home again, welcomed by memories of pleasure and safety of the only sanctuary he had ever known. In his youth, he had spent countless hours secretly perfecting the metal-crafting skills that had later afforded him the means of survival; here he had first imagined a life of purpose and meaning beyond that of financial wealth. Here he had felt his life begin and, ironically, here it might end as well.

There would be but one day at best in which to complete the tasks. Micah forced down the feeling of panic that rose in his chest and tried to organize his thoughts. If he ran out of time, everything would be lost. It wasn't going to work, he thought. He couldn't complete the scroll if he had twice the time than that which remained. Even if the message was already composed, which it was not, the simple act of preparing the copper sheet and then carefully pressing his message into it would require more time than it would take for them to follow him. And then the greater task that awaited him. If that was not completed then Yeshua's life, his own, and perhaps that of all those who walked the face of the earth, would be for naught.

A new wave of fear caught Micah in its grip and with it the realization that hunger, rather than fear, was causing the queasiness. He had not slept nor eaten for a day and a half, and he could push himself no longer.

He dug deep into his bag and retrieved the pouch of food he had all but forgotten. The strong smell of the rancid cheese brought tears to Micah's eyes. This would not serve him. He retrieved his wine skin and a large piece of hard bread from a second pouch. He ate and drank while he worked.

The first section of the scroll, a history of the travesty wrought upon Yeshua, had to be related in detail. Future generations would bear witness to all that had taken place, to the unforgivable betrayal as well as to the unmatched courage of he who had been wronged. While this section of the scroll must be faithful to the events, the words to be chosen were not of critical import.

It was the second section, however, that troubled Micah. It was here in this, the inner part of the scroll, that each mark pressed into the soft copper sheet had to be exact. A single error might render the writings useless, writings that bore the secret that had been passed down to Yeshua and upon which the future of mankind rested.

Yet, though a single error might bring about the

most disastrous of results, too much care might well mean that Micah would not complete his task in time. Too quick and imprecise and all would be lost. Too slow and all would be lost as well.

Micah forced down the fear in his chest. He would not allow himself to think of all that depended on this moment. His skill, his determination, and, most of all, Yeshua's love that lived within him would not allow either message to be lost.

On the way from Joseph's, he had worried that there might not be enough copper to inscribe the tale and complete his tasks. Upon his arrival he had rediscovered the storehouse of copper sheeting from his youth. He had realized there was more than enough copper sheeting for the scroll, enough for two scrolls.

And, with that thought, all became clear. He would make not one but, rather, two scrolls. The first would bear witness to Yeshua's wisdom, his teachings, and the ultimate betrayal of those he trusted most. In this scroll, Micah would include that which would ensure the survival of the generations to come, that secret Yeshua had revealed to him.

In the second scroll, the false one, he would hide a message within the other message, a signpost to the righteous that would point the way to the true scroll.

He would hide the true scroll in a small chamber at the back of the cave that could only be reached by crawling on one's belly through a labyrinth of twists and turns. It was a place that he found when he was a sinewy child. Smiling, he reminded himself that he was no longer a sinewy youth. Still, he felt confident that he could negotiate the passage.

He would place the copper scroll that bore the true message in the tar-covered box that he had used to store his most precious tools. He could warm the tar with the flame of the oil lamp once more so that it might be sealed. He would place the box in the chamber at the end of the passage and there it would remain, to await the worthy soul that might find it and deliver it to the one for whom it was intended.

The false scroll he would hide in one of the nearby caves in which the Essenes stored their most precious documents. This second scroll he would fill with a spurious list of treasures and false locations so as to mislead those unworthy of the message of the true scroll.

Micah smiled at the simplicity of it all. The false scroll, by virtue of it being a listing of treasures, insured that upon its discovery it would be treated well and brought to light as quickly as possible. He who was unworthy of the message of the true scroll would see only the reflection of his greed. He, who was righteous and worthy, would see beyond the simple words, to the message within, the message that would lead him to the true scroll.

Yet Micah could not imagine how he might accomplish so prodigious a task. Two scrolls now, when there wasn't enough time for one. And a hidden message, so written as to conceal its meaning from the eyes of the unworthy while revealing it to the righteous.

I cannot do it.

His heart sank in despair. Could it be that the story of betrayal would never be told? Far worse, might the secret that had been passed down to Yeshua be lost forever and with it, might all of mankind, itself, be doomed?

Micah closed his eyes and brought to his heart and mind the face of his friend.

'Yeshua,' he thought. 'All is lost, for I fear I shall fail you.'

The image of his dear friend seemed to appear among the shadows at the far end of the cave.

'You shall not fail,' Yeshua whispered softly, and then, as quickly as he appeared, he was gone.

Even as the image faded, so a warmth seemed to rise from the copper with which he crafted the scroll, a warmth unlike any that Micah had ever felt.

Where only moments ago his arms were weary, now they pulsed with strength; where his heart had felt fear and his mind was clouded, only power and purpose remained.

Micah worked with deliberation and skill. His mind empty, as if guided by another and, in the ribbon of hours that lay between sunset and sunrise, he completed the task with ease and grace.

By the time he heard the quick clops of hooves on the gravel, all was in readiness. The false scroll lay behind a pile of rocks in one of the Essenes' cave and the true scroll had been secured in the hidden chamber at the back of Micah's cave. Both scrolls had been blessed with prayers. With all evidence of his labor of love well-hidden Micah moved to the entrance of his cave and waited for what God had planned for him.

FIFTY-THREE

Day Eleven, late morning
Hillingdon Town Centre, London

Within half an hour, Gil had withdrawn all the cash he needed from the ATM, hailed a cab, and backtracked his way to Sarkami's. The scene he imagined was always the same. He'd knock, Sarkami would answer, and Sabbie would be looking over the strips of copper and making notes on her translation.

In one variation of his fantasy, she'd be impressed that he had sleuthed his way back without any help. In another variation, she would have been trying to reach him at the hotel. She'd be angry and relieved at the same time to see him walk through Sarkami's door. Either scenario suited him just fine.

What he discovered, however, bore no resemblance to anything he had imagined. Small deep gouges cut into the green paint and exposed splinters of wood around each of Sarkami's locks that had so neatly secured the back door. Two of the locks had been pried half off and the others were missing. Gil hesitated, not certain that he wanted to enter, not able to imagine what other choice he might have.

He glanced at the nearby intersection where cars and trucks rumbled by and planned the fastest route to that haven of activity should the need arise. Soundlessly, he turned the knob, ready to slam it closed at the slightest provocation. The room that greeted him was indistinguishable from the one that had greeted him the night before. No tables had been overturned, no books thrown about, no signs, whatsoever, of a struggle. Gil moved in slowly for a better look, careful to leave the door open for a rapid exit.

The worktables remained untouched. As it did last night, the long clean table bore the same parchment sections, faux facsimile scrolls, and copper strips. Gil didn't know whether to feel relieved or concerned. Nothing made sense.

If Sarkami had begun to cut up the copper scroll, some evidence of his work should have been apparent. A jewelry saw, some copper filings, the cloth on which he would be doing the work, something should still remain. If Sarkami and the scroll had been taken by force, there should have been evidence of a struggle, which there was not.

Gil looked anxiously around the room, half expecting to see Sabbie's two shopping bags as she had left them last night. Nothing. No bags, no scroll, nothing to show that he or Sabbie had ever been there.

Silently, Gil moved toward the bedroom. He had not seen the room the night before. Though quite a bit neater than the living room/workroom, it looked like any bedroom might. Only a yellow flowered sweater, half hanging off the bed, marred the tidiness of the white cotton bedspread. Gil's heart pounded with a recognition that swept up and swallowed him.

This was Sabbie's sweater, the bright yellow sweater she wore every day, the yellow sweater that he had kept in view as they ran through the train station, the silly yellow sweater that he had always meant to tease her about, the one she had been wearing early this morning at the hotel when she went to the empty room to check on what was happening in the street. The flowers he thought it held weren't flowers at all. They were brown splotches of blood. Her blood.

Terror rose in Gil's throat. The blood glistened. *Was it still wet?*

His heart pounded so hard he could barely breathe. Slowly, he reached to touch the sweater. The largest brown stain was wet and sticky. Gil drew it to his nose in hopes that he would discover it was not what he knew it to be. It had no smell.

The only way to be sure is to taste it.

He couldn't. It would be too . . .

Gil never finished the thought. The thin iron rod caught him squarely at the back of the neck. The yellow sweater with its brown splotches fell to the floor and, next to it, so did Gil.

FIFTY-FOUR

Day Three following the Crucifixion, morning
The Caves of Qumran, Judea

The figure of Joseph of Arimathea appeared in relief against the cloudless sky. Micah raced to him in anticipation of seeing Yeshua by his side. Joseph rode alone.

'It is done. Finished. They did just as you said,' Joseph reported flatly. Then he wept into his hands.

'He's dead?' cried Micah. 'Peter, James, the others . . . they . . .'

Joseph lifted his tearstained face and said, 'They came just after the guards fell asleep. They must have been waiting, watching. Even as I entered the sepulcher, they came with some others I did not recognize. Several of them overpowered me and held me while they removed his body.

'I begged them to let me attend to him,' Joseph said plaintively. 'They laughed, pouring the contents of the flask you left for him into the dirt. Then they took him away. Those who remained encircled the sepulcher and, as others approached upon hearing the commotion, these liars began shouting in ecstasy, crying out tales of Yeshua rising to the heavens.'

Micah could not believe what he was hearing. 'The people believed them?' he asked incredulously.

'People believe what they want to believe. Much as you and I, these faithful did not want to know that he was gone.'

'What about the guards?'

'The commotion aroused them from their stupor and, seeing that Yeshua was gone, they became fearful. So grave a transgression might easily mean a reprisal in the form of their own death, so they joined in as witnesses to the apparition's ascent.'

Micah's face reflected the anguish in his heart. 'No,' he cried. 'I didn't think them capable of carrying out such falsehoods. Not about the dead.'

'Nor I,' agreed Joseph. 'These are but mere guards, you know. But their terror made them shrewd. Even now they are claiming that Yeshua foresaw his sacrifice on the cross and, in so doing, foretold of his resurrection.'

Shaking his head in disbelief, Micah asked, 'But

what have they done with him?'

Joseph began to sob once again. 'I know not what happened to him. I do not even know if he was still alive when they took him.'

'They will not let him live,' Micah whispered. 'It would make no sense. Otherwise, why would they have discarded what they thought to be the counteragent? No, they have killed him. As surely as if they had crushed him with their bare hands.'

'I could do nothing,' wept Joseph. 'If only I had been able to give him the antidote.'

'I know, dear friend,' Micah said softly as he wrapped his arm around Joseph's shaking body, 'I know.'

Micah stepped back and in a voice that grew strong, he gave careful instruction to his friend. Though he knew not why, he spoke only of the false scroll. 'There is a scroll, Joseph. I have placed it in one of the Essenes' caves up on the hill. It's hidden in the back, behind the rocks. Flavius Josephus and I ventured there when we were under tutorage together. It was a place for us to play as adventurers. He will remember.'

'What would you have me do?' Joseph asked.

'Do nothing for now. Relate to Flavius my words and bid him take you to the cave, but do not allow either of you to be tempted to look for the scroll. Simply put to memory the cave's location and knowledge of the scroll's existence. The secret of where it resides should be with you both so it is not lost. Then watch and take note if the scroll is discovered by others.'

'And if it is not?' asked Joseph.

'Then if either you or Flavius dies, let the other reveal its location to two others worthy of such

290

knowledge. Two others who are as honest and righteous as you and Flavius are. Good men are neither tempted by greed nor seduced by profit. Entreat them to do as I bid you and Flavius. Let one of those two pass on the secret location to two others who in turn will do the same for generations to come until it is time for the light of day to fall upon the message borne in the scroll. Much time may pass before it is discovered. By that time, man may be in need of the truth, especially if men such as these twelve continue to be revered and rewarded.'

'Do you think they will revere it then, those who uncover it in the time to come?' queried Joseph.

For a moment, doubt found its way into Micah's thoughts. He had not permitted himself the thought until the words of his friend struck terror in his heart. What if no one saw past the first scroll's ruse of treasure? What if no one ever found the second scroll? Suppose the truth was never revealed? Even worse, suppose the truth revealed was of no importance to those who were yet to come? Then mankind would be doomed.

No! He would not allow himself to waiver in his faith. Someday, a righteous man would find the trail he had left. He would discover the message and the truth it revealed and he would use it to undo all of the lies that the Apostles might yet perpetrate in the generations to come. And, when all was done, that soul for which the scroll had waited would recite the words on which man's fate rested.

A soft breeze caressed Micah's check. He breathed it in and was at peace. All would come to pass as it should. He could see it now as clearly as the sun and clouds and trees that stood before him; as clearly as the worried, tired look on his good friend's face.

'You must leave now, Joseph,' Micah commanded. 'You must leave immediately. They will soon be here. I have shown them the way in my map.'

'But there is still time for you to leave, too. You have the horse . . .' Joseph argued.

Micah's face shone with a faint smile. 'There is nothing that I fear now.'

Micah walked Joseph to the horse and turned the steed toward Arimathea. 'Know this before you leave, dear friend,' Micah began. 'Those who will desecrate his memory with falsehoods will not succeed. Yeshua lives. He lives now as he shall live forever more. Not only in our memory but also in the hearts of those who shall never have known him.'

Micah continued in earnest. 'Yeshua once said that it was better to falter in truth than to believe in lies. Because of your help, the Yeshua that future generations will know shall be the real Yeshua. His truth shall live on and it shall, indeed, set them free.'

The two men embraced, and Micah watched as Joseph rode off, the sun already fading over the horizon.

Why did you not tell Joseph of the other scroll?

Micah smiled. Man must fight for that which he holds most dear. In the sacrifice, the soul is cleansed.

He waited. The familiar sound of hooves would soon bring twelve men who would complete that which remained unfinished. He was not afraid.

292

FIFTY-FIVE

Day Thirteen, late afternoon
Muslims for World Truth (MWT)
Video Production Studios
London

Gil struggled toward consciousness. The smell of
sweat was so strong he could taste it. Instinctively,
he jerked his head back then, when he realized it
was the smell of his own body, he fell back
gratefully into a deep sleep.

He was twelve years old again, running free in
the hot country sun, aching with the thrill of
exploring the world on his own. The school term
was finished and he had been liberated. Suddenly,
the bright day of the dream dissolved into the dark
reality of a filthy mattress in a stifling warehouse
room. He was anything but free.

Pain shot from deep within his groin; a
paralyzing ache that grabbed his spine and twisted.
He moaned.

'The toilet's in there,' the small man said,
pointing to a gray door at the far side of the room.

Gil leaped from the bed and bolted into the
bathroom, dry heaved into a filthy toilet, then
urinated for a full minute. The pain vanished.

God. It must have been a year since I peed.

Some vague memory of a hulk of a man flashed
across his mind then disappeared.

A jackhammer began in the back of his head,
and he leaned his forehead against the cool
bathroom wall. It felt good. He wanted to stay

there forever. Feeling the softening growth of beard, he judged it had been more than two days since his last shave, which meant he'd been here for at least twenty-four hours, maybe thirty-six. He was weak and his stomach cramped with hunger. It must have been that long since he had eaten.

The voice from the other room interrupted his thoughts. 'There's water and food waiting for you when you're done.'

Gil strained to identify the accent. It sounded British. From the quick look he had managed on his rush to the toilet, he assumed the accent would be Middle Eastern.

Formal training. He probably comes from oil wealth. So what is he doing in this pit?

Hunger twisted in his stomach. With a promise to himself that he would not speak—no matter what the consequences—Gil returned to his kidnapper and to the food and drink that waited.

Beyond noncompliance, his plan was simple. He would accept nourishment in order to retain his strength. He would gather any information he could, wait for the right time and place, then make a move to break free. He wasn't fooling himself; he knew it wasn't much of a plan, but it made him feel less panicky. Most of all, it allowed him to satisfy the nagging voice that accused him of selling out to the enemy for the price of a little food.

Returning to the filthy bed, Gil tried to focus on the face of his kidnapper. A crescent scar was set deeply into his dark cheek. He wore a camel hair sport jacket that looked as if it had been tailored to fit his well-toned body. His captor smiled pleasantly. This was not the expected image of a ruthless killer.

294

The image of Sabbie's bloodstained sweater flashed across Gil's mind. This man had taken Sarkami, waited for Sabbie, and had done God knows what with her. Then he had lain in wait for Gil and had kidnapped him. This was the one that Sabbie had spotted outside of Ludlow's apartment. This was the new player that had her so worried.

Gil knew it with a certainty that sickened him more than his empty stomach. Wherever this man went, death followed. Now the perfectly dressed little killer had him in the palm of his hand.

Gil looked into the eyes of his abductor. The man stared back with obvious amusement, introduced himself as Abdul Maluka, then offered Gil a cold bottle of Perrier and a plate of crackers.

'These will ease your stomach. When you can tolerate more, it will be brought,' Maluka said. 'We take care of our guests.'

Guest, my ass. I'm your prisoner.

Gil's mind snapped to attention.

He said 'guests.' Plural. Who else are they holding? Sabbie perhaps. Or Sarkami.

Gil accepted the food and drink and tried hard not to show his desperation. He turned from his kidnapper and allowed his eyes to scan the room as he ate.

The gray walls were twenty-feet high; twice that in width. No windows and just two doors, one of which led to the bathroom. The only light came from overhead fluorescent lights. His prison looked like any of a million warehouse rooms. He could be anywhere.

'You have been drugged,' Maluka began. 'You will experience a variety of unpleasant aftereffects including cramps and nausea but they will wear off in time.'

In time! Well, at least you're not intending to kill me straight away.

'The pain in your head and neck are due to the impact you sustained from Aijaz,' Maluka continued. He pointed to the hulk of a man who stood at the door. Maluka nodded and Aijaz disappeared.

Gil turned and faced Maluka. 'What have you done with Sabbie?'

Maluka's eyes narrowed as he nodded his head approvingly. 'Very clever, Mr. Pearson, but that approach won't work on me.'

Gil tried to make sense of the response.

'Within moments of our hasty departure from Sarkami's home, the police arrived. Even they were not fooled,' Maluka went on. 'It was a very amateurish crime scene, you know. Obviously staged.'

'What crime scene?' Gil asked.

A thin smile formed on Maluka's lips. 'The one that Sarkami and Sabbie staged to make it look as if she had been injured and captured, of course. But, now, we have more important things to discuss.'

'Why the hell would Sabbie and Sarkami stage a crime scene?'

'I must assume that you were truly ignorant of their plans or you would have left with them. I cannot, however, bring myself to believe that upon seeing the evidence, you did not conclude that you had been duped,' Maluka concluded.

'She wouldn't do that,' Gil said simply. He hoped his words carried more conviction than he felt. 'Look, I know you took her. Why don't you just tell me the truth? I can't do anything to you.'

'Exactly. Neither could she, so why should we murder her?'

The image of Maluka's man, lying flat in the Monastery courtyard, flashed across Gil's mind. If Sabbie had killed him, Gil felt certain Maluka would not hesitate to take revenge.

'Hassan's death was an unfortunate accident,' Maluka answered as if he heard Gil's thoughts. 'He had a bad heart, an affliction that I learned about only after his recent demise. Besides, I do not kill for revenge.'

Then you do kill for other reasons. Well, that's certainly comforting.

The whole thing made no sense. Maluka obviously had no clue as to Sabbie's whereabouts. Why else would he be asking him? And if Maluka had the scroll, which he would have captured along with Sabbie, Gil wouldn't be sitting there. So Maluka needed something from him. The question was, what was it?

'And what about Ludlow?' Gil asked. The best way to learn about someone was to ask them a question to which you already know the answer.

'Ludlow's death was not of my doing. I should think Dr. DeVris would be the more appropriate person to ask.'

DeVris!

Gil had expected Maluka to place the blame for Ludlow's death on McCullum. That would have confirmed Sabbie's report to Sarkami. But DeVris!

There was only one conclusion: Maluka didn't know about WATSC's involvement. Without knowing about McCullum, it would have been a safe assumption that DeVris had been directly involved in Ludlow's death. It was the most reasonable and logical conclusion. And it showed where Maluka's blind spot was.

But why doesn't Maluka know about McCullum? Or is he just putting on a good show to see if he can catch me in a lie?

Gil's life could depend on the answer. If, on one hand, Maluka was just pretending to have no knowledge of McCullum, then withholding that info could prove to Maluka that Gil could not be trusted. Gil, then, would be expendable.

If, on the other hand, Maluka truly had no knowledge of McCullum, providing information about McCullum could give Maluka all that he needed. Once again, Gil would be expendable.

What was it Sabbie said to Sarkami? McCullum must have stopped using e-mail and was, therefore, invisible to her detection. McCullum must have remained invisible to Hassan as well. That would have left Maluka without a clue as to McCullum's involvement.

Maluka spoke more sternly. 'Now, I think I've been extremely patient. I could use drugs to obtain the information I need, but I rather think you might be bright enough to resist them. Besides, I prefer a good match of wits. In any case, I would hope that you cooperate so that there will be no need to bring Aijaz in to assist. He's watching television right now, and when he's disturbed, he can get very cranky.'

Maluka's demands were very simple: a complete recital of all that had transpired between Sabbie and Sarkami. 'If there were times when you were not privy to their communication, I need to know that as well.'

He reminded Gil that he believed Sabbie and Sarkami had not included Gil in their little conspiracy, but explained that he thought Gil knew more than even he might be aware.

'Whatever you saw, heard, even what crossed your mind, may be of great use to me,' Maluka said. 'Your job is to tell me what you've seen and heard. Mine is to interpret.'

Gil needed time to think, time to figure out what the hell was going on. Was it possible that Sabbie and Sarkami had staged the whole thing? Was the bloody sweater nothing more than a ploy to throw him off track?

Why else would Sabbie have had to leave the room to talk to Sarkami in private?

Everything indicated that he was being played for a fool. Her secrets, her aloofness, her intimacy with Sarkami. The last thought cut like a knife. She left him at the hotel and had taken off with Sarkami and the scroll.

And left me holding the bag!

A single thought played at the back of Gil's mind.

McCullum's boys.

Suppose McCullum's boys had taken her and Sarkami and the scroll. Gil had no proof of either scenario yet each would dictate a completely different way of dealing with Maluka.

If she had gone with Sarkami of her own free will, she could be expected to sell the scroll to the highest bidder. Since there were people who would pay a lot more to hide something than to reveal it, the scroll would most likely never see the light of day again. In that case, Gil had nothing to lose by telling Maluka all he wanted to know. At least with

299

Maluka, there was a chance, depending on what the scroll might yet reveal, that its message might still be shared with the world.

On the other hand, if Sabbie had been taken by McCullum's boys, everything could be lost by telling Maluka all he knew. Just the mention of McCullum's name might give Maluka the information he needed to put Sabbie's life, Sarkami's life, and the scroll's message in jeopardy. It was a lose-lose situation with nothing to go on, everything at stake, and seconds to make a decision.

FIFTY-SIX

A few minutes later

It was a stupid decision, but he had no other choice. There was no way he was going to tell Maluka the truth. Screw the evidence, there was no way she had betrayed him. Or the scroll. It simply was not possible. And if she had, nothing else mattered anyway. He was going to bluff the bastard all the way or die trying.

Wrong choice of words.

The hours that followed were filled with the most creative line of bullshit Gil had ever manufactured. Fueled by what he pretended to be his fury at being duped, Gil recalled imaginary conversations about fictitious parties.

Gil had no difficulty keeping track of the lies. He simply assigned each imaginary person a method, means, and opportunity for a given outcome, then wove their actions into patterns that were easily remembered. More than one of Gil's previously apprehended suspects, complete with new names and motivations, made their way into his supposedly recalled conversations.

At first, Gil wasn't certain that his captor would buy his well-crafted lies but, as the hours passed, and Gil was able to keep his facts consistent and believable, it looked like he was going to pull it off.

Luck had been with Gil from the start. He had begun by prefacing his bogus report on information he had supposedly gleaned from Sarkami's conversation with Sabbie. It had been a particularly fortuitous premise. Like McCullum, Sarkami was a blind spot for Maluka. Sarkami's comings and goings, his connections, his dealings, were all unknown to Maluka. Gil's information, then, could neither be verified nor disproved.

Had Gil chosen Sabbie as his source, Maluka might have known instantly that he was lying. Assuming that Maluka was holding her captive as well, Gil had no desire to linger on what those consequences might have entailed. Or, for that matter, what might be waiting for him when he was no longer considered useful to Maluka.

No matter. He had no control over that. For now, he'd keep spinning his tales and hope that he didn't lose track of the dozens of threads he was weaving.

*　　　*　　　*

Maluka had been quizzing Gil on the details of Sarkami's information for at least four hours. Probably more. Gil closed his eyes. He needed

301

rest. He needed it desperately.

The food he had been promised had never arrived.

'We're in the warehouse above my production office,' Maluka had explained. 'You will be getting food shortly, as soon as the late shift retires for the evening.'

He wasn't certain how long he could keep his mind clear. Twice in the last half hour he had caught himself just before he contradicted himself on a previous lie. Maluka was quick, but he was quicker. At least for the moment.

Maluka checked over his notes. Gil waited for him to make his next move. It came not from Maluka, however, but from the sound of the door being slammed open.

Aijaz unceremoniously dumped the body before them like a rag doll. The man's hair was gray and greasy, his face was pale and slack. Aijaz smiled with childlike affection at Maluka, much like a cat that had delivered a tattered mouse to the feet of his owner.

'He don't know nothin',' the mountain of a man reported, then he waited for confirmation.

Maluka rose, walked over, and lightly kicked his semi-conscious captive in his ribs. Satisfied that his victim was alive enough to groan, Maluka nodded.

'You want me to take him out 'til he comes around?' Aijaz asked.

'No,' Maluka answered. 'But pick him up and prop him in a chair if you would.'

Maluka returned to his seat and faced Gil. 'This unfortunate soul is Robert Peterson, former assistant to the now deceased Professor Arnold Ludlow. Mr. Peterson's condition is the result of

302

his regrettable unwillingness to be forthcoming with the truth when first asked. I don't ask twice,' Maluka added, then returned to the stack of lies Gil had just dictated.

Maluka looked up from his notes. 'There is one thing that puzzles me,' he said. 'Why would Sarkami reveal all of this to you if he and Sabbie intended to walk out on you the following day?'

Gil frantically fought to come up with some logical answer to Maluka's question but, before he could speak, the door opened again.

Saved by the bell.

Aijaz stood in the door and pointed to the cell phone he held in his ham-hock hand. Maluka approached and Aijaz whispered in his ear.

Maluka turned to Gil. 'Good news,' he announced, then left the room with Aijaz at his heels.

FIFTY-SEVEN

An hour later

The door didn't open again for quite a while. In all that time, Gil's fellow victim never stirred. Peterson lay in the chair into which Aijaz had dumped him, his head back, mouth open. At one point, Gil tried to rouse him, to offer him a bit of the remains of his water, to find out anything that might prove useful. Peterson awakened for a moment, sobbed, then slipped back into a merciful stupor. Gil returned to his filthy bed, feeling far more anxious than he thought possible.

Aijaz returned, bearing yet another semi-lifeless form.

What's he got, a factory back there?

The newest addition bore a striking, though decidedly unkempt, resemblance to the person Gil once knew as DeVris. Aijaz pulled the Director of Acquisitions to his feet and smacked him lightly on both cheeks.

'Wake up, you piece of shit,' Aijaz said with a laugh, then attempted to heave DeVris across the room. The Director balanced precariously for a moment, then collapsed against Aijaz's ample chest, clinging to the large man for support.

'Get off me,' Aijaz snarled. He flung DeVris' limp body headfirst onto the bed and Gil.

Gil struggled to move DeVris' dead weight off of him.

Aijaz watched in amusement for a moment, then drew up a box from the opposite corner and settled down on it. He pulled out a package of bubble gum from his pocket and stuffed five pieces into his mouth. Smiling with pride at the greatness of this feat, he grunted and chewed at the wad while Gil quietly waited for the next episode in his bizarre nightmare.

Unsatisfied with the entertainment level of massive gum chewing, the hulk left the room and returned with a portable DVD player that blared the antics of the Three Stooges.

Perfect. Just perfect.

DeVris roused himself quietly, apparently not so insensible as he had been pretending to be. He eyed their guard and spoke to Gil in a loud whisper.

'They call this one Aijaz. He barely speaks

English. You can say anything you want in front of him.'

At the mention of his name, Aijaz flashed his best semi-toothless smile. Having mastered the art of gum chewing, he removed the wad and unceremoniously plastered it onto the side of the box on which he sat. He seemed to rethink the matter, most likely reviewing Maluka's response to such untidiness, then meticulously unstuck the gum with a tissue and deposited it in the trash basket.

All of this Aijaz did with the pride of a prima ballerina, aware that every move was being watched by those who held great interest in his actions. He licked the sticky residue off each of his sausage fingers, then returned to the box and involved himself in the intricate task of peeling a large orange, a fruit that from Gil's estimate was likely to have an IQ greater than the man who now consumed it.

'You give me trouble, I peel you, too!' Aijaz said. Apparently enjoying his witticism, Aijaz repeated the joke in his native tongue for his own amusement and turned back to his DVD player.

Gil rolled on his side and faced DeVris.

'Where's Sabbie?' Gil demanded, then glanced to see if Aijaz had heard him.

'I told you he can't understand us,' DeVris repeated.

Eyes fixed on Aijaz, Gil remained silent.

To demonstrate, DeVris called to Aijaz and, in English, told the Muslim that he should eat his juicy mother in the same way as he did the orange.

The big man recognized only his name and the word 'orange' and laughed. He apparently assumed that DeVris wanted some of his much-coveted fruit and, shaking his head, he teasingly held up the bit of remaining fruit before popping it into his mouth.

DeVris nodded toward the third captive, still lifeless in the chair.

'That's Peterson, Ludlow's assistant,' DeVris said in a voice loud enough for the unconscious Peterson to hear. 'Maluka's reward for cooperation, ehh, Robert?'

Gil pressed his thumb into the hollow of DeVris' neck, just below the adam's apple, and stared meaningfully into his captive's eyes.

'Enough. Do you understand?' Gil asked.

DeVris nodded, almost imperceptively. Gil let go his hold, clearly ready to resume it as needed. 'Now, I'll ask you once again. What's happened to Sabbie?'

'How should I know? They say you staged her kidnapping,' DeVris answered.

'Why the hell would I do that?'

DeVris shrugged. 'It's academic now. If they don't have her yet, they will soon.'

Gil grabbed DeVris on either side of his head and pushed his face close to the Director's. The desire to crush his skull was overwhelming.

'You don't know that!' Gil shouted into DeVris' face.

'Cut it out!' DeVris wailed. 'All I'm saying is that it's just a matter of time.'

Aijaz apparently enjoyed the show and joined in with a shout of encouragement. Gil let go of DeVris, fought the urge to take on Aijaz, and dropped his face into his hands. It was the only bit of privacy left.

'Look, you're fighting a losing battle,' DeVris said. 'I mean, you can hold out hope if you want but, if you think they're not going to find Sabbie one way or another, and the scroll as well, you'd better keep one thing in mind.'

'And what's that?' Gil asked mechanically.

DeVris flashed a sardonic smile. 'They found both of us, didn't they?'

FIFTY-EIGHT

Day Fourteen, morning
Muslims for World Truth (MWT) Video Production Studios London

Gil looked across the Thanksgiving table at Sabbie. She smiled and offered him more turkey. He couldn't eat another bite, he said. Well, maybe just a little. It was a wonderful dream.

George was there, too. When he had left the room for a moment and they were sure George was out of earshot, he and Sabbie had a good laugh over the huge portions that the big guy had eaten.

Sabbie disappeared into the next room to get dessert. As she returned, apple pie in hand, she transformed into George. As she laughed at Gil's astonishment, she stuffed great handfuls of pie into her mouth in anticipation of the final delicacy—Gil himself.

Gil awakened and faced another predator, this one real and barreling toward him. Aijaz's enormous hand seized Gil by the back of his collar and dragged him from the filthy mattress on which DeVris still slept. Without explanation, Aijaz hauled Gil from the room and down the hallway.

Maluka said Aijaz didn't like to have his TV shows interrupted.

Aijaz slammed open the last door in the hall and unceremoniously deposited his charge into another room and onto an even filthier bed. In broken English, Aijaz informed Gil that he would be returning in a minute and that, in the event Gil made any trouble . . . Aijaz finished his warning with an index finger that pantomimed a horizontal slice across his own neck accompanied by a hissing 'tzzt' sound.

If it were possible to compare chambers in hell, the new room seemed somewhat less horrendous than the last. It was larger and, though the sun filtered through a wide filthy window, the room was cool.

Three card tables had been set up, end to end, forming a serving area or workspace along the windowed wall. Each table was covered in clean white fabric that stood in sharp contrast to the shabby surroundings. A stack of papers and a plastic drinking glass that contained felt markers had been placed on one corner of the center table. The beauty of so civilized a setting made Gil ache with longing and plunged him into a deeper depression than any threat of violence could have done.

He wanted to go home. He wanted to walk through the door and find Sabbie there, well and happy, telling him everything was okay, that she had just gone along ahead to surprise him.

Though he risked Aijaz's wrath, Gil slipped off

the bed and headed toward the window. His eyes drank up the color and movement. Buildings, streets filled with people, cars, the city landscape, all of it spread before him in a wonderful buffet of civilization and normality.

Yesterday, the panorama might have exemplified man's disregard for his fellow man and unconcern for his planet. Today, Gil couldn't have cared less about pollution, the deterioration of the work ethic, or the meaninglessness of superficial pursuits. The world outside the muddy Plexiglas windows was his world. He loved it and longed desperately to be part of it again.

Lost in thought, Gil never heard the footsteps that approached from behind. 'We're in the middle of London but we might as well be on another planet,' she said. Gil turned.

For a moment, he didn't recognize her. She was bloody and bruised. Her right eye was swollen shut, and the cut on her left temple, caked with dried blood, gaped open in need of stitches. Her clothes were filthy and wet and her hair was matted with mud and blood. But she was alive. Alive! And there she stood.

He surrounded her with his arms and pressed her to him, almost fearful that it was another dream. She cringed in pain, and he released her.

'Are you okay?' he asked.

She cocked her head to one side as if trying to understand the unabashed show of affection. 'Yes. I'm okay, just some pain.'

Gil opened his mouth to ask her what happened but she interrupted with a warm smile that lasted a total of about two seconds. Then she was all business once again.

'Don't say anything,' she cautioned. 'I've got to talk fast. It all went perfectly but now we'll have to hurry and get our stories coordinated,' she said.

'What went perfectly?'

Without responding, she picked up the familiar blanket-wrapped box that he had not seen behind her on the floor.

Gil placed his hands on the box to receive its warmth. None came.

Aijaz slammed the door open and entered. Unconcerned with their conversation, the hulk settled himself on the floor in the far corner and raised the volume on his DVD to best block out their apparently useless chatter.

'We'll talk as we work. Now, help me,' Sabbie said. She had been struggling to remove a fine silken cloth from the lumpy mounds it covered. The cloth, spotted with red-brown stains, caught and snagged the many thin strips that lay below it.

'Is that blood?' Gil asked.

A dozen cuts on her fingers, some jagged, oozed.

'If you cut a scroll into strips, you've got to expect to draw some blood,' Sabbie explained with a shrug.

'One would have expected to see less gore on Sarkami,' she added, 'but he uses diamond-cutting tools, a dissecting microscope, and precision instruments.

'These are the kinds of cuts you get from an old pair of manicuring scissors and tweezers,' she continued.

'You'll need a tetanus shot,' Gil said. He gently cradled her ravaged hands.

She laughed, apparently at his concern, and

310

continued to lay out the bands of copper.

The strips that had once made up the scroll, lay neatly flattened in piles, each with its own numbered tag. It was like seeing a cadaver where a beautiful body had just been in soft slumber. Perhaps that was why the scroll no longer held the power that had once filled him with such warmth and joy.

Gil's stomach seized with a sudden realization. 'So you *did* stage the kidnapping,' he said. 'Complete with the sweater. It was all fake.'

Sabbie held up her battered fingers. 'The blood part of it was real enough,' she said with a wry smile.

She laid out the last of the strips in earnest. 'We've got to talk fast. Maluka thinks we're in here translating. He has no idea as to what we have discovered and, assuming you haven't told him anything, we can fudge it for a while.' She waited for confirmation.

Gil nodded, thankful he had not trusted Maluka's depiction of Sabbie's betrayal.

'Good. I'll go through the motions of setting these strips up for translation and you make some marks on the paper that look like you're trying to figure it all out. While you do that, I'll fill you in,' Sabbie said.

Gil wrote some random numbers and words on the paper.

'There was no way we could keep ahead of them forever,' she continued. 'One way or another, either McCullum's WATSC boys or Maluka's men were going to find us. It was just a matter of who would get to us first. I needed time to figure out what the rest of the scroll said. That way I'd know who had the most to gain by getting hold of it. Or by destroying it,' she added.

She carefully arranged each strip of copper on the white covered tables in numerical order from right to left.

Gil's gaze fell on the strips once more. The scroll had been perfect, complete, a monument to human communication and ingenuity that had survived two millennia. And she had cut it up with manicuring scissors!

Sabbie continued to explain her sudden departure. While Gil was sleeping that last morning in the hotel, she had seen a news flash on TV about the discovery of Hassan's body at the Monastery. Their photographs had been aired along with their names. Though she knew it had been a distinct possibility, seeing their photos on the news catapulted her into action. The newscaster announced that they were bound for London and added that Scotland Yard was asking for the public's help in apprehending them.

'The Yard couldn't have put all this together that fast,' Sabbie said. 'Not only did they air our passport photos, they had pictures of me that I've never seen. They also had your correct name. If it had been the Yard investigating without outside help, given your passport info, they would have identified you as Arnold Ludlow, not Gil Pearson. Somebody else had to be feeding them the info.'

'McCullum or Maluka? Why would they want the Yard in on this?' Gil asked. 'It makes no sense.'

'Hounds for the hunt,' she said. 'Whoever gave them the info wanted Scotland Yard and the good people of London to point the way. Flush us out, if possible. That way, they could swoop in and pick us off. Which means either McCullum or Maluka has a source within the Yard,' she added thoughtfully.

She knew she couldn't fight them all, she explained, so she faked her kidnapping. At first, she planned on bloodying her own sweater to make whoever was tracking them think that someone else had already succeeded in capturing her and the scroll.

'You didn't do a very good job,' Gil said. 'Everyone knew it was staged, including the Yard.'

'I know. I said that it was my *first* plan. When I realized I didn't have time to make it look convincing, I decided to use the obvious lack of authenticity to my advantage. I made it look totally amateurish, so they'd figure Sarkami and I had staged it so we could run off with the scroll.'

'And leave me holding the bag,' Gil said.

'I couldn't tell you. I didn't know what Maluka would do when he caught you. If you didn't know anything . . .'

'You *knew* he would catch me? For Christ's sake, you might have warned me,' Gil shouted.

Aijaz looked up, put his index finger to his lips, made a 'shhh' sound and, before going back to his entertainment, frowned to show his displeasure.

Sabbie lowered her voice. 'It wouldn't have mattered. There were too many people after you . . . I mean, us. This way at least I had a chance to save the scroll . . .'

'I thought you were dead,' Gil interrupted.

'. . . and come back for you. Which I did,' she concluded.

'I thought you were dead,' Gil repeated.

'I didn't know you cared,' she said flippantly.

He locked her in his gaze. 'Well, you were wrong.'

She looked away. 'I figured without me or the scroll, they wouldn't have much need for you. Besides, I told you, it was the only way I could buy time to find out what the rest of the scroll said.'

Gil waited.

Suddenly she smiled at him as she had smiled at Sarkami. 'Don't you want to know what it said?' she asked.

Gil nodded and held his breath.

'The last piece proves that the scroll is everything Ludlow hoped it might be—and more. It's a doorway to history like none other before.'

FIFTY-NINE

'What the hell is a doorway to history?' Gil asked. Aijaz seemed to be getting impatient and Maluka might return at any minute. This wasn't an opportune time for a detailed report.

'Look, this is very important. You need to know it,' she said sternly.

He stopped himself from asking why. Better to just let her talk.

'Remember when Jesus spoke of the tzaddikim, the righteous ones? It was in the garden, the last time he and Micah ever saw each other. Jesus asked Micah to take his place when he died. But, at the same time, Jesus said that he could not claim to be a tzaddik himself because a tzaddik has no knowledge that he is, in fact, a tzaddik.'

Gil nodded, urging her to hurry.

'But, remember, Jesus also said he could not deny it?' she added.

Gil shrugged.

'Well, the question you should be asking is how could Jesus ask Micah to take his place as a tzaddik, if Jesus was not a tzaddik?' she concluded triumphantly.

Gil shook his head. He had no idea where she was going with this one.

'Look. Micah gives us the answer in the last thing he says to Jesus, the word *Elyon*.'

The word *Elyon*, she explained, means the highest, as in he who ascends to God. According to ancient writings, each millennium there is born a Tzaddik Elyon, a High Tzaddik, who is not counted among the other thirty-six but, rather, stands alone. It is on this High Tzaddik that the fate of the world rests, for he is entrusted with three great tasks. If these three tasks are not completed each thousand years, mankind will no longer be permitted to walk the face of the earth.'

'Go on,' Gil said more patiently.

'In order for the Tzaddik Elyon to complete his tasks, he is given knowledge of his remarkable obligation. Until that time, he lives as any who strives for a life of righteousness. Others may help him along the way but, in the end, he must walk the final steps alone. If death threatens to take him before he is able to complete all three tasks, he must choose another, who has been cleansed and is pure of heart, so that the promise will yet be fulfilled. If he fails to do so, all mankind will be lost forever.'

'You mean that if this special tzaddik . . .'

315

'High Tzaddik,' Sabbie corrected.

'If this High Tzaddik dies without completing certain tasks, mankind will be wiped off the face of the earth?' Gil asked incredulously.

'It happened before,' Sabbie said. 'According to Genesis, during the time of Sodom and Gomorrah, God called for fifty tzaddikim to testify to the goodness of man. By their very existence, those fifty would prove man's worthiness to continue on the face of the earth. When fifty righteous souls could not be found, Abraham asked God to accept ten righteous souls instead. God agreed. In the end, only one righteous soul could be found and Sodom was destroyed. With that destruction, the need for a quorum of righteous souls was established. Since no tzaddik ever knows for sure if he or she is one of the chosen, each of us must act as if we were, indeed, tzaddik to insure that man's days may be long upon this earth.'

'And you're saying that Micah is telling us that Jesus was a High Tzaddik because he uses the world "Elyon" as his final word to Jesus?' Gil asked.

'Yes, but he's saying much more,' she continued excitedly. 'He's telling us why he made the scroll and what we're supposed to do with it!'

Her face was joyous. 'Look. Micah talks with Jesus in the garden at Gethsemane. In that single conversation, Micah is entrusted with the tasks that must be completed by a High Tzaddik. That's no accident!'

'Then Jesus was a High Tzaddik?' Gil asked.

Sabbie nodded. 'Yes, and when the Twelve made it impossible for him to complete all three tasks, the Thirteenth Apostle was chosen to

316

complete the tasks in His stead. He passed on all that was needed in the scroll, so that it would be waiting for the next High Tzaddik.'

'Then a thousand years later, it was William, Elias' brother, who found the scroll,' Gil concluded. 'So he was the next High Tzaddik?'

'No, William was a knight. He had killed in battle. No High Tzaddik may have taken a life. William was a messenger who brought the scroll to Elias, the righteous soul for whom the scroll called out.'

'And now?' Gil asked.

'Now we must protect the scroll until it can be placed in the hands of the next High Tzaddik,' she said. 'Before it's too late.'

'How long do we have?'

'There is no fixed date according to mankind's calendar, which changes around the world. The time must ripen according to the natural order of things, but it will happen once each millennium, more or less. Elias wasn't called until a hundred and fifty years after the turn of the century. This time it may be sooner.'

'How do you know?' Gil asked.

'I can just feel it. It's soon,' she said.

'But how can we get the scroll to him . . .'

'Or her,' Sabbie corrected.

'But how can we get the scroll to the High Tzaddik before it's too late, if we have no idea who the High Tzaddik is?' Gil asked.

Sabbie smiled and cocked her head. 'What makes you think we don't?'

SIXTY

Gil never got the answer to the obvious next question. Maluka strode through the door and slammed it behind him. Aijaz, obviously heartened by the promise of violence, smiled widely.

Maluka would not be stalled any longer. 'I do not have time to play games,' he said. He turned and left with Aijaz at his heels, once again.

'For Christ's sake, give him something,' Gil urged. 'He knows you're bullshitting him. Give him some simple translation from the beginning of the scroll. Just tell him about Micah's life or his love of his craft.'

But even as Gil imagined what contrived message they might claim the scroll contained, he knew it wouldn't work. Maluka would not be conned into believing this piece of antiquity was nothing but the story of a metalsmith and his daily trials and tribulations. And, if they did succeed for a short time, what good would stalling do them?

'I won't do it,' she said. 'I will not give him one single word. Not one. And if you are so willing to give up the scroll to save your own skin, you're far more of a liability than I thought.'

Her cold, calm look was one Gil had seen twice before, once on the way to the bathroom in the restaurant in Weymouth when she thought they were being followed and, again, in the early morning light when Hassan lay at their feet in the Monastery courtyard. It was a look that scared the hell out of him. There was no doubt that she would give her life to save the scroll or, just as

318

willingly, take his.

Gil's gaze dropped to her crotch.

Is she still carrying the gun in there?

He wasn't certain if an answer to that question would make him feel better or worse.

Gil tried a more reasonable approach. 'Look, not every single word in the scroll is sacred. What would . . .'

'Yes, it is,' she said. 'Every word is sacred. That's what you don't seem to understand.'

'But all Maluka has to do is get rid of us and get someone else to translate the scroll. He's going to find out what it says anyway.'

Her face softened. 'Oh, my God,' she said. 'You think this is the real one.'

Gil stared in confusion.

'Of course. If this were the real scroll, it would make no sense to withhold anything from Maluka,' she said. 'You're right. He could just kill us and bring in the next translator. I'm good but I'm not indispensable,' she added with a shake of her head. 'I assumed you knew it wasn't the real one when you touched the box.'

Suddenly he understood. No wonder he felt no warmth from the strips as well. They were fake, cut from a faux facsimile that Sarkami had made. That was why she and Sarkami ran. To give Sarkami time to finish it or to make it look like they were trying to get away. Or both.

No matter. The Cave 3 Scroll was safe somewhere. This was nothing more than a collection of useless pieces of copper. If he and Sabbie didn't tell Maluka what he wanted to know, their abductor would never get it from this worthless scrapheap.

319

'But you said the gashes on your hands came from cutting up the scroll,' Gil said.

'No, I think I said something like, "If you cut a scroll into strips, you've got to expect to draw some blood." In other words, I had to cut up my hand because that's what Maluka expected to see, you moron.'

She was brilliant. In fact, he had seen only what he had expected to see, and so had Maluka. 'Then where is the real . . .'

Maluka returned. He was accompanied by the beast that held a semi-conscious body by the scruff of its neck.

'As you both know,' Maluka began, 'this is Mr. Robert Peterson, former assistant to Dr. Ludlow. Mr. Peterson is the proud father of two little girls, the youngest of which is severely disabled. He would do anything to get his daughter the medical help she so desperately needs. He has sold his soul, and for that he was generously rewarded. Now, he withholds additional information.'

Maluka waved Aijaz to bring the body closer.

With what must have been all the energy he could possibly muster, Peterson raised his head in protest. He knew nothing more, he said, then his head fell forward limply.

'It may be that he does know nothing or that he is withholding information,' Maluka continued. 'In either case, he is of no use to me.'

Gil watched as Aijaz's free hand disappeared behind his back. Gil's chest ached with certain knowledge of what was about to happen.

'Since you two insist on acting like stubborn children, let us turn to a very effective method of instruction. I will count to three. One, two . . .'

320

The sound of the gun was deafening. Pain shot through Gil's ears. Instinctively, he covered them and looked to see if Sabbie had been injured as well. She stood with her hands at her sides, her face impassive, her forehead and cheeks covered with bits of Peterson's bone and brain. Gil could not tell where Sabbie's old bruises ended and Peterson's remains began.

'You seem surprised,' Maluka said, obviously pleased with the terror he had instilled in Gil. 'You may have assumed I intended to show you the importance of responding by the time I reached three. But the lesson was meant to do just the opposite, to remind you that you cannot always predict another's actions. Especially mine.'

Gil glanced at Sabbie. She had not wiped her face. She stood straight, without emotion, and stared directly ahead, past Maluka.

'Now, do either of you have any information to offer me?' Maluka asked.

It was useless to protest. Gil remained stoically silent. Then, as he awaited his fate, something in him changed. A calm washed over him like none he had ever felt. No conflict, no fear. He was powerless to stop this man. Maluka would do what he wanted. This murderer might even escape punishment. That Gil could not control. He could only refuse to help him and that he would do. Even if it cost him and Sabbie their lives.

Maluka turned to Aijaz. 'Let's raise the stakes, Aijaz. Go get the other one.'

Gil prepared himself for Aijaz's return and the massacre that was sure to follow. He was ready. No matter what they did, he would not look at Aijaz or Maluka. No matter what he saw, he would not

321

speak. He would let whatever happened, happen.

As long as she's not next.

The thought brought a cold terror to his soul.

The door flew open a minute later and, despite Gil's promise to himself, the massive form that filled the doorway captured his attention.

In place of Aijaz and his next victim, stood George, smiling, confident, and quite obviously very healthy. Aijaz remained behind him, his face strained and set, his usual toothless smile strangely absent.

SIXTY-ONE

When Gil would think back to the moment he first saw George in the doorway—and he would every day for the rest of his life—he would always remember the unexpected look of delight on Maluka's face. As strange as it was to see his boss suddenly appear in the middle of his own personal hell on earth, it was even more incongruous to see his captor smile at George as if he were an old friend.

Sabbie's reaction was just as bizarre. 'Shit!' she cried. 'I knew it. Son of a bitch, I knew it. Don't kill him!'

Why would Maluka want to kill George?

Gil stared in disbelief as Maluka walked toward George with open arms of greeting.

Gil turned to Sabbie. 'He's not going to kill him, he's going to . . .'

Her hands were in her crotch. She desperately pushed her pantyhose aside and pulled her gun

322

from its hiding place.

In the time it took her to aim, George had moved forward and to one side of the doorway. The blast of a gunshot echoed off the naked walls. She looked at Gil in surprise. She had not yet fired.

Aijaz stood alone in the opening, his mouth open in surprise. In the middle of his ample belly a hole spurted blood like some bizarre fountain. As if in slow motion, Gil watched the huge man look down at his stomach and insert his huge finger into the hole that had suddenly appeared, as if in an attempt to plug up the stream of red that shot forward. Without a word, Aijaz looked into Maluka's eyes, held them for a moment, then he fell to the floor.

Aijaz's killer emerged through the doorway. He was tall, blond, and though he was not dressed in white, Gil knew instantly who he must be.

McCullum's WATSC Nazi!

The Power Angel stepped forward to reveal his mirror image behind. His clone dumped a struggling DeVris on the floor. The second angel of death fired three bullets in quick succession, one into DeVris' head, then two more into the back of Maluka's neck.

It was some mad dream where everyone kept changing places. Except there'd be no waking up from this nightmare.

George stood stock still, a Power Angel on each side.

Gil waited for the inevitable, but wondered why McCullum would send his Power Angels to kill George?

Sabbie remained frozen with her gun pointed

323

toward George and the WATSC bookends. 'Get over here,' she instructed.

'Now!' she repeated.

She wasn't talking to George, she was talking to him! Gil hesitated, trying to make sense of it all. It was a fatal mistake.

The two Power Angels had stepped away from George. Each had Gil in his gun sight. Sabbie's gun could not cover both killers. At most, she could take down only one of them. With a jolt, Gil suddenly realized that she hesitated not for herself but, rather, because it would leave him totally vulnerable.

'Take them,' George ordered. As one Power Angel kept his gun trained on Gil, the other walked forward without concern and took Sabbie's gun from her. Though she said nothing and stood unmoving, tears streamed from her eyes.

'Now clean up this mess,' George ordered. He held out his hand. One Power Angel began to bind Aijaz's legs, apparently for easier transport, and the other handed George his gun so that George could keep watch on Sabbie and Gil.

'Get *his* gun,' George ordered his twin assassins. He pointed toward the heap that had been Aijaz. Both men bent in unison over the bloody mountain, and both men collapsed onto it as George shot both of them squarely in the back.

Gil stood face to face with the fat man he had once pitied and who now pointed a gun at his chest.

'What the hell is going on?' Gil demanded.

'It's nothing personal,' George said simply. 'You know me, Gil. Business is business. Sometimes you can't afford to be a softy.'

Gil waited to become part of the carnage that covered the warehouse floor. Two shots rang out, but Gil felt no pain. He looked down, and, remembering Aijaz's surprised expression, half expected to see himself spilling from his body.

Instead, George dropped to the floor. He hit hard and his gun flew from his hand.

Sabbie crouched low, her gun still pointed. The weapon she held had belonged to Aijaz. Gil had seen him use it on Peterson. She must have pulled it from Aijaz's back waistband, where he had been so fond of keeping it, while George was saying his brief good-bye to Gil.

'Get the guns,' Sabbie said in a throaty whisper. 'Quick.'

'No one's going anywhere,' Gil began.

She didn't answer. When he turned he understood why there was, indeed, no time to waste.

SIXTY-TWO

Sabbie's body lay sprawled on the floor.

Gil bent over her and searched desperately for any source of injury. There was nothing.

'You're okay,' Gil said. 'He missed you.'

'I don't think so,' she replied softly.

Gil told her to straighten her leg. It was twisted at such an odd angle.

'That's the problem. I can't move.' She looked into his face, less than a foot away. 'My head, that's all I can move,' she said in a hoarse voice. 'I can't feel anything else.'

'But you haven't been shot!'

'See if there's an entry wound somewhere on my chest,' she whispered with eerie calm.

The small hole in the hollow above her collarbone was barely bleeding. Large enough for a bullet, it nevertheless looked like any benign injury that would heal on its own.

'George's bullet must have hit my spine,' she said hoarsely. 'Just a bit below the fourth cervical vertebrae . . . I think. Breathing is okay . . . but difficult. Not able to move my . . . arms or legs.'

Instinctively, he started to reply, 'I know, army training,' but the words died in his throat. Sabbie said it for him. Tears streamed from her eyes and pooled on the floor beside her neck.

Gil gently pulled her leg from under her. 'Tell me . . . who's alive,' she said in a weak voice.

He ignored her question and answered the one he assumed she was asking. 'Nobody can do anything to you now, don't worry. I'm going to call an ambulance. I'll be right back.'

'No!' she cried weakly and attempted to lift her head. 'Tell me . . . who's dead.'

'The only thing that matters now is getting you help . . .'

She struggled to get the words out. 'Tell me, Goddamn it!'

'Everybody,' he answered.

'How do you . . . know? Did you check them? Each . . . of them? Do it!' she ordered in a whisper.

Gil pushed and prodded his way through the bodies and reported as he went.

'Power Angel number one, dead.' Pull him aside. 'Power Angel number two, dead. I'll need to flip him over to try and get to Aijaz. Okay, Aijaz bites the dust, too,' Gil said flippantly.

'It's not funny,' she whispered. 'You're going too quickly. Take your time and make sure.'

Gil doubled the pulse-searching time he was spending at the neck and wrists. 'Maluka, dead. For sure,' Gil added.

No need to check Peterson. The next was more difficult. 'DeVris, dead,' Gil said.

'What about George?' Sabbie insisted. 'Did you check him?'

George was the last and closest to Sabbie. He lay face up, his shirt, jacket, and pants covered in red. There was no way he could still be alive. He wouldn't have enough blood left.

Sabbie had turned her head and was watching George intently.

'I think he's still breathing,' she said.

'He's not sharing the ambulance with you, if that's what you're . . .'

Gil never got the last word out of his mouth. As he approached, George turned on his side like a beached whale and, as he held his firing arm up with the other arm, took direct aim at Gil's chest.

'Move!' she screamed with more breath than Gil thought possible.

And he did, just in time. In five strides, Gil was behind George and had wrested the gun from his hand. But somewhere between the first and the last of those strides, George had taken aim at Sabbie and fired.

'This one . . . hit higher,' she whispered. 'Can hardly . . . breathe.'

Gil knelt beside her. He cradled her head in his hand.

Each of her breaths was more labored than the

327

last.

'Where?' he asked desperately. 'I don't see it.'

She stared into his eyes. Tears streamed down her cheeks.

'I'll get the ambulance . . .' he said, laying her head gently back on the floor.

'Wait,' she said. It took everything she had.

His eyes met hers and followed her gaze to his hand. He knew what he would see before he let his eyes drop. The stickiness he felt there was already turning his stomach. A strange clear fluid and thick blood dripped from his hand to the floor. He fought to keep from wretching.

'Sarkami . . .' she whispered.

Was she calling for him? Gil stared, not knowing what to do.

'Sar . . . kami,' she repeated.

'You want to know what happened to Sarkami, is that it?' Gil asked desperately.

'Gone,' she responded.

So, Maluka got Sarkami, too. Or did she mean that she was gone? Oh, God! These were her last words and he had no idea what she was saying.

'Scroll,' she whispered with less breath.

Gil shook his head helplessly.

'Sarkami . . . Don't kill him,' she said. Her words were barely audible.

'Who? Don't kill who? Sarkami?'

'Don't . . . kill . . . George,' she whispered.

Gil's heart pounded madly. George had just shot her. Twice! Why the hell was she worried about him?

'Best place . . .' she started.

'The best place to go is?' Gil said. He was trying desperately to imagine what she wanted to say.

'No, the best place . . .' Then there was no breath left, for words or for life.

She was gone and the silence was deafening.

For a moment, there was no sadness, nothing at all. Then a giant hand within him grabbed his chest and crushed it beneath its grip. Tears of rage poured from his eyes. He reached down, grabbed George, and with all his strength shook the huge flopping body.

'Why the fuck did you do it?' Gil screamed. 'Why?'

George stared at him and said nothing. Gil released him in a heap.

'Why?' Gil cried. 'Why? What good did it do to kill her?' he wailed to no one.

George's head, cocked oddly to one side, continued to stare, not at Gil, but at the nothingness of his own eternity.

Gil returned to his Sabbie, knelt beside her one last time, cradled her in his arms, and cried from the depths of his tortured soul.

SIXTY-THREE

A few hours later

It was like waking from a terrible dream. In the fading light of the day, what had been bloody bodies on the warehouse floor, now appeared as abstract shapes and shadows. Only Sabbie's pale face, cool and still, bore testimony to all that had happened only a few hours earlier.

Gil was filled with an emptiness he had never

felt before. Still, his mind was clear and remarkably focused. There was nothing he could do here now and, sure as hell, Sabbie would have hated to see him wallow in the pain and loss.

She would have yelled at him that he had a job to do and to get the hell out of there. And she would have been right.

He needed food, a place to sleep, and a plane ticket home, in that order. The first two would have to be taken care of immediately. The third would have to wait until he completed the task that he and Sabbie had begun together.

For now, Sarkami's house would do. There should be something in the refrigerator and, if Gil traveled at night, he was less likely to be recognized by—how did Sabbie put it—the good people of London. He was still a fugitive, Gil reminded himself, and he needed to think like one.

Gil gathered up the strips of copper scroll littered across the table and around the floor. Though they were only copies, still he placed them gently within the old wooden box and wrapped it, once again, with the blanket. A strip or two of the faux scroll might still remain beneath the scattered bodies, he thought, but he had neither the time, strength, nor the stomach, to roll them over and search beneath. The police would be certain to unravel the whole matter in time. The removal of these key pieces of evidence, and hopefully leaving no others behind, might just buy him a few extra days.

Unless, of course, they conclude I was the one responsible for all of this.

Had Sabbie been alive, they would have joked about his growing list of criminal offenses. Now, suddenly, he was facing the very real charge of multiple homicide.

*   *   *

The back door to Sarkami's lay open. Broken locks still hung askew. Once inside, Gil wedged some furniture against the door. It offered only an illusion of protection, but he doubted that anyone was after him, at least for the moment. Besides, if somebody wanted him badly enough to knock down the pile of furniture at the door, they were welcome. He'd had enough.

The hummus was dried out, the pita bread was stale, and the iced tea was too sweet. He was starved so, all together, it was one of the best meals he had ever eaten. Gil wolfed it down in a few minutes and rested before his next foraging expedition into Sarkami's kitchen.

He glanced around the room. There was an order beneath the disorder, a logic to the placement of the lights, tools, notes, and books and an organization beneath the debris when you took the time to look past the obvious.

The best place to hide a tree is in the forest. And the best place to hide an organized counterfeiting— or rather, faux facsimile project—is in the midst of a . . . mess.

Suddenly, Gil straightened. 'The best place . . .' Those had been Sabbie's last words. He rose with confidence, walked to the table neatly covered in white cloth, and placed his hands on the copper scroll that lay amid a mound of copper strips and facsimile scrolls. A familiar warmth greeted him. It had not been cut up after all! Gil's heart was filled with an unexpected joy.

This was the scroll, the one for which everyone was willing to kill or die, yet Maluka's men had been in this very room with Gil when they took him prisoner and had missed it. It had been there, right under their noses, but they had seen only what they expected to see; worthless faux facsimiles waiting to be sent to the Museum for display.

It was a brilliant and courageous plan. Sarkami knew his enemy and his enemy's limitations, and he had trusted what he knew to be true. Gil wondered if Sabbie had been part of the decision to leave the real scroll in full view. He got his answer more quickly than he would have guessed.

With an apartment full of possessions at his disposal, Gil prepared the scroll for transport. As he carefully wrapped the scroll in the bed sheet he had torn into quarters, Gil realized he had no idea where he was going. He had assumed that he would head back to the U.S.

On second thought, with McCullum still out there, going home didn't appear to be the wisest of choices. Besides, what would he do with the scroll? He couldn't exactly take out an ad in the *New York Times* for a High Tzaddik in need of a two-thousand-year-old piece of antiquity required for the salvation of mankind.

Gil slipped the scroll into the backpack that lay empty and waiting in the corner. The scroll would need cushioning, he thought. He pushed the faux facsimiles aside, added the strips he had taken from the warehouse to the pile, and slid the soft white cloth from the table. As he watched, a small envelope fell from its hiding place beneath the fabric. It landed at his feet. It bore the words 'To Whom It May Concern' in Sabbie's distinctive script.

Inside, in her handwriting, once again, was the well-known Robert Frost verse. With a simple change of pronouns, poetic licence she would have claimed, Sabbie ended the poem with carefully worded instruction. 'You have miles to go before you sleep.' In those few words, she told Gil all that he needed to know.

He gently laid the note on the scroll nestled safely in the backpack. Beside it, he slipped the passport that bore the name Arnold Ludlow beneath his own picture.

With anticipation, he raised the white cloth to his face. As he had hoped, it smelled of vanilla, like the sweater Sabbie wore in the chapel, only a few days earlier.

Gil held the white cloth to his chest and, with his free hand, pulled closed the backpack. Tomorrow, the soft fabric would cushion the precious cargo. But not now.

Tomorrow he would fly to Israel in hopes of discovering for whom the scroll was intended. Tonight, he desperately needed sleep and a reprieve from thought.

Gently, Gil laid the white cloth on the pillow next to him. Most of all, for just a few minutes more, he needed to close his eyes and to imagine that he was, once again, holding Sabbie.

SIXTY-FOUR

Day Fifteen, late afternoon
Israel Museum Library, Jerusalem

The hand that grasped Gil's shoulder stopped him dead with his fingers poised on the computer keyboard.

You'd think I would have learned by now.

He had arrived in Israel only that morning and had headed straight for the Museum's library, glued to the mainframe computer for most of the day. By accessing their Aramaic program, Gil had hoped to double check Sabbie's translation in search of some clue she had overlooked. If the scroll was going to tell him how to proceed, he'd better be able to speak its language.

After eight hours, Gil had to admit he was no closer to interpreting the scroll than he had been at the start. Within each phrase he thought he had translated correctly, Gil discovered a discrepancy that put a previous section in doubt. Still, he couldn't bring himself to give up. Though he was making no real progress, the challenge, itself, had been immensely satisfying.

Now, the sudden clasp on the back of his neck sent a wave of electricity up Gil's back. He turned slowly. He half expected to see another pair of blond Power Angels behind him. Instead, he was greeted by the swarthy face of the man he assumed to be dead.

'Sarkami!'

'I've been expecting you,' the older man

334

whispered. 'Let's go in the other room where we can talk.'

The library conference room provided them with all the privacy they needed.

'I thought you were dead,' Gil began.

Sarkami looked surprised.

'Sabbie said you were gone.'

The older man laughed. 'I am,' he said. 'Gone . . . you know, gone away. Gone to Israel, to wait for you.'

Gil recounted the events he never wanted to think about again. Sarkami showed no surprise and made no comment. As Gil described George's unexpected second attack on Sabbie, Sarkami nodded sadly as if he had been anticipating the strange twist of events. Gil continued, then waited for Sarkami's response.

Sarkami hesitated, as if expecting Gil to add something beyond the finality of Sabbie's death.

Gil had no idea what else there was to say.

A single tear rolled down the old eagle's cheek. 'She was well named, you know,' Sarkami said softly. 'I got her out of Israel, you know, and brought her to Ludlow in London. Even though they knew everything, he and his wife, Sarah, took her in like the daughter they never had. They helped her establish a whole new identity. Actually, Ludlow was the one who gave her the name, Sabra.'

'It means someone who is born in Israel, doesn't it?' Gil asked. It seemed like an odd thing to do for someone who was trying to leave the past behind.

'Yes, it comes from the name of a type of cactus; a prickly pear that maintains a thorny tough exterior that protects the sweet, softness inside.'

335

After the Second World War, the first Israeli settlers chose the word to describe the children born to their new homeland. To survive, these children would have to have qualities similar to their namesake. Ludlow had chosen the name as both a description and a reminder to his new charge.

Gil's throat tightened. 'She let me in, you know,' he said.

'I hoped she would.'

'It was important for her,' Gil confirmed solemnly.

Sarkami laughed. 'Oh, and not for you?'

Sarkami motioned toward Gil's notes. 'So, you have the scroll, of course,' Sarkami asked.

'Yes, how did you know?'

'Sabbie and I figured you would be able to play connect the dots. Tell me, what have you learned?'

'Nothing,' Gil admitted. 'Nothing Sabbie didn't already read to me from the back seat of the car. The translation is never going to tell me what to do with the scroll.'

'Of course it won't,' Sarkami said agreeably.

Gil looked at him blankly.

'You are like the man who dropped his keys in the street,' Sarkami continued.

Gil shook his head. He had no idea what the older man was talking about.

'There's a wonderful story about a man whose wife finds him on his hands and knees beneath a street lamp one night. He's searching desperately amid the debris and muck of the gutter. When asked what he is doing, the man explains that he is looking for his keys and requests his wife's help. "Exactly where did you drop the keys?" she asks.

"Down the block," he answers. "Then why are you looking here," she asks. "Because the light's better here," he explains.'

I've just turned the corner and entered the Twilight Zone.

'The point is,' Sarkami continued, 'that you're looking for your keys where the light is good but not where you lost them. You're searching where it's easy to look but not where you'll find your answer. Surely, you must have realized that you're spending your time trying to confirm what Sabbie has already told you is written in the scroll because that's the easiest thing to do. After all, you have the scroll, you have the translation program, and you have a job to do that makes you feel like you're getting somewhere. The only problem is, the whole task is pointless and you know it. What you need to learn next cannot be found in any scroll.'

The anger that flashed through Gil was unreasonable. He knew it and he didn't care. Hadn't he been through enough? What did this man want from him?

'What's your point?' Gil asked coldly.

'That depends on your goal,' Sarkami responded calmly. 'If you want to enjoy the diversion of going over what has already been translated, then continue your attempt at confirmation. If you'd like to discover how to get the scroll to the person for whom it was meant, then you need to explore a different path.'

Gil remained aloof. 'And that would be . . . ?'

'You're the cybersleuth,' Sarkami answered. 'What have you been trying to tell yourself? Or rather, what thoughts have you been avoiding?

337

What's that little voice inside trying to get you to hear?'

It was true and Gil knew it. Since he left the warehouse, he had carefully constructed a barrier within his own mind between the horror of what had happened and the clean, unmarred reality through which he was now navigating. He had been forcing himself to stay focused on what could honestly be called 'busy work.'

Gil looked at Sarkami. The great eagle seemed to be waiting for something. A hundred scenes flashed across Gil's mind. He had been avoiding so much, for so long. When Lucy was dying, he had worked longer hours than ever before, which left her alone when she needed him most. At the time, Gil had blamed the doctor for offering the false hope that necessitated making more money. Now Gil could see that, in truth, he found it far easier to avoid dealing with Lucy's pain as well as his own. With Sabbie, as well, he had refused to take her fears seriously, until it was far too late.

But what was he avoiding now? That was the question. And where to find the answer.

'That would seem like the appropriate next step,' Sarkami said, as if he had been reading Gil's mind.

'But I have no idea where to go from here!' Gil protested.

'Well, that's a start,' Sarkami replied, and turned to leave.

'Just a thought,' the older man added before closing the door behind him. 'When you discover the reason why Sabbie didn't want you to kill George, you'll have the answer you've been looking for.'

SIXTY-FIVE

Day Twenty-three, late afternoon
Israel Museum Library, Jerusalem

Perhaps it had been George's weight or his greediness. Perhaps it was because the huge man had been such a damn good actor. Or all of the above. Whatever the reason, Gil had seriously underestimated him.

'You've had eight days. What did you learn?' Sarkami asked succinctly.

Once on the hunt, Gil had been able to access virtually every one of George's files at CyberNet Forensics, Gil explained. Through CyberNet's system, he had tapped into George's home computers as well. He could have done it at any time in the past but, as George probably knew, Gil would have had no reason to even considering doing so. Throughout those eight days, a single document eluded Gil. It was an e-mail that had been created on the day George sent Gil to Israel and had been encoded with a special password.

'At first, I figured it couldn't be that important,' Gil said, 'but there it was, sitting all by itself, in a separate partition of George's hard drive. That bothered me.'

For a while, Gil repeatedly attacked the defiant little document. The more it resisted each of Gil's inventive assaults, the more determined he became. Then, after nearly a dozen attempts, Gil abandoned the futile game. In the past, he would

339

never have walked away from a challenge, especially a chance to prove he was a better cybersleuth than George.

'Now, it just didn't seem to matter that much,' Gil said.

George had left a mountain of electronic jumble behind. Much like the hard copies that littered the big man's desk, the pile seemed endless. Then an odd pattern began to appear, Gil explained.

With each new document he accessed, Gil discovered a pattern to the maze that made up George's secret life. The trail was long and convoluted, a mammoth three-dimensional jigsaw puzzle of illegally intercepted e-mails and Internet searches as well as unauthorized entries into secured hard drives and databases. When the pieces were dissected, then laid in clear view, they told a story of frightening genius.

It took Gil more than a week of fourteen-hour days to work his way backward. The seed that led to the spread of George's influence was a simple program, developed years earlier for Ludlow. It had enabled the Professor's less affluent Museum interns to gain easy access to his communications and texts.

'George was a graduate student back then, freelancing to make money for his tuition. He charged Ludlow half the going rate, then installed a hidden access program in Ludlow's e-mail system.'

'Ingenious,' Sarkami said.

'You ain't heard nothin' yet.'

Nicknamed 'Darwin,' the program began to evolve with the first e-mail the Professor received. The initial evolution provided Darwin with the

340

ability to attach itself to every message that the Professor sent or received. The design was flawless.

From that moment on, each piece of e-mail that entered or left Ludlow's computer, carried within it a bit of the Darwin program. Once the bit of program took root in a new computer, it completed its own programming, providing George full and easy access. Once established, the newly established program began to evolve again. Later evolutions added websites, chat rooms, and instant messages to George's sphere of accessibility. Whatever the user saw, George saw. Whenever he desired.

As the final stroke to his masterpiece, George endowed the offspring of his Darwin program with their own powerful ability to replicate. Each bit of program carried orders to reproduce, immediately and often. With his cyber moles in place, George was free to sit back, read sensitive e-mails and peruse the website records of thousands of potential targets.

'How many people are involved?' Sarkami asked.

'*Were* involved,' Gil replied, 'but I'll explain that in a minute.'

The cyber trail led from Ludlow's little laptop through DeVris' mainframe to the Museum's most confidential records. From there, Darwin traveled to the computers of all of the Museum's contributors, some of the wealthiest and most influential individuals and foundations in the world.

Gil listed a few household names from the ranks of the rich and famous and waited for Sarkami's shocked response. The old eagle looked unimpressed. Gil continued.

With the world at his fingertips, George could sit at home, feet up, and while munching on his favorite snack—with a few strokes of his keyboard—could enter some of the most private recesses of banking, communications, and world politics.

'I could tell he was planning something of gigantic proportions,' Gil said. 'George trimmed his access lists daily and kept only the biggest and most powerful names. He seemed to have been biding his time because for a long time he wasn't actually doing anything with the information.

'Then, out of the blue, a couple of months ago, George began to access every e-mail, Internet search, or other communication that came or went through the Museum's computer system. Anything that carried the word "diary" or "scroll" in it.'

'That must have been an incredible amount of data,' Sarkami said.

Gil laughed. 'Yes, at first, it must have kept him hopping. But George knew how to minimize the workload. He simply wrote a subprogram to filter out e-mail that contained certain keywords.'

'Is that how he picked up Hassan's communications to Maluka?' Sarkami asked.

'Yes. How did you know?'

'Go on,' Sarkami said.

George's interest in the diary was first piqued when an early e-mail from Ludlow to DeVris described the diary as the discovery for which Ludlow 'had been waiting all of his life.'

'I never knew George to give a damn about anybody's opinion,' Gil said, 'but, apparently he

342

trusted Ludlow's judgment far more than most. From what I can tell, George figured that if the old boy thought it was important, it was well worth George's time to check it out.'

Once he learned about the diary, George was obsessed with collecting and cataloging all correspondence and Internet searches that came from Ludlow, DeVris, Hassan, or Maluka.

'He even kept copies of documents and searches that didn't directly relate to the diary or to the possibility of locating the scroll at Weymouth,' Gil added. 'Anything they were interested in, George was interested in.'

'He was quite thorough,' Sarkami said matter-of-factly.

Gil stifled his irritation at what appeared to be praise and continued, intent on presenting George's failures for Sarkami's review as well.

McCullum never used e-mail, Gil explained, and so remained invisible. Only when George accessed DeVris' phone records, did he find evidence of frequent phone calls to and from WATSC headquarters.

'That single piece of information, the fact that McCullum was involved, spurred George into action. From that point on, George's collection of e-mails to and from Maluka, DeVris, and McCullum provided me with all I needed to know.'

'I thought McCullum didn't communicate by e-mail,' Sarkami said.

'With George, McCullum broke his rule,' Gil answered. 'George offered him a deal he couldn't pass up.'

As a first step, George contacted the three men, individually, and informed each of the activities of the other two. In order to ensure each man's interest, George included e-mails that proved the other two were ahead in the hunt for the scroll. Then, when all three were convinced that only George could help them get to the scroll first, to each in succession, George offered the same deal at the same price.

Each was offered exclusive inside information on all activities, e-mail communications, phone records, and computer documents related to the other two. Each man thought himself to be George's sole partner. In exchange, each agreed that, upon discovery of the scroll, George would be given exclusive access to it for three months. After that time, the owner of the scroll would be free to dispose of it as he saw fit.

'Interesting arrangement,' Sarkami said thoughtfully. 'Why only three months?'

'George claimed that three months was all he needed in order to pinpoint the locations of treasure detailed in The Cave 3 Scroll using the new scroll as a guide. George told them that the location of the treasure was all he cared about.'

'And they believed him? Even Maluka?' Sarkami asked skeptically.

'From the little I know of DeVris, George's hunger for money would have made sense to him and McCullum, as well.

'Maluka was a harder nut to crack, so George saved him for last. By that time, George had so much essential information on the other two players, Maluka couldn't turn down the offer. Though, I think he always remained somewhat suspicious.'

'So,' Sarkami concluded, 'in the end, each of the

344

three agreed to the deal they thought to be theirs alone.'

'Yes, and George began to deliver each the information as promised.'

'With each man receiving updated information on the other activities of the two, the chase would have grown more frenetic as the distances between their advantages closed,' Sarkami said thoughtfully.

'And each naturally turned to George for more help,' Gil added.

'So, George was the puppet master with no stake in who won because no matter who got the scroll, ultimately, it would be delivered to him, at least temporarily.'

Gil nodded. 'And you can be sure that George had no intention of allowing any of them to live once the prize had been secured.'

George had a blind spot, however, Gil added, and it cost him dearly. For all his planning, George had underestimated Sabbie. 'That was his biggest mistake,' Gil said.

Even when George realized that she had accessed his computer system, George dismissed her as insignificant. It turned out to be an Achilles Heel for him and, in the end, for her as well.

'Ironic,' Sarkami added. 'Years ago, George was the one who suggested that Ludlow pressure DeVris into giving Sabbie a job at the Museum.'

'He probably thought she'd be just another ace-in-the-hole if he ever needed it.'

Sarkami nodded and sighed deeply. 'Anything else?'

Gil said that, even with all of the answers in place, he hadn't been willing to call it quits, so he

345

had probed a little deeper. Two questions had still remained. Number one: what lay hidden within the one piece of George's e-mail that he had been unable to open? Number two: in answer to Sarkami's previous question, why was Sabbie so worried about George being killed?

Sarkami looked up in surprise, but motioned Gil to continue.

The answer to the first question, Gil explained, arrived in the form of a message from George as Gil was exiting George's system.

A QuickTime movie appeared in the middle of the screen, complete with George's smiling face.

'I hate those "if-you're-seeing-this-then-I'm-already-dead" messages, don't you?' George began. 'In case you haven't figured it out by now and—knowing that your first priority is not necessarily the potential profit in things—let me fill you in. The amazing network you have just discovered constitutes what I refer to as my peach orchard, acres of sweet fruit just ripening on the vine. Each of the Fortune 500 companies, each of the billionaires, each of the obscenely well-financed foundations that you see in my system, share one common fear, a terror of having their most intimate secrets exposed to, shall we say, unsympathetic eyes.

'One by one,' George continued, 'I have brought each of them forensic evidence of the less-than-legal actions, secret stashes, and underhanded deals they have perpetrated. I offered them the information freely, with concern, and suggested only that they protect themselves from future exposure by employing CyberNet's services.

'No one ever refused and as you know,' George

346

added with a mocking laugh, 'the company has done amazingly well. I have taken, as my commission, what I consider to be my fair share of the profits. It's a greater percentage than my contract stipulates but I think I more than earned it.' George's computer image seemed to look directly into Gil's eyes as if, once again, they were both in his office.

'So, Gil,' George continued, 'if you've ever wondered why the company had such high profile customers but still does not seem to be swimming in profit, voilà, now you know that I've been holding a little in reserve for myself.'

George leaned in close to the camera. 'Now, I gotta tell you that being found out isn't fun, but two things make it totally unacceptable. The first is knowing that, after uncovering all of my hard work, being the boy scout that you are, you will probably feel obliged to dismantle the most perfect data gathering system ever devised.

'To make matters worse,' George went on, 'you did not take the bait I so carefully placed in your path. That little annoying e-mail that you could not access contained an attachment, my own electronic little time bomb actually. It was set to detonate on your twelfth try, I figured you'd go for the even dozen.'

Had Gil activated the e-mail, all record of those infected with the Darwin program would have been erased. While the program itself would continue to evolve, there would have been no way of deactivating it. George was hoping that, with some luck, the living program would have provided access for some very smart fellow in the future, someone who would make good and profitable use

347

of it. And, when he did, George would have emerged as the ultimate winner of his game of wits with Gil.

George's screen image panned a dramatically sad face. 'But, if you are hearing this message, you didn't take the bait and you didn't activate the self-destruct. That's not like you, Gil.' George shook an index finger at the camera. 'It means that, like my program, you're evolving as well. What's the matter, lost your old will to win, boy?'

George backed away from the camera that had been recording his message and continued without the sarcastic tone. 'You beat me, kid, but good. And I concede. But before I go, I have one last surprise. While you've been listening with great interest to my parting thoughts, my last little Darwin has been quite busy. It has created a self-destruct subprogram that will erase all record of my activities and the identities of those infected with my Darwin program. In many ways it is quite similar to the e-mail time bomb that you did not activate, with one important exception.

'Since you have disproved my hypotheses that people do not change, you deserve a reward. So, when Darwin's records and connections self-destruct—in honor of your evolution—the Darwin program itself will likewise self-destruct. No continuing evolution, no future game for any future bad boy like me. We'll call Darwin an evolutionary experiment gone sour, and you can rest assured that it will never see the light of day again. Even as you hear these words, my grandest creation, like myself, is fading into oblivion, All because you refused to play the game anymore. I hope that makes you happy.'

The screen went black.

'So, you figured out what George had been up to all along without detonating the e-mail time bomb,' Sarkami said. 'That must make you feel very good.'

'Of course. It makes me feel great.'

'What about the other question?' Sarkami continued.

'Why Sabbie didn't want George killed? No, I don't have a clue.'

'That's because you're still looking under the street lamp,' Sarkami replied and, once again, moved toward the door.

'Wait a minute, you!' Gil said breathlessly. His hand grabbed onto Sarkami's shoulder to prevent the older man from taking one more step. Sarkami broke free and moved rapidly through the busy library corridor with Gil racing to catch up.

'I haven't done all this work just so you can give me some cryptic remark and leave,' Gil snarled.

'No, you haven't,' Sarkami confirmed.

'What do you *want* from me?' Gil asked. Desperation was seeping into his voice. 'What does it matter why Sabbie didn't want George killed? Who cares anyway?'

Sarkami stopped and faced Gil. The great eagle's voice bellowed in the vast library lobby. '*I* care and *you* care, even though you would do anything to pretend you don't. Every living soul on earth cares and they don't even know it.'

'Everyone on earth?' Gil scoffed.

'Yes, all of mankind, even though they don't know it. And you still think it doesn't matter,' Sarkami bellowed. 'There is nothing on earth that matters more!'

The man had gone mad, Gil concluded. What could Sabbie's last request mean to anybody but him? What could it possibly mean to anyone else, much less the entire world?

'You might want to know one more thing,' Sarkami said, his great nose inches from Gil's face. 'Sabbie didn't say that she didn't want George killed, she said she didn't want *you* to kill him.'

Gil's mind fought for an answer. The only possible conclusion was too great to even imagine. The High Tzaddik must be one who had never taken a life. If she had been trying to say that *he* must not kill then . . .

'Then I'm the High Tzaddik,' whispered Gil.

Sarkami looked at him in disdain. 'My God, Gil. Your arrogance is astounding. You are most certainly *not* the High Tzaddik. I am.'

SIXTY-SIX

Day Twenty-five, twilight
The Concourse of the Israel Museum Library
Jerusalem

Gil waited outside on the Library steps. He squinted at his watch in the fading light. He'd give him five minutes, no more. Sarkami had said to meet him in the little conference room inside but Gil wasn't feeling well. It took all that he had to not give in to the nausea and weakness that threatened to overtake him. The thought of a tiny room filled with hot, stale air filled Gil with a sense of panic.

350

He'd catch Sarkami on the way in; there was nothing new to report anyway. The old guy had insisted that Gil take a break for two days. Two totally wasted days with nothing to do but sit on his hands and think about Sabbie.

Gil had agreed to the hiatus only because he didn't know what else to do next. And because, apparently, Sarkami did. Still, if Sarkami was the High Tzaddik, why hadn't he just taken the scroll off Gil's hands himself? Gil shrugged. The whole thing was crazy and he was feeling lousier by the minute.

He sank to the steps and put his head between his legs.

'Feeling badly?' Sarkami asked. Gil had neither seen nor heard him approach.

Gil wiped the cold sweat off his forehead with the back of his hand. 'Must be something I ate,' he answered.

'Or something that's eating you.'

Gil's head snapped up to offer protest but he had neither the will nor the energy to take on the fight. Besides, as usual, the bastard was right on target.

He looked up into Sarkami's eyes. Funny that he had never seen the sadness in them. Or the compassion. At least, not for him.

Sarkami nodded and, in that single gesture, urged Gil to surrender to that which would no longer be denied.

The pain came hard and fast. Silent twisting shrieks tore at his chest. There on the steps, in the middle of the busy Museum campus, Gil sobbed as he had never cried before. Its power took him by surprise, though Sarkami seemed to have been waiting for it.

'Good,' Sarkami said, then waited patiently until the first wave subsided. His arm guided Gil inside, to the library conference room. The golden light seemed to welcome Gil and rather than stale, the air seemed as cool as the fresh night air outside.

'Very good,' Sarkami said as he helped Gil into a chair.

The older man leaned back against the table, waited patiently and asked no questions.

'I did it,' Gil said simply. 'I killed her. If I hadn't . . .' There were so many sentences that started with 'If I hadn't . . .' he could barely keep track of them. If he hadn't dismissed Sabbie's concerns about George, they might have stopped him while there was still time; if Gil hadn't laughed at the idea that Global Positioning Systems could work in two directions, he might have thrown away his PDA which, most likely, would have cut George's access to their every move. If only he had listened to Sabbie when she said she thought George might not be dead . . . So many ifs and that one was the worst of them all.

Sobs overtook Gil once again. He wept for all he had done and all he had failed to do. He wept for the consequences of his arrogance and for the life they would never share together.

'Good. Those two days were well spent,' Sarkami whispered half to himself.

He turned to Gil. 'You've done well. Sacrifice cleanses the spirit. It is the first task of three that you will have to complete for the scroll to find its way to its rightful heir.'

'I thought you were the rightful heir,' Gil said accusingly. 'You said you were the High Tzaddik and Sabbie said the scroll was to be delivered to the High Tzaddik, so why don't you just take the damn thing?'

'Sacrifice cleanses the spirit,' Sarkami repeated as if Gil had said nothing. 'It is the first task of three that you will have to complete.'

'What are you saying? That Sabbie had to die so you could get the scroll or that her death was my sacrifice.'

'Neither,' Sarkami answered. 'Sabbie's death was not your sacrifice. Nor was it hers, if that's what you were thinking. Sacrifice requires the loss of yourself not another, the loss of the certainty that you are right and others are not, the loss of the illusion that you are in control.'

Something in Sarkami's words called to him. And terrified him at the same time.

'Sabbie lost the person she knew herself to be with the rape and the death of her friend,' Sarkami continued. 'That first transformation was not her choice and it left her a lesser, rather than a greater, person. Fortunately, she was transformed again, this time by choice, after she killed her assailant.'

'You mean *when* she killed her assailant,' Gil corrected.

'No, I meant exactly what I said. She did not *lose* herself when she killed the man who raped her. Killing him was well in keeping with the person she had become after the rape. Sabbie's sacrifice came after she had killed him.'

'After she killed him?' Gil asked.

'Yes. After she killed her first attacker, she chose to abandon her plan of vengeance on the others. It was a great sacrifice for her; there was little doubt that, had she chosen to, she would have been able to complete the job.'

'But . . .' Gil urged.

'But, instead, she refused to continue as the violent animal they had made her into. She chose to spend the rest of her life reaching for something greater, for something she believed in.'

'Did you know that she said you saved her that day, the day she killed him?' Gil asked.

'She saved herself.'

'She said you gave her a reason to live,' Gil continued.

'That I did and you did as well,' Sarkami added.

'*I* did?'

'Yes,' Sarkami explained. 'You discovered it in Weymouth Monastery.'

The Scroll. What Sarkami said was true. It was what she and Sarkami and Ludlow had dedicated their lives to. And he had found it for her, for them all. And for himself.

The guilt eased within Gil's chest. He had given Sabbie something greater than anyone else could have. Sobs of relief pressed to be let out but he pushed them down. There was more he had to know.

'The way she looked at you. I've never seen such love,' Gil said simply.

'It was far more than love,' Sarkami said. 'She trusted me.'

'Why?'

'Because of what I did when I found her with the young man she had killed,' Sarkami continued.

'But he was scum and deserved to die. Anyone in their right mind would have allowed her to get away before the body was discovered,' Gil replied.

354

'Yes, he was scum and yes, it was better that he was dead. And most certainly, it was fitting that she was allowed to flee. But, you see,' Sarkami added, 'he was also my son.'

Gil stared in disbelief.

So, that was Sarkami's sacrifice. Not the death of his son but of himself, of the man who had still carried hope of what his son might have become, of the father who, no matter what, still blindly loved his own child. In that moment, Sarkami had relinquished it all, simply because it was the right thing to do.

'You may not know it yet, Gil, but you have been transformed, as well,' Sarkami said softly. 'You will never again feel self-righteous in the face of another's misdeeds, you will never lack compassion for another's regrets. Your guilt and anguish were honest and in their truth, they cleansed your soul.'

Two other tasks lay ahead, Sarkami explained. Upon their completion, Gil could deliver the scroll to the righteous soul for whom it was intended.

'But if you are the High Tzaddik, isn't the scroll meant to go to you?' Gil asked. 'Why can't you just take it from me and do what you want with it?'

'Because it isn't intended for me,' Sarkami replied. 'And because if I were to accept it, its message would be lost on the occasion of my death.'

Gil's blood ran cold. What was Sarkami saying? He pressed the man who had now become his mentor for an explanation. None was forthcoming.

'Well, you're going to be with us for a good long time,' Gil concluded on a lighter note. 'After all,

355

you're reasonably young and healthy.'

'The Chinese say that we own nothing that can't be lost in a shipwreck,' Sarkami replied with a gentle smile. 'Now, let's get back to work.'

The second task was at hand and that came more easily. Over the next two days, at Sarkami's request, Gil designed and uploaded a message that would serve as a digital signpost in cyberspace for the next millennium.

Gil had written the message using an advanced binary pattern, a language he believed would be understood by the High Tzaddik of the next millennium. There the message would remain, in cyberspace, until it was needed to lead the High Tzaddik to the scroll of the Thirteenth Apostle, a thousand years in the future.

Only the third task remained unfulfilled.

'Soon,' Sarkami assured Gil. 'McCullum is not far now. And he is more determined than ever. You will know when it is time.'

SIXTY-SEVEN

An hour later
Library Conference Room, Israel Museum Library

Sarkami chose his position carefully. With his back to the open conference room door, he would appear unsuspecting. McCullum would believe that his arrival had been unanticipated. That assumption was essential to Sarkami's plan and, if all played out well, it would buy Gil the few extra days he would need.

McCullum was certain to bring two new Power Angels, capable of an equal or greater brutality than the now-dead twins. Oh, how that loss must have infuriated the old Nazi, Sarkami thought. No matter, the freedom of having George out of the picture had probably done much to sooth McCullum's loss.

The old eagle's eyes glanced over the props he had so carefully arranged. On the floor, to the right of his chair, partially obscured by his coat, sat a beautiful new leather travel case, now empty. Handwritten notes, highlighted and underlined, open texts of Aramaic translation, and computer printouts, covered the conference room table. Sarkami's hand instinctively touched his right pocket. The key to the library locker remained where he had carefully placed it.

If only he hadn't had to cut short his last meeting with Gil in anticipation of McCullum's imminent arrival. There was so much left unsaid; so much that could have helped Gil with the last of his tasks. Sarkami shook his head. No, Gil would have to discover it for himself. That was the way it was. And he would succeed. Of that, Sarkami was certain. So, perhaps, it was all for the best.

Now, everything was done but the waiting. And even that went far more quickly than Sarkami had calculated.

In one blur of sound and movement, the door to the conference room had been closed, Sarkami had been lifted to his feet by one of the infamous white angels from hell, and a very angry McCullum awaited the answer to a single question.

'Where's the scroll?' McCullum asked.

Sarkami remained silent, unmoving, and

awaited the enactment of the script he had gone over a dozen times in his mind. It was remarkable, he thought, how utterly predictable this kind of man was almost certain to be.

'There are only so many places you could have hidden it and from what I can see,' McCullum said as he leafed through the notes strewn across the table, 'it's not far away.'

Sarkami repressed a wry smile. The fool had completely missed the empty travel case on the floor. Power Angel #1 emptied the contents of Sarkami's pockets onto the table. McCullum's excitement over the discovery of the library locker key was almost palpable. It was all so banal. Somehow, Sarkami would have preferred a bit of imaginative challenge at the end.

A momentary flash of panic brought Sarkami to attention when, for an instant, it appeared that McCullum was incapable of deducing the location of the locker.

Christ, do I have to draw you a map?

In the end, Sarkami concluded that McCullum's stupidity worked in Sarkami's favor. The beating and threats stretched out McCullum's discovery of the scroll and allowed Sarkami to relinquish its location only after suitably persuasive techniques had been put to use.

After stuffing his mouth with his socks, they had broken three of his fingers and had cut the Achilles tendons on both of his feet. In anticipation of permanent damage to the tendons of his fingers, and the end of his life as an artist, Sarkami had surrendered the hiding place, only a few feet from the room in which he had just been tortured.

Key in hand, Power Angel #2 returned with the prize and laid the tarnished scroll into McCullum's hands. A final stab to the heart left Sarkami barely able to hear his attacker's last words.

'How do we know it's the real scroll?' one of the white assassins asked. 'I mean, after all, he makes fakes for a living, doesn't he?'

'He would not die so hard for a mere facsimile,' McCullum said with a satisfied smile, then closed the door behind him.

Sarkami's last thought brought him inexplicable peace.

No, but I would gladly do so for the real one.

SIXTY-EIGHT

Three days later, pre-dawn
Sculpture Garden, Israel Museum

The sixth-page newspaper article testified to the fact that the waiting was over. 'MUSEUM EMPLOYEE FOUND DEAD. ROBBERY NOT MOTIVE.'

Gil had not known what shape the violence would take, but Sarkami had prepared him for the inevitable. Now, the old eagle was dead.

'I've achieved more than I ever thought possible. I've produced replicas of antiquity that the world will experience for centuries to come. The wisdom and love of two millennia have transformed me. I have loved and have been loved. Though I will not see my last wish fulfilled, I am content knowing that you shall complete the task

359

that was entrusted to me.' Sarkami placed his hand on Gil's shoulder.

'Who could ask for more?' the older man asked with a grin that, for a moment, revealed a young, handsome Sarkami of yesteryear.

Sarkami had presented Gil with a soft, white caftan made of the same fabric that had covered the table on which the scroll sat at Sarkami's house. 'This robe was given to me by the High Tzaddik who came before me. Now, it will be yours.'

Sarkami's instructions had been succinct but exact. 'You will know when it is time to cleanse yourself and to put on the caftan. Likewise, you will know what must be done. Leave your mind and heart open. Let the lessons of those who have touched you throughout your life become part of you. Do not linger on the memories but, rather, on what wisdom they have bestowed upon you.'

'Those are your instructions?' Gil asked incredulously. 'Trust the wisdom that has been bestowed on me? So how come, if I'm so wise, I have no idea what you're talking about? Come on, don't do this to me.'

Sarkami had smiled, the same loving look that Gil had once witnessed between Sabbie and the old eagle.

'Then know this,' Sarkami began. 'On the shoulders of the High Tzaddik rests the greatest of responsibilities. It is he who calls forth God and entreats Him to count the righteous among us. It is to he, the High Tzaddik, to whom God's judgment is revealed. It shall be made known to him alone whether, according to the Covenant, man shall be granted Continuance for yet another thousand years or, having proven himself unworthy, man shall no longer walk upon this earth

'The scroll shall guide you. Become as a channel through which the message of the scroll may flow.'

'But I can't read it,' Gil had protested. 'How can I deliver its message?'

'The scroll does not require an understanding of the language in which it was written. Its words are merely a reflection of history. The message it bears is far greater than words could ever express.'

'How will I know what to do?'

'If you are found worthy, the scroll will tell you.'

'And if I'm not?' Gil asked.

'Then the Covenant of Continuance shall be broken,' Sarkami said simply.

'You can't be saying that the fate of mankind, God's determination if man is worthy to remain on this earth for the next millennium, depends on me?' Gil asked cynically.

'No, it will depend on what God finds when He is called to come and count the righteous ones, the tzaddikim, who walk upon this earth,' Sarkami explained.

'I will call . . . who!'

'You're not listening!' Sarkami bellowed. '*You* will call no one. You will be the channel through which the message of the scroll shall flow. It will come as a prayer, a song, not *of* you but *through* you. You must be pure of heart and mind. You must offer no impediment.'

It was the most obvious question but one to which Gil wasn't certain he wanted the answer.

'Why me?' Gil had asked.

Sarkami had looked puzzled. 'Why not?' the old eagle replied with sincerity.

'Come on. I'm not the most religious person in the world or the most righteous. There are a hell of a lot of other people who would make a better High Tzaddik than me.'

'Oh, I see,' Sarkami said with sudden understanding. 'The whole media image thing. Very American, you know. No, my friend, you're confusing Cecil B. DeMille with God. God doesn't require you to be the best at anything in order to win His favor. To become the High Tzaddik, like any tzaddik, you must be a good person, a righteous person, but not necessarily the best person in the world. This isn't some kind of cosmic contest. You need to have lived a decent life, doing your best with what you have been given, but no heroes need apply. Just a decent human being, who has tried his or her best, and who has never taken a life. Though at times he might have desired to,' Sarkami added with a laugh.

'I still don't understand, why me? I mean with millions of good, honest, righteous people out there . . .'

'Good timing,' Sarkami said wryly. 'Or bad timing, depending on how you look at it.'

Gil cringed at the thought of the last few weeks.

Sarkami shook one long bony finger at Gil. 'The funny thing is, you are absolutely right. There is nothing special about you, and that is exactly the kind of person God wants to find when he returns to consider His Covenant of Continuance. You hold the answers God seeks.'

Gil looked up in surprise.

Sarkami continued, 'When you call, God will come. The song within the scroll will bring Him to you. Within you, He will find the essential answers:

Who is man today? What has he become in the last millennium? Is he still worthy to be given more time to grow and develop, to become more like God in His own image?'

'And I'm going to stand and be judged for all of mankind? You've got to be kidding!'

'No, my egotistical friend. Remember what I have said. You will serve as nothing but the channel, the vessel through which God will touch the soul of man. You need only to open yourself and allow Him to enter.'

Gil suddenly understood. 'That is why a High Tzaddik cannot have killed,' he said with certainty.

'Yes. To carry that evil within your soul would prevent God from entering. You could not be a channel if you were already filled with the malevolence of such a past.'

'But suppose the killing was justified?' Gil argued.

'This is not a matter of fairness,' Sarkami answered. 'Sabbie is not on trial here, if that's what you are thinking. And she did not die so that you could be High Tzaddik, so don't feel that you must defend her. In life, you are not punished *for* your deeds but, rather, *by* them. She did what she had to do at the time she did it. Later, she found redemption and peace. She accepted her role in the scheme of things and you must, too.'

Sarkami was quiet for a moment, then added one thought. 'You were part of the redemption, Gil. Sabbie had to make certain that, since she could not take my place when the time came, someone else would. A good person, someone who was decent and, in his own way, righteous, although, perhaps, a bit ordinary, at that,' Sarkami added with a smile.

These were Sarkami's last words to Gil. There was, however, one final act that awaited completion before he left. This one, a gift from Gil to Sarkami.

Gil had taken Sarkami's fingers in his hand and gently guided his mentor to the backpack that lay in the corner of the room. Wordlessly, Sarkami knelt and, as Gil removed the scroll and delivered it into Sarkami's waiting arms, a deep serenity engulfed them both.

Now Sarkami was gone and a new High Tzaddik had emerged.

*   *   *

Gil rose at three in the morning. He showered and dressed in the white caftan Sarkami had given him. Somehow he knew it was similar to the one Micah had taken from his back and had given Yeshua in the garden.

From its place in the corner, Gil gathered up the backpack, slipped it over his shoulders, and walked the empty streets that led to the entrance to the Museum Sculpture Garden. The break in the fence that Sabbie described, far from view of the security control pavilion, remained, and offered him easy access.

The enormous sculptures within the garden greeted Gil as if they had been waiting. Built on the hill called Neva Shaanan, Place of Tranquility, the flowing, square, curved, and stark monuments, some dozens of feet high, all seemed to join together as if to say that, though they were shaped by man, they stood in tribute to something greater than man himself. Gil made his way across the five acres of garden to his destination.

The massive white granite sculpture of a staircase shone in the pre-dawn light. It seemed to reach to the heavens. In the moments before the first rays of light would hail the new day, Gil climbed to the top of the monument and seated himself.

There, next to him on the top step of the sculpture, Gil removed the scroll on which Micah had inscribed his story more than two millennia before. Innermost was the section Sabbie had been unable to unroll and, within it, had been hidden the scroll's true message, the prayer that could not be allowed to die. Here was the only hope for mankind. Within its prayer lived the plea that would beckon God to come and judge man's worthiness. Here it would be determined if, indeed, thirty-six righteous souls might yet be found to testify on behalf of mankind's fate. Here it would be decided if the Covenant of Continuance, between man and God, would be recast for yet another thousand years.

Here, then, the third task would be consummated. As Sarkami had instructed, Gil waited for the final star to disappear from the morning sky. When the final bright point on the horizon winked one last time and was gone, Gil lightly touched his fingers to the edge of the copper scroll. The familiar warmth filled him once again.

Without effort, the sound of prayer made itself heard. Gil knew nothing of the words he sang. They moved through him as the air passes in and out. He was but the empty channel through which two thousand years passed. Gladly he surrendered himself to it.

Even as the sacred sounds made their way to the heavens, Gil knew the ancient thoughts of one whose wisdom still lived.

Grieve not, my brother. Be healed. We are all flawed, we fall and fail. Each of us, with knowledge or without, contributes to the suffering around us, if not with forethought, then by our pretense of innocence, comfortable condemnation, and arrogance. When these frailties are relinquished, all becomes right in thought and action. Therein lies everyman's sacrifice and his salvation as well.

The last boundary between his body and the presence that approached melted away. Now he understood.

Each is the teller of the tale, the bringer of the word. Each soul has his own story and each story is a vital link in the chain of truth, a chain that reaches across the generations, from one millennium to the next. As long as the story is told, as long as struggle and sacrifice bring forth truth, the Thirteenth Apostle lives within each of us. So may God find us worthy to continue to serve and so may our days be long upon this earth.

The Thirteenth Apostle is not one man, not merely he who walked with Jesus and assumed His burdens when He could no longer do so Himself. We are each of us, as Micah, a Thirteenth Apostle, spanning the great abyss between that which we are and that which we would seek to become.

As countless others who have gone before us, we may never know if we are the righteous ones, the tzaddikim, but in this changing and challenging world, we must each live as if we are.